THE
OCCUPATION

Published by Sapere Books.

20 Windermere Drive, Leeds, LS17 7UZ,
United Kingdom
saperebooks.com

ISBN: 978-1-913335-27-4

PROLOGUE

Jersey, The Channel Islands
August 1939

Céline

I shaded my eyes with my hand, squinting through the glare of my glasses. The sea stretched out before me, its dark cobalt blurring seamlessly into the duck-egg blue of the sky. In the distance a steamer puffed black smoke from its two chimneys, making steady headway between the small pleasure craft, their sails specks and splashes of white. Below, the beach was filled with multi-coloured deckchairs, windbreaks and beach towels. I sighed. Scarcely an inch of sand was unoccupied.

I trotted downhill, the smell of hot tar in my nostrils. The summer invasion of tourists was a mixed blessing, turning our peaceful island into a kind of mad-house — everything loud and over-bright. Glancing at my watch, I hurried past the billboards that had sprung up on every building, as if shouting in red and yellow for attention: 'Smith's Cream Ices — Jersey's Best!' and 'Tub Race — every child a winner!'

I'd promised to meet my friend Rachel on the Blue Terrace at the Lido, and I was late. I liked Rachel, but she could be exhausting, and I was very firmly beneath her in any sort of pecking order. Hitching my beach bag over my shoulder, I hurried through the turnstile, the sun tingling hot on my bare shoulders.

At first I couldn't see Rachel through the splashing children, but then on the other side of the pool, I could just make out the brilliant red of Rachel's rubber swimming cap amongst the rest of the swimmers. I narrowed my eyes against the sun.

Rachel waved. 'Come on!' she yelled.

The changing cubicle with its wooden slatted bench smelled of seawater and damp socks. I pulled on my old elasticated polka-dot swimming costume, wriggling awkwardly to get into it, and bundled my clothes and glasses into my bag. Barefoot, I tiptoed out of the changing cabin, but then gasped, hopping in an awkward dance as my feet scorched on the hot concrete.

Dodging the squashed remains of an ice-cream sandwich, I headed for a free deckchair to dump my things and waded down the shallow steps. A sharp inhale as the cold water hit my ribs.

Rachel's red cap powered towards me, her arms scything through the water. She disappeared for a moment, then popped up too close, shaking droplets off her face. An armful of cold water flung in my face made me duck.

'You beast!' I shouted, cowering away, before splashing back.

'Isn't it glorious!' she said breathlessly, before turning on her back. 'I'm going up on the diving board. Coming?'

She didn't wait for an answer, because she knew I'd be shaking my head.

I doggy-paddled from side to side, trying not to get out of my depth, but a few minutes was enough for me and I clambered out and towelled myself dry. Once I'd flopped into my deckchair, I was just in time to see Rachel bounce at the end of the board and upend herself into a perfect line. She slid into the water with hardly a ripple. It gave me a pang of envy to watch her. She was completely fearless.

Fred would have had a go at diving, even though he was no athlete. I thought of my husband with a mixture of annoyance and affection. He never took a day off from the bakery, though he was happy whenever I did. On days like this, he knew that cooping me up next to a hot oven was a kind of torture.

Rachel was swimming back towards me now, doing the butterfly stroke, which involved a lot of wild splashing and everyone clearing out of her way. She hauled herself out, shaking her dark curly hair free of its cap. Moments later, she was stretched out on a candy-striped towel.

'I could lie here forever,' she said.

'If you did, you'd be fried,' I said.

A little boy in red shorts rushed past, wailing, clutching a tin bucket. 'Mummy!' He ran back and forth again shouting, his face wide-eyed and anxious. 'Mummy!'

I saw him run past a few more times, getting more frantic and tearful every minute. I heaved myself out of the chair and went over to him. By now he was bawling. 'Are you lost?' I said.

'I can't find my Mummy,' he said. He looked round wildly, and I followed his gaze but could see no-one searching for a small boy. He burst into fresh noisy tears.

'Let's go and see if we can find her,' I said. 'She might be by the turnstile.' I reached out my hand and his hot damp one slipped trustingly into mine.

'Sorry, Rachel,' I said as I led him off.

She grimaced and went back to sunbathing.

By the turnstile, a woman in cork platform shoes and a low-cut sundress was scanning the crowd. Immediately she saw us and hurried over. 'Graham! What in blazes d'you think you're doing?' She grabbed him by the arm and slapped him hard across the back of the legs. The boy cried out and tried to squirm away.

'Don't smack him,' I said, seeing red marks immediately flare up on the back of his legs. 'He was lost. He was looking for you.'

'Can't turn my back two minutes,' she said. 'Little blighter never listens to a word I say.' Ignoring me, she dragged the poor child away, still howling. I watched them go, wishing I could smack the mother the way she'd smacked the little boy.

When I got back, Rachel was watching me. 'Trust you. You're always finding lame ducks,' she said.

'She didn't even thank me,' I said. 'I wish all these other holidaymakers would go home. It's so busy.'

'Better than the winter.' Rachel propped herself on one elbow. 'Nothing ever *happens* here, does it? When the holidaymakers leave, we're just left with the same old farmers and fishermen, and old women knitting pullovers. It's so *dull*. And there's no men worth looking at.'

I surveyed the busy terrace. 'What about him?' I pointed to a skinny man with very white skin that was flaring bright pink across the shoulders.

She rolled her eyes and stuck her tongue out at me.

'You could go back home to Paris,' I said. 'Must be plenty of talent there.'

'My parents would send me straight back. Paris is full of communists and subversives. She's terrified I'll get involved with the wrong type.'

'And she thinks Jersey farmers are more suitable?'

'In Maman's eyes, yes. Because she knows I won't want them. I can't stop her matchmaking. She keeps on at me, trying to persuade me to get married to a nice Jewish boy, have a tidy little house and have lots of babies, but I can't think of anything worse.'

I couldn't tell her that Fred and I had exactly those plans. She'd sneer at it, and I couldn't bear it.

'They approve of you, you know,' she continued. 'They call

you "that nice sensible girl from the *pâtisserie*.'"

I made a face, and she went back to sunbathing. I glanced over at her brown back above her green ruched swimsuit. Was I sensible? If so, it came from fending for myself. I'd had to grow up fast. Dad was killed in the first war, and Mother died of TB more than ten years ago when I was still at school. I could still remember that panicky empty feeling of being quite alone. That was before I met Fred.

I closed my eyes a moment, hearing the screech of the gulls, and smelling the fishy smell of crab from the stall behind us.

'What's it like, being married?' Rachel's question came out of the blue. I sat up, to see her looking at me with curious brown eyes.

I didn't want to tell her. There was something precious about how I felt about Fred that I didn't want to share. It made me want to hug the feeling close, wrap protective arms around it, protect it from too much scrutiny. 'It's all right,' I said. 'Nice to have someone to share things with.'

She turned over again. 'Don't you ever get bored? I mean, being with the same man?'

'No.' There was a sort of criticism in her tone that made me defensive. 'We argue sometimes, but I think that's only natural. He's worried at the moment. He thinks there'll be another war.'

She didn't seem to hear me. She was silent a few moments before saying, 'I don't think I'll get married until I'm about forty.'

'Aren't you bothered about being left "on the shelf"?'

She threw back her head and guffawed at me, as if I'd said something hilarious. 'No, I like the space and freedom of my own apartment. I'd hate to be cooped up with just one person, or have some man telling me what to do.'

The way she said it stung. It made me feel as if my life with Fred was too small; something of no account, to be dismissed with a laugh. It pointed to a nameless unbridgeable gulf between us, the tiny voice inside me that said: though Rachel was my friend, perhaps it was only until she found someone better or more exciting.

She had a sort of vibrant attraction, a fizz about her. Even now, a young man in long trunks was staring at her and whispering to his friend. Neither of them looked twice at me. Beside Rachel I felt pale-skinned and colourless, the damp Lido heat steaming up my glasses.

Rachel was sitting up now, rubbing Nivea into her legs. The lad who'd been staring at her gave her a cheeky wink.

She waved back at him in a careless kind of way.

'Forty,' I said, nudging her.

We both burst into laughter. The lad reddened and turned away, thinking we were laughing at him, and his obvious embarrassment ran through me in a matching frisson of pain.

I slogged up the hill in the late afternoon heat, pausing to look up at the shop, proud of our window with its *"Pâtisserie"* sign painted in gold on a dark green background. I went round the back, knowing the front door would be shut by now, and Fred would be preparing stock for tomorrow's baking.

When I breezed in, it was to find Fred hurriedly closing the paper. He pushed his fair hair out of his eyes and jammed his bakery cap back on his head. His expression was one of guilt, as if he'd been caught doing something he didn't want me to see.

'What is it?' I asked.

'Nothing,' he said. 'Just reading the news. Hitler's just sent a memo to Mussolini telling him that war with Poland is imminent.'

'That won't affect us, will it?' Fred was German. His real name was Siegfried, but we'd been on the island ten years, and nobody ever called him that. We all called him Fred.

He reached out to take hold of me and planted a kiss on my cheek. 'How was your swim?'

'All right.'

I watched him as he strode over to the sack and began to tip flour into the huge mixing bowl. His white coat strained across the shoulders as he worked. He was avoiding my eyes, stirring amid a fog of flour, and I was filled with a sudden rush of affection for him. I loved the solid weight of him; his practicality, the slow measured way he moved about the shop.

'Rachel says she can't see herself getting married,' I said. 'That she'd be bored with only one man.'

He turned. 'Pah. I bet she changes her mind when she meets the right chap.'

'You don't think we'll get bored with each other?'

He stopped what he was doing. 'What's brought this on? Rachel?'

I nodded. 'It's just that next to her, I seem to be…'

He pulled me against his chest. 'Silly thing. Rachel doesn't know what she's talking about. I can't imagine wanting any other woman but you. The first time I saw you, I thought you looked so fresh-faced, so smiling. You lit up the place. We're happy aren't we?' His hug was fierce.

''Course I am.' I looked up into his blue eyes.

'Then why would you want anything different?'

'I don't. It's just that sometimes I think there's things you're not telling me.'

'What things? There's nothing. It's that Rachel, she just stirs things up. Maybe she's jealous of us. Ignore her.'

He went back to sifting flour, and I went back to the shop to put away the unsold bread. But a few moments later he came up behind me, put his hands around my waist and turned me to face him. 'I love you Céline. I love you exactly the way you are, even with your hair full of salt-water and your nose peeling from the sun. I don't want anything to change. I just want to stay on Jersey with you forever and live out our lives here until we are old and grey.'

His eyes were strangely intense and glassy. I kissed him tenderly, lingeringly, on the lips. His response was urgent, like it used to be when we were courting.

'Let's go upstairs,' I said.

It was a moment before he realised I was serious. But then he grinned back at me and pulled me by the hand.

CHAPTER 1

May 1940

Céline

At the sharp ting-a-ling of the bakery door, I turned down the wireless, which was always on now so we could keep track of the hostilities between England and Germany, and looked up to see who the customer was.

'Morning, Céline.' The postman, Ernest Jones, a farmer's son with a ruddy, perspiring face, dumped the letters on the counter, next to the till, and waved as he breezed out again with another jangle from the bell.

'Is that the post?' Fred emerged from the bakehouse, still in his floured apron and the white cloth cap that made him look like a friendly convict. He slapped his palms together and released a cloud of white dust, before giving me a quick cuddle, pressing me to his broad chest.

'Leave off! You'll cover me in flour,' I said, smiling and hugging him back.

'Bet it's another order from the Marine Hotel for our Viennese pastries,' he said, wiping his hands down his apron.

'Might stop you eating them,' I said, pinching at the soft flesh at his waist.

'You love me really,' he said. 'Good to have a bit of padding.'

He sifted through the mail, dividing it neatly into orders and bills. Then he stopped, his fingers frozen in the act of picking up a brown envelope.

'What's that?' I asked.

'Just a bill I expect.' He hurried away into the back of the bakery. I paused, aware of a tightness in the pit of my stomach, but carried on stacking the loaves into the wooden crates for the hotels on the seafront. When Fred came back, his rosy face had drained to grey.

Another jangle. Old Mrs Hedges from the haberdashery just down the road bustled in, coming to collect her brown loaf.

'We're closed,' Fred said.

'Closed?' Mrs Hedges blinked behind her thick tortoiseshell glasses. 'But the sign in the window says —'

'Closed.' Fred turned the sign around and held open the door.

'But what about my bread?'

'You'll just have to come back later.'

'But —'

'Didn't you hear?' His sharp tone made me frown. Mrs Hedges backed uncertainly out of the door, an expression of disbelief on her face. Neither of us had ever heard my husband be so rude before.

'Fred?' I put a hand to his arm.

'You'd better come through to the back.' He stripped off his apron and stared at it a moment before hanging it on the peg.

'Is it bad news? Is it your parents? Are they all right?' Everyone was calling the war with Germany the 'phoney war' because, so far, it seemed to be all talk. I followed him through to the sitting room and perched myself on the arm of the easy chair.

Fred didn't sit, but paced, gripping his head in his hands.

'What is it? What's going on? Was it that letter?'

He nodded miserably. 'I've been conscripted. I have to leave for army training next week.'

'What? But they're demilitarising us. That's what Churchill said. That Jersey's too small to be any use to the Germans.'

'You don't understand.'

'Show me. Show me the letter.' I pushed my glasses further up my nose.

He handed it over. He was still speaking but I heard nothing he said. The brown piece of paper I was holding had an eagle and swastika on it. The long German words preceded a space where his name had been typed — *Siegfried Huber*. A wave of something cold sluiced over me. 'No.' My voice was a whisper.

He looked at me. 'I'll be fighting for the Germans.'

I stood up, my knees shaking. 'No. You're not going. You must refuse.'

'I can't refuse. If I refuse they'll just send someone to arrest me.'

'But you've not been back to Germany for years. You're a baker. A master baker, for God's sake, not a soldier. It's madness!'

'If I don't report, they'll court-martial me anyway and throw me in prison. Look at all this small print.' He held out an accompanying document printed in small type. 'The letter says I'm to leave within two days and report to the German command at Cherbourg. Kommandant Zweig.'

'We'll go somewhere. Anywhere.'

'Don't be ridiculous. Where would we hide? It's a small island, and everyone knows me and —'

'Exactly. You're not German anymore. You live here, on Jersey.' My voice rose in panic.

He put a hand on my shoulder. 'I am German, Céline. It's no use pretending I'm not. Germany's a part of me. Ever since war was declared, I've been thinking of my mother and father in their little house in Dortmund, and whether they're all right.

Every time I read a paper saying the British are going to bomb the Ruhr I feel my insides grow hot and my blood boil, because whatever your English papers might say, it's not just industry in the Ruhr. I know it. I grew up there, and it's houses, and schools and hospitals. It's factories, like my father's engineering works. And they're all full of people. My people,' he said sadly. 'My school friends, my teachers, my parents. Don't you see? I must do it for them.'

'For that madman Hitler?'

'No, of course not for him.' His eyes couldn't meet mine. 'It's complicated. Germany's my childhood, my school days, the smell of pine logs burning and the taste of my mother's cooking. My homeland. Who wouldn't want to protect that?'

'And you'd choose that over me ... over us?'

He pulled me to his chest, gripping me tight and speaking over my head. 'I've worried about it for a long time. It's nearly driven me mad, wondering what you'd say when the summons came.'

'What?' I pushed him away. 'You mean you knew it was coming?'

'They wrote to me once before. Beginning of last year. I panicked because I thought they might deport me. So I was relieved. And I didn't tell you then because Germany wasn't actually at war with England, and once we were, I thought the war would be short, and it would be over by the time my papers came.' He rubbed a hand through his hair. 'And I knew how I felt, that I would have to go, and I didn't know what you'd say.'

'Oh, Fred.' I sighed and shook my head. 'You said we'd never keep secrets.'

'I thought it better to keep quiet than to hurt you. I can't just siphon the German out of myself; it's a part of me, like Jersey is part of you.'

'But how on earth will I manage here, without you?'

'Albert will do the baking. He's learnt a lot since he started, and he's old enough for the responsibility; and besides, I won't be away for long. The war will be over soon and then I will be home again, and we will all be back to how we were.'

I shuddered. The war still didn't seem real, not here in my sitting room. The thought of it being over was no comfort either, because someone would have to lose, and one of us would be the loser.

On the day Fred went, we shut the bakery, and I went down to the harbour to see him off. I'd told no one where he was going; I was ashamed. Our different nationalities had never mattered when we met in Vienna. He was training to be a pâtissier and, as my parents were dead and I was still single, I was working as a nanny to two children. I kept going back to his shop, partly for his vanilla *kipferl*, but mostly for him, for the twinkle in his bright blue eyes and his open face. One day I forgot my purse, we were so busy chatting, and he had to run after me, waving it in the air. When he caught up, I saw what a fine, tall man he was. I'd only ever seen him behind the counter before that, and it took my breath. I still found him handsome, despite his extra weight.

Today we walked arm in arm towards the boats, in an uneasy truce. It was a glorious hot day, and Fred looked out of place in his dark suit, with his raincoat tucked over his arm. His bushy fair hair was pressed flat with water and his leather suitcase, used for so many holidays, swung at his side.

The ferry to Cherbourg was late, the harbourmaster said, for it had run into trouble with a German blockade. It was ironic that Fred was in danger from the very army he was trying to join. I looked out to sea, and the whole thing seemed crazy; that my lovely soft husband was going to go to France all alone, and who knew when I might see him next?

We sat on the harbour wall staring glumly out to sea, not knowing what to say, and watching the gulls dive into the glittering water for any small fleck of floating debris. The war seemed a long way away from our twisting leafy lanes and white sand beaches. *Please, make the boat not come,* I prayed.

I glanced at Fred. His eyes were fixed on the dark line of the horizon where a black dot was growing larger. The boat. And with it, the terrifying thought that in battle people had to kill or be killed. I gripped his arm, overwhelmed by utter helplessness.

'There it is,' Fred said, standing up.

'Wait,' I choked out. 'I love you.'

He drew me close and wiped the tear from my cheek where it leaked out from under my glasses. 'Chin up. Isn't that what the English say? I'll be back before you can whistle.'

When the boat docked, we followed the queue of people to the gangplank, where the harbourmaster and the remaining officers were examining people's tickets and passes. I looked at my shoes as they checked his passport over, aware of one of them whispering to the other and making a private joke. They stamped the papers and handed them back with impassive faces. Fred turned back to me, his eyes glassy.

'Stay safe, *liebchen*,' he whispered, reaching out to give me a last hug.

The German word was a stab in the heart. It was what he'd always called me, but now it made me afraid. That he could be my country's enemy and might have to shoot at us, or worse. I couldn't speak; I was too churned up, one thought chasing vainly after another.

Fred grasped me tight and kissed me on the lips, a kiss like a seal on a letter, like an ending. And then he was walking away.

No. Not this soon. 'Write!' I shouted. 'You'd better damned well write.'

He turned to give a wave and then stood on the deck staring back at me.

As the boat slid away from its berth, Fred was nearest the stern, his eyes fixed on my face.

'Filthy Boche!' It was the officer who'd stamped his papers. He shook a fist at Fred. 'We don't want you here.'

His words were like a physical blow. I pressed my lips together and ignored him, my eyes fixed on the sea. As the boat moved away, I had the urge to claw it back, to tell them it was a terrible mistake, that my husband was just Fred the baker. Like in the game Happy Families. I wiped a tear away. Would he even reach Cherbourg? Or would some English Tommy take him prisoner? Would his boat be shot at, or bombed? I simply didn't know.

I turned to walk back towards the town, a chasm in my chest.

'Jerrybag!' yelled one of the men by the harbourmaster's office. 'Whore!'

A moment later, a stone whistled past my ear. I set off at a run, stumbling up the hill as fast as I could, clutching my handbag over my head.

Jersey wasn't supposed to be in this conflict at all; but in that moment, some sort of war had already started.

CHAPTER 2

Over the next weeks, I oversaw the bakery as best I could without Fred to help me. I had Albert, Fred's nervous young assistant, all arms and legs like a young colt, and Tilly, our shop girl and chief fetcher and carrier, who lived in. Albert lived at home but came at dawn and did the early baking: all the bread for the hotels on the seafront. When that was done, he and Tilly made pies and pastries for the tourists, for we still had plenty of summer visitors, despite the war.

One morning though, when I came down to the bakehouse, there was no smell of bread. I put my hand out to the bread oven. It was cold. There was no sign of Albert. Was he sick? I went to the door to see if I'd missed a sick note, but there was no letter, and the shop door was still locked. Nor was there any sign of Tilly.

I went up to her room, but the bed hadn't been slept in. She'd been to visit her mother on the other side of the island the previous night, but I'd expected her back for the morning jobs. I lit the oven myself and dragged a sack of flour from the brick storeroom at the back of the house.

The doorbell sounded and I hurried into the shop. It was Rachel, her dark hair tousled by the wind, and a look of agitation on her face. She always came in for her boss's bread before she went off to the bank where she was a cashier, and sometimes she'd stop for a cuppa whilst we caught up with each other's news.

Before she could even ask, I was apologising. 'Sorry, Rache, I've no bread yet. I can't think what's happened. Albert didn't come in this morning and the ovens haven't been lit.'

'Haven't you heard? He'll have gone to sign up.'

I was bewildered. 'For the army?'

'No, silly. Evacuation,' Rachel said. 'It's chaos. I've just been down there. They're taking precautions in case the Channel Islands are invaded. There are notices up everywhere.'

'No! Whatever for?' I stared at her, unbelieving. 'They won't come here. The *Jersey Evening Post* says these islands are not worth conquering. At least, not unless Hitler wants an ice cream and a ride on a donkey.'

'We're so close to France though. And my boss, Mr Scott, says that on the other side of the island you can hear the boom of the German guns and see the smoke from bombs. I don't know what to do.' She stopped and bit her lip.

Fred's name hung unspoken between us. She was the only person I'd told that Fred was fighting for the Germans. Everyone else assumed he was fighting for the British. I'd had no news of him, and his absence chafed every minute.

'I thought you'd have heard,' she went on. 'They've called women and children, and men between the ages of eighteen and thirty. That'll be why Albert's not at work. We've got until ten o'clock tomorrow morning to register.'

'Oh Lord. I bet that's where Tilly's gone too. She's probably still with her mother. She could have let me know! Hell's bells, what will I do with no staff?'

'It's so quick. There's been no time to make proper arrangements,' Rachel said. 'They're shipping everyone off to England. Where will we all end up?'

'Will you really go?' I asked.

Rachel leant over the counter, tucked a strand of hair behind one ear. 'You know my situation. It's hard with a name like Cohen. Mr Scott says he'll keep my job open for me, but that I should go if I get the chance. I weighed it up before, and I really think I'm safer here than in England. That's the place the Germans really want, and they'll go all out to get it. And I've no job or house in England. But now, with all this talk of invasion, it's getting scary.'

'I won't go,' I said. 'Someone's got to feed everyone. Do you really think Albert will be going? He's got two small children.'

'A lot will go,' Rachel said. 'There's queues already around the town hall. I came to see if you were going.'

'You're not serious?'

'People are saying that if trade routes to England get cut off, and Germany holds France, we'll starve. But Mr Scott won't budge. He says you can only take one suitcase and he doesn't want to be a penniless refugee at his age. He's nearly sixty.'

I went to the window and turned the hanging sign to *Closed*. 'I'd no idea. I haven't been into town. I'll get my coat. Better take a look at those notices.'

But even before we got anywhere near the port, the queues wound around the town like a thick dark snake. I gripped Rachel's arm, unable to believe what I was seeing. 'Bloody hell. Half the island must be going, and right in the middle of the tourist season too.'

'Do you think they know something we don't?'

As we got closer, waves of panic and indecision came from the queue. A large woman in a flowery apron was begging her husband to tell her if it was better for her children to be bombed in England or starved in Jersey, and meanwhile, hearing all this, the children clung to her apron in tears.

'There's a new notice gone up,' Rachel said, pushing through the queue towards the bank.

I pulled on her coat sleeve. 'Rachel, this looks bad. If this many are leaving, maybe there's some truth in it, and we might be taken over by the Germans.'

'Let's hope it's just scaremongering,' Rachel said, but her usual carefree face was pinched.

The document pinned to the bank door was headed 'Evacuation'.

'Twenty pounds is the maximum withdrawal allowed,' I read aloud. It was signed, 'by order of the Bailiff'.

'It looks terribly official,' Rachel said. 'It looks like the bank will be cleaned out.' She twisted her hands around the strap of her bag. 'What do you think, Céline?'

'I think you should go. I've heard rumours, passed from the French fishermen to ours … about what happens to Jews when the Nazis arrive.'

'I've heard those rumours too. But they must be an exaggeration, surely? Wartime propaganda and all that. I can't believe they can be true. What would Fred say? Does he think they're true?'

I sighed. 'Before all this, he couldn't decide if Hitler was a genius or a madman. But he told me there's strong anti-Jewish feeling in Germany.'

Rachel dragged me away from the crowd around the notice.

'I know one thing,' I said. 'Fred loves the bakery. He built it up from nothing. So I know for a fact he wouldn't want me to abandon the shop.' The thought of Fred, fighting somewhere in France, and then coming home to no shop, made me cover my mouth to stop it trembling.

Rachel put an arm around my shoulder. 'I didn't mean to upset you. He didn't want to leave either, did he? I know he had no choice.'

'Oh, it's all such a mess.' I fished a handkerchief from my pocket, took off my glasses, and angrily blew my nose. 'But one thing I do know is, if the troops come here, we'd never get out of their way. There'd be nowhere to hide. Can you imagine? Jersey's only eight miles long; they'd overrun us in a few hours.'

She blanched. 'You're right. Maybe it's time for me to leave. I'll put my name down, if you will.'

I was caught then. I'd scared myself and I'd scared Rachel.

CHAPTER 3

We queued for six hours at the town hall and finally got on the list for transportation. I immediately regretted it. That night, I couldn't sleep. I wandered around the house and the shop, scrubbing the ovens and the counter, emptying the bins, as if I were going on holiday. One suitcase was all we were allowed, and my small leather suitcase lay open on the candlewick counterpane whilst I agonised over what to take.

How could I do it? Just leave everything — everything Fred and I had worked for since we got married — and set off with just this one case? To England, where I knew not a soul? I stood, dithering, a bag of hair rollers in my hand. I stared down at them. Hair rollers. It seemed stupid to be worrying about how frizzy my hair was now.

In the end I threw the rollers down on the bed in despair and sat in the dark, drinking tea and thinking of Fred, wondering where he was, and where he might have been posted, and agonising over whether or not to leave.

When the clock showed four o'clock, I peered outside to see rain sheeting down from a black sky. Bloody Jersey weather. I stuffed my brown leather shoes in the case on top of the other clothes and dressed warmly in a tweed suit and a mackintosh, and a headscarf over my hair against the rain.

In the hall I put on my galoshes, picked up the case, and braced myself.

Don't look back.

As I shut the door and turned the key in the lock, I had to close my eyes. All my life was behind that door: the shelves Fred had made himself, the curtains I had sewn, the badly painted pictures I'd done at art class. When would I ever open it up again? I gulped back tears and ran down the unlit road, down towards the harbour, the handle of the case making a groove in my palm.

Though it was dark, I knew every inch of the island and had no trouble navigating. Rachel, in her checked swing coat, was hunched under an umbrella, outside the bank where we'd arranged to meet. I joined her standing under the eaves, to keep out of the downpour.

'I can't believe we're doing this,' she said. 'It feels like running away.'

'Let's try to stick together.' I grabbed her arm and we headed for the harbour.

The queues were even worse than earlier. In front of us, a little girl with her hair in ragged plaits was weeping inconsolably. Her mother, a big-busted woman with two suitcases by her feet and a damp cloth bag over her arm, tried to quieten her.

'Dottie's lost her dog,' the woman explained. Her voice dropped to a whisper. 'He couldn't come with us so we had to go to the vets and...' She mimed slitting her throat. 'You wouldn't believe the queues yesterday. The poor man'd done two hundred by the time we got there. I'm Ivy, by the way.'

Rachel and I looked at each other. Killing pets? It seemed barbarous, but of course they couldn't come with us, and there seemed to be nothing we could say. Rachel found a piece of ribbon in her pocket and engaged Dottie in a game of cat's cradle until she stopped crying and Ivy was able to hand Dottie a handkerchief to dry her face.

When the first wave of boats arrived, with a series of short blasts on a horn, the crowd surged forward. The rain was just a drizzle now, but a shove in my ribs from behind made me stagger forward, flailing to stay upright. In front of me, Rachel hauled Dottie into her arms to stop her being trampled. Everyone's feet slid on the wet tarmac, and in the scrum, Rachel's suitcase was kicked out of the way.

'My case!' Rachel yelled.

I fought my way back, but the crowd was pressing forward, all elbows and chests and bags, in a tide that couldn't stop. The case was just out of reach. I saw a woman in high-heeled shoes stamp on it as she was pushed forward. A few moments later and I couldn't see it at all.

Another boat must have arrived, because I feared I'd be crushed to death as the crowd shunted forward again. Rachel's hat flew off, knocked by someone's umbrella, but she still had Dottie clamped to her hip.

'Mummy!' Dottie screamed, as Ivy was carried forward.

By the time we got near the front, my shoulders sagged. Only one boat was left. Suddenly, I was determined to get on that boat. Behind us, a hundred people were pushing. In the water, one was leaving, crammed with people. There wasn't a spare place anywhere on deck, and it looked ominously top-heavy as it motored out to sea, growing smaller and more vulnerable in the swell of the sea.

'Good grief. There's no navy escort,' Ivy said. 'We'll be sitting ducks for planes.'

'My case!' Rachel peered over the sea of faces. 'Did you see what happened to my case?'

'Sorry, Rache. I just couldn't get to it. There's too many people.'

The last boat was almost full, and the next surge crushed us up to the turnstiles. All around was the stink of wet mackintosh and wool, and cries of 'Let my children through!' and 'Please, my daughter must go on that boat.' A tweed elbow dug into my side, and a male voice hissed in my ear, 'Get out of the bloody way.'

I stood firm, though my arm ached from clinging to my case. The moustached official at the gate asked for papers and funnelled the people in front of us through. He held up three fingers and said, 'Only three more.'

Ivy, her face wild with panic, scooped Dottie from Rachel's arms and pushed her way through the turnstile, so desperate to get aboard that she left her suitcases stranded on the quay.

'One more,' the man said.

'You go,' I said, thrusting my case towards her.

'No,' protested Rachel, 'You —'

Our hesitation was enough time for the tweed-jacketed man to shove past us both and through the turnstile. Behind us there was an immediate outcry of 'Shame!' The gatekeeper clicked the padlock on the gates shut and walked away.

Hopelessly, we watched the boat draw away from the quay, and at last the crowd stopped its press so we could breathe.

'When will there be another boat?' someone shouted.

The officials turned away and didn't answer. The harbour was empty. The small boats in the distance were just specks amid the grey heaving sea. The disgruntled crowd milled around for another half hour in the drizzle as the dawn light pinked the clouds, and it became obvious another boat wasn't coming.

'I'm going to see if I can spot my case, then I'm going home,' Rachel said. All over the street were abandoned cases and bags, hats and umbrellas. A man in a trilby knelt on the cobbles next to Rachel's case, trying to open it.

'What the blazes do you think you're doing!' she shouted. 'That's my case.'

We ran towards him.

'Sorry, miss,' he said, standing up and holding his hands up. 'I thought you'd gone on the boat and wouldn't be wanting it.'

'You worm,' I said, snatching it from under his nose. 'Come on, Rache. Come back with me. I've some eggs; we can have a proper breakfast. You look like a drowned rat.'

'So do you.'

We stared at each other, two bedraggled women, both soaked to the skin.

Rachel laughed. 'It's wetter on land than at sea!'

'Looks like we're stuck here,' I said.

'I didn't really want to go anyway,' Rachel said. 'I feel safer here, where my friends are.'

'The Germans won't come here now,' I said. 'Why would they? There's nobody flipping left, except us.'

But despite my bravado, as I walked past the luggage abandoned in the rain, and the shuttered empty shops, I couldn't help wishing we'd been on that boat. There were so few of us left now, and making a living would be harder than ever. There'd be no chance of resisting any invasion, and if the Nazis came, where would we go? The thought kept going round my head: *left behind.*

Neither Rachel nor I spoke. The reality of our situation had struck home. I stared at the cruet and our greasy plates, and wondered what I would do, now that Albert had gone and Tilly too, and there was nobody to help me. I knew hardly anything about baking, because Fred used to do all that. Though I'd never admit it to Rachel, I'd thought by now we'd be starting a family, and as well as keeping shop, I'd be using my hard-won nannying skills.

Unusually for her, Rachel was silent, and I wondered if she was thinking about the rumours again: the stories that all over

Europe, Jews were being rounded up and deported into ghettos. Her hair was still soaked, and she seemed deflated, as if all the energy had drained away with the rain.

'I suppose I'd better go and see if there's still work for me at the bank,' she said.

'Will it be open?'

'I've no idea. I don't know what I'll do for money if it's not.'

'Chin up,' I said. Fred's favourite English phrase.

'I'm just tired. Thanks for breakfast.'

We parted at the door and I watched her hurry away, still carrying her precious suitcase. Coming up the hill in the opposite direction was a stout square woman on a bicycle, obviously finding it hard going. Near the top she dismounted and propped the bicycle against the wall.

'Phew,' she said, flapping her hand in front of her face whilst she got her breath back. 'I'm Mrs Flanders, from Flanders Farm. Who was that coming down the road? Friend of yours was it?' She didn't stop for an answer. 'Will you be wanting milk, because no one's been to collect it in the van?'

'Oh,' I said, 'Albert used to do that, but he's gone.'

'My farmhands too. It's a total disaster. You're our biggest customer and the milk'll go to waste if nobody comes for it. I've done my best to do the milking myself, but I can't manage without more help. Terrible thing, the men all running away like that. And now the women too. Cowards, the lot of them. And me, a poor widow-woman with no man to help. Is Tilly still here? I've come to ask if she'll lend a hand with the milking.'

'I've seen no sign of her. I expect she's gone.'

'She was always a flighty little madam. You'd best get started with the baking then. Don't let me hold you up.'

'Albert's gone and I don't know how the mixing machine works or what temperature to set the ovens.'

'Let's have a dekko.' Before I had chance to stop her, Mrs Flanders was in the bakery, loading flour and yeast extract into the big bowl and setting the electric mixing machine churning. 'Matches?' She held out her hand.

I obliged, and she opened the big oven doors, and for a moment all I saw was the broad beam of her backside in its black serge frock and the soles of her sturdy shoes. Within a few minutes, she'd got the gas going. 'Can you drive?'

I shook my head, feeling even more hopeless.

'Well, you'd best learn, ducks. Have you got the keys to the van?'

'Yes, over here.' I pointed to the board behind the door where all the keys hung.

'I'll take it, then, and fetch you the milk.'

'I'm not sure —'

She already had the keys dangling from her hand. 'You'll need milk for the scones and to make butter, won't you?'

'Yes, but —'

'Let the bread prove,' she called as she opened the door. 'Twenty minutes. Then in the oven on a slow heat. Keep an eye on it whilst you make another batch. I should be back by then. I'll drive you over to the farm later, to help with the evening milking.'

The door banged, and outside I heard the grunt and roar of the van starting up, and she was gone.

I don't know what I would've done without Mrs Flanders. Always in black, always matter of fact, she had more energy than a carthorse. What I wasn't to know then was that she knew everyone's business, and was the greatest gossip in the whole of Jersey.

CHAPTER 4

Cherbourg, France
May 1940

Fred

My raincoat flapped round my knees, drenched from being on deck. The half-mile walk from the docks to Cherbourg's Gare Maritime gave me a chance to push down my seasickness and regain some sort of equilibrium. By the time I reached the concourse I'd put down my case, shown my papers, and made that damn Nazi salute ten times.

Who in the name of God had designed such a ridiculous salute? One that might knock off a hat or catch someone with a stab in the eye? I'd forgotten it, in all my years away, though I'd been proud to do it first thing this morning. It was exciting. But after so much repetition, the novelty had worn thin.

The station was familiar; I'd been here with Céline on holiday. Cherbourg station, with its iron beams and lofty glass roof, had always seemed quite glamorous — we used to laugh at the idea that we were treading in the footsteps of celebrities like Charles Lindbergh and the Roosevelts. Now though, the Hollywood colour and gloss had gone, and the platforms heaved with the grey-green uniforms of my countrymen.

At the turnstile out of the station, I saluted the cheerful-looking Wehrmacht officer, showed my papers again, and asked in German for the barracks. He pointed down the street towards what had obviously once been a fin de siècle hotel, all sinuous curves and stucco, the frontage now festooned with enormous red and black flags. I stopped to stare, unable to help myself. I felt a surge of pride at these giant swastikas as big as a house, a fizz of excitement as I realised my country had really taken over France, and that in some strange sense, I now owned this city.

I dodged a passing bicycle and lugged my suitcase towards the columned portico. In what had once been the car park, a platoon of soldiers goose-stepped past. I stood in awe, envying their precision, their shiny uniforms, the sheer sharpness of their silhouettes. I took a childish thrill in the thought that I was destined to join those gleaming ranks.

I passed behind them, a kind of first-night nerves making me loiter a little before walking through the hotel lobby. My wet shoes squeaked on the red-tiled floor, causing the two older uniformed soldiers at Reception to look up as I hurried forward.

Again the salute, again my embarkation papers, my orders, my Reisepass: my German passport.

I took a surreptitious look at these soldiers and noticed the more senior one sported a small square moustache, a square black stamp, like the Führer. Unlike my elder brother, I thought Hitler's yelling and posturing faintly ridiculous. Still, Hitler was the cause of all this military splendour, so I had to give him grudging respect.

Now I had more to sign: next of kin, and an oath to the Fatherland. A thumb had to be squashed into ink and then pressed into the brown book that I was surprised to see already bore the photograph I'd sent ahead from Marriot's, the photographer's in St Helier.

'Sign here.'

A stab of something as I signed it: a mixture of pride and regret. That I'd gained Germany but somehow lost Jersey, and, waiting at home, Céline. What would she think? Her face swam before me, eyes laughing behind her owl-like glasses, the dimple in her chin. The ache in the pit of my stomach at leaving her was still raw.

I was brought back with a start as the rubber stamp thumped down on my new Soldbuch.

The men gave the ledger a cursory glance. 'Siegfried Huber. Yes. Third floor. Uniform stores. Your platoon drills at sixteen hundred hours. Heil Hitler.'

As the hand shot out, I did the same, but my hand hit the lip of the counter.

I winced but covered it with a smile. They saw, and one of them smirked.

The lift, with its curly iron grille, had tape across it, so I took the wide staircase from the lobby, surprised it still had its plush maroon carpet and brass stair rods. An unlit chandelier dangled lopsidedly from the roof with some of its crystal missing. Tall windows let in the dull afternoon light as, puffing slightly from climbing all the stairs, I followed the German signs to the uniform stores.

The stores turned out to be what had once been a bedroom suite, complete with enormous walnut armoires, and a sink with a mirror, at which another uniformed man was examining his reflection. The corner housed a pile of suitcases just like my own, hung with brown labels, by a door that obviously led to another room.

I approached the long trestle, piled with grey-green field uniforms and concrete grey fatigues, where a soldier barked out, 'Height?'

I hesitated, trying to remember what was on my papers, but couldn't. Not in centimetres anyway. Only in inches. Five foot ten and a half inches. I fumbled to open my Soldbuch to look.

The soldier raised his eyebrows to his neighbour. They thrust a pile towards me. 'These should fit. Boots and pack in room seventeen. Helmets on the numbered racks below.' He thrust a key into my hand. 'Locker key: matches the number on your tag.'

'Thank you,' I said.

The man at the sink turned to me and grinned, patting his tunic front. 'Smart, eh?'

I nodded and smiled back, though his feet ruined the effect as one big toe was poking through his sock. He was an older chap, in his forties at a guess, with a red weather-beaten face and a white mark where a full moustache used to be.

'You need your medical first,' he said, 'then you can change, collect your boots, and go downstairs for your pack.'

The German language flowed over me, thick and growlingly familiar. It reminded me of my father. The hole in my chest at leaving Céline was soothed by my sense of homecoming. But of course that was absurd; I had to remind myself, this was France, not Germany.

'Oh. Thanks,' I said to the other soldier. 'My first day.'

'Mine too.'

'No chat in the ranks,' the soldier at the trestle said. 'Through that door.' He stabbed a finger towards the adjoining room.

Naked except for underpants, I stood goose-pimpled and humiliated before two uniformed medics. Their white coats were buttoned tightly over their uniforms. I surreptitiously pulled in my stomach and pushed out my chest, ashamed of the soft whiteness of my belly and the flabbiness of my chest. I pushed my damp hair out of my eyes and tried to ignore the indignity.

An excruciating twenty minutes later, I was pronounced fit, then shorn, shaved and dressed in a uniform that was far too small around the girth.

I passed through the room with the mirror, not daring to look. I must lose weight, I thought. My jacket was so tight I could barely bend to pick up my new boots, which again were as narrow and stiff as cardboard. What size were these? I checked them again and forced my calves into them.

After emptying my case into a canvas sack I headed for my billet, and every other man I passed on the way was slim and trim, and in a uniform that didn't crease across the stomach. I went into another hotel room with eight beds jammed together. The sight of them reminded me I hadn't slept last night, and now all I wanted to do was lie down. No one else was in sight, so I dumped the sack on the nearest bed and flopped down full length.

When I closed my eyes, it felt as though I was still rocking on the boat. I turned on my side and let out a sigh.

'Hey, that's my bed. Get off.' The tone was not one of friendly jesting.

I shot to my feet. 'Sorry, I didn't know.'

'That one's free.' He pointed to the one crammed up behind the door. I dutifully heaved my sack to the bed in the corner, casting a quick glance at him as I went. A tall young man with a pale, almost luminous complexion, protruding lips, and a look of the upper classes in the raised set of his chin.

'I'm Siegfried,' I said, attempting to make amends with a smile. 'People call me Fred.'

'No first names,' the youth replied, frowning, standing too close and looking down on me from his height. 'You may call me Leutnant Obenauer. And you are Private...?'

'Huber.'

'Huber what?'

The language was no problem at all; I could segue easily between English, French and German, but the army? Well, that was another language altogether. I suddenly understood. 'Huber — sir.'

'Well, Private Huber, we'll soon get you into shape.' He shot a patronising glance to the straining buttons of my jacket. 'What did you do before you joined up?'

'I was a chef pâtissier.' Too late, the French words were out.

'A what?'

The French term obviously meant nothing to the man before me. 'A chef.'

Still a blank stare.

'A baker, sir.'

'A baker. I see.' His few words held a sneer. 'And where did you do your basic training?'

'I haven't done it yet,' I said. 'They told me to report here.'

A pause. Obenauer frowned. 'Not even a basic fitness test? Where do you live?'

'I came straight here from Jersey.'

'Jersey?' His tone made it sound like the moon.

'It's an island off —'

'I know where it is. What on earth were you doing there?'

'It's where I live now. I married a Jersey girl, and —'

'But your family, where are your family from?'

'Dortmund. The Ruhr. My father's an engineer in the Hoesch factory.'

'Then why didn't they send you back there to take your basic fitness test?'

'I suppose they thought it would be quicker to send me here.'

'No training at all? You mean you came straight to France, straight to the front line, from your bakery?' He was staring now, incredulous. 'No weapon drill, no learning of ranks, flags, or orders?'

I shifted uncomfortably. 'I've told you. I was ordered to report here, to Kommandant Zweig.'

A slight smirk enlivened Obenauer's features for an instant. 'That'll be fun,' he said, and sauntered out.

At four o'clock I found myself outside in the car park with sixty other men, a pack on my back, the strap on my helmet chafing at my chin, and a rifle on my shoulder, which, following everyone else, I'd been issued from the coach house at the back of the hotel.

Having no idea what to do, I positioned myself at the back of the ranks and copied the rest.

'New?' the man next to me asked.

'Yes.'

'You should be there.' He pointed. 'You're number 564. You should be there, between 563 and 565.'

I strode purposefully to the correct place. Further forward in the ranks I could see the other new recruit, the older red-faced man I'd met earlier, only now he had his boots on. He seemed quite at home, and snapped briskly to all the orders. Determined to be just as good as him, I followed as the platoon moved out of the car park onto the road. I hadn't done the goose-step walk since I was a child playing at soldiers, and it was hard work, especially in these damn boots.

Down the main road we marched, ignoring the splashes from passing armoured cars and German lorries bound for the port. The streets were empty of French pedestrians. Once I caught a side-glimpse of a dark-haired woman carrying an umbrella, but she lowered her head and hurried out of sight as we passed. Some of the buildings looked deserted, the shutters swinging, windows broken. I daren't look too hard; it took all my effort to keep moving. The arm holding the rifle ached like the devil already, and my thighs were burning.

Though the road signs had been uprooted, a painted shop sign on a butcher's told me we were in Octeville, the Avenue de Normandie. From an upstairs window, a brick sailed towards the men in front. It landed short and broke into bits, but was ignored by the troop. I had the impression of men moving out of sight. Thank God for our helmets. I passed several burnt-out cars, but I couldn't stop to wonder, for the noise of stomping feet had become just background to the pain burning in my legs and feet, and the straining muscles of my arm. To my shame, I could hear myself panting audibly as we came to a bridge and turned left onto a forest track.

There the ranks split into columns of two and broke into a jog. The man next to me was breathing evenly, eyes fixed ahead, the picture of health, his cheeks pink and smooth. Beside him, I laboured to keep up, sweat pouring from under my helmet to sting my eyes. 'Shan't give up,' I chanted in my head, over and over. My legs were slipping to jelly and there was a stitch tightening like a wire in my side. I gritted my teeth. How much longer?

Another mile. Tall pines passed either side in a never-ending blur. I couldn't go on. I was stumbling now and the obligatory pack thumped against my back, winding me with every step. How had I got so unfit? The men in front kept up the relentless pace. But I knew I couldn't stop. To do so would be to show myself up as unworthy, as weak. Another mile. Two. My feet stung, raw from the rubbing of the new boots; the shoulder under the rifle was on fire.

Finally the trees cleared and we emerged onto an old railway track. A glance to the left showed a burnt-out German tank and an overturned English armoured car. Beside it lay untidy brown heaps, which I somehow understood to be dead Englishmen.

Don't look, I told myself.

From there, we came to a road. When the order came to march again in the dreaded goose-step, my legs would barely lift. The men behind me fell into ranks either side. One of them cast a disgusted eye on my overheated face, glanced at my legs stumbling out of time on the tarmac.

At long last the hotel came back into view. I'd never seen a more welcome sight in my life.

'You!' One of the officers fell into step beside me as we turned into the yard. 'Fall out left.'

I staggered from the line and tried a half-hearted salute. Stopping was as bad as jogging. I was pouring with sweat, my collar drenched with it. The uniform stuck to my back.

'What's your name?' The officer who'd pulled me out had a long nose and blue eyes under white-blond eyebrows.

'Huber, sir.'

'You make us look untidy.'

The officer behind caught up, and my shoulders sank. Leutnant Obenauer.

'What's up here?' Obenauer asked. 'Trouble?'

'This man can't march.'

'Not surprised,' Obenauer said. 'He says he's had no training.'

'Why not?'

'Kommandant Zweig's orders.'

'The bugger. Does he expect us to train him?'

Obenauer shrugged, in a slightly pleased sort of way. 'Probably.'

The officer glanced at the backs of the men lining up in neat ranks. 'Then you can have him, Obenauer. Make sure he's up to it by tomorrow.'

'Yes, Oberleutnant Jessel, sir.' With that, Jessel walked off after the platoon.

I waited for Obenauer's orders.

'Well, Herr Bäckermeister,' Obenauer said, using the term 'master baker' with a supercilious smile. 'You look a mess. And I don't like cleaning up other people's messes.'

I wished I could catch my breath enough to reply to Obenauer, but I also knew that, a) I was too bloody unfit, and b) to do so would be fruitless and only lead to more trouble. I knew his type. He was like my brother, Horst. Nothing would be gained by going against him. He was a man who thrived on lording it over people. If Obenauer was anything like Horst, he'd do anything rather than suffer an injury to his pride.

'Have you nothing to say?'

I squared my back and stared impassively over Obenauer's shoulder.

'Well. I don't intend to get into trouble with Jessel. So you have half an hour to tidy yourself up. Wipe your face. Clean your boots. After that, you will practice marching drill in the yard.'

Such bliss to take the weight off my feet. It seemed bizarre to be in uniform. My mind ran over how I'd got here. How, once in neutral waters, the Jersey boat had dumped me on the German motorboat like an unwanted catch of fish. My papers said I was being repatriated, and I suppose to Jersey I was an embarrassment and they were glad to be rid of me. From the formal greeting on the motorboat, I was offloaded in the port, where a group of German soldiers hauled me aboard a docked troop carrier: all grins, full of the news of the failure of the Maginot Line. Their air of righteous confidence was infectious: that everything was to go the German way, that the English were running, defeated, in their tiny boats, scared of the weight of German tanks and men.

Now I was one of those men. If I could ever get fit enough.

The half hour flew by too quickly. I examined my heels. Not good; they were blistered and bleeding, but with no bandages to hand, I had to improvise and put on a second pair of socks. It made my eyes water to force my sorry heels back in those boots. Each step was a torture. Wincing, I washed my face at the sink, shying away from the mirror and the pathetic creature trying to comb his hair with trembling hands. I thought of Father, who'd served in the Great War. He'd be ashamed of me.

Half an hour later, Obenauer was already waiting as I marched over, determined not to limp. He ran through the orders: '*Vorwärts! Im Gleichschritt! Marsch! Im Laufschritt, marsch! Beine höher!*' Forwards. Goose-step. Quick march. Legs higher.

I refused to be defeated. I stoically did as ordered. I'd done a few rounds of the yard before Obenauer was joined by a few of his friends. Their laughter carried across the yard, and the sound of it sapped my remaining strength.

Obenauer preened himself and yelled even more ludicrous orders. 'Right turn! Forward march! About turn!' all followed in quick succession.

'Make the fat pig jump, Fritz!' one called.

I heard him but ignored it.

'*Hinlegen!*' came the order.

Lie down? What the…? I stopped, unsure whether to obey or not. I was tired of this game.

'You heard me!' Obenauer yelled. 'Lie down!'

I let my knees give way and lay flat on the ground. Peals of laughter came from Obenauer's friends.

'Up!' came the immediate call. I stood, a sudden flare of anger burning in my chest. I was half up when the order came again.

'Lie down!'

Damned if I would. I ignored it and continued to stand up.

'Lie down!' Obenauer yelled again.

I pulled myself slowly upright. 'This isn't training,' I said quietly. 'You've had your fun. I had a long journey here and this is my first day. So give a chap a break, lads, won't you?'

'It's my first day,' Obenauer mimicked in a babyish lisp. His friends tittered, enjoying the joke.

So, reasonable requests were not going to work. Still, I'd tried. I took a deep breath. 'If you want me to do more, you can take it up with Kommandant Zweig. I'll answer to him.' I turned and began to walk away.

I felt an icy shock as a pail of cold water hit me with a clout from behind. I paused only an instant but kept on walking, the water dripping down my neck. I wouldn't give them the satisfaction of seeing my face.

I pushed my way into the lobby, which was full to bursting with a crowd of soldiers cramming down the stairs into the dim hallway. Someone had lit paraffin lamps, and the smell of paraffin mixed with the savoury smell of frying onions.

'Still raining is it?' a cheerful voice asked me. The older recruit from the stores. 'Hurry up,' he said. 'Time to eat.'

'I'll just go and get dry,' I said, wiping the wet from my face.

'No time, friend.' He clapped me on the shoulder. I winced. Every jolt made me ache all over. 'A chap told me if you don't get in the first sitting, there'll be nothing left. Come on, you can dry off later.'

We queued by the trestles in the dining hall with the rest. The smell of food made me realise I was ravenous, and surprisingly, the food was plentiful: a German-style meal of potatoes and a veal stew with hunks of black bread. I couldn't help thinking that more salt and real peppercorns would have made it far more appetising.

'I'm Helmuth,' my shorter companion said. 'Helmuth Schulz. You new? Where'd you do your training?'

Again that question. I decided to say nothing. 'Huber. Siegfried,' I said, 'but everyone calls me Fred.'

The other man raised his eyebrows, waiting for more. A brief silence. Perhaps he saw evasiveness in my eyes. He filled the gap. 'Me, I'm from Frankfurt,' he said. 'They wouldn't take me at first. Thought me too old. But in the end I convinced them they needed me. I can mend their boots if nothing else.' He laughed, a deep belly laugh that put crinkles round his eyes. 'I'm a cobbler,' he said. 'Well, was. In case you hadn't guessed, I'm a soldier now.'

I laughed, though almost immediately I'd categorised the man as provincial, a bit lacking in intelligence. I hated that about myself; that I was so quick to judge. And I didn't want to reveal what I did for a living because it was too hard to explain that I wasn't just an ordinary baker, but a skilled pâtissier. It would sound patronising. And if I told him I was a baker, it would make me seem like a working man, when I wasn't. Not really. Not with a university education and a training in Vienna that nearly broke my father. Instead, I asked him, 'You married?'

'Yes. A good girl. Ingrid. She didn't want me to join up.'

I nodded, and waited. He seemed to want to talk.

'She'll come round, once we've sorted out France. She deserves a better life. Her father lost everything in the crash of

1923. His savings, her dowry, all made worthless overnight. What should have bought her a house — well, after, it would barely buy half a loaf of this bread.' He waved the slice in front of my face.

'Must've been awful.'

'Terrible. Ingrid couldn't get over the shock of losing everything. They had to move from their fine big house into a small apartment, a rabbit hutch of a place. That's how we met. I was next door.'

'Must've been fate,' I said.

'She was so beautiful, and I never thought she'd say yes. I overheard her one day as her father went out to beg for bread. She said, "But we are better than this, Father." I couldn't bear it. So I offered to marry her and told him I'd work night and day to build up my little business, and one day I'd keep her in the manner to which she was accustomed.'

'And did you?'

'Ha! What do you think? I was so naïve. A stupid youth, full of big ideas. No. The white Jews swarmed in from the east and took over our neighbourhood. They were the ones with the money; they bought up all the best shops. The big houses with gardens. We just couldn't get premises. Oh, Ingrid hasn't ever complained. But I saw it in her face every day, that life had disappointed her. She'd sit in her best silk dress, gazing out of the window of our shabby apartment, as if to look inside it offended her. It broke me. Just broke me. Every day she'd see the Jewish women walk by in their jewels and furs. That's when I joined the party. I saw that National Socialism was the answer.' His face was pink with heat and enthusiasm.

'Do you have children?'

'Not yet. But we will. And when we do, they'll never again become victims of someone else's money and power. And with

45

luck, Hitler's vision will spread all over Europe — we are bringing our forward-thinking to our neighbours.'

Did he mean France? I was uncertain about the idea of Germany taking over France. I loved French culture, and particularly its food. I cleared my throat. 'Do you think we'll be staying here for good? I mean, will France be under German rule from now on?'

He rubbed a knuckle up the side of his nose, surprised at the question. 'I expect so. Some things we'll keep, I think, like better food and wine, and better beaches. Prettier women!' He laughed. 'But the rest — the French inefficiencies, all their moral indecency, their lack of discipline — well, we'll soon clear all that up.' Helmuth paused and leaned towards me, embarrassment creeping over his face. 'I saw,' he whispered. 'In the yard.'

I felt my face grow hot. So I was to have no pride. I pretended not to hear and wiped a chunk of bread over the greasy lines on my plate.

'I was at the window and I saw what they made you do. It wasn't right. The new Germany doesn't need men like him. We're supposed to be setting the French an example.'

'It doesn't matter,' I said. 'Forget it.'

Helmuth's mouth twitched as though he might say something else, but in the end he kept silent and tucked in to his stew again with enthusiasm, tearing at the bread with his teeth.

When he'd done, he said, 'It's good to meet you, Fred. I'm glad there's another new boy like me. We'll stick together, eh?'

I smiled, hoping he didn't detect my lack of enthusiasm. I stood up, shivering in my damp clothes. I had to get away. Away from this man who'd witnessed my humiliation. 'Goodnight then.'

'I'm for an early night too,' he said. 'I'm looking forward to getting my orders tomorrow. Don't know what my duties are till then. You?'

'No. No idea.' I was about to walk away when he kept me talking.

'As you can see, there's no electric or gas to read by. Our boys took it all out. Thank God for our army kitchens, eh?'

I laughed politely.

'Goodnight then. You should get into your fatigues before you catch your death,' Helmuth said.

I quashed the irritation that he was telling me what to do. He obviously meant well. 'You're probably right. Goodnight, Helmuth,' I said.

'Hey Fred, better check the chalkboard by Reception before you go up,' he said. 'Routine schedule for the week's posted there.'

I gave a nonchalant wave as I went. Out of the dining hall, I limped to the board and saw a timetable chalked in neat capitals. Reveille was at 5.30am. Later there was foot drill, artillery drill and briefings in the hotel. Perhaps then I'd meet Kommandant Zweig. But for now I was too tired to think. I peeled off my boots and uniform and climbed under the itchy grey blanket. I expected to sleep, but there was no chance. I heard the other men stumble in, laughing and jesting, smelling of schnapps. Much later, I heard snores from a neighbouring bed. I thought of my bedroom at home, Céline's comforting arms around me and the lazy tick of our hallway clock. Finally, just as the dawn light crept through the window, I fell into a fitful sleep.

A piercing bell woke me. I squinted at the clock on the wall. Five o'clock. German time, I realised. The room was full of figures scrambling in the half-light, throwing on their clothes, smoothing down their beds. I glanced towards Obenauer's bed, but it was already empty. Gingerly, I swung myself out of bed; every muscle had tightened overnight. One ankle was swollen; how had I done that? The thought of more marching filled me with dread. The other men were intent on dressing and making beds. No sign of Helmuth; he must be billeted elsewhere. Most of the men were of a type, thinner versions of me — pale, straight-nosed Aryans with fine blond hair.

I hurried to dress like the others, fastening my still-clammy jacket with fumbling fingers. I reached under the bed for my boots.

My hand felt empty air.

I'd left them just there, behind the door, I knew I had. Cursing my aching thighs, I groaned as I crouched down, then crawled under on hands and knees. Nothing.

'Has anyone seen my boots?' I asked.

Seven pairs of eyes turned to look. One of the men wore a half-smile, and I suddenly understood. Another of their little jokes.

'Maybe you left them in the Lokus?'

Muffled titters.

'I don't need to take my boots off to pee,' I retorted. 'Has Leutnant Obenauer taken them?'

The men shrugged. 'It's not our fault you've lost them.'

'Then I'll go to the stores, explain someone's taken them, and ask for another pair.'

This answer was met with indifference. I glanced at the clock. Five fifteen. I'd have to be quick if I was to get out on parade. I lurched for the door, but was forced aside as the others elbowed past.

Hobbling, trying not to feel foolish in my socks, I hurried to the stores. The door was locked. I couldn't go on parade without boots. For a moment I leaned against the wall, defeated.

A soldier approached purposefully along the corridor. From his peaked cap, I realised he must be of a superior rank.

'What do you think you're doing? Why aren't you on parade?' The voice was cold, impersonal.

'Sorry, sir. I know this sounds a little odd, but someone took my boots.'

By now, the square mountain of a man was right in front of me. 'Why would anyone want your boots?'

'Don't know, sir.'

'Well what do you expect me to do about it?'

'I was hoping —'

'There's a penalty for losing property of the Reich. I suggest you find them as soon as possible. Now get out of my sight.'

I'd no choice but to walk away. From the corridor window I saw the men lined up in the yard, but I daren't stop by the window to get a closer look. Jessel bellowed the orders, followed by the crump, crump of marching feet. Had I been missed?

Another quick glance from the window showed that the yard had emptied. My shoulders sagged with relief. I found my way back to my billet, only to see my boots standing there at the end of the bed. I was about to put them on, when a foul smell made me step back. Closer investigation revealed they were full of shit. Bastards. I should've guessed.

For the next hour I pondered it all. Why? What had I ever done to Obenauer? Was it just because he'd spotted the weakest person, like the runt of the litter, and had to bully someone? I gagged as I washed out my disgusting boots in the sink, but I couldn't bring myself to put them on now they were cold and damp. Already the idea of being a soldier had lost its glamour. I made excuses for the men. Perhaps they'd seen horrendous fighting with the British. Lost friends in the fighting. Perhaps a weak platoon member would put them all at risk.

At the sound of the men returning, I hastily hauled on my boots, even though they hurt like hell. My stomach twisted with nerves. Ridiculous, I thought. But deep down the fear made me hurry to get out of the room; out of their way.

As a result, I missed breakfast, hiding out in the toilet until I was sure they'd gone.

It was ridiculous to hide like that. I'd have to do something. I went back to Reception and asked the stone-faced soldier behind the desk after Kommandant Zweig. 'I've been told to report to him,' I said.

'Name and rank?'

'Huber. Private.'

He leafed through a diary, ran his finger down the pages. 'Yes. There's a note. Yes, Huber 565. Next Monday fortnight at zero eight hundred hours, after the morning run.'

'Not earlier?'

The man behind the desk just shut the book with a snap.

From then on, I struggled through the routine, trying not to draw attention and keeping well out of the way of Obenauer and his friends. Cleaning the billets I could manage, and when it came to rifle drill, after a few attempts, I soon picked up what to do with the weapon from my neighbour, and though not as sharp in my movements, I think I passed muster.

Though I hadn't been particularly drawn to Helmuth Schulz, I found myself looking out for him at lunch, and I was disappointed to see him ensconced in a group of lively, laughing men. It would have been good to have some company. Too embarrassed to join him, I took a table as far away from Obenauer as I could and found myself near the draught from the open door, at a table that every other soldier was keen to avoid.

Between drills, I kept out of the billet and loitered miserably in the corridor. In the afternoon there was something called combat exercise for some of the men, whilst others were to go in groups, with instructions to search empty houses and collect anything useful and transport it back to the hotel. Apparently, many French families had fled before the approach of the Germans, and French goods were much in demand by the officers.

I was down for exercises in the yard. When I got there, I was dispirited to see that Jessel was in charge. The exercises were knee bends, or squats with the rifle held out in front, followed by sprints running between two lines marked with string. As I puffed and panted and strained, Obenauer whisked through the routines with the prowess of an athlete. His squats were as fast as if his boots had grown springs, and he was first every time across the line. He barely drew sweat. The man was like a cross between an Olympic god and a machine. He was good, and he knew it. Satisfaction was written all over his face, and in his wake panted all the other men who could not quite reach his level of physique.

The other man who struggled was Schulz. If I could get away with it, I stopped as soon as I could, never quite reaching the fifty required repetitions, whereas the stupid fool Schulz doggedly kept on, long after everyone had stopped, finishing his fifty squats, or fifty sprints across the line.

The training must have been having an effect, because over the weeks both Schulz and I got gradually fitter. I surprised myself. I must have lost a good few kilos, and I began to feel I might even have grown a few muscles. All this would have made me feel good were it not for the fact that Obenauer still made my life a misery. One night I came back from supper and was about to get into bed when I smelt the stench of piss. The bastards had pissed in my bed.

As usual I was the only man in the room.

It was Obenauer's piss — I was sure of it — so Obenauer could live with it. Hastily, I stripped my bed and changed my wet sheets for Obenauer's dry ones. Then I got into bed. Of course, I couldn't sleep, knowing that Obenauer would come back and instantly know what I'd done.

Even as they came down the corridor my heart thudded in my chest. I heard the men bang against doors, heard their ribald laughter.

'Look. Sleeping Beauty!' I knew they meant me, but I feigned sleep, my hand clutching grimly to the sheets.

'Pig must stink,' Obenauer said.

I heard the springs as the men sat on their beds, and I could barely breathe. The noise of brushes as someone polished his boots.

Then Obenauer's shout. 'Some bastard's pissed in my bed.'

I held my breath.

Next thing I knew I was hauled bodily out of bed. 'Think it's funny?' Obenauer said.

'I was just returning the compliment,' I said, with an attempt at bravado.

'The Lokus,' Obenauer said, and three pairs of hands grabbed me.

I kicked out, connecting with Obenauer's knee.

Immediately he swung his fist back and the punch blinded my eye. The ache in my head seemed bigger than his fist. I staggered back and felt myself being dragged down the corridor. I heard the clang of the cubicle door and a crunch as my knees buckled and hit the floor.

Head cracking down on porcelain. White and stars.

Water over my nose. *They're going to drown me.* I fought my head upwards, but hands pressed me down. The noise of the flush and the cistern whooshed in my ears.

I gasped like a fish, managed to take a gulp of air before my head was rammed down again under the water. Someone kicked me from behind between the legs. The pain bloomed to make me curl up, crash to the floor. The room turned silent.

More laughing. I lay there a while, brought a hand to my eyes to wipe away the water. My nose felt soft against the white tiled floor and I could see a smear of blood. Was it mine? I didn't want to sit up. My vest and shorts were soaked. Everything hurt.

I had to get up. If I didn't, they'd have won.

I crawled to the doorway and hauled myself up by the door frame. It was several minutes before I was stable enough to move, hand on the wall, back to my billet.

When I gingerly stepped back into the room, there was not a sound. The men seemed to be sleeping. My bed had been stripped back to its bare ticking mattress. My pillow had gone. I lay down and my head throbbed. My breath whistled through my broken nose.

CHAPTER 5

I asked in vain at Reception to speak with Zweig. They made me wait another week until my designated appointment. Zweig's office was a palatial hotel bedroom on the first floor, with a view over the town instead of the yard.

When his secretary called me in, Zweig himself was seated behind a large leather-topped desk.

Double-damn. Zweig was the stout square man I'd met in the corridor when I was looking for my boots. A woman in an apron stared at me from behind a trolley with a hostile expression. Another soldier was in the room too, lounging on a chair facing the window, with his back to me. A curl of cigarette smoke rose into the fug above his head.

'Ah, Huber. Heil Hitler,' Zweig said. His eyes showed a trace of amusement at my discomfort.

I replied with the salute.

The man in the chair turned, and immediately I saw it was Obenauer. Could I never escape him? What did the bastard want with me now?

'Sit,' Zweig said, pointing to the chair and leaning back in his. 'Coffee? Tell Louise how you like it.'

I sat. Zweig was still awaiting an answer.

'Oh, milk and sugar, please,' I said, as calmly as I could muster.

The maid, Louise, ignored my smile and brought it over, her expression set. I sipped at the scalding liquid, because the cup rattled too much for me to leave it in the saucer.

Zweig dismissed the maid and fixed me with a dazzling smile. 'You're our man from Jersey, isn't that right?'

'Yes, sir.'

'The Führer has a soft spot for the Channel Islands. It is a nice place, yes? How long have you lived there?'

'Ten years, sir.'

'And you can speak English and French?'

'Yes, sir.' I was wary.

'And now you are back with your own people, so?'

I took another gulp of the coffee. It was good, a proper French café au lait. Zweig's eyes were fixed on me, like twin needles.

'And how are you finding army life?'

Hell, I wanted to say. And I knew my nose looked like a car crash and my eye was still bruised. 'Fine, sir.'

Zweig exchanged a look with Obenauer. 'You don't find it hard? A man with no training?'

What was I expected to say? 'I'll get used to it, sir.'

'You know Paris has fallen?'

I didn't, but he was going to tell me anyway.

'The French government have fled to Vichy. But we have a job in mind for you ... one that's a bit less ... physically demanding.'

A warning bell went off in my chest. I looked to Obenauer, his smug face, with sudden realisation. The bastard. He'd made my life hell on purpose. Under orders from Zweig. I'd been taken for a fool. I stayed calm.

'What is it you had in mind?' I asked.

'You have a choice, Huber. You can stay here and complete your training ready for front-line action, or you can go to Paris. We need a translator. If you stay here, Obenauer will make sure you enjoy your stay.'

It was a threat. No doubt about it. I sat upright, my elbows tight to my sides. I swallowed but kept my eyes fixed on Zweig's jowly face.

'Alternatively, you can go to Paris and do a little translation and surveillance work if we require it. Plain clothes of course.'

I was being played. 'What sort of surveillance?'

'We will supply you with a cover story ... and all the relevant documentation.'

'I'm not sure I can pretend to be French,' I said, suddenly stubborn. Something in me wanted to fight back.

'You won't need to,' Zweig said easily. 'You will be a Jersey man who has arrived in France before the occupation. So your French need not be perfect. But your main job will be to translate regulations before we issue them, all that sort of thing.'

Thoughts rushed through my head. They wanted me to be a spy. What would Céline think? Obviously it would be dangerous. But the thought of getting away from this hotel, from the humiliation of the drill yard — God that was tempting. But I didn't like the feeling of being under Zweig's thumb. It made me resistant.

'I'll need to think about it,' I said, keeping my hands firm on my knees.

He sighed. 'All right, Huber. But don't take too long. The Führer is to visit Paris next week, and there is much to be done in the way of orders and protocol. Whilst you are deciding, perhaps we will give you more training. Obenauer can give you a little more physical instruction.'

I swallowed, knowing what that meant. 'I'll let you have my answer in the morning,' I said firmly.

'Obenauer, bring Huber to my office at eight o'clock. Make sure he has decided by then. And Huber, not a word to anyone else.'

'How did it go?' Schulz asked me when I passed him in the coach house collecting his rifle for cleaning.

'All right.'

Schulz sat down next to me and began to disassemble his weapon. 'What did he say? Did he tell you why you were sent straight here and not to training camp?'

'No. He just asked me how I was getting on, that's all.'

'Didn't you ask him?'

'I told him I was managing.' I picked up a rag and began polishing, turning my face away from Schulz's curious eyes.

'It's not fair, though, is it? It's too much to learn all in one go. Did you tell him about Obenauer, about the fight? About how they all pick on you?'

Better not to tell him that Obenauer was there. 'I didn't like to.'

'You didn't want to grass on him, you mean.'

I pretended to be busy cleaning.

'If they did that to me, I'd have something to say. The regulations say troops should treat each other with mutual respect. That's what they used to tell us in the *Jugendbund*, to build trust in each other. Obenauer should have respect for his men and vice versa. Otherwise, who can you trust on the battlefield?'

I gave a non-committal grunt of assent.

'Was that my name I heard?'

I looked up, via shiny boots and cavalry trousers, to Obenauer's self-satisfied smile.

'No, sir,' Schulz said, but his blotched red face told another tale.

'Show me your rifle, Schulz.'

I knew instantly he'd find fault with it. No matter that Schulz had polished every part of it to within an inch of its life. I knew he'd find something wrong.

'I can see dirt, here, and here. Get it cleaned up. Your Saturday night pass is rescinded, Schulz. You will take guard duty instead.'

Bastard. It wasn't fair. No need to take it out on Schulz, the poor sap. 'Sorry,' I said.

'Huber. Yours, please.'

I handed it over with sullen resignation. He looked it over as I waited. 'Now assemble it. At the double.'

He shoved it back to me and I fumbled to slot it together.

'Quicker!' he yelled.

When it was finally there and resting on my shoulder, he came right up to where I stood and thrust his face towards mine. 'Not quick enough, Huber.'

He called over one of his friends who was inspecting further down the benches. 'Grossman! Take this man to the yard and have him assemble and reassemble the rifle until it's time for artillery drill.'

'But that's hours away —'

'Do you want to join him? Just do it, Grossman.'

Reluctantly I stood up to follow Grossman.

'Look sharp!' came the command.

Grossman set off at a march, and I followed.

It was no good resisting. Wearily, I stood in the yard and began. After the fifteenth time my hands were moving automatically, and far from being a punishment, it became a pleasure to feel I really knew how the thing worked, that my hands had become familiar with its workings. I got quicker, until the thing just seemed to happen. Meanwhile, Grossman had become bored and was leaning against a wall, and ceased to watch what I was doing.

Zweig's offer was on my mind. I didn't like being manipulated and I knew that Céline regarded Jersey as British. It was all right so long as I was just obeying orders. I'd have some excuse then for what I did. But to be a spy would mean lying to people, betraying them when they were most vulnerable. How would I be able to excuse that?

I'd have to say no.

'You ready, Huber?' The unwelcome figure of Obenauer loomed over the table.

Schulz and I had only just sat down to plates of pink tinned meat, rubbery cheese and the slice of bread that was the Wehrmacht breakfast. I gulped at my coffee and stabbed a fork into the cheese. I held up my hand. 'Five seconds.'

Obenauer reached over to my plate, grabbed the meat and the remains of the cheese and stuffed it in his mouth.

'Hey!' Schulz said.

'You complaining?'

Schulz looked uncomfortable but shut his mouth.

'You're done now,' Obenauer said to me, his breath stinking of cheese.

I had no option but to get up and follow him. Schulz raised his arms in a sympathetic shrug.

Five minutes later and I was back in Zweig's office. This time there was no sign of the maid with the coffee, or his secretary, and Obenauer was told to wait outside the door.

'Well?' Zweig said. 'Have you decided?'

'The answer is no. I'd rather stay here.'

'Don't be awkward, Huber.' He paced up and down behind the desk. 'You might like to know that our Führer's plans are advancing. Our men will be on the Channel Islands within the next few weeks. Your wife lives in St Helier, yes?'

I frowned, disconcerted by the mention of Céline. And what did he mean? Was he serious? Was Germany intending to occupy the Channel Islands like France? A jolt of fear ran up my spine.

Zweig saw it had affected me and pressed his point. 'Women who cause us any trouble there will be deported. To a camp for enemy aliens, in Germany.'

'Céline would never cause any trouble.'

'This is wartime, Private Huber. Mistakes are easily made.' He fixed me with a regretful look. 'I'm sorry, Huber. But you're not making this easy, and you should know by now that in the army we rarely take no for an answer. Of course, we could give you orders, but it will be more productive for both sides if you volunteer.'

'If I go to Paris, will you give me your word nothing will happen to her?'

'I cannot swear to anything in wartime. How can I? But yes, I believe she will be much safer if you agree.'

I hated the idea of caving in. But what would happen to our house and shop if Céline was gone and Germany invaded Jersey? I suddenly realised that I minded it very much. Jersey was tiny, a little jewel of an island. We'd been happy there for ten years, and he was telling me that all that would have to change? This wretched war.

The more I resisted, the more little men like Schulz would get in the line of fire. And Céline? Well, I was helpless, I realised. I couldn't live with myself if anything happened to her, because I, in my infinite wisdom, was too stubborn to obey orders. Her face as she saw me off on the quay swam before my eyes. The trusting look in her eyes.

'When do I leave?' I asked, my voice less steady than usual.

'Good man.' Zweig exhaled, opened a desk drawer and took out a cigarette. He tapped it on the desk, then lit it with a book match and inhaled deeply. Carelessly, he threw the book of matches on the desk. I stared at it, aware of the smell of sulphur and the eagle and swastika design printed on the red background.

'Keep it,' Zweig said, gesturing at the matches.

As I pocketed them, I had a feeling of wheels being set in motion, of being pushed along by an invisible force.

'Your passes are already prepared,' Zweig said. 'You will take a train for Paris in two days' time, but first — you need briefing to get to know your *Kriegsname*.'

An alias. Already my stomach swooped.

Zweig took another drag of his cigarette and said, 'You'll find Feldmeister Trott in room twenty-seven. He's expecting you.'

CHAPTER 6

Céline

As summer came, gradually things in the bakery got organised, despite the fact that the population of Jersey was half what it had been. My bread was not the best, to be honest. It was a bit tough and chewy, but at least I was baking, though I had to be up every day before it was light. Mrs Flanders came to help with it, and in return, twice a day, I trekked over to Flanders Farm four miles away to help her with farm work and milking. She'd managed to commandeer several other women who owed her favours, and we gradually came to a rickety routine.

The result of this was that by the time the shop opened at eight o'clock, I already felt like I'd done a full day's work. Today was a wet day and it just made everything harder. Many bakeries had ceased to run, so the shop was always busy, despite the rationing.

One morning, Mrs Flanders was still there helping me lay out loaves when the shop door flew open and Rachel blew in, shaking a flurry of raindrops from her wet umbrella. Since our night at the harbour, we'd grown even closer, and now Fred was gone, she called in every day on her way home from work so we could share supper. This morning's visit was unusual.

'Can we talk?' she said. The set of her jaw told me she was angry.

Mrs Flanders stood up from under the counter from where she'd been stacking loaves in a crate.

'Morning,' Mrs Flanders said, with a breezy customer smile.

A sudden silence.

'I wanted to talk to you on your own,' Rachel said, glaring at me.

'Don't mind me,' Mrs Flanders, said huffily.

I put down my basket. 'Just give me a few minutes and —'

But Rachel was already out, tugging at her umbrella, which was tangled in the door. Finally, she swore and abandoned it.

'Wait! You'll get soaked!' I yelled. But by the time I went after her, she was already halfway down the street, going in the direction of the sea, her head bowed against the rain. I stood on tiptoes, brandishing the umbrella like a fool. 'Rachel!'

She must have heard me, but she didn't turn back. Already drenched from the squall, I dragged the umbrella back inside and shook it out onto the doormat.

'Well,' Mrs Flanders said, hands on hips. 'What on earth was all that about?'

'No idea,' I said, handing her a loaf to wrap in brown paper.

'Heavens, you don't think she could be...?' Mrs Flanders mimed a bump on her stomach.

'Not Rachel. I've known her ages, and I know there isn't anybody.'

'That's the thing with young girls,' Mrs Flanders said. 'They're always getting themselves in trouble. Take Albert's wife. I bet you didn't know he married her on the rebound. It wouldn't surprise me if one of those kiddies wasn't even his.'

Mrs Flanders continued to tell me all Albert's private business as we wrapped the bread, but I wasn't paying any attention. I was worried about Rachel. Since the night we'd tried to leave, I felt connected to her somehow, and today there was something about her accusing manner that had told me it was bad news, and that it was somehow my fault.

Mrs Flanders and I loaded the crates with loaves and crusty rolls for the hotels, and I stacked them in the van, thumped on the roof, and waved her off.

I breathed a sigh of relief. Though I couldn't manage without her, just being with Mrs Flanders was exhausting. At lunchtime I put a 'Closed for Lunch' sign in the window and, grabbing Rachel's umbrella, hurried down to the bank in St Helier.

She's off sick, they told me. Sick? She hadn't looked remotely sick this morning. I'd have to go to her apartment.

Rachel lived on the second floor of a small dilapidated Victorian boarding house near the seafront; faded and peeling, it had communal stairs that always smelt of boiled cabbage.

When she opened the door, I tried to give her the usual kiss to each cheek, but she withdrew. Her eyes were red and wouldn't meet mine.

'What is it?' I asked. 'What's going on?'

She held out a letter to me. 'From my mother's neighbour. Read it.'

The envelope was addressed to Mrs R Jones. But Rachel wasn't married, and her name was Cohen. I raised my eyebrows at her. 'I know,' she said. 'I wasn't sure it was for me either. But it was my address, and my initial, and the sign on the envelope told me I should open it. Go on, read it.'

I pulled it out and took it to the window where there was more light. Though the rain had stopped, the windows were misted up and splattered with gull droppings. There was no address on the top of the letter, and no date. It was in French, but on Jersey, everyone could speak both French and English, or Jèrriais, our own Jersey language from the old Norman. I translated easily:

Mr and Mrs Cohen of 6 Rue Balard, Paris, were ordered to report to the train station yesterday, and by now they will be on their way to a resettlement camp. Given that they are unlikely to return, their house has been requisitioned for use by the Sicherheitspolizei.
Heil Hitler.

At the bottom of the letter was a small symbol that looked like a cat's face. The same little drawing was on the envelope. 'What's this?' I asked, pointing.

'That's how I know it's from Madame Bouffard. It's their cat, Otto. He's dead now, of course. It was when I was a little girl. I used to feed Otto when they went on holiday, and he always wrote me a thank you note, signed like this, but of course it was Madame Bouffard who wrote the notes.' She swallowed. 'I haven't seen a note signed like this for twenty years.'

'This woman, is she a Nazi sympathiser?'

'Of course not.' Rachel sighed. 'She's just an ordinary woman, like my mother. She's not doing it out of malice. She's my mother's best friend; they used to gossip over the garden fence and exchange recipes for tarte au citron. I suppose, now France is occupied, Madame Bouffard must pretend to toe the line. Not to, might be too risky.'

I stared at the note again. 'She doesn't say where they've gone. You don't think it's just someone making trouble?'

'No. Look, I trust her. She wouldn't write me this unless it were true, and I can't bear to think of it. Of where Maman and Papa are, I mean. I'd heard rumours of this, of the mass transportation of Jewish people out of the cities and into ghettos, but...' She stopped, picked at the frayed edge of her cardigan.

'When did you last hear from them?'

'Maman's letters kept coming as usual until about six weeks ago. Then they suddenly stopped, and though I've been writing, I've heard nothing since. I suspected England wouldn't let our mail through to them, now France is under German occupation.'

I turned the letter over to look at the postmark. The words 'unlikely to return' had sent a chill through me. 'When was it sent?'

'That's just it,' Rachel said. 'I don't know. You can see the censor's mark, but it came this morning and the rain has blurred everything.'

'What will you do?'

'I can't go there to look for them, can I? I don't know where they've gone, or where to look. How can they do this?'

I put the letter back in the envelope. Her voice had an accusing tone. And suddenly I realised that she meant Fred.

I bridled. 'It's not Fred's fault,' I said. 'It's this stupid war.'

'His brother's a Nazi Party member though, isn't he? You told me yourself before the war. Can't he do anything? Can't he find out about this resettlement camp?'

I saw the desperation in her eyes, but I knew Fred couldn't get involved, even if I could contact him, which seemed impossible given the circumstances. It was bad enough that England and Germany were at war. How hard he'd worked, to become English, ditching his German name Siegfried, to make himself plain Fred. Now all that was ruined.

I sighed. 'Fred doesn't want to be involved, not in Nazi politics. He hasn't lived in Germany since before we were in Vienna.'

'Not involved?' She scoffed bitterly. 'He's fighting for the Germans isn't he?'

'They forced him. I told you!'

'But can't he do something? Write to his brother, pull a few strings?'

'You know he can't. Jewish sympathisers are … well, I mean—'

'Fred won't help me because I'm a Jew.' She set her lips in a thin line and went to open the door.

'Rachel, it's not Fred's fault.'

'He's a German, isn't he?' She almost spat the word at me.

CHAPTER 7

Fred

I shifted in my seat towards the train window and peered out at the seamed patterns of the dry summer landscape as we rattled past. Beside me, Helmuth Schulz leant back in his seat and turned the pages on his paper, a smile of contentment on his face, pleased he'd been designated the duty of accompanying me to Paris. He had volunteered, apparently. He was always volunteering for something. I, in turn, was offended that they felt they couldn't trust me to reach my destination on my own. What did they think I needed? A babysitter?

So, after a few attempts by Schulz to make conversation, we had remained silent, and after an hour or so, when neither of us spoke, I finally felt able to lean towards the view and take in what I could see of France. The further we got from Cherbourg on our six-hour journey, the more people I saw: long lines of people in cars and trucks, even horses and carts, like dark pencil lines against the pale crops in the fields. France was on the move, and I knew they were running from us. Were we really so intimidating that they'd give up their lives to run away from us?

But I could see we were everywhere. Every crossing and every station was manned by armed men in our distinctive uniforms.

'Look,' Schulz kept saying, pointing them out with evident pleasure.

There's something ghastly about a uniform and a rifle; it commands unwarranted respect. I was glad to be dressed in my old Jersey raincoat over my well-worn suit.

Schulz was still in his field grey, with his cap pressed over his close-cropped hair and all his Nazi insignia shining. He caught my look, grinned, and said, 'You look different out of uniform. Not like one of us. Still, I expect that's the point.' He laughed.

'I'm glad to get out of the thing. Itched like crazy.'

'I'll make sure you don't get any trouble,' he said. 'I'm looking forward to Paris. Ooh la la!'

I laughed with him. He was a good sort, but it was mildly irritating that he should see himself as my protector. I returned my gaze gratefully to the window. I was aware I looked like a prisoner and not part of the German Army at all. My clothes no longer fitted me, I'd lost so much weight. My shirt was loose around the collar and my trousers were held up by a safety pin. I was to be in civilian clothes from now on, but I did wish they'd thought to supply me with clothes that fitted.

There was not much sign of battle, just long swathes of people heading away from us. The sun still shone, the birds still sang. I thought of Céline, and how I was moving further away from her. I should have written or sent a telegram. But what could I have said? Just warning you, *liebchen*, the German Army are about to invade the Channel Islands? I didn't even know if it was true. Or if they were telling me this just to frighten me.

If it was true, I wanted her to be prepared. But if it wasn't, it would just cause her unnecessary worry. If I wrote, what would she do? Would she leave? She couldn't come to France.

My head buzzed with unanswered questions, until at about seven o'clock we creaked and rattled into the Gare du Nord. Paris was worse than the station at Cherbourg. Even more saluting and showing of papers, this time as if I was in Schulz's custody. As I suspected, the other Germans looked down on me now I was no longer in uniform. I began to feel what the French must feel, and it rankled.

I was no longer Siegfried Huber. I had to get that in my head. I repeated in my mind Édouard Vibert, not Fred. And I was to live life as if I was a Jerseyman, born there, but stuck in France, who just happened to have been caught out when the Germans came. I was to speak French or English, and never German unless I was in the Reich's translation offices. They hoped people would think my slight accent was from living in Jersey, but though my French was pretty good, I feared the Germanic gutturals in my voice would give me away. The translations I'd be working on would be sent to me from the adjutant by a trusted courier, and I was to work from my apartment unless summoned by the security headquarters.

A car awaited us outside the concourse, with a soldier in Oberleutnant's insignia who greeted Schulz with an enthusiastic 'Heil!' He stowed Schulz's case carefully in the boot and slammed it shut, leaving me to sit with mine on my knee.

If I'd thought there were many Germans in Cherbourg, I'd seen nothing until I got to Paris. The Arc de Triomphe was thronged with uniformed men. Nazi swastikas the size of bedsheets hung from all the official buildings.

'Will you look at that!' Schulz slapped his knees with excitement.

I leaned to the car window, rubbed a finger in the condensation. Half the male population of Germany must be here. Plenty of French too. I'd imagined from the numbers on the road that the city would be empty of the French, but no.

To my relief, the shops and cafés were all open, and I began to think I might actually enjoy being in Paris.

The car pulled up at a tall building on the Rue Dupin, close to the Jardin du Luxembourg. The officer pointed, gave me a key, and said, 'Third floor. Number five. Your instructions will be waiting for you. Curfew is from ten until five; make sure you are off the streets by then. Mark it well. You are still in the army, and any misdemeanour, you can be sent to a fighting unit.'

'I was in one at the barracks in Cherbourg.' I pointed to my black eye.

My attempt at black humour fell on stony ground. Both of them looked at me blankly.

'We could meet up later, explore the city, hey?' Schulz was full of boyish enthusiasm.

'That won't be possible, Schulz,' the driver said. 'I'm to take you to be briefed. They're sending you down to Dijon in a few weeks. From now on, you don't know each other. Got it?'

Schulz frowned. 'But we —'

'You'll get your orders later.' The Oberleutnant cut him off.

I sensed Schulz's dismay and felt sorry for him. I took his hand and shook it. 'We'll meet again, I'm sure.'

'When we're both generals, eh?'

'You bet!' I smiled and stared up at the stone corbels and wrought-iron balconies. 'Is this where I'm to live?' It looked rather grand.

The officer didn't answer, just got out and opened my door.

'Heil Hitler,' he said.

'Goodbye, Huber,' Schulz said. 'You lucky devil.' He punched me affectionately on the shoulder.

I got out and lifted my hand in a wave to Schulz. In reply, his arm shot into an over-enthusiastic 'Heil'.

With my case swinging, I strode into the dark lobby of the house and started up the echoing stone stairs. No concierge or other person was in sight. On the first-floor landing, I looked from the window to watch the big black car draw away. I closed my eyes and exhaled. I supposed it was too much to hope I'd never set eyes on either of them again.

My key turned easily in the lock, and what a relief to lock it and know no one else could get in. I flicked a switch and a light bulb flickered into life. The apartment smelt of vinegar, and something floral. Lavender?

The blackout blinds were down, and it was pitch-black, so I groped for the switch and turned on every light. The apartment was three rooms — a salon, a kitchen with a partition to a bath, and the bedroom. A double bed, made up. Bare walls, almost spartan. It smelled as if the whole place had been recently scrubbed.

It was hardly welcoming. Though it was clean, there were marks on the wall where pictures had once hung. The kitchen table was old and scratched. In the middle was a French Triumph typewriter, quite a good one, and a box of paper. Neatly lined up next to it was a newspaper, *Der Deutsche Wegleiter für Paris* — some sort of guide for the German troops — and a brown foolscap dossier. The dossier was labelled 'Édouard Vibert'.

I wondered what sort of a person Vibert would be. Perhaps he would be one of those arrogant French chefs who smothered everything in sauce. I pulled myself up to be more erect, tried out a sneering smile. I sighed. I'd never keep it up. But I couldn't afford to be the Fred I used to be, scared of Obenauer and the rest of the army. I'd have to get a bit more backbone if I was to survive. Vibert was an enigma, but he'd have to become braver than Fred ever was.

I flipped the dossier open to reveal what looked like several pages of information and instructions, along with official-looking papers in German, all in buff binders with the eagle stamped at the head.

Later, I thought, folding it shut. The journey had made me tired, but I was also restless, and hungry, and I'd seen what looked like a café on the corner. I'd go there. I could probably just make it before curfew, and the thought of French food made my mouth water.

I belted my raincoat, put my hat on at an angle that might pass for jaunty (was Édouard Vibert jaunty?), and picked up my keys. I hesitated at the door. On the doorframe were some etched lines in pencil. I smiled. When I was a child, my mother had measured me against the door frame in the same way. I tilted my head to read the name next to the lowest mark. *Emil.* I touched the highest mark, measuring it against myself. I guessed Emil would have been about seven or eight years old when they moved away.

Had Emil done his homework at my kitchen table? The thought of him filled me with unaccountable sadness. I had a sudden urge to get out of the apartment as quickly as I could.

The café was called *Les Deux Pigeons.* Two pigeons. Inside, there was only one other table taken, and that was by two elderly Frenchmen in old knitted jumpers, one with a bushy moustache, and one without, but wearing a dusty, faded beret. The sight of them made me smile. Both had their braces pulled over the top of their jumpers, their trousers up past their waists. They watched me come in with beady eyes. I sat outside at one of the two rickety tables that were set on the pavement.

'M'sieur?' A short, stout woman appeared by my side. She had expressive black eyebrows over bright blue eyes, despite the bristling grey hair that stood straight up from her forehead.

In French, I ordered the cassoulet and a glass of *vin ordinaire*.

She nodded, her eyes flicking to my bruised eye, and strode away with a bouncing, energetic step. I put her in her late forties, despite the grey hair.

The cassoulet must have been bubbling on the stove already, because she was back within a few minutes, the plate steaming with a tempting aroma of cloves.

'*Bon appétit,*' she said.

I tucked in, and, I swear, it was one of the best things I'd ever tasted. I was about halfway through it when two German soldiers came and sat at the neighbouring table. I smiled at them, but they ignored me and continued their conversation in loud German. I expect they thought I couldn't understand.

'We've put the fear of God into them,' the older one said. He had a nasal voice and a thin, mouse-like face. 'Pétain's asked for an armistice, and the Führer's agreed. From now on France will be split into two zones. Ours and theirs.'

'Surely that won't work,' the one with the wire-rimmed glasses said. 'Where do these zones begin and end?'

'We'll have Paris and the north, and the Frenchies have fled to Vichy.' The thin one gave a choke of a laugh. 'They're calling themselves the French State.'

'Did the Führer agree to this?'

'Seems so. Don't think it will last though. The south's the best part of France. Best wine, best weather, anyway. And I fancy a chateau when the fighting's over,' thin face said. 'How about you?'

'A spell on a nice hot beach. Palm trees and sun. St Tropez or Nice. What if we get leave and want to go down to the south?'

'We'll have to have a visa. You won't get leave anyway. Too much shit to do here. But the French are fools. They've burned their boats. If they want to cross back over the border now, we can keep them out.'

His friend grunted and reached for my ashtray. He didn't ask or say 'excuse me'. Just took it, as if everything was his by rights. I might as well not have existed. I glared at his profile, but he was oblivious.

'Hey, can't we get any service round here?' Thin face stood and shouted in German into the café.

The grey-haired woman came out but gave no greeting, just waited for their orders with a stony face. I could see she hated to be summoned in such a rude way.

They ordered a carafe of wine, and pâté de foie gras. So they were obviously intent on three courses. I didn't like the two men, and their presence, and the fact they were my countrymen, made me uncomfortable. I was about to ask for the bill, when I realised, with horror, that I had no money. Neither French nor German. And I wasn't even sure which I was supposed to pay with. Francs or Reichsmarks? Or should I have a ration card? I should have read the instructions in the dossier before coming out. Hell, I wouldn't last long if I didn't get more on the ball. I hadn't even thought.

I searched my pockets but found only fluff.

I hovered by the table. A sneaky getaway? No, it would draw attention to me and have every flic in Paris after me. Maybe I should ask the two Germans for a loan? Impossible. It would mean explaining, and I'd been well briefed to keep my identity secret.

There was nothing else for it. I went inside and headed for the counter. The woman was just making up the bill for the two Frenchmen outside. She raised a hand in apology. 'One moment, M'sieur.'

She delivered their bill with a friendly smile before returning to me.

God, I hoped my French was up to this. I began, 'So sorry, Madame, but I find myself in an embarrassing situation. I've only just arrived in Paris, and find I have left my wallet behind.'

She stared at me.

'I can leave my name and address, and I promise to bring you the money tomorrow, as soon as I can get to the bank.'

'You have no money? No ration card? Are you in trouble?' She was looking at my eye now.

'No, no. I had a stupid accident. I fell down the stairs in my new apartment.' Her expression was sceptical. I apologised again. 'I'm sorry about the money. I'll bring it tomorrow, you have my word. I never usually do this. I can leave my name and address.'

'The two men outside will know what to do with you.'

For a moment my heart plummeted. I'd no wish to have this conversation with the Germans outside.

'Hey,' she called, 'Sebastien! Henri!'

The two old French men shuffled in. Thank God, not the soldiers. But by now I was thoroughly rattled.

'This man says he can't pay for his dinner,' the woman said. 'What should I do?'

'How much did you enjoy it?' the one in the beret asked me, wrinkling his moustache and looking up at me with sharp eyes.

'To be honest, it was delicious,' I said. 'The meat was so tender, and the cloves … well, possibly the best cassoulet I've ever tasted.'

'So, worth your money then?' the other asked.

'Yes. And I'm quite happy to pay, as soon as the banks open.'

'You shouldn't give credit, Berenice,' the first Frenchman said. 'It might set a precedent. You should make him wash dishes, that's the usual penalty.'

'Or clean the floor,' the other said, winking.

'Now, Sebastien —' the woman began, but I held up my hands.

'He's right,' I said. 'That seems fair. Show me to your kitchen.'

The two Frenchmen looked at each other and shook their heads, exchanging shrugs.

'Don't mind them,' Berenice said. She gave me a conspiratorial smile. 'They were spoiling for an argument. It entertains them and there's nothing they like better, as long as the argument's not with them.' She cast a disparaging look through the window at my countrymen.

'I meant it,' I said. 'I don't mind doing dishes. I'm used to cafés.'

'Well, actually, I could use a hand. My kitchen assistant, Nicole, has her day off today, and we've been pretty busy. There's a stack of plates, since there's only been me.'

'Right then, lead on.'

She hesitated a moment, and I could almost see her weighing me up. I seemed to meet with approval, despite my black eye. Or was it because of it? She led me into the kitchen behind the café, past a big scrubbed table to an enormous sink, where the draining board was piled high with dirty dishes, and the wooden racks above were ominously empty.

'No hot water,' she said. 'Electricity's still rationed. You'll have to manage. You get started, whilst I deal with the two customers still outside. What's your name?'

'Édouard. Édouard Vibert.' The name still felt strange but I held her gaze.

'Berenice,' she said. She went to check on the stove where three pots were still bubbling. She must have opened the oven to check on something, because a smell of apples, cinnamon and pastry wafted past my nose. It made me immediately homesick.

To counter this, I stripped off my mackintosh and jacket, rolled up my sleeves and plunged my hands into the freezing water in the sink. I began to scrub. It was pleasant to do something familiar, but a tension still lodged in my stomach. I wished I could have told Berenice my real name. She was not like most Parisian women; her face was devoid of lipstick or powder and her short, square figure exuded an air of efficiency.

As I scrubbed conscientiously, getting rid of every scrap of grease, she bustled in and out in her canvas apron, pushing the door open and closed with her hips. After a half hour, I'd started on the big greasy potato skillet, when she appeared again.

'Phew,' she said, running a hand through her bristly hair. 'They've gone. Not a word of thanks, and no tip. Mind you, they paid, which I suppose is more than some.'

I began to apologise again, but she laughed. 'Only teasing. You've earned your dinner. I watched you; you were thorough. You wiped the draining board down afterwards and didn't wipe your hands on the glass cloth. You did a good job. You say you worked in cafés before?'

Now I was on safer ground. 'Yes, I used to own a bakery. In the early days I worked in a patisserie with a café attached.'

'Ah. That explains it. Where are you from? I can't place your accent.'

'Jersey. But I trained in Vienna — but that was before the war,' I said hurriedly. 'And now I have a bakery in St Helier. But since the hostilities, I find myself stuck here. I can't get a boat back to Jersey whilst the Germans hold the ports.' So far, so good. She was listening in a relaxed way, the tea towel slung over one arm.

'So what were you doing in Paris?'

The question came too quickly, and my answer wasn't ready. 'Oh, just business,' I said, floundering. 'I mean, I needed some new recipes, so I thought I'd research what was selling well in France.' I was improvising furiously.

'A spy, you mean. Pinching all our ideas.' She grinned. 'The cheek of it. What will you do with yourself whilst you're in Paris?'

The clock saved me by pinging the quarter hour.

'You'd better get on home,' Berenice said. 'Curfew in fifteen minutes. Have you far to go?'

'The Rue Dupin, just around the corner.'

'Oh, I've friends on the Rue Dupin. Which number are you?'

I didn't want to tell her, but couldn't see a way around it without being rude. 'Number sixteen. I overlook the street.'

'My friend Anneliese had an apartment in that one. They were forced to leave though.'

'Oh? When the Germans came?'

'No, I've said too much. I shouldn't bore you with my woes. We all have our stories. War's not easy, not for any of us. At least I'm not locked out of my country, like you.'

I hung up the glass cloth on the row of hooks next to the sink.

'Thank you,' I said to her. 'I actually enjoyed that.'

I'd unhooked my mackintosh from the back of the door and was about to leave, when a voice from the front called, 'Berenice?'

'Pierre! Just wait a moment.'

She ushered me towards the door. The young man who'd just come in had an anxious, harried look and was stepping from foot to foot. She put a hand on his arm, and I saw her whisper something to him as she passed.

'Your debt's paid, Édouard,' she said to me. 'But I hope you won't be a stranger, now you've found us.'

'Not if that cassoulet was anything to go by.' I bent to embrace her in the French way, kissing the air either side of her cheeks. As I walked away, I heard the door being locked. I turned to see her and the man Pierre in the light of the window. They were in earnest conversation. Perhaps he was her son? He had the same high forehead and he looked too young to be a lover. Something about the way his eyes darted around the café, as if checking no one else was there, arrested my attention.

CHAPTER 8

The next day I opened the folder and began work on the translations. There was a note telling me I would be issued with further files in due course. I assumed someone would come by and deliver them or further orders would appear. The documents I'd to translate seemed to be radio transmissions, some in French, some in English. They were weirdly cryptic. 'The swan has flown.' 'Meet Laura at the usual place after the opera.'

Other documents were official notices. Mostly orders about rationing and curfews, and the language of these made me smile. They were so typically Prussian, and sounded horribly stilted translated directly into French. The French had a much more relaxed way of expressing orders.

I was enjoying the work. After three weeks of square bashing, it was a relief to use my brain. Late in the morning, I came to one that had 'urgent' attached to it with a paperclip. It was a list of orders. I scanned it, translating and then typing into formal French as I went, but the words ceased to be just words and suddenly loomed into sense. I paused, elbow on table, resting my head into my hand. Was this really what I was reading?

The Executive Order on Family and Personal Names requires Jews bearing first names of 'non-Jewish' origin to adopt an additional name: 'Israel' for men and 'Sara' for women.

Were they serious? Had it come to this, that they were really expecting people to change their names?

The Decree on the Confiscation of Jewish Property stipulates the transfer of assets from Jews to non-Jews. The Decree concerning the Surrender of

Precious Metals and Gems currently in Jewish Ownership requires Jews to turn in these items to the state without compensation.

Without compensation? Surely not? It was sheer robbery. There was more.

The Decree on the Exclusion of Jews from French Economic Life stipulates that all Jewish-owned businesses be immediately closed.

The Reich Ministry of the Interior herewith invalidates all German passports held by Jews. Jews must surrender their old passports, which will become valid again once the letter 'J' has been stamped on them.

I stood up from the table. I knew there was anti-Jewish feeling in Germany, for my brother Horst was not the only one who felt strongly that Jews were the cause of all Germany's hardships. Schulz, too, had expressed the same opinion. But on Jersey things were different; one of Céline's best friends, Rachel, was a Jew, and nobody thought anything of it.

Now the stark reality of what that meant was right in front of me. I squirmed, deeply uncomfortable. It was all very well and good in Germany, but now the same rules were to apply in France? I didn't want to be responsible for writing down these orders in French.

On impulse, I took the German document and tore it in half. If the paper never existed, I wouldn't have to translate it. I knew this was dodging the dilemma I was in, even as I held the pieces of torn paper in my hands.

A knock at the door.

God in heaven. Panic-stricken, I started to shred the paper into tiny pieces.

More thumping at the door.

Hastily, I scooped the bits off the table into the waste bin and scrumpled up a page of the troops guide to Paris and thrust it down on top.

When I opened the door I was breathless. 'Sorry,' I said, 'I didn't hear the door.' I felt heat rise to my face. What a stupid excuse. The first thing I saw was a German uniform. Then I realised it was the thin-faced man who'd been at the café last night. I opened the door to let him in.

He introduced himself in German. 'Leutnant Freitag. I've orders to take you to the Avenue Foch,' he said. I must have looked blank, because he said, '*Sicherheitsdienst.*'

Security headquarters. Could they know what I'd just done? Of course not. I was just jumpy, that was all. I forced myself to smile and look relaxed.

'Shall I bring my work with me?'

He shrugged. 'They didn't say. So yes, friend, better had.'

I gathered up the papers and my translations. To make conversation, I said, 'You were at Les Deux Pigeons last night, weren't you? I was at the next table.'

He raised his eyebrows. 'Were you there? I didn't see you.'

I was beneath his notice, he meant.

'The food there's not bad, is it?' Freitag said. 'Over-priced to us Germans of course. Not a patch on Maxim's, or Lafage's, but all right if you want something simple. Though the service is terrible. They should employ a few young waitresses. That woman who owns it is so surly. Ugly too.'

I made no comment, because I'd rather liked Berenice.

'What happened to your eye?'

'I fell over,' I said. This was so manifestly untrue that I saw him trying to find a reply.

'How are you finding your apartment?' he asked.

'Fine,' I said. 'But I have no ration book. It must have been an oversight, and I can't eat without one. It caused some awkwardness at the café.'

'You are sure? You haven't misplaced it?'

'Quite sure. I should have been issued with one.'

He frowned. He obviously didn't like me remarking on the army's inadequacies.

'This way,' he said, tersely, holding open the door. 'You need to look as if I'm taking you somewhere to question you. Understand?'

I locked up and he escorted me to the waiting car. There was less traffic on the road since I was last in Paris, and all seemed to be driven by uniformed men. Hundreds of bicycles lined the streets and pavements though, so I guessed that petrol was rationed to the occupying forces only.

If Frenchmen were in any doubt of who was in charge, the National Assembly building soon put them right. A huge banner shouted in capital letters: **DEUTSCHLAND SIEGT AN ALLEN FRONTEN!** — Germany is victorious on all fronts! To me the sign exemplified the hectoring manner of Hitler and the Nazi Party, and made me sigh and shake my head.

'What's the matter?' Freitag asked.

'Nothing,' I said. 'Just a little tired.'

The Avenue Foch was a wide tree-lined boulevard close to the Arc de Triomphe, and we pulled up outside a substantial five-storey building. All the wrought-iron balconies on the whole row were hung with the obligatory red and black. One of the flags had come adrift and was flapping at half-mast.

'I'll have to get that fixed,' Freitag said as I scrambled out.

We went in through the solid square entrance, my folder under my arm, and up the broad staircase. When we got to the fourth floor, I could see doors flanked by armed guards.

'Sturmbannführer Kieffer's private quarters,' Freitag said, pointing down the corridor.

We continued our ascent. I was relieved I could do it now without puffing and panting. On the top floor the windows were small and square, and the corridor had six numbered doors, all with black-plated rim locks on the outside.

'Interrogation cells,' Freitag said. 'The most soundproof rooms in the building. Still not good enough though.'

'Is there anyone in there now?' I asked.

'Two. Both saboteurs. Once we've questioned them, there'll be more, God willing.'

I hesitated a moment and had to hurry to catch up. Freitag stopped at an open door where several bare-headed men in shirtsleeves were gathered round a table playing cards.

They looked up as we paused in the doorway. 'Stop salivating, lads,' Freitag said. 'This one's not for you. He's one of ours. No name though, and you don't know him, understand?'

'Never seen him before in my life,' came the reply, amid a mixed response of friendly banter. 'The guardroom,' Freitag explained, 'in case you haven't guessed.'

The last door was labelled with a plaque: 'Interpreter's Office'.

As we entered, several female secretaries in uniform looked up, and a dapper man in civilian clothes stood up from his desk, apparently enthusiastic to meet me.

'Ah. M'sieur Vibert. Of course, I know that isn't really your name, but still…' He winked. 'Ernest Vogt.' He held out his hand. 'I'm in charge of our little translation department. You'll be answering to me from now on.'

'Good to meet you, Herr Vogt,' I said, relieved to be dealing with someone so cheerful, and a man not wearing an army uniform. He looked to me like a German version of Agatha Christie's Hercule Poirot. My shoulders relaxed.

'Come through to my office,' he said.

His office was small, comfortably furnished and immaculate. Not a speck of dust anywhere. I noticed a shelf with a radio transmitter and many dictionaries in different languages arranged in size order. 'Sit down, sit down.' He tapped a finger on a thick folder. 'I've been reading your file.'

I stared at it. It was as thick as a doorstep. I didn't think there was that much to know about me.

'Educated at the Humboldt University, Berlin. Chemistry, I believe.' He smiled.

'That's right. Though I don't work as a chemist now. In Germany at that time it was hard to find research work, so I decided to —'

'Yes, it's all here. You went to Vienna to retrain as a pastry chef at the famous *der Demel*, and that's where you met your wife.'

How did they know that? 'Céline, yes. She was working in Vienna as a nanny.'

'It was unexpected for your family, this marriage and change of career?'

'No, not really, I've always loved cooking.' An image of my father's red-faced fury was quickly quashed. 'They are not so far apart as you might think, the culinary arts and chemistry,' I said, feeling a sudden need to defend myself.

'Quite so. And now you have a little bakery business on Jersey, taking our Austrian pastries to the English. Am I right?' If he knew all this, why was he asking? 'From now on though, you will be unmarried, at least here in France. Oh, don't worry, you may write to your wife, using the army channels, but Édouard Vibert, he is a bachelor, yes? It could be useful.'

I frowned and crossed my legs. The idea of pretending not to be married felt disrespectful to Céline.

He opened the file and clicked his jaw, as if to free it. 'I believe you've never had any proper political affiliation, though your brother, Horst Huber, is well known to the party. I am wondering … why did you not join the National Socialists and take a part in youth leadership when your brother did?' His manner was relaxed, but there was a quiet intensity to the question.

'I suppose because I was living in Jersey by then. I never imagined I would return to Germany. And I'm afraid I'm not like my brother. I've never been a very political animal, Herr Vogt.' Already I felt under pressure. I sensed his disapproval, even though the genial smile was still pinned to his lips.

'But politics is life, is it not? If you care about Germany, you must realise by now, an intelligent man like you, that National Socialism is the only answer. I have some forms here for you to fill in. A formality only. We have copies of your brother's credentials and can verify your parents and grandparents through him.' He pushed them towards me. 'You can take your time to fill them in.'

I glanced over my shoulder to see if Freitag was still there, but he had gone, and two stone-faced armed guards were waiting at the door. The sight of them gave me a jolt.

Vogt saw my look. He passed a hand over his oiled hair. 'A precaution, merely. Do take your time.'

The green paper documents were an application to join the Nazi Party. Could I refuse? I thought of the interrogation cells and inwardly shuddered. The four categories listed on the front of the document were: German-blood ('Aryan'), Mixed-Blood — First and Second Degree, or Jew. Inside, there were spaces on the form for my parents' and grandparents' names, their places of birth and nationality. Part of me was proud that I could trace back my family, and we were all of pure German stock. But another part of me had been amongst the Jèrriais, the French and the English, for so long, that the question of my race seemed almost irrelevant.

Sweating slightly, I filled in the form, but I hesitated with the signature. 'Which name should I sign?'

He snapped the answer. 'Your own, of course, Herr Huber.' But immediately the impatience was glossed over by his former jovial manner. 'Édouard Vibert is a *nom de guerre*, just fiction, isn't that so?'

I felt like saying that this particular Siegfried Huber felt like a fiction too, but kept my mouth shut. I was in a predicament, a game in which they were the cats and I was the mouse. I was under army jurisdiction, so I'd do well to be cautious and play their game.

I signed it, and he told me to write down my new identification number, before I passed it back.

Again, the click of the jaw. 'Of course, it must be checked and ratified by the Office of Racial Policy. And you can't carry it, not as Édouard Vibert. I will keep it here, in case you encounter any … difficulties. Then you must give your number to any arresting officer. Memorise it well. Understood?'

I nodded, and he stowed the thing in his desk.

'You have my translations?'

I pushed the folder over to him, and he took a few minutes to check it all through. The building was ominously quiet. Up here, we were away from the traffic, and it was so still I could hear my own breath. Vogt pursed his lips, a finger tracing my translations. He read slowly, meticulously, his face close to each paper. I stared at his bald head with the few strands of hair oiled across the pink scalp.

He lifted his head and turned on the charm. 'Good, good. Very good. They did not send you the new orders?'

I feigned puzzlement.

'They should have sent you ... oh, never mind.' The impatience was back. 'I'll have my secretary send them on. Now —' He opened the door and called for a secretary to bring him another dossier. 'Pierre Severin.' He pulled out a photograph. 'Here he is in the café near your apartment, Les Deux Pigeons.'

The photograph was blurred, but I recognised the café.

'We want you to find out where he lives. He's a slippery animal, and our uniformed men can't track him down.'

'Then who took the photograph?' I asked.

'One of our operatives. Unfortunately, he's no longer ... operative.' He smiled at the play on words. 'You're his replacement.'

'So why is Severin of interest?'

'He's been delivering a horrible little Resistance rag called the *Musée de l'Homme*, and we suspect his group of cutting our telephone lines at the exchange.' He held up a hand as if I might speak. 'I know, I know. All petty things, but they all add to our inconvenience. We want Severin stopped, but he moves from house to house, and so far the devil has eluded us.'

I nodded and picked up the photograph. Could that be the Pierre I'd seen last night? It could be. I'd only glimpsed him, and many young men looked the same. He had no distinguishing features that I could see. Just a dark-haired young man with dark eyes and a serious expression. Pierre wasn't exactly an uncommon name either. 'So if I see him, what do you want me to do?'

'Find out where he lives, that's all. The Gestapo will bring him in for questioning.'

'Sounds simple enough.'

'Don't compromise yourself though. We need M'sieur Vibert, the Jerseyman of French parentage, to be operational for as long as possible. If you think they suspect you of being anything other than an ordinary citizen trapped here by mistake, we will have to redeploy you in a fighting role.'

'I'll be careful,' I said. He meant I'd be cannon fodder. How had I got here? A sense of unreality made me shiver. Was I being threatened by my own countrymen? 'I don't like to mention it, Herr Vogt, but if I'm to eat in the café you mention, I need a ration book,' I said.

'Ah yes. Of course. And some clothing coupons. You don't look at all French in those old clothes; buy something that looks less … English.' He pulled two cards from my file and placed them before me.

Carte individuelle d'alimentation, I read. *Carte de vêtements et d'articles textiles*.

Vogt sucked his lips, then said, 'I'm afraid it'll be the same rations as every other French citizen. But you won't go hungry. I'll make sure a few extra items are delivered to your apartment.' He stood up and went to a metal filing cabinet where he extracted a slim leather briefcase. 'Reichsmarks in the front pocket, occupation francs in the back, and an unfit for employment card. You've a weak heart, by the way. And inside, more documents for translation. I've a large workload, as you can appreciate, and I'm expecting it to increase once those cells are full. I need an extra pair of hands.'

'Thank you,' I said. My initial impression of Vogt was of a charming little man, but our conversation so far made me sure he'd a backbone of barbed wire.

'It's sensitive material,' he went on, 'so don't let these papers out of your sight. Best take them straight to your apartment, and never leave your door unlocked. The French are all petty thieves.' He gave a little laugh, and I smiled in return as he unlocked a drawer and took out a gun. He pushed it towards me. 'MAB D pistol. Bullets in the briefcase. You can't be too careful. You can go out of here the back way and find your own way home. From now on, you will have no contact with us, unless we send for you. I'll send our uniformed man, Freitag, or a plain-clothes man, Foucault, as go-between. If anyone asks why we visit you, you can tell them we are investigating your background because you are a foreign national. Got all that?'

'Yes. Seems straightforward enough.' I slipped the gun into my pocket with a sense of unreality.

'Heil Hitler.' His arm shot out.

It was obviously my dismissal.

CHAPTER 9

The night was warm and sultry, and the café was busy when I arrived, with a mixture of French customers in shirtsleeves and summer dresses, and Germans sweating in their uniforms. I heard one of them complain about the heat, and I was about to give him a sympathetic smile when I realised I wasn't supposed to speak German. And German speakers were everywhere. I grabbed the menu. I had to get used to ignoring them.

I glimpsed Berenice, rushing from table to table with her notebook and pencil, and then hurrying out from the kitchen with baskets of bread and carafes of wine.

Finally she got to my table. I patted my wallet, on the table before me. 'I'm ready to pay my debts now,' I said.

'Don't be silly. They've been paid. Now, what can I get you? I'm afraid we've no more rabbit stew, and the duck's no longer on the menu. Rationing's hit us hard this week. But I can recommend the soup; it's a good hearty mix of vegetables and barley, and our bread's fresh.'

I ordered the soup, and when it came it was delicious. For a few moments I was thoroughly content, sitting outside under the stars, with a full belly, watching the world go by. After my meal, I ordered coffee, but still there was no sign of the mysterious Pierre, if indeed he really was Pierre. I'd have to find an excuse to stay later. Last night, he'd arrived late, after the doors were closed.

I could hear the sound of a child crying. The well-dressed woman at the table next to me turned to look up the street. The café fell silent. Helmeted soldiers were pushing a family ahead of them at gunpoint. I placed my spoon to the side of my plate as they passed. A stoop-shouldered man, his face a mass of bruises, led the way, carrying two suitcases, followed by a dishevelled-looking woman clinging tight to her children. The older one was a girl of about twelve in socks and sandals; she was the one who was sobbing so audibly. The younger child, a boy, just looked white-faced and terrified. Behind them, and the cause of the girl's sobbing, trailed a yellowish dog with a brown collar.

Immediately, everyone's eyes turned back to their plates.

The father turned to the dog. 'Guismo! Go home!'

'No, Papa,' the girl sobbed, 'we can't leave him behind. Please! Let him come with us!'

The dog whined, its tail between its legs, uncertain what its orders were. Finally, he slunk after them, still whining.

The soldier bringing up the rear turned, aimed his pistol and shot the dog in the head at point-blank range. The movement was matter of fact, like swatting a fly. The dog yelped once, crumpled, twitched and did not move again. Still nobody looked up. The café was silent. Not even a single clink of cutlery. It was as if all life was suspended.

The mother's whispered words rang out … too loud. 'Come on, Chantal.'

The girl was suddenly quiet, dragged away by her mother, her eyes wide with shock and confusion. The little boy's mouth quivered, but he didn't cry, just clutched his mother's arm tighter.

When they'd passed, conversation resumed. I heard the word 'Juifs' whispered again and again. The dog lay there, but nobody went to it. Everyone carried on eating as if nothing had happened. I did the same, swallowing though my appetite had gone, because I didn't want to draw attention to myself. Presumably, Édouard Vibert would have seen such things before. Siegfried Huber, on the other hand, was ashamed that any German could do that to an innocent animal.

I pushed the half-finished soup away and ordered coffee, and Berenice brought it without speaking, her mouth set tight. The cup rattled in the saucer as she placed it down. I hung around until the café was almost closed. Finally, I was the last one at a table.

'Don't tell me,' Berenice said, 'you want to wash up again.'

I smiled. 'No. It's just … I like to watch the world go by.'

'Then you are a crazy man.' Her outraged gaze swung over to the dog, still lying there.

'Of course, I didn't mean that. That was awful. That poor girl.'

'I know them,' Berenice said. 'The mother plays tennis at my tennis club. Or rather, she used to. Alain and Sonia Finkelstein. I don't suppose she'll be playing tennis where they send them. They owned the jewellers on the Rue du Cygne. Now I expect the Boche own it.'

'Where will they send them?'

'Hush. Come inside. We can't talk here. Even the walls have ears.'

She took my plates from the table and gestured for me to follow.

'Nobody really knows what happens to them,' she continued. 'We know they'll go north to a holding camp, and then they'll be deported. A Jewish settlement in the east, they say. But where, nobody seems to know. It's happening to all the Jews. The couple I knew from your apartment, they were deported too, along with their little boy, Emil. The father was a professor at the Sorbonne — fled from Germany in 1934 when he saw which way the wind was blowing. Used to come here every morning for his pain au chocolat. Such a nice man;

wouldn't harm a fly.' She shook her head, piled the dishes into the sink. 'But he had communist sympathies, and someone must have said something. Even in Vichy, it seems, they are not safe. Many people bear grudges, or they inform on people for payment.'

'Can't we do something?'

'Not unless you want to join them, no.' She took on a casual tone. 'Of course, there are ways in which we French fight back against this occupation. But we have to choose where to put our resources. It is sad to say it, but though we might wish to save every family … well, the bigger picture; that's what's important.'

'Will you stay in Paris?'

'I worked for ten years to build up this business, so I'm sure as hell not going to hand it to the Boche on a plate.' She gave a rueful grin. 'Sorry about the pun. But it's harder and harder to find things I can cook. The rationing is so stingy, and unless I can find cheaper provisions, only the Germans will be able to afford to eat here.'

'What ingredients can you get? Maybe I can help with some recipe ideas … I mean, I don't want to be presumptuous, but perhaps two heads…?'

'Have a look in the stores.'

'In here?' I headed to the door to the cellar.

'No!' She leapt in my way.

Confused at her reaction, I hesitated.

'No — over there behind the curtain.' She pointed to a partitioned alcove. 'Our supplies have gone haywire; there's nothing down there. Everything's here, where I can lay my hands on it easily. It's tiring, going up and down there, and I still can't get used to having to adapt when I can't use butter or cream, or even potatoes. And I hate to use the black market; it prices us out of Frenchmen's pockets. But go ahead; have a look. I'd be glad of anything you can come up with.'

I headed behind the bead curtain and surveyed the jars of broad beans, the eggs, the sack of flour, and the pigeon breasts under the meat cover. She was right; this wasn't much. We'd have to come up with a way of getting more ingredients. Already I was thinking 'we', as if Berenice and I were on the same side.

A male voice from outside. 'There's a dead dog just outside in the road, didn't you know?'

I froze, pretending to examine the crock of pâté I'd just found on the shelf.

'Yes,' Berenice said wearily. 'They found the Finkelsteins. It was their dog. Poor Chantal. They shot Guismo right in front of her. Bastards.'

'How did they find them? I thought Madame Fournier was a safe house?'

'Hush.' Whispers I couldn't hear.

I came out from behind the curtain. 'I suppose it's beans with everything then,' I said brightly.

'So you see my problem,' Berenice said.

I looked to the young man who was staring at me with interest. 'I'm Édouard,' I said. 'I was just helping Berenice.'

'Édouard, this is … this is my friend, Antoine,' Berenice said.

'How do you do?' Surely this was the same man Berenice had called Pierre only yesterday.

'Édouard's from Jersey,' Berenice explained. 'But he's stuck here. Can't get home.'

'Tough luck,' Antoine said. 'Where are you staying?'

I told him, whilst aware it was the very question I wanted to ask him. 'And I think I'm living in the apartment of your friends,' I said to Berenice. I told her about the marks on the door, and the name 'Emil'. 'The landlord was glad to let me have it at a cheap rent. A French friend arranged it because I couldn't travel to Jersey.'

'They haven't sent you to a work camp yet then,' Antoine said. 'My friends have all been delegated to camps or factories. Separated and sent God knows where.'

'So how did you get out of it?' I asked.

He looked to Berenice. She gave a nod, as if to confirm I could be trusted.

'I dodged them,' he said. 'I was a mechanic, so I wasn't in a reserve occupation like farming or feeding the bastards, so I'm what you might call "on the run". Berenice helped me find a place to stay. She has many friends and we help each other.' He turned to Berenice. 'Have you a tarpaulin?'

'There's one in the larder, under the shelf,' I said. 'I saw it earlier.'

'Good, then let's get that dead dog out of the way before curfew, and bury him before he starts to stink. Will you give me a hand?'

We took the tarpaulin out and he lifted the dead animal into it. 'Fine-looking dog,' he said, stroking his soft yellow ears.

Between us we rolled it up. Antoine took one end and I the other. 'Where will we take it? We've no spade,' I said.

'The river,' he said. 'Best we can do.'

We carried him to the embankment, found some loose stones to weight it down and knotted it all up tight. 'Poor Guismo,' I said. 'He didn't deserve to die. Bloody pointless, and you should've seen the girl's face.'

We lowered him in and watched him sink. It was a strangely emotional moment, watching the bubbles rise, glinting in the black oily water.

'Rest in peace, Guismo,' Antoine said. His voice was serious. He looked at his watch. 'Almost ten. We'd best get off the streets unless we want to go the way of Guismo here.'

We shook hands and I gave him a wave as he disappeared back towards the café. Was he staying there? In the rooms above? I was fairly sure this was Pierre Severin. Of course, I'd no real proof. But he'd seemed genuine, despite the false name, and I really didn't want to know his address. If I knew, I might have to confess it to Vogt.

CHAPTER 10

Céline

The meeting with Rachel left a bad taste in my mouth. The thought that people were being uprooted, with no way to resist, appalled me, and that somehow Fred was implicated in this horror made me squirm with guilt. Writing to Fred's brother would do no good. Horst and Fred had always argued over politics, and as Horst was the older one, he'd always insisted he was right and that his little brother was naïve. According to Horst, the Jews were sucking all the wealth out of Germany and must be stopped. Writing to him would merely point Rachel out as another Jew and make things worse.

A few days later, I needed to go from the farm to the greengrocer's and before that to the bank to withdraw some money, so I took my bicycle. It was a glorious day, the verges fragrant with cow parsley and purple vetch, and the hedgerows buzzing with bees. As I freewheeled down to town, I saw evidence that the farms were struggling; fields were emptier of cattle than usual and many houses had broken windows. Weeds were strangling their vegetable gardens, cars with missing wheels rusted outside. Mrs Flanders, never one to miss a juicy bit of gossip, had told me that whole herds of cows had been slaughtered because there was nobody to look after them, and that there'd been a rash of looting since the evacuation.

When I got to the bank, Rachel was helping another customer at the counter. I couldn't think what to say to her, so I deliberately chose another cashier, but when I saw her watching me, I attempted a smile.

She turned away, cutting me dead, as if she hadn't seen me. I swallowed and pretended not to care, but it smarted deep inside. Dispirited, after I'd queued with my ration book for my shopping, I went to the beach. It had been work, work, work all week, and surely I could spare myself an hour in the sun before cycling back to do the milking. I parked my bike against the railings and walked down the promenade towards the steps to the beach.

I was vaguely aware of planes flying low overhead, but they were a common sight, and my attention was taken by Rachel coming towards me from the direction of the bank. I steeled myself, debating whether to avoid crossing her path, but I decided to make one last attempt to speak to her.

She was going to go past me, but I grabbed her arm and had just opened my mouth to speak when there was a deafening staccato noise. Further down the promenade, people jerked and fell to the ground.

I threw myself flat, my nose to the concrete pavement. Machine-gun fire. My mind finally caught up with my body. Rachel was on the ground too, and I realised I still had hold of her arm.

There was a tremendous bang, and all the glass from the windows of the hotel flew out. Another huge blast. The ground reverberated under my chest, and I covered my head with an arm as debris rained into the road. Rachel hauled me to my feet and we stumbled to shelter at the back of a tea shack and pressed up against the wall, our backs to the beach.

A woman pulling two small girls by the hand ran crazily in zigzags, unsure where to go. By the bandstand, a man in shirtsleeves crawled on his belly towards us for shelter, and he paused to look up. I followed his gaze into the summer sky and saw two more German planes flying low. Against the blue, black pencils of bombs rained from their underbellies.

'Christ Almighty.' I couldn't believe it.

'Duck!' Rachel yelled.

A shudder and crash, and the hotel right in front of us burst into flames. Further down the road, plumes of smoke rose up behind the chemist's in the direction of Voisin's on King Street. A man in shorts and sandals ran past screaming, blood pouring from his head and down his shirt.

When the noise of the planes receded, there was a deathly silence. Rachel didn't move.

'Are you all right?' I asked. But I couldn't even hear my own words.

Rachel nodded, dazed, and let go of my arm. Into the silence came a distant wailing. A siren. My ears had stopped working. I hit them with my palms and shook my head.

'What the hell's that?' Rachel said.

'Only the bloody air raid siren,' the man who was propped next to us said. 'What use is that? Too bloody late. And it's not as if we've even got any shelters to go to.'

I stood up and peered out from behind the shack. The beach was deserted. On the promenade there were two holidaymakers still lying down. Blood leaked from their bodies in dark pools. Close by us, an elderly woman lay on her side, her handbag spilled open on the pavement, her hands clutched to her bleeding stomach.

'Why isn't anyone doing anything?' I asked helplessly. 'Where are the fire services and the ambulances?'

'Gone to join up, or evacuated,' the man said glumly.

'Well, don't just sit there,' Rachel said. 'We have to get them to hospital.'

We ran over to the woman groaning in the street.

'Lie still,' I said. 'Help's coming.'

Rachel didn't look at me, but she took off her nice new cardigan and covered the woman to keep her warm. A black-uniformed hotelier rushed out with a bottle of brandy and a basket of china teacups and thrust one in my hand, before moving to others who were helping. From behind us the sound of screaming made the hairs on my neck stand up, as black smoke billowed overhead.

I held the teacup to the injured woman's lips, but she couldn't stay still enough to drink it, as she twisted and writhed in pain.

'Here.' I thrust it at Rachel, and wordlessly she downed the lot.

Finally, a fruiterer's van arrived and we were able to load the woman in the back and send her to hospital. We watched it go in silence.

'I never thought the war would come here,' Rachel said, still not looking at me.

'Where are the RAF?' I said. 'Why didn't somebody do something?'

'We've been demilitarised,' Rachel said.

'Someone should tell that to the bloody Germans.'

A pause. Fred's unspoken name loomed large.

'Suppose I'd better go and see if my apartment is still there,' Rachel said. Her dress was stained with blood. She gazed down at the stain as if it might disappear.

'I'll come with you,' I said.

'There's no need.' She was still frosty.

'I'm coming, Rache, and that's that. Just hang on whilst I fetch my cycle.'

Miraculously, it was where I'd left it. The tyres crunched over the debris of broken glass, broken tiles and dust, with me trying to steer it away from the worst of it. Every noise made me startle and cringe, and I couldn't stop looking up in case another wave of planes should come over.

Pier Road was completely impassable; the Royal Yacht Hotel had been hit, and the area around the weighbridge. Chunks of masonry and bricks blocked the street, and policemen, their navy uniform shoulders grey with dust, were keeping people away. We averted our eyes from a body covered in blankets on the pavement.

'If the bombers come again, where's best to go?' a distraught woman asked one of the policeman.

'Under the table, love, like the rest of us,' was his answer.

Rachel's apartment had lost its windows, though it was still standing. She pointed across the road. 'Look at that.'

A villa on the other side of the street was half-gone, and a huge crater filled the road.

'Looks like I was lucky,' she said.

She opened the door with an unsteady hand and we went up the stairs.

I followed her into her apartment, although she hadn't invited me. Shards of glass littered the carpet and the curtains dangled awry, blasted from their hooks.

'Lord, what a mess. Have you a dustpan?' I asked.

Between us, we swept the floor of glass, and the sound of the broom gave me a sense of returning normality. As I came to wipe down the mantel, I paused in front of a photograph; I'd seen it before: a pretty, petite woman in a lace flapper dress with a long wedding veil swathed down to the ground. She carried a huge bouquet of roses and was looking up at a dark-haired man in a stand-up collar and bow tie. Her expression was somehow serious, although there was a smile on her lips.

Her parents.

She saw me looking. 'Still no news,' she said defiantly.

'Oh, Rache, I'm so sorry,' I said.

Her eyes filled with tears, and all of a sudden we were both crying, clinging to each other, weeping like children.

'You must hate me,' I said.

She said nothing, just pulled out a handkerchief from her pocket and held it out.

I took it and cried some more. 'It's the shock,' I said. 'Don't mind me.'

'Tea,' Rachel said. 'The answer to everything.'

The feeling that she had somehow forgiven me made me almost light-headed.

Saturday brought many tales of horror into the shop, so by Sunday I was glad of my day of rest. But the next morning, church bells startled me awake with their clanging. I pressed my face back into the pillow. I kept seeing the bombs falling, and the bodies on the pavement twitching under the onslaught of bullets. A noise of an engine made my heart race, and I leapt out of bed even before the insistent hammering at the door made me hurry down the stairs.

'Mrs Flanders?' I paused and listened before unlocking the door.

'Let me in!'

I opened the door. She was dressed in her best hat and coat and stepping from foot to foot in agitation.

'What's the matter?'

'We've had it. They'll bomb us again if we don't surrender. Look.' She unfolded a creased piece of paper onto the counter. 'Planes are dropping these all over Jersey.'

I unfolded the paper and read it. It was in English — a demand that white crosses be painted on the airfield, and that white flags should be hung out to indicate surrender. My heart did a flip. 'We're surrendering already?'

'There's white flags flapping all over the place. Never seen anything like it. It's barmy. We've no soldiers, and there's not a single anti-aircraft gun on the island.' She paused to suck in a breath. 'The Jerries can just walk in, and there's not a damned thing we can do to stop them. Makes me sick, it does. Your husband should be here, fighting them off, not in France where they've already lost.'

I felt guilty, but I didn't enlighten her.

'Have you a white sheet?' Mrs Flanders asked.

'I don't know ... yes, I suppose so.'

'Better get it out then. Don't want to get shot.'

'They wouldn't shoot us, surely?'

'I've heard the Germans are the worst. They say they've been bayonetting babies in France and shooting anyone who resists.'

'Rubbish. It's just a stupid rumour.' I screwed up the paper again and threw it into the wastebasket. 'Germans are just people doing their job. Just ordinary young men, like our Tommies. Get a grip, Mrs Flanders.'

'But what will happen? Will we all have to speak German, or what?'

'I'm sure we won't. The Bailiff of the island, he'll get it all under control. Now calm down and let's go and get those cows milked. Invasion or no invasion, the cows know no difference, and we'll still need milk.'

'I'm not dressed for milking.'

'I can see that. Why are you all dressed up?'

'We have to have some pride. I'm making sure they see we're a respectable people. That they can't just ride roughshod over us like the Frogs.'

I closed my eyes. God give me strength, I thought.

But as we travelled up the lanes in the hazy dawn, with the hedgerows sparkling in the dew and the mist hanging low in the folds of the fields, my hands gripped tight to the seat. I couldn't imagine what it would be like, to be under German law.

Don't worry, I told myself, they'll be like Fred. But inside I felt a resistance growing. Despite Fred, I didn't want to be German. I was English and a Jerseywoman, and I didn't want anything to change my dear little island home. And I remembered with a shudder the letter about Rachel's parents, who had been shipped off somewhere and would probably never come back.

The day after the Germans came, the shop telephone was eerily silent. Usually it rang constantly, and the shop was full of people wanting bread and cakes. I was so disturbed by the eerie quiet that when the paperboy brought the paper, I almost snatched it out of his hand. Gone were the usual headlines about fishing or milk yield, and instead there were proclamations from the new German Kommandant ordering the handing-in of weapons and the surrender of all British soldiers on leave. There was to be a suspension of sales of spirits and petrol — did they really think we would make bombs? — and we were to be forbidden the use of a boat without a permit. All the phone wires to England had been cut. Immediately, I went and dug out the wireless, but frustratingly, no mention was made of Jersey on the BBC.

We didn't see any soldiers for two or three days; apparently the Germans had flown in, and they couldn't yet land their troops for fear of the English blowing up their troop carriers. The hot summer weather had returned at last, and the first time I saw a German was when two of them came into the shop for bread. They weren't in full uniform. In fact, they looked like any other tourist on holiday, except for their shiny army-issue boots. One of them looked about sixteen; he had white-blond hair, and his shirtsleeves were rolled up over pale, freckled arms. He had caught the sun, and his nose was peeling.

'Good morning, miss,' he said in perfect English, 'I would like a small loaf, and do you have an apple pie?'

'It's too early for apples, but I have rhubarb.'

'Rhubarb?' He looked to the other older German, who shrugged.

'It's very nice,' I said. '*Sehr gut.*'

The sunburned one grinned broadly. 'You speak German. *Wunderbar!*'

I was about to ask them where in Germany they came from but bit my lip, my cheeks hot with embarrassment. Should I be nice to them or not? Were they the enemy or not? I didn't know. Hurriedly I fetched the rhubarb pie and put it on the counter. They paid in Reichsmarks and pfennigs, and I baulked, but I didn't feel I could refuse. Already, the feeling that I couldn't refuse bothered me.

When the door clicked shut behind them, I sifted the coins in my hand, full of unease. I wondered where Fred was — whether he was buying bread somewhere in France — and my heart ached.

Later that day, another older, stiffer German came in. 'Is that your *Wagen* outside?' He held the door open and pointed at the van.

'Yes, my husband's. But he is away —'

'All transport is to be surrendered. Give me the keys, if you please.'

'But Mrs Flanders needs the van to collect the milk, or I can't bake. I can't drive, you see. And we use it to collect flour from the mill, and to deliver bread to all the big hotels.'

He stared a moment. 'Mrs Flanders, who is she?'

'From the farm at the top of the hill. We help each other. I help with the milking, she drives the van.'

'I will talk to the Feldkommandant. In the meantime, no driving.'

After he'd gone, I sighed. It was clear things were going to be different, and by the evening Mrs Flanders was on my doorstep again, out of breath from cycling, her glasses steamed up from her efforts.

'It's a good job my Walter's dead and gone,' she said, without preamble. 'He'd turn in his grave. The farm's to be completely taken over. We're to grow wheat and barley and potatoes. And to make room for their crops, we've to abandon grazing and slaughter some of the cattle. It took years to build up that herd of Jerseys! The policeman who delivered the message was very apologetic, but he says they need to feed the German garrisons that'll be stationed here.'

'Oh Lord. What will you do? You've no men to help, have you?'

'I don't know. It seems an unholy muddle to me, and the harvest's going to be a joke. But the policeman said no food will come from England, not now; so I suppose it's do that or starve.'

'They came this morning about the van and —'

'That's another thing. To keep the van, I'm to deliver all the bread to the officers stationed in the Grand Hotel in St Helier.'

'Don't I get a say in this?'

'Seems not. We get to keep a tenth of it, they're saying.'

CHAPTER 11

July 1940

Fred

Finding Pierre Severin, I decided, could take me a very long time. Was this treason to the Reich? Probably. I shut my mind to the thought. I decided not to go to the café that evening, but to have breakfast there instead and explore Paris a little more on foot. As I passed close to the Métro, I saw a German paper for sale. It was out of date, but I bought a copy anyway. 'To light the fire,' I said to the vendor.

The headline stopped me in my tracks. '**JERSEY ERGAB SICH!**' Jersey has surrendered. The heat drained from my body in an instant. There it was in black and white. Germany had invaded Jersey.

I read on, only vaguely aware of the other people passing by. In St Helier, bombers had attacked the harbour. Had Céline been there? She enjoyed a stroll on the quay, looking at the boats on her way to the market. 'Mooching,' she called it.

I read and re-read it, unable to decide what to do. Finally, I stuffed the paper in my pocket and began to run back towards my apartment. What about our shop? If anything had happened to Céline, I would...

Could I ask Vogt? I had strict orders not to contact him unless sent for.

Berenice. She might have a radio, might be able to tell me what was happening on Jersey. I broke into a faster run, dodging pedestrians. A German soldier turned to look at me sharply. Panting, I slowed to a brisk walk. Somehow I had to get a message to Céline, find out if she was all right. By the time I arrived at the café, my armpits were soaked with sweat, not from running, but from fear. I strode past the tables of customers to the counter. The other Germans in their uniforms looked at me with a disinterest that made me want to punch them. I arrived panting at the counter. Berenice was making out a bill. Her eyes widened at the sight of me.

'What?' she said.

'I need to find out what happened in Jersey. My home. My wife.'

'Your wife?' She was confused. 'You didn't tell us —'

'I know, I know. It's complicated. But I need to find out. I mean, have you a radio?'

'Hush. Keep your voice down.' Her matter-of-fact voice calmed me. 'Be calm. I'll do what I can. Take this coffee and go back outside. When the officers have gone, I'll come and fetch you. Then we can talk.' I was about to protest, but she pushed the coffee towards me.

I took a deep breath and went to find a table alone, where I sipped the bitter coffee, my leg tapping an involuntary tattoo of impatience. True to her word, when the officers had gone Berenice appeared.

'Quickly,' she said. 'Follow me.'

She led me through a side door of the café that went up some narrow stairs to the apartment above. I was too panicked to notice anything except that one wall housed an enormous bookcase and a sideboard held a pile of gramophone records and a player. From a cupboard she pulled out a small Bakelite radio and turned the dial to tune it in.

'It's tuned to Radio Londres, not Radio Paris. I don't know if you'll hear anything about Jersey, but it's your best hope. You can only listen for a short while, fifteen minutes, and with the volume very low. If anyone finds out we are listening to that and not Radio Paris, we can be arrested. Understood? Tune it back when you're finished.'

'Thank you. I'll be careful.'

'And Édouard, I hope she's all right.'

Berenice disappeared downstairs, then back to her customers, leaving me alone with the radio.

I pressed my ear close to it. It was playing an old French tune, one Céline and I had often heard at fetes and festivals on the island. It gave me a sweet pang of nostalgia. But after fifteen minutes, I still had no more news about Jersey, just more news about Vichy France and how it was doing little to help the occupied half of the country. Pétain apparently wanted the occupation to be peaceful with no more bloodshed, a sentiment I couldn't help but agree with.

Reluctantly, I switched the thing off. It was tempting to keep listening, but Berenice had been kind; I couldn't betray her trust. If Céline were in trouble, surely I would feel something? I listened, straining for some sort of instinctive response. Nothing. The best I could do was to send her a sort of prayer, though I wasn't much of a believer these days. Science had knocked that out of me. But I sent a yearning hope she was well.

I imagined her sitting with her library book, knees tucked under her skirt, on the proddy rug in front of our fire. She was right. We should have fled to England. But even then there'd be no safe place for me there, not as an enemy of the state.

'Nothing?' asked Berenice when I came down.

I shook my head. She rested a hand on my arm. 'You would hear if anything was wrong. Try not to worry.'

'I'm fine,' I said. I hated the look of sympathy in her eyes.

But when Freitag came later in the week for my files, I slipped in a letter to Vogt, asking him if he could find out for me if Céline was okay. I received no reply, and there was nothing in the new folder the next week to indicate he had ever received my note. I ground my teeth and cursed him, but I knew it would do no good.

From then on it got no easier, but I developed a routine that helped me stave off the worst feelings of not knowing. Breakfast at the café, followed by my translation work, followed by a long walk in the city. I liked my new trim waist, and the feeling of good health that fitness gave me. I refused to carry the gun Vogt had given me. I left it in my apartment drawer, because I worried it might fall from my pocket and give me away to Berenice. In the late afternoon, I'd go back to the café and go through the menus with her, trying to find some way of making the ever-dwindling supplies make a meal. '*La débrouille*', she called it. Resourcefulness.

One day in the kitchen, she asked me about Céline. 'Why didn't you tell me you were married?'

'I suppose I just wanted to keep her out of it,' I lied. 'I didn't want the Germans to hear her name.'

'You could have told me. After all, it's what friends are for.' It was a gentle reprimand, but I still felt guilty.

In fact, I told her hardly anything. I was on my guard the whole time, as if to relax even a little might lead to some *faux pas* I could never undo. What with that and the struggle to keep on top of the language, I had become a stiff and humourless person, the very opposite of the easy-going man I'd been on Jersey. Even with Berenice, I felt we couldn't quite be friends, that her gentle probing might lead me to crumble altogether.

CHAPTER 12

Céline

And so it began. Months of new regulations, and by Christmas there were four thousand German troops on the island and a programme of fortification began. I couldn't get used to seeing it. When I cycled down to the town, I passed platoons of soldiers marching up the road on their training drills, or German trucks ferrying bags of cement. It seemed so odd, with the blackbirds still singing away, oblivious to these interlopers in our midst.

Many things had to change. In the next six months our libraries were censored, the village school had to teach German, and the newspapers' front pages were devoted to German victories. Our clocks changed to make us part of French time, and suddenly cars had to drive on the right.

For a while we did our best to ignore it all. As food became scarcer, the best bread was sent to feed the Germans, and the grandest houses on the island were taken over by German high command. Of course, to Jersey people they were always the enemy, but to me I couldn't help but think of them as Fred's countrymen, and it made me uneasy to be both patriotic and a traitor to my country at the same time.

We came to dread the knock at the door which meant we had to open it before someone broke it down. One day the knock came just as I was taking the kettle off the hob and it made me jump so hard that scalding water shot out of the spout and over my arm. I opened the door to find two uniformed Germans there, one tall with sandy hair, the other thickset and darker.

'Have you a wireless?' The taller one asked.

'Yes,' I said. 'But it isn't working.' I mentally crossed my fingers they'd believe me.

'Show me.' He stepped over the threshold without an invitation and I backed away as they both came in. They made me nervous in the way big dogs did, that they might suddenly do something savage and unexpected.

I pointed them towards the sideboard, where the wireless sat in its usual place, and they walked over and switched it on. Nothing. 'See,' I said. 'It's broken. It's not working.' The fuse was in my purse.

'We will take it anyway,' he said. 'All radios are forbidden.'

'But it was my husband's,' I said. 'He's a soldier like you in the German army. He won't like it if he comes home to find it gone.'

I might as well not have spoken. The shorter man unplugged it from the wall, but I lunged towards him and grabbed the set in my arms. My scalded arm burned, but I clung on.

'No! It was a gift; I know it's broken, but it has sentimental value,' I protested. I was desperate. How would I get any news of the war in France without the wireless?

'Put it down,' the taller one said.

I gaped at him. He was pointing a gun right at me. Even here in my own sitting room. Slowly, very slowly, my eyes fixed on him, I lowered it to the ground. The shorter man picked it up and I watched him walk away with the Bakelite box under his arm. The other man kept the gun trained on me, with a superior smirk on his face. When they'd left the house, I looked out of the shop window to see them swaggering away, the wire with its two-pin plug still trailing on the road.

The sight of it made me feel powerless, as if I'd lost more than just the radio. I went to the kitchen table and thumped my fists down on it as hard as I could until I was hot and breathless. It still didn't ease the feeling of frustration, and even my scalded arm seemed trivial compared to the anger welling up inside.

Later that day, Rachel came by the shop on her way to work.

'I try to act normal,' she confided, 'but I can't. I still can't get used to the way they parade about, as if they own the place, and us with it.' She saw my arm, which I'd wrapped in a wet tea-towel. 'What happened to your arm?'

'I scalded it. But it's nothing.'

'Let's look.'

I unwrapped it to show her the blister and she sucked in her breath.

'Ouch.'

'They've confiscated my wireless,' I said.

'Oh no. What happened?'

'I made a bit of a scene. The soldier actually threatened me. With a gun.'

She was incredulous. 'Here?'

'Yes. It was my fault. I didn't want to let it go. But still, I can't get over it. He would have shot me for my wireless. I couldn't take it in, that my life was on the line for something so small.'

'It's happening all over. They've banned them. I hoped somehow they'd never get to you.'

'But how the heck will we know what's going on in the outside world?'

'That's just it. They don't want us to know, do they?'

CHAPTER 13

Paris, October 1941

Fred

For a while I heard nothing of Antoine (or was he Pierre?). Nor for that matter did I see Vogt or my German masters, and in one way I was glad. I had a routine of helping Berenice at the café; I'd lay tables or clear away, or wash pots for the pleasure of some company. It was an odd and lonely existence working for invisible paymasters with no colleagues to talk to. I missed Céline, and with no news from home I feared what she might think of me now the Germans had taken over Jersey. Freitag appeared regularly at my door with a fresh folder of translations. Sometimes another Frenchman brought them, a wiry pimpled youth who introduced himself as Foucault. A youth in the pay of Vogt, obviously. I did my work thoroughly and efficiently and hoped to be as invisible as possible.

Many of the German pronouncements made me fidget as I tried not to be the man who put them into French. Some documents were for Section IV, what Freitag called the *Funkspiel*, or Radio Game. Captured Allied wireless sets were being used to transmit fake messages to try to flush out enemy radio operators and members of French Resistance groups. Whoever did the transmissions would have to have perfect English, I thought. So many agents. Were they willing, or had they been 'persuaded' just like me? As the months went by, I realised that these men rarely lasted more than a dozen messages before their signal was found, and I was both grateful not to be one of them, and guilty about my part in translating the messages.

Today I was to translate another batch of these transmissions. In one way, it was fascinating. In another, harrowing. My translations could mean life or death for these people. I thought of the interrogation cells at Avenue Foch and closed my eyes. Céline was right; I should have resisted joining the army. I wasn't much good as either a soldier or a spy.

When I'd finished my work, I was forced to queue with the rest of the French for my rations in an icy wind. As a single man, with a supposedly weak heart, and no hard manual labour, my entitlement was meagre. The waiting was long, the day bitter, and my feet were numb by the time I got my quota of milk and bread and climbed the stairs to my curiously deserted apartment block. Two other Jewish families had lived there, but both had fled. Now only one elderly Frenchman remained, and me.

I stared at the table. A large crate had appeared beside another folder of translations. My previous work had gone, even though it was only half-finished. Someone had been in here. Someone — someone other than me — must have a key to this apartment. And if they had a key, then nothing I owned would ever be private. Of course, I should have known they would keep an eye on me.

I peered in the box. A small pat of butter, a few rinds of bacon wrapped in greaseproof paper, a small German sausage, some earthy carrots, a screw-top bottle of peas and a jar of red jam: the provisions they'd promised. If I'd known, it would have saved me queueing.

With my fingers still clumsy with cold, I pulled out a small bottle of brandy and put it to one side. Thank God they thought this essential. If there was one thing I needed right now, this was it. I unscrewed the top and took a large swig. The fumes in my throat made me wheeze, but the warmth began to thaw my stiff muscles. The taste reminded me of Céline, of how we sometimes used to stroll to the harbour before coming back to our nightcap of cocoa and brandy. Maybe I'd pour myself a nightcap later. I hated to eat on my own; I missed Céline, and I missed Jersey, where everyone knew me and I didn't need to keep watching my step in case I forgot to be Édouard Vibert.

I was too worried that I was being watched to stay indoors. I needed distraction. What to do? I rummaged through the food on the table. It was hardly a feast, yet already I was conjuring a recipe, so I packed it all back in the box, except for the brandy which, given the weather, was too tempting to give away. I carried the box over to Les Deux Pigeons. For the first time, I looked over my shoulder to check I wasn't being followed. The fact someone had been in my apartment made me cautious.

The café was quiet. Few soldiers ate in restaurants in the middle of the day. I took the box through and stood it on the counter. 'A few extras for tonight's menu,' I said.

Berenice picked through the contents. 'My God. Bacon. And butter!' Her eyes lit up. 'Where did you get these?'

'An aunt of mine,' I improvised. 'She lives in the country. It was a gift. I'd like to share it.'

'Nice aunt. Brandy too, by the smell of you. But I can't give you anything for it,' she said, pushing the box back towards me. 'In fact, I've been told to call it a day. Been given my notice.'

'What? You're giving up the café?' The thought of it hurt me, as if I'd had to give up my own shop. 'But you said you'd never give up. What about those two old guys who come every day?'

'I know, I know. But I had a letter this morning telling me I'm to be closed down unless I serve only soldiers. Then I'll be entitled to a special licence. All the cafés that serve the French, especially small ones like me, are having their rationing licences revoked.' She moved her index finger round and round on the counter, tracing circle after circle. 'And I think there's a political motive too.'

'Like what?'

'These are places where the French get together and talk ... or plot. I think they don't like that idea.'

'But what will you do?'

She shrugged. 'Find war work, I suppose. I don't suppose I'll get much choice. And they don't like women running things either. They think all women should do is sit at home. Haven't you heard their slogan? The three "Ks"?'

Kinder, Küche, Kirche. I'd heard it of course, but I pretended I hadn't.

'Children, kitchen, church,' she continued. 'The kitchen I'm fine with. The others — well, if you want my opinion, it's just an underhand way of producing more obedient citizens for Hitler. As if women have no minds of their own and are just there to be the Reich's baby-producing machines.'

'Can't you get work in a bigger restaurant?'

'What, and serve Nazis all day long? You've got to be joking. But the worst thing is, I'll probably lose my apartment too.'

'Won't they let you stay?'

'Doubt it. It'll become Boche property, another brothel probably. But it's not just me. Sometimes I take in ... lodgers.' Her expression became guarded. She was watching my reaction.

Now was the moment. I felt it, even though nothing was said.

I caught her eye, spoke carefully. 'Lodgers like Antoine?'

'He said you were a good sort. He took to you. He doesn't trust many people; we've learned not to. Look at the Finkelsteins — betrayed by a neighbour.'

The air between us bristled. 'Where's Antoine now? I liked him.'

'He's not living upstairs anymore; we … move them around. Makes it harder for the Germans to get a fix on them.'

'Are they all work dodgers like Antoine?'

She lowered her voice. 'They're all people who want to…' She paused, waiting for me to fill in the word. When I didn't, she said, 'People who don't see why they should collaborate.'

'I see. If there's anything I can do…'

'No, no. It has certain … dangers. And I'm not sure how long I will be able to stay in Paris. I told you, I'll have to close unless I pander to the troops, and once the Germans get an idea, it's as if it has to be done yesterday.'

'I hope you're wrong. Where will I eat if you're not here?'

'You'll survive. After all, you can at least cook.'

'Let's look on the bright side. It might never happen. We should make a decent casserole with that bacon before it goes bad. For your loyal and regular customers only, I mean.'

She smiled, and the stiffness seeped out of her. 'Then we will have to work out a way it doesn't get to German mouths,' she said. 'Food has always been the first act of resistance, all through history. The invader always fills his own belly first.'

'Not today, though,' I said. 'Today we keep our bacon off the menu and under the counter.'

The first act of resistance was easy.

The next morning, I was up early and at my desk. From the sheer number of transcripts I'd received, I guessed more illegal radios had fallen into Vogt's hands. I paused and sucked on my pencil, trying to distance myself from the task. There were orders to grapple with too. I hadn't been able to avoid translating the new rules for Jews in Paris, and here were more of the same.

I walked to the window and stared into the street, and I was just in time to see a black car draw up outside and the spiky figure of Freitag get out. He straightened his cap and looked up at the apartment. I shot out of sight and hurried back to my desk and put everything into order.

Sure enough, there was a sharp rap on the door. I let him in, and without preamble he said, 'Herr Vogt wants to see you. I've to drive you over.'

A summons. Never a good sign. I took up my work, and as I locked the door, I asked, 'Was it you who brought the food?'

'That, yes. All right?'

'Fine. Do you have a key?' I couldn't keep the accusation from my voice.

'Of course. You weren't in, and I didn't want to leave it outside. It'd be snatched by the thieving French as soon as my back was turned.'

All very reasonable. But still I resented it. I led the way downstairs with him following behind. As we got to the bottom, I looked back, and I was in time to see a white-haired man in an ancient cardigan emerge from his apartment and stare at us over the bannisters.

Seeing Freitag, he retreated hurriedly behind his door.

Vogt looked exactly the same as the previous time I'd met him. 'Ah, Vibert,' he said affably. 'How's it going?'

'The work's pretty straightforward — main problem is that sometimes the coded transmissions make no logical sense, so I can't rely on context.'

'True. But you manage. The other task — another train line was incapacitated last week by an explosive device, and it has all the hallmarks of our friend Severin. I'd almost forgotten about him until this incident. He's a mechanical engineer — manages to make bombs out of old motorcycle cylinders filled with gelignite.' His manner was as if it was my fault.

'I've kept my eyes open, but I haven't seen anyone of his description. In the day, the customers at the café are mostly our men, and the Gestapo. The food's good, and it's popular.'

'The woman who owns it, have you spoken to her?'

'Yes. I've made a friend of her, but I don't want to arouse her suspicion. An old Frenchman I was talking to says she sometimes takes in lodgers, young men who are dodging the work conscripts.' The closer I could stay to the truth, the less chance of messing up.

'Ah, that sounds more like it. And?'

'There's nobody lodging there at the moment, though just before curfew I've seen several men arrive and then leave quietly one by one, dodging the patrols. They could just be illegal drinkers, or they could be the men you're after. It's always too dark to identify anyone. I heard, though, that you're thinking of shutting the café down. That seems a shame. If you shut it, if it really is a meeting place for the Resistance, they'll scatter. There might be a chance to root out the whole network if we had a little more time.'

'Hmm. Better to just to close the place and deport the woman.'

I tensed. 'I don't think she does much except provide the premises. They'll soon find somewhere else, then we'll have lost them. If it's Severin and the young men we're after, we should turn a blind eye, let them get over-confident. Once they think they're getting away with it, that's the time to strike. We could have them in for questioning, and we'd get much more out of them that way.'

'We've *been* turning a blind eye.' His eyes narrowed, and I could see him grudgingly weighing up what I'd said, but he was a man who was reluctant to accede to anyone else's ideas. 'See if you can wheedle your way into their group. Otherwise, as inconvenient as it is for your stomach, we'll just close her down.'

There was nothing to do but nod, agree, and give him the damn salute.

I was left to walk home again. It irked me that they drove me there on a whim and then didn't drive me home. As if Vogt's time was too precious to be wasted but mine was utterly disposable.

I'd bought Berenice a little more breathing space, but I could already see that this wouldn't end well. I was deceiving both parties, and sooner or later one of them would rumble it. The thought made me unaware of the traffic until a horn blared, and I leapt back from the road I'd been about to cross. I held up my hands: 'Sorry, sorry!' I said, but then repeated, '*Pardon!*' Good job the traffic was too noisy for them to hear my English apology.

Panic rose in my chest. I was always so close to the edge, as if fear had lodged in the seams of my clothes and I could never get away from it. I liked Berenice, who was supposed to be my enemy, but Vogt, who was supposed to be my friend, made me shrivel inside.

CHAPTER 14

Céline

The winter of 1941 was hard. Temperatures were below freezing, and the Germans needed our fuel, our electricity, and our cars; even our blankets and spare pillows were requisitioned. I took to wearing two jerseys when I served in the shop, and even then, my wrists and hands were blue.

With coal being rationed, I allowed myself only a few lumps of coal a day for a few hours warmth in the evening, and gleaned as much wood as I could from the copse behind the farm. When the gas ovens were hot in the morning I huddled next to them, only moving when the shop bell went and a customer needed serving.

The evenings were the worst: no gas, no electricity, and little light. There was little we could do in the cold and dark, except go to bed early. I often looked at the wooden bread trays and wished I could chop them up for firewood, but they were needed for the German bread deliveries.

One morning, I'd just seen Mrs Flanders off on the bread run, when two soldiers came into the shop, carrying a bulging sack. 'You have soap?' one of them asked.

My mouth must have fallen open because it seemed such an odd request, but they pushed past me into the house and headed to the kitchen and the bathroom. I followed and was in time to see them take the half-used bar from the sink, and look through the cupboards and drawers for more. I was helpless to stop them; what could I do against armed men? And yet it seemed such a trivial thing to demand. They took every scrap of soap including the hard carbolic from the kitchen and the soap flakes for washing clothes from under the sink.

'I must have soap to clean the bread tins,' I protested, as they were about to take the remnants of my packet of washing soda, 'unless you want your bread to be dirty.'

The young soldier shrugged. 'It is orders. The men need soap, so we must bring soap.'

It seemed ridiculous, but there was nothing I could do. When Mrs Flanders got back, I told her and she said, 'that's nothing. One of my farmhands says they waltzed in one night, bold as you like, and took his whole dining suite. A table and four chairs, to go to an officer's mess in St Helier. How the Boche knew he had 'em, no-one knows. But it seems that if they need it, we have to give it up. Mind you, he can't really complain — he's the one that went to his neighbour's house, the one who'd been evacuated, and stole his best bedroom suite.'

After I'd helped Mrs Flanders with the milking and was back in the shop, the first customer in the queue was Mrs Galen, a colourless little woman with her hair squashed under a hair net. She lived opposite, and was often at her window to see when my queue was the shortest. She asked for her weekly bread ration, and I wrapped it as usual and pushed it across the counter.

'That's not the full weight,' she said, her eyes accusing. 'You've sold me short.'

'Four pounds,' I said, placing it on the scales so she could see. 'That's the ration for a woman, unless you're a manual worker.'

'Your scales are rigged. Just like in the butcher's. You think we don't know, but we're not stupid. Your bread's full of chaff and sawdust.' She turned indignant eyes to gather support from the woman behind her.

'It's got bran and rye in it, that's all. We can't get as much wheat flour now, so we have to make do.'

'The Germans don't make do, though, do they?'

'Do you want this bread, Mrs Galen, or not?'

She grudgingly held out her ration card and I passed her the bread. She pushed it into her basket, but not without making a parting shot. 'All you care about is the Germans, because they line your pockets. A nice little fortune you're making for yourself, and I bet their bread hasn't got chaff in it.' She flounced out.

'Ignore her,' the woman behind said. 'I know her husband gets his baccy on the black market, so she can hardly talk.'

I served the rest of the queue, wondering how it was we'd all become so suspicious - of each other, that instead of the common enemy bonding Jersey people together, somehow distrust was driving us apart.

Rachel arrived to share my fire as she often did. In her building, one of the apartments had a German soldier billeted there and his presence in the building made her uncomfortable. I was unravelling an old blue Guernsey sweater to knit up into socks and asked her to hold out her hands so I could use them to hold the wool taut. She was quieter than usual, her gaze troubled as she stared into space.

Finally, I whipped the wool off her hands and put it down. 'What is it, Rache?'

'I had to deliver a customer's file to my boss, Mr Scott, today. There was something on his desk … a paper.'

'Go on.'

'An order. I couldn't help seeing it. It said no Jew was to be — let me see if I can remember the words — yes, no Jew was to be "engaged as an employee who comes into contact with customers" and that Jewish employees should "be dismissed and replaced by non-Jewish employees".'

'Has Mr Scott said anything?'

'No. But it said the penalty for disobeying the order would be a fine or imprisonment. Honestly, Céline, I've been dry-mouthed all afternoon, wondering if he'd come and dismiss me, or take me off the front desk and put me in the back, but he just carried on as usual. He asked me to cash up just the same as always, and told me he'd see me tomorrow.'

'D'you think he knows you saw the notice?'

'I expect so. I was so shaky when I read it that I just left the file on his desk right next to it. But what worries me more is that other people will have had the same order, so it looks like soon I'll be not only out of a job, but unemployable.'

'Maybe Mr Scott will just ignore it. He will if he's any sense, anyhow. You're a good worker, and it would be cutting off his nose to spite his face if he were to lose you.'

'But it isn't fair on him. He'd be risking prison, just to keep me on.' She picked up the wool and began to wind an end around her fingers. 'D'you think I should talk to him about it?'

'I don't know. You probably shouldn't have been spying on his desk in the first place, so it's a bit awkward.'

'I know. I've always been too nosy for my own good. It's just I saw the word "Jew" and couldn't resist reading it.'

'If I were you, I'd just leave things as they are. If he doesn't mention it, then you needn't, and we just have to hope he doesn't follow their instructions.'

'That's you all over, Céline. Never rock the boat.' She put the wool down in her lap and sighed. 'But maybe you're right. It'll be hard to just carry on as if I don't know. It makes me feel so … so indebted. I really hate that feeling.'

'Hate it or not, I don't think you've much choice.'

After she'd gone home, I picked up the wool but had no heart to wind it into a ball. I'd intended to knit socks for Fred, but now the idea chafed. Surely he couldn't approve of this sort of thing, of sacking people with no notice? And I worried for Rachel. She was right, Mr Scott was putting himself at risk, and how long could he do that before they caught up with him?

CHAPTER 15

Fred

Throughout the winter and into early 1942, the café became my second home. I'd grown to enjoy a game of chess with Sebastien whilst old Henri looked on sagely and muttered advice. Both of them had wives at home but preferred to sit at the café.

'After forty years wed, she's glad to see the back of me,' Henri said.

I appreciated his good humour. The French seemed stoical, but the city felt greyer, people smiled less, and the weight of the German orders grew heavier as the war rumbled on. The food had become steadily less appetising as the winter weather came and rationing bit harder. Berenice and I used to sit together most evenings muffled up in coats, breath steaming before us, trying to fathom out what we could do with the few ingredients at our disposal. Early mornings, whilst I was at my translation work, Berenice bought what she could on the black market. Mostly eggs, rabbit and vegetables. Food was the constant topic of conversation. What we could serve, how to cook it and where we could get it.

'You've been such a help,' she said one day, after I'd walked three miles in driving rain to collect a dozen eggs, 'but I can't pay you.'

'You feed me. That's payment enough.'

'How do you manage though? Are they still investigating you?'

I knew the question would come, and I was well prepared. 'To be honest, I think they've forgotten about me. I'm just one man, and I'm trying to keep my head down. I was lucky; they gave me ration cards because I was born here in France, but now Jersey's been taken over, I'm terrified they'll transport me to a labour camp or something if I make a fuss about going home. I'll have to sit it out and hope the war ends soon. There aren't many men left in Paris, so I try not to stand out.'

'Still no news from your wife?'

'No. But the papers say there were very few casualties on Jersey, and the occupation of Jersey is more peaceful than here in France because it's so small. No news is good news. The British had disarmed the island, and we ... the Germans just marched in.' Berenice hadn't noticed my gaffe. I exhaled, though I felt adrenalin race in my veins.

'How's the book going?' To cover all my hours at the typewriter, I'd told her I was using the waiting time to write a recipe book.

'It's the only thing that keeps me sane. We're all obsessed by food, aren't we? It feels good to channel it into something useful.'

'I hope you don't mean recipes from Les Deux Pigeons?'

'No. From my research from before all this. *A Taste of Jersey*, it'll be called.'

'I understand, Édouard. You've been away so long, and it reminds you of home.' She smiled in a sympathetic way, and I turned away, because I couldn't bear for her to look in my eyes and see the guilt.

A few days later, just before lunch, I was summoned back to Avenue Foch. I followed Freitag up the stairs with my stomach churning in trepidation. This time the guards were on duty outside the cells, and from that I guessed the cells must all be full. An old woman in an overall was cleaning the walls with a cloth and bucket, and a strong smell of bleach and disinfectant hung in the air. I stared as I passed, and the woman moved aside to let me pass, her cloth dripping on the wooden floor. The marks on the walls looked like smears of blood.

We turned into the interpreters' office.

'You're to take this one,' Freitag said, indicating a leather-topped desk with its back to the door and facing the back of the building. 'Vogt's busy with the interrogations today. There are some radio messages for you to translate here. Then leave them in that tray — they'll go downstairs to be decoded.'

'Can't I take them away?'

'No. Too sensitive. You've to do them here. Vogt's orders.'

I sighed and sat down. No café lunch for me today. I reached for the file and began translating the French and English into German. As usual, the messages were opaque, presumably in code. I'd been at it about fifteen minutes when the noises began. Thuds and shouts, then groans. A man was moaning, not just once but over and over. '*Non! S'il vous plaît... Non, je connais rien!*' I know nothing.

The blonde secretary who was typing a memo ignored the sounds as if they were no more than the buzz of traffic passing below. Freitag continued to talk on the telephone, a slightly irritated look on his face, turning his back to the door and cupping one hand over his ear.

A scream, instantly stifled, then whimpering. The words were too indistinct for me to hear, but I couldn't help trying to decipher them. I could no longer write; my attention was distracted entirely by the noises outside. A moment's silence, then another cry, this time a cry of agony. Every hair on my body stood on end.

Freitag calmly got up and went over to the bookcase where a radio stood. Moments later, the room was filled with the crashing sound of a Wagner concerto. The music was designed to drown out the noise from the corridor, but somehow it had the opposite effect, making me listen even harder for the noises outside.

At her desk, the secretary was unwrapping a half-baguette and eating it between typing. I couldn't work. I read the same phrase over and over. '*Le cerf est dans les bois*'. The deer is in the woods. It was followed by some numbers: 7, 16, 26, 53. I could make no sense of it. The world seemed to have lost its meaning. A man was screaming and I was translating nonsense and a pile of numbers into German.

I rested my head in my hands, blinked.

The screaming had stopped. Freitag leapt up and turned down the radio, and the secretary looked up from her typing, suddenly alert and thrusting her sandwich into a drawer. From this, I realised Vogt had come in behind me.

'A clean shirt, please, Elise,' Vogt said. He was drying his hands on a towel.

As he passed, I saw his cuff was splattered with blood. Elise opened a cupboard and drew out a new shirt, still packaged in cellophane. She passed it to him and he took it and went through into his office.

The door behind me was open, and there were still groans echoing from further down the corridor. I ached for the men who would hear those noises from the cell next door, knowing they might be next.

The two guards outside the door behind me were laughing and joking. 'You weren't in long, Fritz.'

'I'll have you know I timed it. Seventeen minutes.'

'You win. I reckoned he'd only last ten. I owe you five francs.'

The banter continued. They were betting, actually betting, on how long it would take a man to give in to torture.

I turned to see who was speaking. A large loose-limbed man with a misshapen nose that looked like it had been broken like mine, more than once. He gave me a grin. 'I'm gagging for a smoke,' he said.

'Tell you what, Schuster,' the other guard said, 'I'll watch the doors whilst you go. Vogt won't come back, not now he's got his clean shirt on. He's meeting Baroness Orlov for lunch.'

'Tip me the wink if he's coming, then.' Schuster disappeared down the corridor.

A few minutes later, Vogt appeared again. I turned to catch a glimpse of him, his white shirt pristine under his suit jacket.

'Bauer?'

One of the guards replied.

'Where's Schuster?'

'Toilet, sir.'

'Again? That boy must have a weak bladder. Number six is done with, so take him out the back way to the Bois de Boulogne. You know what to do.'

'Yes, sir.'

Having given his orders, Vogt passed by with a whiff of starch and hair oil.

Although I tried to concentrate, I couldn't. I heard Schuster return from his smoke and Bauer complaining. A few moments later, there was the rattle and clank of a lock, the slow creak of a cell door opening and the scrape of a man being dragged out. A moan, and the words: '*Prie Dieu.*'

I saw them go from my window. The tall belted figures of Bauer and Schuster, their breath steaming in the cold air, hauling a young man by the armpits, his dark blue shirt bloody, an almost-corpse. One bare foot dragged in the wet dirt. I couldn't see his face, but his useless hands hung misshapen like lumps of raw meat. At the end of the street they disappeared into the thick of the woods.

A half hour later I saw them return, and Schuster stopped for a sneaky cigarette just off the main thoroughfare on one of the riding trails. Bauer rubbed his hands and stamped from foot to foot. He was obviously keeping watch as they skived. Of the prisoner, there was no sign.

My hands were shaking so hard I could barely hold a pen. My only thought was to finish as soon as possible, but my mind didn't seem to want to function. I realised I'd been staring at the same words for more than five minutes.

Towards the end of the afternoon Vogt approached me, a whiff of garlic on his breath. 'You've finished?'

'Not quite,' I said.

'How much longer?'

'A half hour perhaps.' My voice was calmer than I felt.

'Give them to Eva when you're done.'

I watched him go, watched how everyone in the office followed his progress but nobody looked at him directly. Once he was out of sight, the room itself almost exhaled.

I did as he asked, and when I went out of the office I saw the same elderly woman still in the corridor, mopping and cleaning. The stink of disinfectant made me gag.

Back in my freezing apartment that night, I made myself a meagre meal of stale bread and tomatoes, which I left untouched on the plate. I couldn't face going to the café, but I couldn't eat either. The thought of what I'd heard at Avenue Foch made my stomach queasy. I tried to reason it out: that this was war, and no doubt the other side used just such methods. But the man's cries haunted my thoughts, the feeling that I should have done something.

Over the next few weeks, they called me to the office several more times. Often the radio was on loud, and Schuster and Bauer were stationed outside the doors, when they weren't inside with Vogt. Sometimes the prisoner was taken out to the woods and never returned, sometimes he was taken away in a van from the front of the building, presumably to a prison camp somewhere. I did my best to ignore everything, fixing my eyes on my desk and resolutely blocking out what was around me. Each time, my disgust grew. Not just for them, but for myself.

One afternoon, the sounds were different, higher pitched. A woman. My heart jumped. Was it Berenice? There was no way of knowing. Nobody but Vogt and his 'special' guards, Bauer and Schuster, went in the cells.

Calm down, it can't be her, I told myself.

The muffled screaming went on until I had to get up and go to the window and put my head outside. Feeling nauseous, I inhaled the sharp cold air of the street.

'Getting to you, is it?' Vogt had come up behind me.

'A little,' I said.

'That's war for you,' he said. 'It's what the Kommandant fails to realise. The front line exists here, as well as the one in the east with the tanks and artillery. At least we won't be blown to bits by cannon fire. Warfare's always bloody. Now take the ancient Greeks. They thought nothing of tearing their enemies limb from limb by tying a man to two different chariots and having them gallop in different directions. Do you read the Greek myths?'

I gave a non-committal grunt.

'Worth reading if you want to know what a hero looks like. The interrogations … well, it always takes a while to get used to it. You have to ignore it because they rely on us weakening. Of course, if you let them go without breaking them, and they carry on their operations, more of our men will die. The important thing is the German lives we're saving. Think of those, Huber. Last night, thanks to information from one of those internees, we uncovered a cache of machine guns and ammunition that would have been enough to wipe out a whole platoon. The bastards would kill our men as soon as spit on them. And if we don't stop them now, it'll spread like a fungus.'

He clapped me on the shoulder like my uncle used to do when he came to visit. 'Come on, I'll show you something.' He beckoned me towards his office. Reluctantly, I followed him in as he shut the door behind me. His office was oppressively hot; a coal fire glowed furnace-like in the hearth.

'It's bloody, this game,' he said. He rummaged in his desk and brought out a brown glass bottle. He stood it in front of me and tapped the lid. 'Cyanide capsules.'

I was about to pick it up, but he slapped his warm damp hand over mine so it was pinned fast to the desk.

'There are eight capsules in there, all removed from enemies of the Reich. This is what we are up against,' he said, his eyes on mine. 'They'd rather die than give us what we need to know. The true sign of a fanatic.' He released my hand, patted it reassuringly. 'When we're less busy, I'll have time to show you. We have to search everywhere — all the body's hiding places. They even drill a hole in a tooth to hide the capsule from us. But we always find it.' He smiled. 'We don't let them cheat us.'

I looked down at my knees and caught a glimpse of a metal waste paper bin, into which he had stuffed his blood-spotted shirt.

CHAPTER 16

Fred

By the time the spring came, birds were beginning to return to Paris, but the sounds of Avenue Foch haunted me. I could hear the nightmare screams in my head even when I was awake. How could I look the French in the face? The guilt made me avoid the café, until I became so curious as to how Berenice was doing that I had to call in, just to set my mind at rest that she was still there. I was relieved to see her sturdy figure rushing between the tables just as she usually did.

'Ah, Édouard!' she said. 'I'm so glad to see you. Where've you been hiding? You're just the man I need! I wondered if you'd mind helping out again? Just for a night. I wouldn't ask, but I'm desperate. I'll pay you of course.'

'What is it you need doing?'

'It's Nicole. She's just given us notice.'

'And left you in the lurch?'

'Says she's got a better offer. Stupid girl. Gone to be a receptionist at a Soldatenheim. The big one on the Avenue de la Motte-Picquet. Of course, she'll get her perks, like all collaborators do.' Judging by Berenice's scathing expression, and the scorn in her voice when she said 'perks', there was no greater sin.

'What needs doing?'

'Kitchen duties. Sorry.'

Berenice would struggle if there was no one else in the kitchen. And I felt for her. Paris was fast becoming nothing but a Nazi playground. There were now cinemas especially for the troops, and cafés that served only Germans. And I knew her time was limited. I feared the threats might really materialise and they'd ship her off to a work camp somewhere.

Washing the dirty pots felt like sanity. I liked the clatter of plates and cups, the swish of the water. Washing felt like a sacred act after a day at the Avenue Foch. Being in Berenice's ordered kitchen was like breathing clean air. We smiled at each other as we worked, in the simple companionship of stacking the clean plates back in the cupboards, and polishing the glasses.

'Édouard, did you mean what you said?' Berenice asked me, in a low voice. 'About helping us?'

'Of course,' I said, replacing an ashtray carefully on the draining board. 'I'm happy to do this any time.'

'No, not that. I meant … well, I think the Germans might be watching us,' she said. 'There's a couple of soldiers who hang around more than necessary.'

'Perhaps they just like the food,' I said.

'Ha! Not unless you like beets and cabbage. But still, it makes me uneasy. And I had a message: Antoine needs a safe place to stay. Just for a couple of nights. I thought of you.'

I spoke too quickly. 'I've not much room; my apartment's tiny. And I've only the one bedroom.'

'Oh.' I saw her face fall, and it bit into me hard. She masked her disappointment. 'That's quite all right. I'll try and find somewhere else.'

What to do? In a split second, my mouth had opened again. 'It's fine, Berenice. He can come to me. He'll have to sleep on the floor or something. When will he come?'

'Tonight. Are you sure?'

'Quite sure. I'm glad to help.'

Her warm smile was reward enough. 'He's only passing through. He's on his way to meet some other friends of ours near the coast.'

'How did you get to meet Antoine in the first place?' I asked.

'You might as well know,' she said. 'He's my son. Antoine Chaput is just a nom de guerre.'

'Is his father...?'

'His father and I are separated.' A pause. 'He died last year in an automobile accident. Pierre blames me. Since then we've been...' She shrugged and looked away.

'Oh.' There was obviously a history there she didn't want to share. I had never asked Berenice's surname, though I had seen the name Severin on the café's stationery and knew there must be a family connection. Apparently, that too had been a fact missed by Vogt at security headquarters.

She turned back to me. 'So if he comes, look after him, won't you?'

When I got back from the café that evening, I was in a cold sweat. What had I done? I was caught in a cleft stick now, one of my own making. I just had to hope that Vogt didn't decide to send Freitag or Foucault round. I should never have got involved with Berenice in the first place. What if the Gestapo were watching me too? I closed the shutters and pulled the curtains tight together. Meticulously, I cleared the place of German papers, the German soldiers' gazetteer, and burned the contents of the wastebasket in the empty grate. As I passed, I caught sight of the photograph of Céline that was propped on the mantelpiece.

I stared at it a while, at her smiling face, her eyes bright with humour. She'd taken off her specs for the photo, and it made her look younger. I'd written from Cherbourg through the army but could tell her only basic facts. Now, no letters would get past the German blockade unless I asked Vogt to send them. I didn't like the idea of Vogt's fingers on my letters. What would she think? It was all so complicated. I just had to hope Antoine's visit would be a one-off.

In the event, Antoine didn't arrive until bang on curfew. I ushered him inside.

'Sorry, it's not much,' I said. I indicated the small sofa, which was far too short for his rangy six-foot frame.

'I'm used to it,' he said simply, dropping a battered holdall down beside it. 'Don't suppose you've got a drink?'

I remembered the bottle of brandy and got out two small tooth-glasses.

I filled them half-full, and he downed his in one gulp before flopping onto the sofa. 'That's better. Thanks for this, Édouard.'

I sat down opposite him in the easy chair and sipped at my brandy, grateful for the sudden flush of warmth. He ran his hand through his fine brown hair. He was filthy, I realised, his hair sweaty and fingers black.

He saw me looking. 'I know. I look like a down-and-out.'

'Bathroom's through there,' I said. 'Have you eaten?'

'Can't eat,' he said. 'I just need to calm down. I'm still all of a jigger. I had two of them on my tail, and they got a shot at me, but I managed to get in the car just in time. We dumped the car of course, and I walked the rest. Félix has gone to a different house. Doesn't do to be seen together.'

'Sabotage?' I just stopped myself asking if it was a railway line, information I wasn't supposed to know.

'Yep. We wanted to disrupt the coal going to the armaments factory. The blast was bigger than we reckoned, and we didn't get away quick enough.'

'What were you using?'

'Simple pipe bomb. Couldn't get gelignite, so it was gunpowder. From the old firework factory. Bloody awkward to work with, but it's more or less impossible to get explosives anymore.'

'Have you tried making your own?'

He stared. Too late, I realised I'd have to continue the conversation now I'd started it. I said the words in English, hoped they were the same in French. 'Nitromethane, and an oxidising agent — ammonium nitrate, say — and you've got something with just as much firepower as gunpowder.'

He understood. 'Really?' he said in French. 'But where would we get ingredients like that?'

'Ammonium nitrate's just fertiliser,' I said in English, before reverting to French. 'Nitromethane — well, that's more awkward, but it's found in some paint solvents.'

'You're not serious?'

'That's what chemistry at university does for you. As a student, all you want to know is how to make the biggest explosion.' I realised that in my enthusiasm I'd nearly said the German name of where I studied. I shut my mouth quickly. What the hell was I doing? This wasn't childhood chemistry, it was bloody war.

'Could you find us the right things?'

'Well, I suppose I could, but...' I tailed off. *Shit.* I'd let my mouth run away with me again before I'd thought it all through.

'It's risky, I know,' Antoine said. 'It won't be on any ration card, so you'd need to be a thief. It's the same for us all. We've had to get used to the idea that we're all criminals. All Resistance members are wanted men. In our own country.' The bitterness made his bony face seem older.

I took another larger swig of the brandy, to cover the fact my face was blazing. I'd just done something really stupid.

Antoine's forehead furrowed as he held out his glass for a top-up. 'Never mind chemistry, we could do with a few proper burglars on our team, though I must say I've got quite good at getting over the wall into the paper plant. Printing paper's strictly controlled now, and there's always Nazi guards on the gates. I expect it's the same with fertiliser. Though walking about with a sack of fertiliser might be a damn sight safer than stealing stuff from Nazi garrisons or munitions dumps. Tell you what, I'll get you the stuff, and you can show us how to make the device.'

'No, you can leave it to me,' I said, hastily backtracking. 'I know what I'm looking for.' I couldn't have them bring explosives here, not with Freitag liable to drop in for a visit at any moment.

'Oh, good man. Berenice said you'd be up for it.'

I tried to divert him. 'She's your mother, isn't she?'

'Yes, but I've been calling her Berenice for years. She's just not a "Maman" type, too intellectual. Oh, I know you think she's just a café owner, but she's a bloody good businesswoman. Single-minded as hell, that's my mother.'

It wasn't a compliment, I could tell. 'It takes a lot of work running a café. I used to be in the same trade.'

'Did she tell you she gave up her life to school me and put me through university? Insisted on it, when all I wanted to do was race cars, like my father. All that studying, and now there's a war on. Bloody useless. Anyway, I don't tell people we're related. It's safer. I'm supposed to be dead; my papers are all false. I have several aliases, in case I get caught.'

'Must be awkward.'

'You get used to it. We'll have to find one for you.'

'No. I'm happy to take the risk.' Lord, not another name. I couldn't cope with that. I thought frantically for an excuse. 'Besides, it's not like you and Berenice; there's nobody here I'm protecting. It will make no difference to me. I'll stick with Édouard, thanks very much.'

'If there's any hope you can get it, we'll need your explosive in a month. There's a bridge — a viaduct actually. If we can bring that down, it will cause no end of trouble for the Boche. But we have to wait a while, because there are some Allied airmen who need to travel that way before we blow it to smithereens.'

'Allied soldiers? Are there any left? Aren't they all prisoners of war by now?'

'Nope. These have been parachuted in, to try to get more intelligence about German troop movements and targets. We help them land and then get them out of France and back to England. I can't tell you any details; we have to keep it all under our hats.' He slugged back the rest of his brandy and slammed down the glass. 'To be honest, I don't know why we do it. Haven't we got enough trouble without the Brits expecting us to babysit them in and out of France?' He was angry. His fist was squeezing the edge of the sofa.

I stood up, suffocated by him, by the intensity of the emotion that was somehow compressed inside him.

'What will you do tomorrow?' I asked. 'It's just … well, I'd like to work. I have a sort of routine.'

'Berenice said you were writing a book. I'll keep out of your way. I've to collect some printing, then drop the papers off at the collection points. I'll be gone before you wake, before it's fully light. Safer that way.'

'I'll turn in then,' I said. 'I hope you sleep well.'

144

He didn't answer, but peeled his long frame from the sofa and headed for the bathroom.

From the bedroom, I heard the cistern belch and gurgle. Sounded like he was using more than the two inches of water we were supposed to take. I lay awake in my pyjamas, fretting over the fact there was an enemy agent on my sofa. Or rather not on my sofa, because the walls were thin and I could hear him pacing the room, then the clink of a glass as he helped himself to the dregs of my brandy. A moment later, I smelled the pungent waft of his cigarette smoke.

From the noises next door, I could tell he didn't sleep, and neither did I. Was I really going to source explosives against my own people? Yet who were my people? I felt far more allegiance to the struggling Berenice than to the bullies of the German Army, who would deport people simply because they didn't share their religion. The relationship between Berenice and Antoine was obviously complex. And in the back of my mind were my mother and father, German to the core, and my brother Horst, who fiercely believed that all other nations were somehow inferior to ours. They would hate me for thinking these thoughts.

In the room next door I heard Antoine cough, and the flush of the cistern for the umpteenth time.

The front door clicked shut before it was light, and I felt a surge of relief that Antoine had stuck to his word and was off the premises. I wasn't looking forward to another night of no sleep.

I took the folders from the wardrobe where I'd hidden them under a pile of blankets and set to work. One of the letters I was translating was a memo from Pétain about something called a 'Jewish Statute'.

As of now, all French Jews were to be divested of businesses, premises and citizens' rights. The Crémieux Decree, which had granted French citizenship to a hundred thousand Algerian Jews more than fifty years ago, was hereby revoked. Under the new legislation, no Jewish doctors would be permitted to carry on their medical practice. It seemed to me that the free French state of Vichy was just as bad as the occupied zone at persecuting the Jewish population.

The thought of it made me angry and restless, so much so that by lunchtime I was ready to escape it, and I went over to the café. All the tables were inside now to preserve warmth. Sebastien and Henri were huddled over their chess as usual. They nodded at me as I arrived, but the German soldiers ignored me as beneath their notice.

I watched Berenice working, her bustling square figure rushing in and out with plates of steaming food. She was always polite to the customers, but I detected extra warmth for the French. '*Non, désolée! Pas de pain aujourd'hui.*' No more bread today. Yet everyone could see the German soldiers' sleek plumpness, whilst the French grew daily thinner and more lacklustre.

Finally Berenice got to my table. 'All right?' she asked. I could see from her eyes she meant Antoine.

'Fine,' I said, and I reached to give her shoulder a reassuring squeeze. I saw her exhale.

She brought me coffee 'on the house'. It wasn't as good as usual, and the cup had dark grounds floating at the bottom.

'Sorry,' she said, seeing me grimace. 'It's chicory. All we could get.'

I noticed the tables were bare. 'What's happened to the tablecloths?'

After a furtive glance to check no one was listening: 'They're not fit to be put back because we can't get them washed. The laundry's been closed down. Seems the laundry employed some Jews, and men came two nights ago and smashed the place up. People are disappearing all over the place. Antoine says there are camps in Vichy France, and they're holding them all there. Jews, communists, anyone who disagrees with the Nazi regime.'

I was afraid she'd read something in my face, and I looked away. Fortunately, some soldiers sat down at one of the tables near the window and Berenice was obliged to go and take their order. As she hovered around them, I saw one of them was Freitag. He caught my eye and gave a faint smile. Immediately I busied myself stirring the grounds in the bottom of my cup, and praying that Berenice hadn't seen that look.

CHAPTER 17

As the weeks passed, and summer came, I began to see more and more people wearing the yellow star on my daily walk. I myself had typed up the notice in French that was to go to the printers — the one telling Jews to collect the stars from the gendarmeries, and that this tiny bit of cloth would use up a whole month's worth of their precious textile rations. Today, as I passed through the city, there were green and yellow buses on every corner, hordes of uniformed police, and ragged groups of Jews herded together with their suitcases.

Outside an old cinema, a small girl with black braids wept as she was suddenly separated from her father. A harassed gendarme in a peaked cap gestured him onto the already-packed bus, waving his gun. The mother begged and protested, with the child clamped to her side, her face screwed up in fear. I looked back over my shoulder as the police insisted the father go without them and saw him try to make light of it, kissing the girl hard on the forehead before climbing aboard with a wave and a smile full of tears. The bus drove away in a cloud of choking exhaust fumes.

What was going on? These were not German soldiers, but French policemen. But what incensed me more was the little crowd of rich Parisiennes that had gathered to stare. Well dressed, and each wearing the Paris woman's trademark of a tiny veiled hat and high-heeled shoes, they pointed and whispered. The war was right there on their streets, and yet they behaved as if it was an entertainment specially laid on for them.

The rich seemed to be thriving everywhere I looked. The restaurants were still full of beautiful young women wearing jewels, hanging on the arms of German officers. If you had money, everything could be bought on the black market. Unless of course your name was Epstein, or Abrahams, or Benmohel. My thoughts turned to Rachel, Céline's friend. I had sent several brief notes to Céline telling her I was safe, for I could tell her little else. I love you, I said. At least that could not be censored by Vogt's office.

But from Céline there could be no reply, and this was the hardest thing of all.

When there came a soft tap at my door I was almost asleep, but I shot up out of my chair. 'Who is it?' I asked.

'Antoine.'

I looked at my watch. Only nine o'clock. He was early. This was the third time he had used my apartment as a place to stay, and each time made me wired with apprehension. When I opened the door, he smelt of red wine and motor oil. He walked past me and took possession of the sofa straight away. His expression was closed off.

'Had a good day?' I asked mildly.

'There's never a good day whilst those bastards hold Paris,' he said. 'I can't tell you what I've seen today, because you wouldn't believe it.'

'Try me. I saw them taking Jews out of Paris.'

'I'm ashamed of my own people. Why don't they do something?' He shook his head. 'Any more of that brandy?'

'I'm afraid not. There's nothing to drink, except water in the tap. It's not been switched off yet if you want to wash, or fill your glass.'

'Then I'll just sleep, if you don't mind.'

I felt it like a dismissal. I was annoyed that he hadn't even attempted to behave like a guest; that he hadn't asked after Berenice, or tried to make any kind of small talk; his eyes were closed as if to shut me from his mind.

I left him and went through to the bedroom. It was too early to sleep, and I wished I had something to read, but I'd put everything away in the wardrobe again. There was nothing for it but to get ready for bed. I was half into my pyjama bottoms when there was a loud knock at the door.

I froze mid-movement. It could only be Freitag or Foucault. Nobody else ever called. I hauled my pyjama trousers up and tied the cord.

Antoine appeared at my bedroom door. A muscle twitched in his cheek.

'In here,' I whispered. 'Hide. I'll see who it is and get rid of them.'

When I opened the door a notch, it was Freitag. 'Bit late to come calling,' I said, in French, whispering and hoping Antoine couldn't hear. 'I was getting ready for bed.'

'What?'

I repeated it in German.

'Early to bed, early to rise, eh? It won't take a minute. Orders from Vogt.'

I winced. His voice was loud and filled with the Germanic certainty of his uniform.

'Keep your voice down, you'll wake everyone.'

'It's only nine thirty. Most of them won't be in bed for hours. Anyway, I'll not keep you long.'

'Wait there then,' I said, trying to close the door, but Freitag pushed his way in and stood in the living room, staring at the empty table. 'There's a collaborator just been brought in for questioning. He's got an illegal radio, so Vogt wants those papers he gave you, the transcripts. I said I'd collect them tonight so he could have them first thing in the morning.'

'They're in the bedroom,' I said. 'I hide them, in case anyone should break in.'

He nodded, accepting my explanation. I pushed the door open and slipped through. Antoine wasn't hiding, he was statue-still, arm outstretched, pointing a gun at me.

I froze.

His expression was cold, his jaw tense. The scent of something about to erupt hung in the air.

I raised my hands slowly in a gesture of surrender, keeping my eyes fixed on him, and walked carefully to the wardrobe. I took out the file, and as I turned to go through the door I felt the presence of the gun as if it was actually pressing into my back.

No shot. So he wasn't going to risk a shootout with Freitag.

In the living room, Freitag had lifted a corner of the blackout curtain and was peering out. 'Quiet street,' he said. 'You're lucky.'

'Here,' I said.

Freitag turned, smiled and extended a hand. All my senses were tuned to the room behind me. Freitag reached for the file.

'Are you all right?' he asked. 'You look very pale. You're not sick are you?'

I realised I was still gripping the cardboard edge of the folder as if it might hold me up. Abruptly, I let go. 'Just tired,' I said. 'I was about to go to bed.'

'Sleep well,' Freitag said, and strolled to the door.

I followed him, wanting to shout, 'Don't go! There's a man in my bedroom who'll surely shoot me just as soon as you've gone.' But how could I explain Antoine; what he was doing there? Freitag gave me a leisurely 'Heil Hitler' and the door closed with a bang.

The room ricocheted around me; my legs felt like feathers.

'Don't move. The gun's loaded,' Antoine said.

I turned at his voice. He kept on walking up to me until I could smell the engine oil and Gauloises.

'I can explain,' I said. 'I didn't give you up, did I?'

'Nazi bastard. You can explain why you were talking German, can you? What was in that file? No, don't move.' He nudged me forward with the gun. 'Sit there.'

I staggered back and sat in the sagging chair, cold shivers racing down my back as I gripped its arms. 'It's not what you think —'

He scowled. 'You don't know what I think, so keep your mouth shut.' He looked at his watch and seemed to be calculating time. The minutes ticked by in silence. Outside, a distant siren wailed.

'Now.' He gestured for me to stand. 'Get moving.' He turned me round and pushed the gun up against the back of my neck.

'Antoine, just listen a moment, let me explain —'

'Shut it. I shan't tell you again.' The muzzle of the gun nudged me forward. I wasn't wearing shoes, just a shirt and tie and pyjama bottoms. The hall floor was icy underfoot. Antoine had hold of my shirt collar and that was pulling back as the gun forced me forward and down the stairs.

'Where are we going? Can't I just get my shoes?'

I hoped someone might come out and scare him off. But we were minutes from curfew, and all sensible Parisians had retreated behind their locked doors.

Should I run for it? He'd shoot me if I did. I couldn't think, just had to keep moving. On the street, he steered me into a dark alley. 'Make a sound and you're dead,' he said.

The ice and grit of the street stuck to my feet. The streets were impenetrable, all lights out for fear of British bombs. I was a blind man lurching into the dark. My foot stubbed against a kerb. Five minutes? Ten? Suddenly, he steered me sharp right into a doorway and knocked. A burst of knocking in a staccato pattern. No one came. He began the knock again, the door opened and I nearly fell inside. A shove from behind and I was in a dimly lit hallway. Wrinkled linoleum under my feet and the smell of grease and fried onion.

'What the hell?' a deep voice said.

'Is Félix still here?' Antoine's voice cut through the other man's protests.

'In the back.'

A push between the shoulder blades and I was hustled through into a back room, where another shorter, stouter man leapt up from the floor and grabbed a rifle from where it lay under the table. This must be Félix. He had a cigarette in his hand, and a tin ashtray full of butts remained on the rug before a cold hearth.

'Who's this?' he asked, staring at my pyjama pants. 'What's with the gun, Antoine?'

Antoine nudged me again with the barrel. 'This, gentleman, is the German bastard who offered to take me in. And we all know why he might want to do that, don't we?'

Both men came round to stare at me. The bigger heavy-set youth came right up to me, too close for comfort, his mouth curling in disgust.

'I can explain,' I said, in French.

'Take off your tie,' Félix said, swinging the rifle and delivering a crack to the side of my head. My eyes blurred, but I obeyed. Safest to comply, a small panicked voice in my head bleated over and over. They tied me tightly to the back of a chair, with my hands behind me.

'Jérôme, your braces.' The big man grunted a protest but took off his braces to tie my feet. I didn't struggle and this made me ashamed. Stupidly, I wondered what would happen if I wanted to use the toilet.

'Will they be looking for him?' Jérôme asked.

'Don't think so,' Antoine said. 'My guess is they won't find him gone until morning.'

'Then we can dispatch him and dump him once we've got what we need.'

I closed my eyes; the side of my head throbbed. The bone above my eye ached and made my right eye stream with tears. I thought of Vogt, his words that all Resistance men were fanatics.

'Who are you?' Félix stood in front of me, and even though he was short, my position made me shrink away.

I swallowed. What should I tell them? Whatever I said, it wouldn't look good.

The hesitation produced a punch from him that set my head reeling. 'They call me Édouard Vibert,' I said. 'But that's not my real name. I'm from Jersey. I'm married to a Frenchwoman, Céline Dupont.'

Antoine kicked the chair. 'Liar. I heard you talking in German. You were sent to spy on me; that's why you were hanging round the café. I should have guessed. It's my mother, stupid woman, she can't resist an intellectual, even if he's a Nazi spy.'

'I'm no Nazi. My name is Siegfried Huber. I'm German but I haven't been back to Germany for ten years. Not until now. Not until I was told to join the German Army or go to prison. That's the God's honest truth.'

'So why aren't you in the army now?'

'Because I speak French and English as well as German. They threatened my wife if I didn't do as they said. I was caught, understand? I didn't want this bloody war. I didn't want to do any of it, but they're not people you can resist.'

They glanced at each other.

'He gave a file of papers to the German officer who came,' Antoine said.

'What was in the files?' Félix asked.

'Translations. Transcripts of radio transmissions, German orders.'

'Who for?'

'Vogt at security headquarters.'

Félix gestured at the others to go into another room. I guessed it was the kitchen. I heard muffled voices arguing in there. I guessed they were arguing about whether to kill me on not. I thought of Antoine disposing of that dead dog and shuddered. Only now did I wonder how many others he'd dispatched into the Seine.

Whilst they were gone I tried to wriggle my way loose, but the tie was cutting into my wrists and was too tight to budge. Shouting for help would achieve nothing except more blows to the head. I was caught like a fly in a trap.

Félix was first back in the room. From the others' body language, I guessed he was the leader of the little group. His belligerent gaze raked over me as if I were a worm. 'If you don't tell us everything that was in that file, then you'll not see the morning,' he said.

'And if I do tell you everything, then I still won't see the morning. I'm not stupid,' I said. 'So it makes little difference. As far as I'm concerned, nothing's changed. I sheltered Antoine — or Pierre, or whatever the hell he's called — a man the Gestapo are looking for, and I didn't give him up. I could have, but I didn't.'

Antoine snorted. 'Pah. Only because you planned to let me lead you to my friends.'

'No. Not because of the Gestapo. I took you in because Berenice was my friend. And because of her, I thought you were my friend. It wasn't about the war, it was a simple act of kindness and respect for a woman who asked me a favour. That's what the war has made us forget. The very thing that we're fighting for, for Christ's sake.'

'Crap. Don't believe him, Antoine,' Jérôme said. 'No one could be that naïve.'

I shrugged. 'Believe what you like. But I'd be a damned sight more use to you alive. I can get in the security headquarters. I've got access to all their papers. And I'm a chemist. Antoine wanted me to use my knowledge of explosives to build a bomb.'

'What?' Félix turned on Antoine.

'He's lying. I never said that.'

But Antoine's face flared red and Félix turned on him. 'You damn fool. I'll sew up that mouth of yours.' He grabbed Antoine by the shirt. 'What else did you tell him?'

'Nothing, I tell you. I told him nothing!' He wrenched himself away.

'You plan to blow up the viaduct at Morlaix,' I said.

Félix shot another vicious glare at Antoine, put a palm to his forehead and sighed. 'What a fiasco.'

'I still say we should dump him,' Jérôme said. 'He's not worth the risk. He could take us all down.'

'Shut up, Jérôme,' Félix said. 'Let me think.'

Antoine and Jérôme looked at each other warily. Although Félix was short, he had a dynamism in all his movements that made him unpredictable. By now my hands were going numb, and my back ached from my shoulders being forced back.

'Whoever you are,' Félix said to me, 'you're a coward. All along, you just took the easiest route. A single word in a German ear and you could be interrogated by the Gestapo. Think your head hurts? That's nothing to their methods. They will pound your fingers to a pulp with a hammer. They will hang you from a bar and beat you with iron flails. That is what Vogt's men do. So why should we show you mercy? They have none.'

The sounds of the room at Avenue Foch came back to me, but I held my nerve. 'You're right. But if you want my information, then you'll need me alive. I tell you, I could be useful to you. Who else can get in Vogt's office?'

'You could also be a liability.'

'No, Félix, it's too risky,' Jérôme urged, with a warning look.

'Can you get files out of there?'

'I can try.' God help me. I knew now what men under pressure would do — say anything for another day of life.

'Blindfold him,' Félix said.

I heard Jérôme complaining under his breath as he fetched a cloth shopping bag from the kitchen and shoved it over my head.

'Take him back where you found him,' Félix said to Antoine.

'You're letting him go?' Jérôme was incredulous.

A prod in the back. 'I'll risk it for one week. If a single word gets out about us from you, you'll be finished.' A thump in the chest. 'You will copy every file you receive and give it to Berenice at the café. From now on we own you, Vibert.'

By the time I was back inside my room and had taken the wretched bag off my head, the whole thing felt unreal. Everything was the same as it had always been. The silence seemed to be asking me questions. Whose side was I on? If I were to run, what then?

The answers were not encouraging. If I ran, I'd have both Antoine's mob and the whole German Army after me. If I stayed, I'd be liable to be executed by one or the other as a traitor. I had liked Antoine, but now I saw another side of him. The men in that house were ruthless. They were probably all killers. But what was an army, other than trained to kill?

I could make no sense of it. All I knew was, like a puppet, to stay alive I had to somehow find the courage to dance to two different tunes.

CHAPTER 18

Céline

Time creaked by, with more rationing and stricter enforcement by the Bailiff in his determination for a peaceful occupation with no trouble. Arrests were made of anyone chalking 'V' for Victory signs on walls or promoting anti-German propaganda. Meetings of the Women's Institute or any sort of groups that could be used for resistance were banned. Rachel and I grew closer as life grew tighter and meaner.

Initially, the Germans seemed content with our details from the Bailiff, but recently they had become more stringent about knowing exactly who, and where, everyone was. On the autumn day the Germans came to register me, I knew they were coming because they'd been to Flanders Farm earlier, and I'd seen the list of occupants nailed up inside Mrs Flanders' front door. She had several older men staying at the farm, and some young school-leavers who helped with the hard labour of ploughing and digging up the beets, potatoes and turnips, which were now our staple diet. It made me shiver to see the piece of paper with names, ages and nationalities scrawled there. Everyone was listed, and if you weren't, there would soon be nowhere to hide. Immediately I feared for Rachel. What would she do?

The men who came to the bakery were polite in the distant way of all officials. Up until that time, I had never had to reveal to any German my married name. Now, two of them were in my sitting room, one with a ledger in front of him and the other with a box camera slung around his neck.

'Name?' Oberstleutnant Fischer paused with his ledger open on his knee. He was a thin, tough-looking man, who squinted at me as if I were a specimen in a museum.

'Céline Huber.'

'Huber? A German name. Are you of German descent?'

'No. I was born here. My husband is German.'

'Really?' He glanced sceptically to his younger friend with the camera, who looked embarrassed and tried to shrink further into the chair. 'And where is this German husband now?'

'Somewhere in France. He was conscripted into the German Army.'

'He is fighting for the Reich?' Fischer's eyebrows shot up.

'Yes. We met in Vienna before the war.' Just the talk of Fred made a lump form in my throat. I struggled to maintain my composure. 'But I haven't heard from him for more than six months, and then only a brief note. Perhaps the mail isn't getting through.'

'Excuse us, Frau Huber.' Fischer beckoned to his comrade and they had a whispered conversation in German in the shop.

When they returned, Fischer bowed and said, 'We are sorry to distress you. We will tell the Feldkommandant and make him aware of your husband's service for our country. It is a difficult situation, no?'

'Have you a photograph of him?' Müller, the younger man with the camera asked. I could hardly refuse, so I fetched our album with proof of our stay in Vienna and turned the pages, although my stomach was churning. Me, on the beach at St Helier, sun-hat in hand, smiling. Fred standing in front of the Donnerbrunnen fountain in Kärntner Strasse, posing like Neptune. It made my chest hurt and my eyes prickle to think of our two countries at war. Such good times we'd had.

'Your husband — he is very handsome man,' Müller said in broken English.

'Yes, yes he is,' I said, feeling my eyes tear up again. I thudded the book shut.

Oberstleutnant Fischer supplied me with a handkerchief. It was large and starched, and smelt of tobacco.

When they'd taken my photograph, they went.

'I am sorry,' whispered Müller as he left. 'Sorry to intrude.'

I just shook my head. Keeping the white handkerchief bothered me. I'd seen them hanging from people's windows, and it seemed to me to be a symbol of Jersey's surrender. So I burned it on the oven flame until it charred to ash, feeling guilty. Fred would have called me stupid. I looked at our wedding photograph on the mantelpiece for a long time afterwards, my mind full of thoughts of him. Would he have agreed with what the Germans were doing? Was he doing the same thing in France? Too many questions that couldn't be answered.

A week later we were issued with identity booklets, which we had to carry with us at all times. Somehow, these small bits of cardboard made us all feel more like an oppressed people. When I opened mine up, the left side showed my photograph, which was deeply unflattering. It had seemed traitorous to try to make myself attractive in front of those Germans, so I was immortalised as a woman in a threadbare summer blouse with untidy wisps of hair. My eyes stared out widely.

On the right of the card were my *Particulars* — *Nähere Angaben*. These included colour of hair: brown; colour of eyes: blue; and a section for '*Besondere Merkmale*', or special physical features. I was glad this section said 'None'.

We were told we could be arrested if we couldn't immediately produce these cards, and as time passed many forgot to carry them, and the newspaper became full of people who'd been caught out and imprisoned. Complaints to Mr Coutanche, the Bailiff of Jersey, fell on deaf ears.

One breezy autumn day, I was helping with the milking when Mrs Flanders brought the paper and waved it in front of me.

'It's not right,' she said, giving me no time to read it. 'There's thousands of English people here. And now they're deporting them.'

My heart gave a flip. I grabbed the paper. 'Who?'

'Anyone of English descent. Not just soldiers, but women and children. And people with a criminal record, and anyone Jewish,' she said. 'But I don't mind getting rid of them. Look.' She pointed out the passage to me. Undesirables on Jersey were to be deported to Germany, according to the notice, which was signed by Feldkommandant Knackfuss.

Thank God. It wasn't me. I was a Jerseywoman through and through. But Rachel wasn't. If they deported her to Germany, who knew what might happen to her after that?

'They've got twenty-four hours. Look.' Mrs Flanders leaned over my shoulder to stab an arthritic finger down on the small print commentary below.

Twenty-four hours? It was impossible. A welter of emotions flooded through me. Fear, for Rachel, and guilt, that it was somehow Fred's fault, and, by extension, mine. 'Mrs Flanders, excuse me, but I have to go.'

'What? You're not English are you?'

'No. But I've a friend I want to see … to ask if I can help.' I'd already thrust away the milking stool and was rushing to the house for my coat, with Mrs Flanders hurrying after me, still in her milking overall.

'Céline! You can't do this,' she shouted. 'You can't just run off and leave me with all the milking to do!'

'Sorry, Mrs Flanders,' I called as I shrugged my way into my gabardine and leapt onto my bike.

The streets of St Helier were full of hurrying anxious-looking women. I passed what used to be a high-class man's tailors and saw a notice taped to the window: *Juedisches Geschaeft* — Jewish Business. The window was smashed and no stock remained, just a tailor's dummy, nakedly leaning. My feet grew leaden. So it was happening here after all.

At the bank there were queues stretching out of the door. What is it with war that it seems to produce such queues? In front of me, a well-dressed man clutched a cardboard box obviously full of the family silver. Two candlesticks poked out, and what looked like a gold clock.

I peered over the line of people. There was only one cashier, and it wasn't Rachel.

I dashed out of the door and down the road to where I'd chained my battered Raleigh to the railings. When I got to Rachel's, I propped it inside the gatepost and hooked the chain around it. Her house still had boards at the windows to keep out the rain; there were so few tradesmen left to do any repairs. The downstairs door, its blue paint peeling, stood open, so I took the stairs two at a time.

Voices. As I looked up to the landing outside Rachel's apartment, I saw two men, in grey-green German uniform, forcing the door.

I froze. They hadn't heard me. As I held my breath, I saw one of them give a great kick with his boot, and Rachel's door sprang open. I knew I should run, but I wanted to know what they would do, so I stayed where I was. A scrape of drawers being opened, of cupboards slamming shut. The rattle of china, followed by heavy thuds.

'*Nichts. Sie ist weg.*' She's gone.

The boots came out of the door, and I fled down the remaining stairs. '*Fräulein! Stehen bleiben!*' The voice called after me, but I didn't wait. I unhooked the bike and was on it in three seconds, pedalling for all I was worth towards the town centre, along York Street and Union Street, wiggling past the parked cars outside Ahier's the newsagent. Only when I was past the library on Beresford Street did I dare to look behind me.

A pair of German soldiers were strolling there, in the middle of the road, as if they owned it. As I whizzed past them, one whistled and called out something, and both men laughed, but I pretended not to hear. Once out of their sight, I jumped off the bike and began to push it down towards the beachfront at Havre des Pas.

All the time I was walking I passed men and women with suitcases and hatboxes. Everyone seemed in a great hurry, but no one smiled. Instead, the air around them bristled with tension.

When I got to the outdoor bathing pool, it was closed and barricaded with barbed wire. I found a green-painted bench nearby and stared out to sea, where, instead of white-sailed yachts, German military vessels blotted the horizon. Seagulls wheeled and dived, squalling with hoarse cries over the water. Was Fred calling out or wolf-whistling at the French women where he was? I had received only a few letters from Fred in the years he had been gone, and they were all heavily censored; it seemed he was allowed to tell me nothing of what he did, except that he was now in Paris. His letters consisted of lists of his meals and details of his daily walks. Everything else had been blanked out by the censor.

The thought of it made me angry. Was my husband putting the fear of God into the French the way the Germans put the fear of God into me? Now post from outside the island was forbidden, unless it was for the Germans. How I hated that word, 'verboten'. So much was verboten now.

I stared at the glistening blue water and thought of days gone by, when Rachel and I had picnicked on this beach. Wherever Rachel was now, she wasn't at home, and life for her looked precarious. Had she volunteered for the boats? It didn't seem likely. Why would she, when we knew how it was for Jews in Germany? But I knew she wouldn't have been given the choice, and my heart grieved.

CHAPTER 19

The next day I was explaining to old Mrs Hedges, over her stout leather handbag that rested on the counter, that she'd already had her four pounds and ten ounces of bread ration for the week, and she couldn't have more. It was becoming rather heated when the shop door swung open and the tiled floor filled rapidly with German soldiers. Mrs Hedges let out a little cry, as the sheer bulk of so many men with rifles seemed to suck the air from the shop.

Oberstleutnant Fischer emerged from their midst and placed one palm on the counter as if to stake ownership. 'I am very sorry, Frau Huber, to interrupt your business.' His manner was placatory, a thin veneer of pleasantry, as he pulled an identity card from his pocket and handed it to me. 'We are searching for a young woman, Rachel Cohen.'

My mind raced. I stared down at Rachel's face, hoping my eyes didn't betray my connection to her. I read her details, all in neat, sloping handwriting. Hair: black; eye colour: brown; distinguishing marks: none. Her card, unlike mine, was stamped with a red 'J'. Where had they got this? Why wasn't Rachel carrying it in her bag anymore? A thousand questions skittered through my head. I took a breath. 'I haven't seen her,' I said. It was the truth.

'But you know her?'

'She buys her bread here; she's a customer. Is something wrong?' I pinned a pleasant smile to my face.

He passed the card to Mrs Hedges, who scrutinised it carefully. 'It's that young woman who works in the bank,' she said. 'Nice young woman, always got a smile.'

'Not anymore,' Fischer said. 'She's…' He stopped abruptly, stretched his jaw and pulled his collar away from his neck as if it was too tight. 'You won't mind if we search?'

'No, of course not. Go ahead.' Mrs Hedges and I exchanged glances. There was something they weren't telling us.

The men headed for my sitting room door. Far more men than would be needed for my small house, it seemed to me.

'*Achtung!*' Fischer called. '*Macht es vorsichtig. Ihr Mann ist Deutscher.*' Be careful, her husband is German.

'*Danke,*' I said.

He ducked under the lintel and followed his men.

For the first time I felt the invasion viscerally, that I must stand by and do nothing. Even if they were careful, the thought of these men in jackboots tramping over my rag rugs, of them opening up my drawers and looking into my personal things, made me angry. I found myself tearing one of the paper bags on the counter into shreds.

'You never told me you spoke German.' Mrs Hedges fixed me with an accusing eye.

'Only a little,' I lied. 'You have to try to get on, don't you?'

'Your husband's German,' she said. 'That's what that man said, isn't it? I understand them, but I don't speak to them. Not if I can help it. I learnt it through music. Bach. Beethoven. I used to love opera, especially Wagner.' She braced her shoulders and frowned. 'Can't stand them now, of course.' She didn't give me time to answer. 'That poor girl. She's a Jew, isn't she? It's on her card. I've heard what they've done to them in France. If she's not dead by now, she soon will be.'

'I'm sure —'

'Some of us have principles,' Mrs Hedges said, raising her voice and pushing out her chest. 'I won't be buying my bread from you again. Good day.' And she plucked her bag from the counter and went.

I leant on the counter and pressed my forehead into my hands. I felt her words as a sharp twist in my guts.

I pulled myself upright as Fischer returned, followed by his men, who were grinning broadly as if searching houses was their favourite hobby.

'If this young woman comes to you again, you will tell us, *ja?*'

'Of course. Whatever I can do to help.' I wiped my hands on my overall, aware of the patter of my heart under it, and my shallow breath. These men weren't the enemy, I reminded myself. My husband's kin. Just men like him.

Fischer swiped Rachel's identity card from the counter, squinted at it once more, and pushed it into his breast pocket. When he left, I went through to the house. Everything was as it should be. There was no disorder. Yet still, I couldn't get out of my head the fact that only a few moments earlier uninvited guests had been trawling through here in their helmets, examining everything, prying and peeking into my business. The drawer on the sideboard was open, exposing its innards of old telephone directories, wires and plugs, scissors, string, and old birthday cards.

They'd had their hands in there. There was nothing of any importance, just bits and bobs that might come in useful. But their searching left an atmosphere behind, one I couldn't at first find a label for, but later I had it. The room smelt of suspicion.

My bicycle was an effort to ride now because we couldn't get inner tubes for the tyres, and so I'd improvised, like everyone else, with lengths of hosepipe filled with sand. It made for a lumpy ride that evening, as I forced it through the blustery autumn wind. Halfway up the lane to the farm, I saw the glint of helmets. Instinctively, I pulled off to the side and slid off the saddle.

The thud of German boots was interspersed with another sound. The first cohort of soldiers got closer, marching in formation, boots gleaming as they splashed through the puddles and leaves on the lane, their rifles poking upwards from their shoulders. I dragged the bike further into the field gateway. They were right beside me now, their polished leather holsters stuffed with guns. So many guns. Lugers, I think they're called. Guns on Jersey streets would have once seemed unthinkable. But behind them…

I stared, unable to believe my eyes. About thirty men, all stick thin, unshaven, bruised and filthy, dressed in an assortment of rags. The worst of it was, they had no shoes. Just mud-encrusted cloths tied around their feet, and they were marching on this stony dirt track. One of them glanced my way, but his eyes flicked only briefly to mine before they returned to the heels of the man in front. Something about the beaten quality of those men made me rigid. It came to me in a sudden rush of heat. The Germans were using these people as slaves.

One of the last men to pass had a shirt that was torn at the back and through its flapping vent weals showed, stripes darkly encrusted with blood. I pressed myself back against the gate. The man had been whipped. Actually whipped. Yet this was no gladiator in a film of ancient Rome, it was happening now, in twentieth century Jersey.

As I watched, a leaf blew from the sycamore tree near the gate and landed on the man's shoulder. He paused to pick it off, holding its fragile yellowing bowl in his upturned hand. A smile almost broke at the corners of his mouth. Immediately, one of the guards poked him in the back to make him move quicker. The man winced and stumbled, crushing the leaf in his fingers, but righted himself quickly and lurched forward, and I pressed my fist to my mouth. The fragments of leaf careened away in the breeze.

The second group of soldiers tramped past, after the workers, their faces fixed and impassive. Shaken, as soon as they rounded the corner, I mounted my bike and pedalled furiously up the hill.

'Did you know they were using slave labour?' I asked Mrs Flanders.

She sucked her lips. 'Aye. Well, they're only foreigners. Russians and Poles mostly. There's a camp for them. Something called OT. Organisation Todt. They work at the quarry near L'Étacq.'

'I just saw them. They looked barely alive.'

'It's them or us, though, isn't it? With rations so low, we have to feed ourselves and the Germans first. They will keep bringing in more workers, and it stands to reason we can't feed them all. It's not up to us.'

'But those people were starving. Legs thin as twigs. It can't be right.'

'Well, you'd do best not to complain. Or they'll say it's anti-German and deport you. And then who knows where you'll end up?'

Fear twined around my throat. And that horrible feeling that I'd once had in the playground, when I'd watched the school bully kick a boy repeatedly on the shins but I was too scared of the bully to report him.

I milked the cows in silence, hearing the squirt of milk sing into the pan, but my mind lingered on those men. Seeing the state of them made me realise that we were also expendable;

that they could deport us, just like the Jews, or choose to use us as slaves. We were all equally at their mercy. Yet there must be something we could do. Something. The reality of living under enemy occupation had begun to bite, but within me a stubborn resistance was growing.

Mrs Flanders led the cow she was milking out of the milking parlour, and I heard the latch of the gate and her hearty slap on its rump as she let it into the field. When she came back, she said, 'I was sorry to hear about your friend. It is her, isn't it? What a terrible thing.' She waited expectantly.

I stood up and stretched my back. 'Which friend? I don't know who you're talking about.'

'That girl from the bank. Rachel, is it?' Mrs Flanders took her pail to the churn and poured in a long stream of milk.

'Yes,' I said. 'They came looking for her at the bakery. Have they been up here to you too?'

'Looking for her?' Her eyes widened as she plonked her empty bucket down with a clatter.

'Wanted to know if I'd seen her.'

'But why?'

'I don't know why,' I said. 'Why do they do anything?'

'But I'd heard…' She was biting her lip now, and her hand crept up to cover her mouth.

'What? What's the matter?'

'I don't know how to tell you. Oh Lordy. I thought you knew. I went in the bank on the way back from the morning deliveries and they said … well, they told me she'd passed away.'

'Rachel? That's ridiculous. She can't have —'

'Just walked into the sea and drowned herself. Can you imagine?' Mrs Flanders' eyes lit up with beady glee. 'She didn't turn up for work and she's not been seen since. Of course, they knew she was a Jew at the bank but had let it slip by. Now Mr Scott, the bank manager, has been arrested.'

The news gave me a jolt, even though I'd known it might happen.

'His own fault, of course,' Mrs Flanders went on. 'Employing Jews is forbidden.'

That word again. 'But how do they know Rachel's dead?'

'An off-duty soldier found a note. She'd left it on the beach with all her clothes. Said she'd rather die in the sea than in a camp.'

'But Rachel would never do that. She just wouldn't.'

'She might. If you were a Jew and knew that if they found you you'd be deported to a German prison camp, what would you do?'

I shook my head. 'I don't believe it. And why are they still looking for her in the town if she's drowned? Surely they should be searching the beaches?'

But I knew the answer. They were suspicious, just like I was. I took the cow back to pasture and sent her on through the gate, before turning back to deal with the milk. Where was Rachel? Was she really dead? I couldn't believe it, not a strong swimmer like Rachel. But if she wasn't, then where was she?

A yell from the yard. 'Céline, you idiot! You left the gate open! There's cows all over the yard.'

CHAPTER 20

The paperboy brought the paper as I was having breakfast. Oats with milk, and a pot of weak tea with recycled tea leaves — the only reasonably sustaining meal of the day. I opened the *Jersey Evening Post* to see an announcement about Rachel on page two. I leant closer, my tea forgotten. It showed her identity card photograph and offered a reward for information leading to her whereabouts. The article said she was 'deliberately evading the German authorities' and that anyone withholding information about her would be punished.

As I pored over the small column on the kitchen table, I wondered where she could possibly go. Perhaps Mrs Flanders was right, and she'd drowned herself. But then I dismissed that thought; Rachel wasn't a person to give up; she was far too stubborn. No, she was out there somewhere.

Troubled, I folded the paper and pushed through the door to the shop, glancing at the clock over the empty shelves. After nine, and no customers yet. It was quieter these days as we had so little to sell. The days of buttery fingers, sugar icing and Viennese pastries were gone. Now it was grey bread that wouldn't rise, because all the flour was adulterated with sawdust or straw to bulk it out. Our good bread had to go to the Germans in the hotels first, and what was left was tough and almost inedible. We were all thinner, all tired, and all of us carried tension like a wire in the pit of our stomachs.

I heard men's voices outside the door, and through the glass I could see helmets. What now? Were they still looking for Rachel? I tensed as the door opened.

'Céline! So I have found you at last!' The man in the German officer's uniform grinned broadly at me and held out his arms as he came around the counter. For a moment, I thought it was Fred and hurried to meet him, but then I took a step back, confused. He was too tall for Fred.

The man folded me in a bear hug and then noisily kissed the air either side of my cheeks.

'Horst?'

Fred's brother grinned, showing even white teeth. 'What luck I have, to be posted here. Can you believe it? I asked of course, but I didn't expect it.'

He was taller and broader than I remembered, with the same nose and the same fair flyaway hair as Fred. But his features were flatter, as if squashed to the edges of his face, and he was ramrod straight, unlike Fred's soft roundness. His eyes were roaming around the room, unable to be still. I couldn't work out what it meant, him being here. Was it good, or bad?

The two men behind Horst stood respectfully at the door. Horst must be their superior, I realised.

'But what are you doing here?' I asked.

'I am posted here. Lucky, *nicht wahr*?'

'Since when? When did you arrive?'

'Just yesterday,' he replied. 'I came straight here this morning. I can't stay long today, because I have been selected for the Organisation Todt.' He waited, eyebrows raised, as if I should be impressed. 'I was posted here because my English and French are so good.' It made me smile, because he pronounced 'have' as 'haf' and his English accent certainly left a lot to be desired. 'Why you are smiling?'

'Nothing, Horst. You must excuse me; I am still getting used to … to the situation.'

174

'I understand. It is big change for you. But do not worry. Things will be better for you now I am here.'

'Where will you be working?'

'One of the camps in the north of the island,' he went on. 'Where they quarry for stone. I am to be Kommandant there; the other man, well, he could not keep control.'

I suppressed a shudder. Fred would never believe it, that his brother could work there, where people were treated so badly.

'Have you heard from Fred? No letters are getting to us here.'

Horst smiled. 'No. But I get reports. I ask where he is. If you know the right people, you can find out. Last I heard, he was still in the *Besetztes Gebiet* in northern France — how you say, the occupied zone?'

'Was he all right, though?'

'You know Siegfried. He will not make a fight — too lazy. He will stay there until they build the New Order Hitler makes.'

My face froze in its smile.

Horst was still talking, oblivious to the fact he'd insulted Fred. 'France will be a new place. They will move out the undesirables and they will be cleaning the place up.' He strode past me to the door to the sitting room and peered through, wrinkling his nose. 'It is not what I imagined, this bake shop. I thought it would be bigger. I thought to stay here, keep lookout for my brother's little wife. How many bedrooms you have?'

No. He couldn't stay here. 'Just one,' I said. 'Mine and Fred's. And a maid's room. Oh, but it's very tiny. Our housemaid Tilly used to have it, but she's ... she's left now.'

'A maid's room?' He stuck out his chin. 'That will not be suitable. I stay at the hotel for now.'

I made an effort to relax. 'Which hotel are you staying at, Horst?'

'They put me in the Pomme d'Or, but only for two nights. It is reserved for the navy, not army men like me, and I need to be nearer my work. Do you know anywhere, Céline? A nice big room with pleasant people? With a view of the sea?'

'Sorry, I can't think of anyone immediately. But I'll ask around.' Didn't he realise that nobody would want a German living with them if they could avoid it? And a sea view. I almost laughed.

Horst turned to his two colleagues at the door. 'My brother's wife,' he said. 'Pretty, *ja*?'

I cringed and blushed, but the two men at the door nodded enthusiastically and Horst looked pleased.

'We will dine together. At the weekend,' he said, tapping a fingernail on the counter. 'I will arrange it and send car to fetch you. Then we can talk. Will be nice, no?'

'Very nice,' I said. Then, as he was still staring expectantly, 'Thank you, Horst. It's a good idea. You can fill me in on what you know about Fred.'

He saluted me then with a neat Heil Hitler, and I wasn't sure what on earth to do in return, so I just raised a hand in an uncertain wave. Moments later, there was the roar of car and motorcycle engines outside the door, and all returned to silence. When they'd gone, I exhaled and turned the *Closed* sign on the door. I needed to think.

Work at the farm that day passed in a haze. We had to work quickly as the nights were drawing in, and I had to help Mrs Flanders with her main potato crop before it got dark, as well as the milking. Now there was less baking to do, I spent more time at the farm. All the time, as I yanked the cold and filthy lumps from the freezing ground, I worried about where Rachel was, out in this cold weather, and what to do about Horst. Eventually, I realised there was nothing I could do. Horst was a fact; and that was that.

But after Mrs Flanders delivered me home in the van that night, I locked the door firmly against intruders and, to be honest, against Horst. What if he should come back? I ran my hands under the tap and scrubbed the dirt from under my nails. It would be awkward, being seen with a German officer. So far, I had managed to keep Fred's whereabouts a secret. But Mrs Hedges had already realised I was married to a German, and no doubt the word would spread like the proverbial wildfire.

And what would happen if I was seen dining out with one of them? Perhaps I should just tell Horst to keep his distance, explain to him how awkward it was. But Horst wasn't a listener; he never had been; he was too full of his own self-importance. He'd be in his element here, I realised — bossing everyone about the way he used to boss Fred.

Three days later, I was still worrying about Horst as I got the Aga ready for baking. It would be too wasteful to use the big oven, and Mrs Flanders had given me a bag of corn kernels she'd saved from gleaning in the fields so I could make my own proper bread. 'Don't use the German flour they issue,' she'd said. 'It's poison.' As I wound the handle on my coffee grinder to make the precious flour, I realised I'd need yeast from the outside storeroom. It was after the nine o'clock curfew by now, but I could risk it, claim I was baking for the Germans.

I fiddled with the padlock in the dark and finally got it open. The yeast was kept on a shelf behind the door. I felt for it with my hand.

'Céline?'

I gasped and nearly shot through the ceiling.

In the darkness I could just make out a human shape, a dark silhouette against the half-empty sacks of flour. I'd no time to think before Rachel emerged towards me, shivering in a thin cotton dress and shoes with no socks or stockings.

'You idiot! What the hell do you think you're doing? How did you get in here?' My heart was still thudding like crazy.

'How d'you think? I pushed the water butt up to the wall and climbed through the window.' Her face was pale but defiant.

'You nearly gave me a heart attack! Do you know they're searching for you?'

'Of course I do. I've been hiding for days. I don't know where to go. It's getting too cold now for the woods, and yesterday German soldiers were in there, looking for firewood.'

'You're supposed to be dead.'

'I know. It wasn't very clever, but it was all I could think of. There was no time for a better plan.'

'Sorry, Rache, but you can't stay here. Fred's brother is in Jersey.'

'Horst? The Nazi?'

'I don't know about Nazi, but he's a German officer and he thinks he should keep an eye on me. It wouldn't be safe for you to be here. And what would you have done if I hadn't come, stuck in a locked storeroom? How would you have got out?'

'You weren't supposed to know. I climbed through, but then I fell in, and I couldn't get out of the blasted window again. That's what comes of being short. I thought this place would be full of sacks of flour and provisions, like it used to be, and I'd be able to eat something and then climb out. But now there's only these two half-empty sacks and I can't reach the window.'

'But what will you do?'

'If you could just let me have something to eat, and leave the door open, I'll get a few hours' sleep and be gone before morning. If they catch us, it will be deportation for me and arrest for you. But that way, if anything happens, you can say you just forgot to lock the door and you know nothing, right? You haven't seen me.'

'But where will you go after that?'

'I'll be fine; I'll find somewhere.' Her words were brave, but we both knew the whole island was swarming with soldiers. She looked at me as if daring me to contradict her, arms crossed as if to hug herself, and her fists clenched into the thin material of her dress.

'I was going to make bread,' I said uncertainly. 'That's why I came for the yeast. So I can feed you at least.'

'No. Go now. I'm scared someone will hear us. But leave the door open.'

I hurried inside clutching the packet of dried yeast, with my heart hammering. I still hadn't got over the shock of seeing Rachel there, like a wild animal, forced to forage and live in ditches and outhouses. Yet harbouring her would be dangerous. All Jews were supposed to have left the island. Those who helped them would be arrested.

I took out my worry on the grinding and made bread. It was a tiny loaf, hardly big enough for the loaf tin, but as soon as it was in the oven, the smell made my mouth water. All the time I thought of Rachel, huddling in the dark in my storeroom, hungry and frightened, in that thin cotton frock, whilst I was inside in the warm. What on earth would she do in the winter? I thought of her parents, their wedding photo, and wondered if they were still alive, or in a concentration camp somewhere. And I thought of Fred, and how Horst said he was too lazy to fight. It all ran round in my head, like rats in a maze, until I could bear it no longer. I threw open the back door and ran to the store.

As I burst in through the door, Rachel cowered back against the sacks, hands up to protect herself.

'It's me, you fool,' I said. 'Come inside. You can't stay out here. Not whilst I've a spare bed.'

'No,' she said. 'It wouldn't be fair.'

'Just get inside.' I grabbed her by the arm and pulled her to her feet. 'Quick, before someone sees.'

We ducked and scarpered around the corner, and as soon as we were in the shop I slid the bolts home on the door.

Rachel went straight to the range and stretched out her palms to the heat. She turned then, eyes unexpectedly full of tears. 'You don't have to do this. I don't want your charity.'

'It's not charity; it's common sense. And you'd do the same for me, wouldn't you?'

'I don't know. It could end badly.' It was a bald statement of fact.

I stared at her, at her lank, unwashed hair, the dark shadows under her eyes, at her arms prickled with gooseflesh.

'Wait there.' I bounded upstairs and came back with one of my thick wool pullovers. 'It'll be huge on you, but warm,' I said, thrusting it towards her. 'We can heat water on the range for a bath later.'

She held it up. 'Chanel, darling, how luxurious!'

'Fool!' But it broke the tension to hear her jest the way she used to.

She struggled into the pullover and already looked better with the scarlet wool next to her face, but I noticed her hands shake as she edged closer to the range.

I leaned over her to open the oven door, but the bread was so small a loaf it was already cooked, and I left the door open to bring more heat into the room.

'I've no butter,' I said, 'only dripping. Mrs Flanders let me have the scrapings from her pantry.' I handed her a plate and tore the loaf in half, wincing as the hot crust burned my fingers.

'Doesn't matter,' she mumbled, cramming the bread into her mouth.

I wasn't much more restrained myself, for it was steamily fragrant and startlingly good after the grey gravel we'd been calling 'bread' for the last six months.

'I knew you weren't dead,' I said, once we'd emptied our plates. 'You'd never drown yourself. You're such a good swimmer the waves would just laugh and throw you back.'

'Pity of it is, the Germans think the same. Should've known they'd see through it.' She gave a little laugh. 'Stupid idea. Still, it was either that or end up herded into a camp like my parents. I've thought a lot about it, dying. There might come a time where it's a choice I'd make. But not willingly. So much has changed in these last years. I've begun to see that the Nazis really do intend to cleanse the world of Jews.' She gave me a rueful look. 'It still seems faintly unreal, that they can do that and nobody will lift a finger to stop them, but then I've seen this whole island begin to cave in to fear. It only took a few deportations and arrests before people began to be too scared to stop them.'

'I know. I can feel it, the terror. It's like an undercurrent, as if we're all looking over our shoulders the whole time. We thought the war would be short, but it drags on. Lord, how I wish it were over.'

Rachel stood up and went to sit in the sagging armchair. 'But what if it's never over?' There was a desperate edge to her voice. 'What if the Nazis win?'

'Don't even speak of it. I refuse to live on Bratwurst and Sauerkraut.'

'You'll be all right. You'll have Fred.'

'I never really think of him as German. He's just … well, Fred.' I heard the catch in my own voice. To cover it, I pushed my specs further up my nose and got busy. 'You hang on there, and I'll go and get a pail of water, and we can heat it on the range. You can have your bath in front of the fire.'

I ran the tap, blinking back tears. 'Stupid,' I said to myself.

By the time I'd got the bucket to the range, Rachel had pulled off her shoes and was asleep, feet curled underneath her bottom. Exhausted, I guessed.

I set the bucket down quietly and fetched a blanket from Tilly's room. Rachel didn't even stir when I covered her. She'd have to stay there for the night at least. I checked the curtains were pulled tightly shut and fetched the alarm clock with its big bells. I'd set it to ring at four in the morning, before dawn. She must go by the morning, I knew that.

I also knew that turning her out of my door to an unknown fate would be the hardest thing I'd ever done.

CHAPTER 21

The rapping at the front door made me leap out of bed, bleary-eyed and fumbling for the alarm. Light seeped through the crack in the curtains. With horror, I groped for my glasses and picked up the clock. Six thirty. How the heck did that happen? Oh Lord, I hadn't forgotten to set the alarm, had I? I'd meant to, but could I actually remember doing it...? What a blethering idiot. And now here was Mrs Flanders, come to get started with the baking.

I threw on my candlewick dressing gown and shot down the stairs, almost tripping over the dangling cord as I went.

Rachel was hopping up and down putting on her shoes.

'Quick! Upstairs!' I hissed at her.

The knocking was even louder now, and I heard the letterbox open. A voice boomed into the shop. 'Céline! Get up, you lazy lump. It's six thirty! Let me in.'

I was about to go and open the door when I saw our two plates still on the table. I shoved them both into the cupboard under the sink and ran to the door.

'Sorry, Mrs Flanders,' I said, out of breath, 'I must've overslept.'

'I can see that. You look like you've spent the night in a hedge. Well, get out of the way, then, and let me in. And get yourself dressed whilst I get the oven lit. There's a frost this morning and that wind's sharp.'

I rushed upstairs again, and seeing no sign of Rachel in my bedroom, I stuck my head around the door into Tilly's room. A tap on my shoulder made me yelp. Rachel was behind the door. I flashed her a warning look and put my fingers to my lips.

'You all right up there?'

'Fine,' I called out. 'Just stubbed my toe.'

I dressed in a panic, throwing on an old skirt and a darned jersey, and splashed my face in the bedroom washbowl. There was no soap of course.

By the time I got downstairs, Mrs Flanders had got the ovens heating and was kneading the first batch of bread. 'We'll have to get a shift on,' she said. 'Best leave it to prove whilst we do the cows, and then you can finish it off when I drop you back.'

Deliberately, I got into the van without my coat. As the engine roared into life, I shouted, 'Wait! I forgot my coat!'

'You'd forget your head if it wasn't screwed on.'

I leapt out and into the house. 'Rachel,' I hissed, 'it's only me.'

Her head poked out from the top of the stairway.

'I'll only be a few hours. Don't answer the door. Get your bath and take some of Tilly's clothes, whatever she's left. We'll decide what to do later.'

'I'm not staying —'

'I haven't got time to argue. You can't leave in the light — too risky. Just do as I say, okay?'

'All right, Miss Bossy Boots.'

I was a long time coming back from the farm, because Mrs Flanders was teaching me to drive the van, and I kept stalling the damn thing. After I waved her off, I unlocked the shop door to smell the aroma of baking. My mouth watered, but these days the loaves often smelt better than they tasted. I followed my nose and there was Rachel in the bakehouse, already kneading the next batch of bread.

'I had to do something,' she said. 'Sitting about waiting is just too nerve-wracking.'

'I like your outfit,' I said. She looked better already, dressed in one of Tilly's plaid kilts and a jersey. They were still too big, and she looked like an orphan, but at least they were more practical than the thin cotton frock she'd been wearing yesterday.

'I couldn't take anything from my apartment,' she said, 'or it would have looked suspicious. My dress had to go on under the clothes I left at the beach, in case the neighbours saw me go out. I carried the shoes wrapped in brown paper. Good job I had a spare pair, even if they're more hole than shoe. I tell you, I was scared I'd be blown to bits by a mine. The beach is littered with them.'

'Soldiers went to your apartment. I went to look for you and they were kicking the door in.' I explained what I'd seen.

'I got out just in time, then.' Her smile was the same, but there was a tension around her jaw. 'Would it be all right if I took Tilly's coat?'

'Well, she's not coming back from England for it, is she?' I caught her eye, and we held each other's gaze. 'Look, Rachel, you can't just leave. You can stay here. If you go out there … well, anything could happen.'

'No. I told you. It would be too much of an imposition. If they catch us —'

'I know, I know. Don't keep saying it.'

She pulled the oven door open and dragged out the tray of loaves and set them on the table. 'Ugh. Those look horrible. But beggars can't be choosers I suppose.'

'Rachel, you're changing the subject.'

She sighed. 'Do you think I don't want to stay here? But I know what it will mean. It will change your life. You will never

185

be able to be easy again. And I ... I will always have to be grateful. I'm not very good at being grateful, Céline. And I can be bad-tempered and awkward, and bloody-minded. And what about Horst? I couldn't live with myself if something happened and they caught us. You'd get the blame.'

'Then we'll just have to make sure they don't.'

She shook her head, but I could see she was tempted.

'God, you're stubborn. And I don't care how bloody-minded you are, if you're still alive.'

'You might just regret saying that.'

I rushed over to hug her. For a moment, we stood just gripping each other.

'We'll make it, you'll see. And you can help in the bakery. They'll wonder why my bread suddenly tastes decent. And you can have Tilly's room, but you'll have to be still and quiet when customers are in the shop — her floorboards creak and they're right above it.'

CHAPTER 22

Paris, September 1942

Fred

Berenice was thinner and more careworn, and her clientele were all uniformed Germans now. She'd had to agree to serve only the German Army. The French were visibly shrinking as the Germans grew fat on black market beef and potatoes. Of course, Henri and Sebastien still sat at their usual table to play chess and watch the world pass by, but no longer were they allowed coffee in front of them. The Nazis tolerated them only because they were old and harmless.

Whenever I was driven to Avenue Foch, I waited until Vogt was in the interrogation rooms before taking my translations through to the in-tray in his office. There, I'd try to empty the filing cabinet of at least one file by slipping it inside my own file.

It was hit and miss, because my heart nearly beat out of my chest at the thought he might appear. Today, I just had the cabinet open and had leafed through the files to 'V' for Verkehr — transport communication — when I heard his voice in the outer office. I slammed the cabinet shut just as he came in.

He glared at me. 'You've no need to be in here. You can give the files to my secretary. What were you looking for?'

'I just needed to cross-reference a translation with a previous one. The transmission I'm doing, well I'm almost certain it's the same man, the one from last month where we lost the trail.'

187

'I don't keep files of enemy agents in that cabinet. They're in the one in the outer office.'

'My apologies, Herr Vogt. I won't disturb you any further.' I eased myself towards the door.

'Wait.'

I swallowed, dreading him calling for Bauer and Schuster.

'Here.' He picked up an envelope from his desk and held it out.

'For me?' I couldn't believe it. My first thought was that the letter might somehow be from Céline.

But then I saw it was franked in June with a German Army interior postmark and addressed via the Wehrmacht command at the Paris office. The army-issue envelope bore my brother's fat, childish handwriting.

'I'm sorry, it's taken a while to get to you,' Vogt said.

It was unlike Horst to write unless someone forced him to. Was everything all right at home?

'Allow me.' Vogt passed me a paper knife.

I slit it open and withdrew the stiff regulation postcard.

Dear Siegfried,

I asked after you and all they'll tell me is you've been given 'special duties'. Knowing you, that means sitting on a sofa with a pretzel and a book! You'll never guess — when the chance came up to volunteer for field duties, I took it, and I'm being posted to Jersey. All these years and I never got there, so my fingers are crossed. I know you will be relieved that I will be able to check on Céline for you whilst I am there. Make sure she's behaving herself! Good news from me, I've been promoted TWICE. So you must call me Oberleutnant Huber now! Mother and Father both so proud, and send love. They ask me to tell you to write; Mother had no birthday card from you and she worries so.

Give Paris hell from me, Heil Hitler. Horst

There was no return address. How could I have forgotten Mother's birthday? Guilt washed over me, along with a prick of resentment that Horst was so clearly a success when I was floundering. And worse, he was going to be posted to Jersey.

'It's from my brother,' I said.

'Ah yes, a very good man in the party. Nice he is keeping in touch, yes?'

'Yes sir. Thank you, sir.'

I made my exit as soon as I could.

Bloody Horst.

I'm not jealous, I told myself.

But then I realised. He could already be there by now. Imagining Horst in my house, his boots on my carpet, made me want to shout all the German curse words I could.

I was powerless. Would the Germans in Jersey behave the way they did in France? What about Horst? Would he watch as the police rounded up the Jews?

When I got home I struck a match, set light to the letter and watched it shrivel into ash in the ashtray.

My trousers grew baggy at the waist because not only was food harder and harder to come by, but the worry of my double life, and what might be happening in Jersey, ate away at me. I could barely sleep. Every noise outside made me leap from bed sweating. I'd survived more than two years as a Nazi interpreter but knew it was only a matter of time. Radio operators barely lasted a month, and I knew sooner or later I'd slip up and reveal my links to Félix and his undercover Resistance. The reason I'd survived so long was because the focus of the Nazi interrogations had shifted away from Resistance saboteurs and onto people who might be hiding Jews. Thirteen thousand Jews had been 'cleansed' from the city in that awful round-up the Germans called *Opération Vent Printanier* — or Operation Spring Breeze.

In Félix's house, the tragedy of this round-up had given them renewed impetus. It now seemed essential to resist. We sat around the table to plan our next attack.

'Our own countrymen, rounding up whole families like animals,' Antoine said, stubbing out his cigarette. 'I would never have believed it.'

'If we can't trust our own police, who can we trust?' Félix said.

'No one,' Jérôme snapped, with a sharp glance in my direction.

'Lay off, Jérôme,' Antoine said. 'Without Édouard, we'd still be working on guesswork.'

'The police had no choice,' I said. 'The Gestapo wanted to take only the men and women, but the French authorities knew they'd be saddled with their children. There are no separate ration books for children. Of course, if the children starved, Germany would blame France, and it would look bad for the French. More negative propaganda. So the police were ordered to help and round up whole families. What was the fate of a few Jews against the great name of France?'

'Bastards,' Jérôme said.

'Not just that,' I added, 'but they thought it would be more orderly if the whole family went. It would look less threatening. Like a family outing. And they'd go more quietly if they were taken by their own countrymen.'

'Was it really so calculated?' Félix shook his head.

'Have you ever known the Nazis be anything less?'

'Where did they take them?' asked Antoine. 'Have you found out?'

'From what I can gather from the memos, they went from the Vel' d'Hiv stadium to somewhere called Auschwitz — Brzezinka. It's a camp somewhere in Poland.'

'What goes on at the camp?'

'Nobody knows,' I said. 'I've tried to find out, but I just meet a brick wall. But I do know this: they don't come back. And there's a notice I've just had to translate that says anyone hiding Jews or assisting them in any way will be shot.'

Silence.

'All right,' I said, realising I'd hit a nerve. 'I can see I shouldn't ask any questions.'

As food grew scarcer, my extra food rations dwindled to non-existent, and I was forced to queue with everyone else. I passed *Soldatenkaffeen*, where plump-bellied soldiers sat at tables laden with sausage and potatoes, then was obliged to wait three hours in line for my two-ounce ration of minced rabbit. The long queues, the unfairness of it all, made me shift from foot to foot, unable to be still.

I looked down at my shoes, which were already old when I left Jersey. The soles were coming apart from the uppers, and shoes couldn't be had on my coupons. I'd need to get them fixed. When I'd been given my soft brown paper parcel of meat, I shoved it in my pocket and headed to a shoe repair shop I'd seen on a neighbouring street.

The shop sold various sorts of hardware as well as repairing shoes. I showed my coupons to the cobbler in the shapeless dark suit.

'Ten minutes,' he said. 'I'll do them straight away if you'll wait.'

I stood in stockinged feet as he whisked the shoes through to the back where I could hear the tap of his hammer and the whirr of the grinding machine as he resoled them.

I glanced at his calendar with a faded picture of a canal boat and the peeling posters for slug pellets. I browsed the shelves. They were half-empty. A few tins of Paulin's shoe polish, some Bon Ami sink cleaner. Then I saw it. Paint stripper. Nitrocol. Three bottles on the bottom shelf.

I picked one up and turned it round to read the list of ingredients. And there it was: nitromethane. I was about to put it back when a movement behind the door made me thrust it under my coat and wedge it under my armpit.

The cobbler held out my shoes for me to see, then plonked them down. 'All done.' His smile revealed more gum than teeth.

Keeping my left arm clamped to my side, I swiped the shoes off the counter with my right and clutched them to my chest. I sat on the stool provided and shoved my feet into the shoes. What the hell was I doing? But I couldn't put the damn bottle back now. He was watching me.

'Rheumatism,' I said, awkwardly tying the laces.

'That's why you don't fight, eh?'

I nodded and smiled ruefully, thanked him again. As soon as I got on the street, I began walking away as fast as I could. 'You're wrong,' I said under my breath. 'You said I don't fight. But I do.'

The glass bottle was slippery under my arm, but a strange exhilaration filled me, making my steps lighter in my newly soled shoes, my walk full of bounce. I don't know what made me steal the bottle. It was an impulse. But I couldn't untake it.

In doing it, I had made myself free. I was neither in thrall to the Germans, nor to the French, nor to the English. I had made a free choice. It was this that made me feel alive: to be able to choose.

The night was warm, and every time Félix switched on his torch, crowds of moths and midges fluttered into the pencil of light.

'Keep it steady,' Antoine said, as the beam swung away.

'I heard something,' Félix said.

We paused, like deer in a forest. The distant noise of a car. Jérôme was on watch further up the track, on the road near where we'd left our bicycles. His cigarette made a red pinprick in the dark. When he didn't move and the noise faded, we resumed digging. So far, we had destroyed a viaduct and a bridge, and this was to be our third derailment, though the last had failed because the pipe bombs were unpredictable. So much depended on the quality of the ingredients, and in wartime, they were never reliable. Today we had my nitromethane and a new type of fertiliser that Jérôme had found in someone's outhouse.

The rail tracks glimmered under our light as we buried the metal pipes under the creosoted planks and attached the detonators. Four pipes set to go off at ten-second intervals. I wiped an insect from my face, breathing the sour smell of fertiliser. The small nub of plastic explosive was the last thing, jammed into the end of the pipe. I sighed, satisfied, and mentally crossed my fingers. You could never tell with untested ingredients.

'Ready,' called Félix.

The armaments train was due soon. We needed to be well away before it derailed.

Antoine stood up. 'All set.'

'Go.' I dived off the embankment beside the track, rolling in a breathless tangle.

There was a flash like lightning and an enormous boom. I covered my head as gravel and debris spattered over me. A clank of metal. Seconds later, the heavy crump of three more explosions. The ground shook.

'Jesus, that was some blast!' Antoine said. 'Let's get the hell out of here.'

We ran towards Jérôme and leapt onto the bicycles. I wondered what the state of the track was, but we didn't dare look back.

'Car!' yelled Félix.

Ahead of us, an armoured truck with slit headlights was bumping down the road. I swerved off the road to the right, following the others as they dragged the cycles into a brake of trees. Had they seen us?

The truck passed without stopping. Near the rail track a patch of grass was burning, a flare that would surely announce where we'd been. After about a hundred yards, the truck slowed and the tailgate dropped down. Against the light, there were silhouettes of armed soldiers. They climbed the embankment and headed down the track towards the fire.

Another set of lights. A second truck approached from the other direction. The headlights made us all crouch lower.

We'd chosen the place because it was an obscure junction, away from houses. It had taken us half a day to cycle here from the city.

Where had those two trucks come from? It was too much of a coincidence.

Silently Félix gestured for us to lay low. Torches flashed across the road and in our direction, but we were just out of range. We pressed ourselves flat to the ground. It was a good thing we were all in dark clothes. My heart thudded against the ground. I daren't look up. Any movement would attract their attention.

Their voices carried in the still air. They were arguing about whether to search for us or try to stop the train. The train was full of German soldiers on the way east, they said. I closed my eyes. I hadn't known that. Félix had told me it was a train full of armaments. If it came off the tracks, I'd be responsible for the men's deaths.

The noise of engines coughing into life. Shouts of '*Schnell!*'

They'd chosen to stop the train instead of coming after us. One truck to go further up the track past the damage, the other to the main signal box. Thank God. When the road was silent again, I looked up.

'That was unlucky. The blasts were too big,' Antoine said. 'They'll intercept it.'

'It will put the line out of action though, won't it?' I said.

Nobody answered. For some reason I felt guilty, even though the failure was nothing to do with me.

We climbed on the cycles and pedalled into the darkness.

'Why didn't you tell me the train would be full of troops?' I said to Félix.

'The bigger question,' he said, glaring accusingly, 'is how did the Germans know where we'd be?'

CHAPTER 23

Céline

Rachel moved into Tilly's old room and for a few days I almost forgot she was there, except for the fact my shoulders grew knots and I had a permanent feeling of panic every time a German came into the shop. Fortunately, I was not someone people noticed much, and so the fact I was scrounging for extra rations barely raised an eyebrow. The evenings were the best, when I could lock all the doors and we could settle downstairs by the range and chat over weak tea and the cobbling together of meals from whatever ingredients I could glean.

Mrs Flanders was our lifeline. She still had a wireless set — *verboten*, of course — but she was so avid for news that she risked keeping it, wrapped like a baby in blankets, beneath bales of straw in the barn. Ghoulish gossip was Mrs Flanders' reason for existence; without it she'd probably shrivel up and die. So in the evenings after work, as we peeled beet to make sugar syrup, I could tell Rachel the news from the World Service.

Horst telephoned to tell me his driver would collect me on the Saturday evening, so when the day arrived Rachel helped me get ready in my one good dress, a dark floral print with padded shoulders and a cinched-in waist.

'What's he like, this Horst?' Rachel asked, as she fastened the little buttons at the back.

'I don't know him that well. In Vienna, I always found him a bit intimidating. And he treated Fred in a condescending big brother-ish sort of way, belittling his career as a pâtissier. He once told Fred that baking was *weiblich*, womanly, right in front of me. It was clearly supposed to be an insult, and he was totally oblivious to the fact he'd just insulted me too.'

'Sounds like a dream date.'

'I'm hoping he'll tell me some news about Fred. He can find out about him through the German network, and I'm desperate to know how he is. Though it feels really strange; somehow, I can't really imagine Fred as part of an invading force.'

'He probably looks different in uniform.'

I stared at her then. It was something I'd never thought of. How stupid. I'd always just imagined him in the clothes he wore at home. And suddenly I could see it; that the uniforms were a big part of the intimidation.

I shuddered. 'Don't let's talk about it,' I said. 'I just have to get through this one night.'

'I'd better go upstairs. He might be early,' Rachel said.

When she'd gone, the house fell to silence again. I was ready far too soon, but we couldn't risk anyone coming unexpectedly, so I wanted to be waiting. I sat on the edge of the armchair, steeling myself, my palms sweating with nerves. It would be so easy to slip up, to forget and to say 'we' instead of 'I'.

In the event I was at the door as soon as I heard the car. It was a shiny black monstrosity called a Horch, with glaring headlamps and a gleaming chrome radiator like something from a film. I made a great fuss of locking up, although I felt like I was acting a part. The chauffeur held the door for me, with a '*Guten Abend*, Frau Huber.' As I climbed in, I saw the curtain at the window twitch.

Rachel, you fool! I prayed the chauffeur hadn't seen it and gripped tight to the leather seat as the car slid away from the kerb. Wait till I got home, I'd have words to say to her. I began to wonder if I could really trust her to be careful enough. She'd always been a bit flighty, a bit reckless. For the first time, the real spectre of deportation to a German prison camp made me shudder in my seat.

I was deposited by the harbour outside the Pomme d'Or hotel and told to go into the lobby to Reception. In my plain wool coat, I felt too dowdy for the grand entrance and the sleek interior, with its silver bucket for umbrellas and the elaborate display of starched roses on the front desk. I was about to go to ask the porter where I might find Horst when he appeared before me.

'Céline!' he said, grasping me by the shoulders and making two loud air kisses. 'I've reserved for us a table in the restaurant.'

'You mean here?'

He must have seen my consternation. 'It will be more relaxed here,' he said easily.

Relaxed for him, perhaps. For me, it was the equivalent of being inside a wasp's nest. All male eyes turned to me as we passed through the lounge, though the Germans soon looked away through lack of interest. On the other hand, I was greeted by resentful stares from the waiters, who, as far as I could see, were all islanders with whom I was all too familiar.

Horst pulled out a chair for me in the mirrored dining room and sat down opposite. The room was full of uniformed men dining in great good humour. Most seemed to be in naval uniform and were chatting in German in groups of three or four. Glancing around the room, I could see only a few other women, and they all seemed to be in evening dress — accented with red lips and plucked eyebrows, and the flash of white gloves and jewellery.

I flushed as I struggled out of my coat, and I handed it to the hovering waiter. I was woefully underdressed, I realised. But then again, what could I do? I was in my only dress that wasn't used in the shop or on the farm.

Horst laid a small parcel next to my plate.

'Oh, Horst, what's all this?'

'Open it,' he said.

I tugged off the bow on the box and slid it open. *Bas Le Bourget — transparents comme l'air*, I read. French stockings, flesh-coloured and wrapped in cellophane. Again, heat rose to my face, partly because Fred had never in his life given me such an intimate gift, and partly because I knew these had come from France, another occupied country just like Jersey.

'You can wear them next time we dine out,' he said, leaning in and patting my hand. His palm was unpleasantly hot.

'Thank you,' I said, uncomfortable. 'It was a sweet thought.' I withdrew my hand, closed the lid, and asked to see a menu.

'Sorry, but there's no menu. The rationing, you see. But usually we have something reasonable here.'

Reasonable? I was aghast when they brought me fresh tomato soup with a crisp bread roll, roast chicken with runner beans and roast potatoes, and a pear and apple upside-down pudding with custard. We hadn't seen a fresh tomato for years, nor eaten anything sweet, except carrots and turnips, let alone the luxury of custard. I'll swear it was made with eggs too.

I couldn't help thinking of Rachel, at home with my empty larder, and the lumpy flour they supplied us with, which only made hard bread. It was torture. I couldn't help enjoying it, but at the same time I could hardly swallow for the thought of all the other islanders saving their one egg for a special occasion.

Horst packed away his dinner in a business-like way, whilst extolling the virtues of German efficiency. 'We are building everywhere on Jersey — tunnels, bunkers, walls. It will really put this island … how do you say it? On the map. This will be the strongest place in Europe when the Führer he finish it.'

'Why, Horst? Why does he need Jersey? We don't understand.'

'Because from here we are close to France, and to England, which we will have under our control soon enough. It is ideal place for German command. A good stronghold. And besides, it is very beautiful, *ja*?'

'But will it still be beautiful once you've built all that? Everywhere I go, there's the stink of concrete and men building. And as for our beautiful beaches, they are full of mines and barbed wire.'

Horst tightened his lips, picked up a napkin and pressed it to his mouth. I had offended him. 'The English, it is their fault. All the building work is necessary because of the English. Once the English cease to threaten us, then we'll clear the beaches again, and life here will become more … more pleasant.'

'I'm sorry. It's just that we're not used to changes here in Jersey. Everything's been the same here for hundreds of years, since the Normans. Let's talk of something else. Tell me about Fred. Is there any chance he'll get leave any time soon?'

'Leave? Probably not. France has many pockets of Resistance. All men are needed there. We have a shortage of fit men in Germany. It is small in population compared with the rest of Europe, and there is much clearing to do.'

'What do you mean by clearing?'

Horst paused, took out a cigarette and lit it. 'I forgot, you are not a German.' He puffed a moment and blew out a thin stream of smoke. 'It is not something for you to worry about. Tell me instead the most beautiful place on the island.'

He was changing the subject, damn him. I played his game. 'Mont Orgueil, the castle. It has stood there for eight hundred years, and the view is breathtaking.' Too late, I realised that this was the first place the Germans had taken over, and even now they were building gun turrets into its sacred walls. Everything about this conversation made me tense. I found I was gripping the edge of the damask tablecloth.

I reeled off a few more local beauty spots, all of which had lost their peace and charm since the occupation, but Horst seemed to barely be listening. He was watching other people watching me.

'They are wondering who you are,' he said. 'You are a new face here. And a charming one. I thought we might take a stroll, so you could show me the sights. We need to walk after dinner, yes?'

I agreed; anything to escape this stultifying atmosphere. So, after coffee for me and cognac for Horst, we set off to stroll past the bobbing boats in the harbour and towards the church. I couldn't help but see the rubble still being cleared from the harbour front, and the gunboats anchored just off the coast. The evening was chilly, and Horst took my arm. To counter the disloyal feelings this produced, I entertained Horst by telling him about Saint Helier, who lived just offshore as a hermit but was set upon by pirates in the early days of Christianity.

'What happened to him?' Horst asked.

'He was beheaded by the chief buccaneer, who feared his men would be converted to pacifism by the holy man's impassioned preaching.'

'Shame, I would have liked to hear him preach.'

'You're a thousand years too late!' I said.

He laughed, and the ice was broken at last. 'Horst,' I said, pulling away and anxious to seize the moment, 'it feels awkward for me to be seen with you. It will cause trouble with my neighbours and countrymen. You see, to them you are still the enemy.'

'They will learn.' His mouth set in a stubborn line. After a few more steps, he said, 'They will get used to this way now. When they see how we Germans keep everything in order, how we make a prospering *Heimat* for us all, then they will learn our way it is best. And the quicker it come, the better.'

Heimat. A homeland. 'But we were all right as we were, Horst. Imagine how you would feel if the English took over Dortmund.'

He frowned. 'That will never happen.' The bells of the church struck the half hour. 'That time already? It is a shame. Time to get you home, before the curfew.'

He led me back the way we came, and at the front of the hotel he asked a boy to summon the car. To my consternation, he then dismissed the driver. 'I'll drive you myself,' he said, 'then we can continue our conversation.'

My stomach clenched. Would he expect to come in? Already my mind was skittering ahead, to Rachel, and whether she would be out of sight. The headlamps sliced through the dark as I took sideways glances at Horst's face. He kept up constant talk of how he had seen Hitler himself talk at a rally in Berlin, and how inspirational he was, how he had such vision, and would transform the lives of the whole of Europe with his new ideas. 'The old order is dead,' he said. 'Time to build a new world.'

When he talked with such passion, he had a kind of boyish charm. I could almost believe in it, this golden future, except for the fact I'd witnessed the Nazis' far from golden treatment of their Russian and Polish workers.

The car drew up outside the bakery. Thank God, no lights were showing.

'You have coffee inside?' Horst asked.

'No. No coffee. Not what you would call coffee anyway. It's acorns, ground into powder. Very unappetising. We can't get coffee now.' I hoped to put him off.

'Is it very bad?'

'Disgusting. You wouldn't want to try it.'

'On the contrary, it seems like I ought to taste this strange Jersey drink.'

'It's late, Horst, and I'm tired. I was up at five thirty to help on the farm.'

'I won't stay long.' He was already climbing out of the car, and moments later the passenger door opened.

Reluctantly, I unlocked the door and let him follow me inside. Think of Fred, I thought. He'd be pleased I was entertaining his brother. I willed Rachel to keep quiet and tried not to let my eyes stray to the stairs or the ceiling as I lit an oil lamp. No electric lights were allowed after curfew.

There was no sign of Rachel, but the sitting room was warm, and the fire in the hearth blazing.

Horst sat down in front of it and took off his driving gloves. 'You like it so warm?' he said.

Oh no. Why didn't I think of that? It was odd to have left the fire blazing whilst I was out.

'I've been ill,' I said hurriedly. Helpfully, a sweat broke out on my forehead. 'I banked the fire up before I came out. It wouldn't do to catch a chill again.'

'Oh, you are ill? But why you not say?'

'I didn't like to refuse your invitation. Fred would have been disappointed if I didn't come.'

'I see now why you are tired and not like yourself.' He stood up again. 'I will leave you, but perhaps we could meet again soon. It is agreeable to have female company.'

'Perhaps we can do it again in another week when I'm better.' *Or not at all.* I went back through the shop, past the counter and opened the door.

He took the hint. 'I won't embrace you,' he said, 'if you don't mind. Thank you for a delightful evening.'

I watched him climb into the car and drive away, before collapsing against the door jamb. I was drained. Please, let him get busy and forget all about me. Maybe he would, once he got more involved with his odious job. But then, how would I get any news of Fred?

In the sitting room, I pulled the curtains tight shut and called out, 'Rachel?'

Rachel appeared, swamped in an old nightdress and dressing gown of Tilly's.

'You idiot,' I said. 'You banked up the fire. I had to explain why I'd go out leaving a fire blazing away.'

Rachel sat down, leant an elbow on the arm of the chair and put a hand to her forehead. 'Oh jeepers. Sorry. It was stupid. I just didn't think.'

I was exasperated. 'Look, Rache, we have to be more careful. I can't be worrying every time I go out, thinking you'll have done something daft. And I saw the curtain move when we drove off.'

'What did I tell you?' she flashed. 'I told you you'd regret it.'

'I don't regret it. I'm just tired and stressed, and worried to death, that's all.'

'Sorry. I'm just not used to being told what to do. And I hate being cooped up. You're right about the fire; I kept it going because, to be honest, I don't feel too good. I can't get warm, and I feel sort of shivery. And I couldn't find any other heating in the house.'

'I know, they took away all our electric heaters to conserve power. You're not getting ill are you, Rachel?' Now I came to look at her, she did look awful. Pale, with red-rimmed eyes.

'It's probably just a cold. My throat's really sore. I'll be better once I've had a good night's sleep. But I couldn't sleep knowing you were out with that German. I kept worrying he'd come in and I'd snore or give myself away by falling out of bed.'

'He thinks I'm ill. It was the excuse I gave him about the fire being so hot when we came back.'

'Oh heavens.' She swallowed. 'It's not going to be easy, is it?'

'Look, you get back to bed. We can't risk you getting any worse.'

She smiled. 'Yes, it would be a bit inconvenient, wouldn't it, to have a dead Jew on your premises.'

'About as inconvenient as having a live one, I'd say.'

'Ha ha.' But she got up and wobbled towards the stairs. Halfway up, she stopped and turned. 'Thank you, you know I—'

'Stop it with the thank yous. Or I'll have to throw you out.'

But the next morning, far from being any better, Rachel was worse. She had started a hacking cough in the night. The last thing I needed. Just after dawn I got dressed, boiled a kettle and took her a hot drink.

'It's the worst thing that could happen,' Rachel croaked.

'Can't you stop the cough? Mrs Flanders'll be here soon.'

'I'll try. But it just sort of takes me over. I'll have to stuff my head in the pillow. Keep the door...' Another bout of coughing.

'I know, I know, keep the door shut.' I watched as she smothered her face with the quilt. I could still hear her, despite all her efforts.

The noise of the van outside threw me into a panic.

'Don't let her in,' Rachel said. 'She's got the biggest mouth on the island. If she finds out I'm here, we'll both be...' More smothered coughing. 'Céline?'

But I was already in my bedroom, throwing off my clothes and struggling back into my nightdress and an old jersey.

I ran downstairs, slapping my face to make it red. When I opened the door, I put on a forlorn expression and made my voice nasal. 'Sorry, Mrs Flanders, I can't come to work. I've got a terrible cold. I've been coughing all night.'

If I expected sympathy, none was forthcoming. 'Have you? According to Mrs Hedges, you were fine last night. She saw you on the promenade. Have you taken some onion water?'

'I've no onions,' I said.

I kept the door between us, but Mrs Flanders was keeping her distance anyway.

'Well, we can't get lemons, that's for certain,' she said. 'And I don't know anyone with any honey left. But I'll see if I've an onion at home. Are you sure you're not fit? A bit of fresh air might do you good.'

At that moment, I heard coughing from the room upstairs. Immediately I began coughing, though I was aware it didn't sound very convincing. My face grew hot with effort.

When I stood up from being doubled over, Mrs Flanders was looking up at the window with a suspicious expression. 'When did it come on, this cough?'

'Just last night,' I mumbled.

'Wouldn't be anything to do with the fact you were walking arm in arm with one of those Germans, would it?'

'I'm sorry, Mrs Flanders, but I've got to go back to bed.'

Another cough from upstairs.

'Still in there, is he? You're a Jerrybag, that's what you are. And your man off fighting a war! I would never have thought it of you. That's it. I'm done with you. You can drive the bloody van yourself.' She flung the keys at my feet. 'I'll walk back to the farm, thank you very much. And don't you dare show your face there again. You're not welcome.'

I watched her sturdy back retreating down the hill. What could I do? Mrs Hedges had obviously seen me and Horst, and now Mrs Flanders obviously thought he was still inside and the cough had come from him. I couldn't explain without giving Rachel away.

Suddenly it was all too much. I went to the drawer of the bureau and took out paper and a pen. If I was supposed to be ill, I couldn't bake or do deliveries, could I? I scrawled a notice: *Sorry, closed today due to ill health.*

After I'd stuck it in the window, I relayed what had happened with Mrs Flanders to Rachel, who was still coughing.

'Cripes. Do you think the Germans will come to see what's happened to their bread?' she asked.

'I've locked the doors and there's a notice up saying I'm ill. I'll have to telephone the Kommandant's office to explain.'

I picked up the receiver and dialled the switchboard, who put me through to the German Supplies Unit. Making myself sound hoarse again, I explained to the man on the other end that I was too ill to bake.

'Hold the line whilst I speak to my supervisor,' the man replied in English. In the background, I could hear the clicks and whirrs of the switchboard and a whispered conversation, before he came back on. 'Are you still there?'

'Yes.'

'If it persists, they say they will have to send someone else to take over the bakery.' The voice was clipped, official. 'They say you have three days to resume normal production.' Then, in a whispered undertone, 'Mrs Huber? Don't let them take over. You'll never get it back. I hope you get better soon.'

'Thank you,' I whispered back, 'I intend to.'

'V for Victory,' he whispered.

Rachel's cough got worse, and then it turned into a terrible silent rattle. I began to fear she might actually die. Still dressed in my nightclothes in case anyone should call, I bathed her forehead to try to reduce the fever, but it was obvious she was really ill.

By the afternoon, she was burning with fever and delirious. What was I to do? She needed medical help. I couldn't trust Mrs Flanders, even if she'd speak to me, which I doubted. Was there a doctor I could trust? The doctor I'd had since childhood had retired and then been evacuated. I paced back and forth trying to work out a feasible plan.

The insistent 'brrring' of the telephone made me run downstairs. I hesitated, agonising, my hand hovering over the receiver. Finally, I picked it up, not speaking.

'Céline? Is that you? It is I, Horst. They told me you are sick and no bread comes today from you, so I ring to find out how you are.'

'Worse.' I made my voice weak and croaky. 'I need something for a fever and a cough. Can you ask someone to send some tablets?'

'I will come,' he said. 'I will bring a doctor.'

'No! I mean, no need for that. Just some linctus, and aspirin or something to bring my temperature down.' I was gabbling now, in a panic.

'Asp—? What? You must not worry. I will take care of it. Go back to bed and leave the door unlock.'

I backtracked furiously. 'No, no! It's really nothing. Don't worry yourself. I'll go straight back to bed, and I'm sure I'll be all right in the morning. These things, they come and go, I don't —'

'Stop this protest. I will come at six, when I'm off-duty.'

'It's very kind, but there's no need —'

'You are family. It's my duty to help. Now go back to bed.' And he rang off.

Hell's teeth. It was a disaster. I'd have to hide Rachel somewhere. But where? And she was in no fit state to be moved either, and I couldn't expect her to make any kind of decision. Which would be worse, to die of a fever right here, or to be transported to Germany to some unknown fate? I thought of those Todt workers and knew her fate would be worse than theirs.

There was nowhere to hide her. The Germans inspected the storeroom most days, and they hadn't been yet. But then I had an idea.

The van.

It was parked at the front, where Mrs Flanders had left it, but I could reverse it right to the back door to where the deliveries of flour were made to the storeroom. Nervously, I inserted the key and turned it. Nothing. After three attempts, and a lot of choke, the engine spluttered to life, and I inched forward a little until extra pressure on the accelerator resulted in a kangaroo jump forward. Please don't let the neighbours catch sight of me, I prayed. After all, I was supposed to be ill. It would be typical of Mrs Galen to come out at the wrong moment. Still, it was a risk I had to take. Unfortunately, my driving lessons with Mrs Flanders hadn't covered reversing.

After a lot of grinding of gears and cursing, I finally managed to get the damn thing close enough. I unlocked the back doors of the van and left them standing open.

I glanced at the clock. Five thirty. Terrified Horst and the doctor might appear at any moment, I opened up the back door and dragged an eiderdown from my own bed and some cushions from the settee to make a sort of nest in the back of the van.

Now to move Rachel.

I tried to explain to her what I was doing, but she was distracted and didn't seem to understand. She thrashed and groaned and mumbled some sort of gibberish about the sea. When I tried to help her out of bed, her legs gave way under her. Grim with frustration, I tried to drag her to the stairs.

Thank goodness I'd spent all those months doing heavy farm work. I was fitter and stronger that I used to be, and Rachel was thinner. By now she'd gone flaccid, and her face had two bright spots of red on the cheeks. I'd have to carry her, I realised, and I didn't know if I could. She was smaller than me, but she'd be a dead weight.

I gritted my teeth. By stepping down a few stairs and dragging Rachel towards me by her arms, I managed to turn her and hoist her over my shoulder so I could half crawl backwards down the stairs.

A stagger, and I was out of the door and dropping her awkwardly into the van. She groaned and lashed out but then slumped. She'd have some bruises, but worse, her chest still made that rattle when she breathed, and now the rattle was worse, her skin clammy and cold. I tucked her up as best I could.

Should I lock her in? I'd have to. But it would be pitch-black in there.

I explained to her in urgent whispers why I'd moved her and told her to rest until I came to fetch her. 'I won't be long,' I said. 'Please, Rache, for both our sakes, don't make a sound.'

She showed no sign of having heard me. Maybe she'd sleep. I couldn't think any more; I was too scared to come up with anything better, so I shut the doors and locked them.

It was a good thing I'd moved her so quickly, because almost immediately there was a knock on the glass pane of the shop. I shut the back door and glanced through the window. A man in a grey-green uniform was peering in at me, his nose to the glass, hand shielding his eyes. He had a doctor's bag in his other hand.

There was no sign of Horst.

Warily, I opened the door. Standing before me was the young man who'd come with Oberstleutnant Fischer to fill out the registration papers. The one who'd taken my photograph.

'Frau Huber? Your brother-in-law sent me. I'm a doctor.'

'Oh. I thought you were a photographer.'

'Ah, you remember me, Leutnant Müller. In wartime, yes. In peacetime, I'm a doctor. Well, not yet. I'm student of medicine.' He smiled.

'A student?' I remembered I was supposed to be ill. 'A student?' I repeated with a raspy voice.

'All the real doctors are in France, or at the front, or in hospitals at home. I was the only doctor they could find. Are you going to let me in?'

I opened the door.

'Hauptmann Huber cannot come. Some … trouble at the camp.' His expression hollowed and darkened, as if in pain, before he took on a brisker manner. 'He said you were very sick. Please go back to bed. I'll examine you there.'

For a moment, I resisted. I'd heard rumours of women left alone with German men: the rapes and atrocities. And I was in my nightdress! But this one seemed courteous, even a little nervous, his light hazel eyes shifting around the shop. I led him to the settee in the sitting room and sat down.

'Have you brought something for fever?' I asked.

'*Ja*. But I must take temperature first.'

My chest squeezed tight. It would be normal. I should've made a hot drink, but now it was too late.

'Open your mouth.' He shook the thermometer and popped it under my tongue, then took my wrist to take my pulse. 'Is a little fast,' he said.

Whilst we were waiting for the temperature reading, I took a good look at him. He was pale, with a prominent Adam's apple and a slightly beaky nose. His hands were long and slender, and his wrists covered in a downy fuzz.

He pulled out the thermometer and squinted at it. Then shook it again in frustration. 'You are feeling a little better, yes? Are you hot?'

'Yes,' I lied. 'And my chest is very tight.'

He then examined my throat and took a stethoscope to my back, asking me to breathe in and out.

He put his things away in his bag without a word. Something in his manner told me he was angry.

'It seems just a common cold. There is nothing the matter with you that rest cannot mend,' he said.

'But I need something for the fever. And for the cough.'

'I have not heard you cough, Frau Huber. Everywhere there is war, men losing limbs, men destroyed by bomb, men with beatings and shot dead, and you complain of a cough.' His face had turned red and his hand shook as he fastened his bag. 'Shall I tell you what I think, Frau Huber? You are a liar. You think you can use Hauptmann Huber to get something you can sell. I have heard it before from you Jersey women.'

Heat rushed to my face. 'I'm really ill,' I protested. 'You have to give me the medicine. If you do not, I will tell Hauptmann Huber you are a useless doctor, and you insulted me.'

His mouth tightened and his lips turned pale and bloodless. 'Foolish woman. You try to threaten me? If I was a different man, you would pay for that, and for wasting my time.' He avoided my eyes and headed for the door. As he opened it, a noise hit my ears.

Banging and shouting.

Rachel.

There was no hope he'd ignore it — such a racket. I followed him as he strode around the back. The van shuddered with blows from the inside. My eyes raked round the street, praying that Mrs Galen hadn't seen us.

'Is this your van?' Leutnant Müller asked.

I nodded, knowing that it was too late to save the situation.

'Who is inside? Open it.'

I hesitated, but then his hand went to his gun.

'All right, all right.' I ran for the keys and unlocked the shiny black doors, but stood before them. 'Please,' I said desperately, 'don't hurt her. She's ill. She doesn't know what she's doing.'

I threw the doors open, and at the sight of the German with his gun, Rachel backed away into the corner, but a bout of coughing left her wheezing and she collapsed to the floor of the van.

'*Was ist los?* Who is this? Why you lock her up?'

'She's the one who needs the medicine, but —'

He was no longer listening. He'd put away the gun and was climbing inside the van, where he made soothing noises, encouraging Rachel to move a little until he could carry her inside.

When she caught sight of me, she slumped. 'I didn't know where I was,' she rasped. Then her mouth quivered. 'I'm sorry,' she said.

I threw her a sad look and shook my head. This was it; we were finished.

'Quick,' Müller said, hoisting her up, 'open the door.'

I let him carry her inside.

A quick examination was all it took. 'She needs to go to hospital,' he said. '*Lungenentzündung.*'

The word meant nothing to me.

'An infection of the lungs. It is serious, you understand?'

'Like pneumonia?' Rachel asked weakly.

'I don't know this word. Frau Huber, bring me a cloth with cold water, and ring your hospital.'

I hurried to wring out a cloth and passed it to him. 'She can't go to hospital. She'd be deported straight away.'

He ignored me, loosening the neck of Rachel's nightgown and smoothing over her hot face with the cool cloth. Rachel let him do it, too drained to move, and finally, after some minutes, she seemed to quieten and drift to sleep.

'Please,' I whispered, 'just give me the medicine and pretend you haven't seen her.'

He sighed and passed me the cloth, before slumping down on the sofa and resting his head in his hands. When he looked up, he spoke quietly. 'She's Jewish, isn't she? I remember taking her photograph. We had a friendly conversation, you know? We ... liked each other. Later, I heard she was supposed to have...' He shook his head. 'I remember thinking, so this is what we have come to, that women will walk in the sea rather than give themselves up to us. It made me feel ... ashamed.'

'She just turned up one night. We're friends. Was I to turn her away?'

'So, you risk your life for your friend. I apologise, Frau Huber. I thought you were ... well, I thought you were a woman greedy for medicine for the black market trade. But now I have a problem. If I ignore you and let her die, then you will be deported to a work camp, Ravensbrück or worse, and you will become filth, an animal. Nobody survives it. They work you there until you die. Can you believe I am telling you this? Here, too, it happens, with the men digging stone.'

'I saw some slave workers. I didn't believe men could be so inhumane.'

'So you see, I would not want that for any person. On the other hand, if I treat your friend and let her live, then I will be a traitor to my own country, and I will be hanged by my own countrymen. Yes, they are not above this. Small cruelties have swelled like a monster. Where does it come from, this evil? Is it born of war? My medical skills are too small against such suffering. I just wanted to do good. To cure and do good. But now there is no "good" for any German.' He sank his head into his hands again.

I was silent a moment. 'Please, don't tell Hauptmann Huber. I think he would have to deport me to save face, and Rachel is too ill to move. But if you leave now, you can just forget the whole thing. We'll manage somehow. Nobody needs to know. Just tell my brother-in-law I'm feeling better and put us out of your mind.'

'She must have something for the infection, then she will have a better chance. She needs sulfa, this is good for lung disease. I can get it from the German medical store, if I'm careful. But it would need to be soon.'

'Would you?' I held my breath.

'It is selfish. I don't want to kill anyone. It's against the oath I took as a student doctor and a Christian. I will help you by bringing the medicine. She may still die. But we will have tried. And in the meantime, give her this.' He took a bottle of aspirin and a packet of Elliot's Medical Cigarettes from his bag, and after further instructions about dosages and how to keep her cool, he left the things on the sideboard. Something about the way he did this was so ordinary, so like before the war, that it brought tears to my eyes.

I blinked. 'I don't know what to say.'

'Nothing. In these days, always best to say nothing.'

'Tell Hauptmann Huber I am feeling better and that he has no need to visit.'

He stared at me. 'You are a brave woman. You have heart. You are nothing like Hauptmann Huber.'

'He is part of Organisation Todt, isn't he?'

'Yes, he is in charge. We supervise the incoming men at the camp at St Brelade. Before they go to Five Mile Road or to St John's Quarry. I have to...' His mouth twisted. 'Never mind what I do. It is not for women's ears.'

Then he went, leaving me alone with the rattle of Rachel's chest.

I watched over Rachel, who must have exhausted herself with all that banging on the van doors. I bathed her regularly to keep her cool and fed her the aspirin in mint tea.

At four o'clock, the knock at the door came again. After a peek through the glass to check it wasn't Horst or Mrs Flanders, I let the German in.

'I'm Céline,' I said. 'I don't know your name.'

'Wolfgang.' His shy smile suddenly made him seem like the young man he was.

'Rachel's sleeping,' I said, 'but her breathing is terrible. It sounds like her lungs are full of water.'

He went over to look at her and took her pulse. 'She is weak, but we must give her the sulfa now. It will help.'

'Leut— Wolfgang, would you help me move her back upstairs?' I said. 'I'm frightened someone will come and find her here. And she will be more comfortable in a proper bed too.'

He picked her up, like he was carrying a fragile parcel, and took her upstairs. She woke when she was being moved and he was able to persuade her to take the sulfa on a spoon. 'Make her drink plenty of water,' he said. 'I have left the bottle by the bed. Every day in the morning, one spoon. Now, I must go. Hauptmann Huber sends his best wishes for your recovery.'

'Tell him I'm already much better.'

He laughed. For a slim man like him, it was a surprising sound, full and deep.

I saw him to the door. Across the road, Mrs Galen was sweeping her doorstep, ogling at the German car parked at my front door. After it had driven away, she yelled at me, 'Jerrybag! Do you wonder why you've no customers anymore? Dirty Boche.'

There was nothing I could say. It pinched me, deep inside. I missed Mrs Flanders and the farm, and I fretted about the three-day deadline. I'd have to start baking again soon. I couldn't risk the Germans taking over the bakery.

Over the next couple of days, I gave Rachel the medicine and it seemed to do the trick, for her breathing had eased, and she was able to sit up in bed.

She thought she had dreamt Wolfgang, that she had been delirious and conjured him up.

'You mean, he really won't tell?'

'I don't think so. Nobody's come knocking at our door yet.'

'And he brought me that ghastly stuff I've to take every day?'

'Risked his neck too.'

'I'm not sure, Céline. The more people know I'm here, the more likely it is I'll get found. Are you sure you can trust him?'

'Can you trust anyone these days? We'd no choice.'

Our conversation was interrupted by the telephone. It was the German Supplies Unit. 'You will bake tomorrow. If you do not, we will send another baker to use your ovens.'

'There will be bread tomorrow,' I promised.

Later that evening I dragged the flour from the store, though there was barely any left. No new delivery had come from the mill, and all imports were frozen. The autumn harvest had given way to the chill fingers of winter. I'd relied on Mrs Flanders for eggs and milk and potatoes, and now there would be none. Mrs Galen, whose brother kept an illegal pig, had given me the occasional rasher of bacon or pig's trotter, but now? Well, I just didn't know.

Recently, the Germans had taken the whole bread ration to feed their troops. Having my neighbours freeze me out might mean I would starve.

When I saw the German uniform I was expecting Wolfgang, but when I opened the door, Horst was there, filling the doorway. In his hands was a large bunch of dark red chrysanthemums. He held them out to me with a big smile. He was immaculately attired — everything shiny, even his cheeks, which glowed as though scrubbed.

He stepped forward, so I had no choice but to move out of his way and let him in. My blood seemed to skitter in my veins.

'Are those for me?' Numbly, I took the flowers. 'How thoughtful.'

Food would have been a more useful gift, but probably not so appropriate for his vision of himself as a handsome man-about-town.

'You look much better,' he said. 'My man Müller, did he give you the medicine?'

Obviously, Wolfgang had said nothing about Rachel. 'Yes, thank you. He was very good. Very professional.' My ears strained for the slightest sound from above. *Please, Rachel, don't cough.*

Horst beamed, and he sat himself down on the settee as I fussed at the sink with a jug for the flowers.

'These are lovely, Horst!' I said, in a loud, bright voice, so that Rachel would hear me. Her cough was still a danger now, and she was still weak and apt to fall into a doze.

'You will be well enough to come out for dinner?'

'I can't come out this evening, Horst. I must bake.' The relief of an excuse! 'The Kommandant says that, unless I produce bread by tomorrow, he will send someone to turn me out of my house.'

Horst's jaw worked a little, and his gaze shifted away. 'Well, do not blame him. He has a job to do. The troops are hungry. There are more than ten thousand of us now, all hungry men. But perhaps I can be of help.'

I frowned, wondering what he meant. Surely he wouldn't take to baking?

'Céline, it is this way. I find it not to my liking at the hotel. It is too many men. I am with men all day and I miss my home, the pleasure, or — how you say? — the comfort of family, of home-cooked food. I will move in here with you. That will be best. Then they will not take your home. I make sure of it. A good solution, yes?'

I swayed on my feet. 'But Horst, there is only a small box room. It's not suitable; it is cold and damp, and it would be far too cramped.'

'Let me see this room.'

'Now? But it is a mess. Let me clean it up. If you come again tomorrow it will be tidy and —'

But he was already climbing the stairs. I coughed frantically, hoping to send a signal to Rachel to hide. My mouth was dry. Where could she hide? This was it. I steeled myself, already imagining shouts, soldiers in jackboots running in with guns.

Horst turned left and threw open the door of my room. I envisaged what he must be seeing: a double bed, with an iron and brass bedstead, its candlewick counterpane pulled tight and neat over the burgundy quilted eiderdown. He strolled over and patted it, then sat down, bouncing a little on the mattress.

'You are comfortable here?'

'Fred used to like the view,' I said, conjuring my husband into the room. Speaking his name might make me less afraid.

'Did he? Well he will have a different view now.'

He strode over to the window. The blackout blind was open, and down below the port looked calm, the blue of the sea melting into the haze of a grey sky.

'Yes, very good view,' he said.

He put a hand on my shoulder as he passed. 'Now, no need to fear. You have a man in the house.' His words sent a convulsion through my stomach. He pushed open the other door and peered in before I could prevent him. Over his shoulder I saw that the bedside table still had a bottle of tablets on it, and Rachel's scuffed brown shoes were side by side under the narrow single bed.

'The maid is gone, yes? So you can clear this room.'

From my position behind him I could see through the crack in the door, and Rachel's fingers, gripping the flowery fabric of Tilly's nightdress, right behind it. Rachel's closeness made me faint; my blood pounded in my ears.

'Yes, yes,' I flustered. 'I'll clear it straight away. Sorry for the mess. I wasn't expecting anyone to visit, and I've been so busy with the shop.' I spoke loudly to get his attention as I reached for the door handle, and I pulled it sharply towards me until it clicked shut.

He smiled at me. 'I understand. Not easy to keep house with no maid. But things will be easier when I am here. You are right. Thank you. I will take the bigger room. It is good of you to offer.'

In that one sentence, I saw how things were. The veneer of politeness that hid the determination to have his own way. And there was nothing on earth I could do about it.

I followed him shakily down the stairs. His next leave day was in five days' time, he said, and then one of his men would bring his luggage into my house. I pretended to be pleased, though inside I was crumbling. Before he left, he came towards me as if to embrace me. But his hand suddenly reached up and took off my glasses. He folded them into his hand.

'You don't need these,' he said. 'You are very pretty without them.' And he took hold of me by the shoulders and pressed his mouth to mine. His tongue snaked between my lips.

I was so shocked I couldn't move.

From above there was a choke of a cough, hastily suppressed.

He released me. 'What is that?'

'Just seagulls on the roof,' I said, pulling him hurriedly towards me. 'We are by the sea, remember?'

He kissed me again, in a long wet, revolting kiss, and I endured it, willing Rachel to stay quiet.

On the doorstep, he turned to me. 'We understand each other,' Horst said.

I nodded and held out my hand. 'My glasses,' I said.

'You don't need them.' He dropped them onto the cinder path and ground them under his boot. 'Nobody wears them in Germany. Get changed,' he said. 'Something nice. I have some duties to do, but I will come back for you at seven thirty.'

After he'd gone, my legs began to shake. I felt for my glasses, and then I had to kneel with my nose close to the path to find the bits. One lens was completely crushed, the other cracked, and the frames twisted into shrapnel. The world, which had been sharp-edged, was blurred. My image of my brother-in-law had fractured into something I could no longer recognise.

CHAPTER 24

I stripped down to my underwear and, shivering, held open the wardrobe door.

'You're actually going to change to go out for dinner with that Nazi?' Rachel said, as if these were normal circumstances.

'What do you think?' I shouted at her. 'Do I have a choice?'

'Can't you make up an excuse?'

'What excuse? He's going to be bloody living here in a few days.' I dragged a skirt and blouse from their hangers and fought my way into them.

My fingers wouldn't work, and I couldn't see properly.

'Here, let me help,' Rachel said. 'You've got it buttoned all the wrong way.'

'He broke my glasses.'

'Where are they? Let me look. I'll see if I can fix them.'

'You can't fix them!' I said with venom. 'They're smashed to pieces … everything's smashed to pieces.' I was consumed with anger and shame. 'Just leave me alone.'

I heard the soft growl of a car engine outside. As I peered out through the net, I saw Mrs Galen's face appear at the window opposite. We stared at each other, before her curtain twitched shut.

I heard the soft click of Rachel's door as she disappeared, like a cat, into hiding.

When I came out of the house, Horst frowned at my red eyes and my homely skirt. 'Why you not wear my stockings?' he asked.

'I have no … no suspender belt.' My cheeks grew hot as I mimed the belt.

'This is easy fix. I bring you, soon, with new dress.'

He took me to one of the restaurants frequented by Germans and propelled me to a table. At every opportunity, he crept his hand onto the bare flesh of my knee. I had to hold the menu up to my nose to read it, and of course, I saw with a sinking heart that even that was in German.

'I will order for you,' Horst said with a self-satisfied smile.

I ate a meal that almost choked me, keeping a polite distance but fearful of offending him. Offending the Germans was something that landed you in jail, along with chalking 'V' for Victory on the pavements or owning a wireless. Horst regaled me with stories of his childhood. In nearly all of them, Horst was the clever one and Fred the stupid one, or Horst the leader and Fred limping behind. I gritted my teeth and tried not to show my annoyance.

When he drove me home, the house was dark and silent.

'Soon this will be my house,' he said, looking up at it. 'It is humble, but I will endure it. It is better than one room at the hotel.' But then he saw something that made him leap from the car. 'What is this?'

The front window of the shop was daubed with an enormous dripping white 'V' and 'ENGLISH VICTORY IS CERTAIN' in roughly drawn capitals.

'I don't know,' I said, instantly feeling guilty. 'I don't know who did this. But I don't think it will be easy to clean — the paint smells like enamel.'

'It is not to be borne, this Resistance. We will find out. Your neighbours will be punished. I will find out who is responsible for doing this to our house.' He paced up and down the street, a kind of animal tension in the way he walked. 'Stay indoors tomorrow, Céline. It is none of your business.'

'But, Horst, it's probably just children fooling around.'

'I don't think so. Stay indoors. I order it.' Without even a 'goodnight', he forced his bulk back into the car. 'I must go and organise some men,' he shouted through the window. 'If you hear anything else, call me.' He drove off.

My shop had been a deliberate target. One of my neighbours had chosen to do this, to make me feel bad. It was the last thing I needed, to be made the centre of German attention. I wouldn't put it past Mrs Galen, or her husband Anton, to single me out.

Rachel came down from upstairs. She was dressed and looked much better. 'How did you get rid of him? I thought he'd want to come in. I was all set to hide behind the door.'

'Don't jest,' I said.

'I'm not jesting. I was bloody terrified. There's nowhere else to go.'

'Did you hear anything or see anything when I was out?'

'No. Nothing. I heard noises outside, but I kept the curtains drawn and the lights out, like always. Why?'

I explained about the window. 'He told me to stay indoors tomorrow.'

'Guess that means me too. Shame, I was thinking of a nice stroll down to the harbour for an ice cream.'

'Will you stop it with your stupid jokes. It's serious.'

'What should I do instead? Cry? Once I'm on the run, I've probably only a few days before I get caught. I might as well enjoy them. I would've left already, but I wanted to thank you first.'

'I told you before, I don't need thanks.'

'I'd be dead by now if you hadn't fetched Wolfgang. I could hardly breathe, but all I could think of was that I mustn't die, because otherwise it would cause you even more trouble.'

'Don't be a goose. Look, we've five days before Horst moves in. We'll just have to find you somewhere else. Is there anyone else you trust?'

'No. Nobody who would risk their life for me. That's what you mean, isn't it? And it isn't fair. I can't ask that of anyone. I'll move on tomorrow. Meanwhile, let's get on with the baking. It'll give us time to think. Maybe we can stop Horst moving in, and you never know, we might come up with an idea.'

'Have you ever tried to stop the Germans doing anything?' I said.

'What if you ring the Kommandant and get him to send someone to take over the bakery? Then at least you wouldn't have to deal with Horst.'

'It might be someone worse. Or they'd move me out and neither of us would have anywhere to go.'

Both of us fell to silent kneading.

At dawn, we were up again to bake the meagre consignment of bread. Rachel had just got it in the oven when there was the noise of boots on the street outside. I tweaked back the curtain. Even without my glasses, I could see enough to know there was a whole platoon of soldiers in the street.

'Get upstairs out of sight,' I whispered urgently, flapping my hands at Rachel.

From behind the bedroom window, I watched as they knocked at every door and dragged the occupants onto the street, even shy six-year-old Lily and Mr and Mrs Soulier, her schoolteacher parents. If the door didn't open, soldiers shot off the lock and kicked it in. Mr and Mrs Galen were white with terror; the others just looked stunned. They stood in a ragged line, trying to make themselves seem smaller.

A car arrived, one I recognised, and Horst got out. The troop saluted him with rigidly raised arms and a Heil Hitler.

Horst strolled up the line and then pointed to the window. I saw Mrs Galen look up to the crack in the curtain where I was watching, and her mouth pursed in disgust. Still, I couldn't move away.

'Who has done this?' Horst said. 'You are all neighbours. Who saw?'

Nobody answered.

'You?' He grabbed a rifle from one of the men and smashed it hard upwards into Mr Soulier's jaw. I heard myself gasp as he fell to the ground, groaning and spitting out teeth. Another of the men aimed a vicious kick at his stomach. Mr Soulier curled into a bloody foetus, hands over his head, as Mrs Soulier, eyes pools of horror, grabbed Lily and pressed her face into her skirts, her hand on her head. Nobody else dared move.

Horst walked along the line. Sickened, I couldn't look away. I was the cause of this; if I hadn't known Horst, had never had him in my house, then nobody would have painted on my window. I would be one of them, instead of one of the enemy.

The next man in line was the old man, Mr Benoit, who hardly ever came out of his house because he was lame and walked with a stick. Horst dragged him forward, the man cringing, his hands clamped together before his face, pleading for mercy.

'Who will tell me what they saw?' Horst called out. 'Or shall I shoot him?' He threw down the bloodstained rifle and cocked his handgun.

'No, please. I saw nothing.' Mr Benoit was on his knees, a wet stain on his trousers.

'I count to three.' Horst pressed the gun to his temple.

The rest in the line froze, like dummies. Some closed their eyes.

'Three. Two.'

I leapt down the stairs and flung open the door of the shop. The jangle of the bell made everyone's eyes swivel to me. 'Please. It doesn't matter. It's only a window!'

The shot rang out and Mr Benoit slumped. His head hit the pavement with a second crack. So quick? Alive one moment and gone the next? It didn't seem possible.

'Céline —' Horst's voice was calm — 'I told you to stay indoors.'

'Please, Horst.' I met his gaze with mine. 'It's not worth someone's life.'

The neighbours shifted their eyes sideways to look at me, but they didn't move. I felt as if the whole world was staring.

Horst walked the few steps over to me, a cold look in his blue eyes, the gun pointing straight at my chest. He leaned close to me as I stood quaking. His words were whispered, conspiratorial. 'It is necessary. To keep order. Do not try my patience.' He called to his men. 'Schulz, Vogel, *begleitet Sie.*'

Two men grabbed my arms and half pushed, half carried me towards the shop.

'Let go,' I protested. 'I'm going.' I ran inside.

From behind the glass in the door, I watched Horst cock his gun and move back to Mrs Soulier, who was shuddering with weeping and fear, with Lily still pressed to her knees.

Please God, no.

Horst prodded Mrs Soulier in the neck with his gun. 'You want her to be an orphan?'

'Don't shoot!' She fell to her knees, shielding Lily by pushing her behind her. 'It was Mr Galen!' She pointed. 'I saw him with a brush, painting the window! Last night, when it was dark.'

Horst swivelled to look at him.

'You bitch!' Mrs Galen shouted. 'Don't believe her! She's lying. We know nothing about it!'

But anyone could see Mr Galen's guilt. It was written all over his face.

Horst gave an order in German and the men moved forward in a crush of rifles and helmets. The Galens were punched and beaten, and frog-marched away down the road.

When the disturbance was over, the street emptied. Mrs Soulier carried Lily indoors and then came back to help her husband to stagger back into the house. But Mr Benoit was still lying there, like a discarded bundle. The shock of it made my teeth chatter and my stomach roil.

I couldn't think. Couldn't make sense of it.

I ran my hands under the cold tap until they were blue.

Like a sleepwalker, I dragged the dough from the mixing bowl to divide it into loaves. The smell and texture of it, on top of what I'd just seen, were enough to make me run back to the sink to vomit and then hurry on shaking legs to the privy in the backyard.

I scrubbed at my hands again, over and over, letting the clear cold water run. My hands seemed to be someone else's as I loaded the bread into the ovens and busied myself with batches of loaves. When I looked into the street an hour later, the old man was still there, but now there were flies buzzing near his face, and the blood had dried to a dark stain.

There was no noise at all from upstairs. Rachel might as well not have existed. But I knew she'd have heard the shouting and the shots, and the body in the street was plain to see.

I'd have to drive the bread to the German Supplies Unit if I didn't want to be evicted. The thought of driving was bad enough, but the thought of seeing any more German soldiers made my palms sweat.

CHAPTER 25

When I returned, driving slowly because I could barely see the road without my glasses, I avoided the bundle in the street. I was a coward. It had taken only one morning to turn me into someone who would just ignore a body on my own doorstep. There was still an unsettling silence from Rachel's room. If she was still planning on leaving, she must be even more afraid than I was. And leave she must. I had no doubts at all now about the man who would be sharing my house. I couldn't understand it; how could Fred and this man have come from the same womb? The thought of Fred in a German uniform made me uneasy.

I glanced at the clock. Nine thirty, and the day already felt a hundred years long.

Finally, Rachel came downstairs. 'I saw,' was all she said.

Her face was white, and in the oversized clothes she was childlike; nothing like the brazen, confident swimmer I used to know.

'Pull yourself together,' I said. 'Eat something.' I passed her a plate, on which was a nub of the grey bread with a scrape of margarine and a cup of nettle tea.

There was nothing we could say to each other.

Finally, Rachel said, 'I don't want to leave you alone with him.'

I squeezed her hand where it lay on the table. 'None of us asked for this. We just have to survive it. If we can only survive, better times will come.'

'I'll leave as soon as it's dark.' Tears stood like glass in her eyes.

The shop was open, but I had nothing to sell anymore, except what I could filch from the German ration. I'd stretch bread rolls until they were tiny and flat like dried biscuit, and occasionally someone would come to barter — a potato for a small roll. But word must have spread that I wasn't to be trusted, for none of my island customers came near me anymore, and if I tried to speak to them on the street, they cut me dead.

It was lunchtime when a German car rolled up the street. I shouted to Rachel, 'Germans!' and heard her bedroom door close. I stood behind the shop window, behind that ugly 'V'.

The car stopped just in front of Mr Benoit's body, and the door opened.

But it wasn't Horst, it was Wolfgang. He went over to look at Mr Benoit and gently rolled him onto his back. He bent to listen to his chest and feel his pulse, though it was pretty obvious Mr Benoit was dead. Wolfgang looked up and down the street, but seeing nobody, he lifted the man off the road and into his arms. It was a struggle, for Wolfgang, though tall, was slight.

I only hesitated a moment before I ran out, locking the door behind me. 'Where are you taking him?' It was an accusation.

'I hear about this shooting. It is a bad thing. He can't lie there, this old man, in the street. Has he any family?'

'No. Not that I know of. His wife died years ago.'

'Then let's take him there.' He indicated the chapel just down the street with a nod. 'They will bury him, I hope.'

I went ahead to push open the gate. 'There's no graveyard here; Almorah Cemetery is up the road. But the door's always open, and the minister knows him; he will know what to do.'

The iron handle twisted easily and the heavy oak door swung open. The chapel was dim, with high windows and semicircular rows of pews. Wolfgang lay Mr Benoit down just before the altar platform, on the smooth-flagged floor.

We were silent a moment, both looking at the cross on the altar table. This wasn't a high church, but its plainness and simplicity made our presence even more stark.

'We say prayers for him,' Wolfgang said.

We knelt side by side. Instinctively, I felt I could trust him, but I couldn't pray. The taut feeling in my belly, the sensation of being caught on a dangerous ledge, wouldn't let my mind rest.

Wolfgang's hands rested on the pew in front of him, and I saw then a great bruise across the back of his hand. He saw me staring and thrust it into his pocket.

After a while, we stood together and walked silently from the church. It seemed natural for him to walk me to my front door.

'Can I see the patient?' Wolfgang asked. 'Just a few moments. I am supposed to be collecting a man from the boat, but it is delayed.'

'A Nazi?'

'Yes, a Nazi.'

I hesitated, key in hand, blocking the door.

'I do my job.' He looked ashamed. 'But for you, I am just a doctor. Not a German. Not a soldier. Just a doctor.'

'A few minutes then.' I turned the key in the lock. 'It's okay, Rachel,' I called softly. 'It's a friend.'

Rachel emerged warily from the top of the stairs.

'You look better,' Wolfgang said. 'It's good to see you out of bed. The cough is gone?'

'Almost.' She suddenly seemed shy. 'Thank you for bringing the medicine. I was in a bad way.'

'You will be able to rest now, and soon you will be good as new.'

Rachel caught my eye, and Wolfgang saw our exchange of glances. 'You have trouble?'

'Hauptmann Huber,' I said. 'My brother-in-law. He has decided to move in here.'

'In this house?' Wolfgang sucked in his breath. 'This is not good news. He thinks all Jews *Untermenschen*. And outside, there is nowhere for a person to hide.' He turned to Rachel. 'You have to have shelter. Haven't you some storeroom? An attic or a cellar?'

'There is nowhere,' Rachel said. 'We've wracked our brains, but nothing. And Hauptmann Huber doesn't strike me as a man who will listen to reason. No, I must move on, and I'll try to get a boat to England.'

'Impossible,' Wolfgang said. 'The boat patrols stop every craft. Two men were shot only a few nights ago. And trees are being cut down so fast for wood, there's nowhere left to hide.'

'Well, I can't stay here,' Rachel said.

'In the day, yes you can. He is out all day doing his work.' The way Wolfgang said 'work' left me in no doubt as to its ugliness. 'I see him arrive in the morning, and we all thank God when he leaves at night.'

'It's just too dangerous for you, for me to stay here,' Rachel said.

'And too dangerous for you if you go,' Wolfgang said.

We sat in silence, at an impasse.

The next day was a whirlwind of activity. I had the daily baking and delivery to do, and to clear enough space in Tilly's room for all my things. I didn't want to leave anything of mine or Fred's in Horst's room. I also kept Rachel's things and all of

Tilly's. We couldn't get cloth or shoes anymore. Every garment was precious. I stacked what I could under the bed to make room, lining up my own shoes near the front and putting Rachel's at the back.

Wolfgang arrived in the middle of the chaos. 'I can't stay long. Hauptmann Huber has sent me to see to one of his men who is suffering with ache of the stomach. I can spare only a half hour. But I have an idea. You have bread boxes, yes?' He mimed the wooden trays we used for carrying bread.

'Ah. You mean crates?' Rachel asked.

'Crates, yes.' His face was bright with fervour.

'But we don't have any bread,' I said. 'Not since the English cut off French trade routes. They're trying to starve you out. And us with you.'

'That is not important. Show me these crates.'

I took him to the bakery, where a stack of unused crates was piled up near the door. More were stacked under the counter.

He pulled one out. 'We use these, to build a wall.'

'What?' I didn't understand.

'A hiding place for Rachel.'

'Here?' Rachel's face took on a worried expression.

'Wolfgang, I don't think it will work,' I said. 'This isn't a child's game. We don't need a den, we need a proper safe house.'

'What better place? They will not look in a house where Hauptmann Huber lives.'

'It seems like fantasy. I'm still not sure —'

'You will see. I am good builder, but I need nails and a hammer. Can you get these?'

'I have them already. In Fred's toolbox under the stairs. But I still don't think it will work.'

'Let him try,' Rachel said. 'We have nothing to lose, have we?' Brave words, but I could see by her face the idea terrified her.

The next day, Wolfgang arrived even before it was light. Thank heavens the bakery was a detached shop, because the hammering made a lot of noise. Rachel and I muffled it as best we could with quilts and eiderdowns. And of course, people had got used to strange noises outside, and they knew it was best to stay indoors out of the way until curfew was lifted.

For a medical student, Wolfgang wasn't a bad carpenter. We watched him saw strips of wood and join them together, and fit a false wall about two foot six away from the real wall in what used to be Tilly's room but would soon be mine.

'Has Hauptmann Huber ever been in this room?' Wolfgang asked.

'Only once,' I said. 'He just pushed his nose in, said it was too small, and then came out.'

'And I was holding my breath behind the door,' Rachel said.

Wolfgang shook his head and blew out air. 'You have close shaving,' he said.

'Close shave,' Rachel corrected.

'Would he notice, do you think, that the room is smaller?' Wolfgang said, running his hand along the new partition.

'Not if we could paper it and hang the same picture there,' Rachel said. 'The bed can go right up to it just the same.'

'I haven't got any wallpaper. At least I have, but not the same.'

'Fetch it,' Wolfgang said, 'and we'll see.'

It wasn't the same at all, but we had no other option. I worried that Horst would notice.

'We'll need to paste it up with something,' I said.

'Haven't you got anything?' Rachel asked.

'No. If there was any wallpaper paste in the house, I'd probably eat it.'

Rachel stepped through one of the gaps in the wooden wall. 'Gosh. I'd better not put on weight. How will I get in and out?'

Wolfgang pointed. 'A small door, hinged there, under the bed where the join will be hard to see.'

'It might work,' I conceded. 'But I don't think I'll ever get any sleep.'

'I'll sleep in the day,' Rachel said. 'I'll need to stay awake at night in case I make a noise.'

'Let's hope the war is short,' Wolfgang said.

Two days later, the wall was finished. Wolfgang had managed to find a pot of glue the Germans used for postering, and once the paper was up and the picture hung, it looked like any other wall. Of course, it was flimsy and wouldn't stand up to inspection if someone hammered on it, but we just had to hope no one would dare do that where Horst lived.

Rachel and I took a torch and crawled under the bed and through the flap.

'It's tiny, Rache,' I said. Her face looked gaunt and skeletal in the darkness. 'You'll hardly be able to breathe.'

'I won't be able to breathe anyway,' Rachel said, 'in case Horst hears.'

'I'll be sleeping right next to you on the other side of the wall; he'll just think it's me.'

'It is working?' Wolfgang's voice from outside.

We crawled back out. 'It has to work,' I said.

'Thank you,' Rachel said to Wolfgang. 'Because of you, I have a chance. May I?' And she reached up to kiss his cheek.

He flushed brick red, but the smile reached right up to his eyes, though he tried to hide it.

'Forty,' I said, nudging her with an elbow.

'Chance would be a fine thing,' Rachel said, her voice choked.

Wolfgang looked at me, not understanding, but I didn't enlighten him.

CHAPTER 26

November 1942

Fred

Félix never completely trusted me. On several occasions the Wehrmacht appeared at the sites of our sabotage, just too close for comfort, but none of us could work out where they were getting the information. It could be coincidence, or it could be something more.

Occasionally I was summoned to Avenue Foch, and each time my stomach clenched in dread thinking this was the end, that they'd found out I was helping the French activists. I was so jumpy that the last few times I'd taken the loaded pistol with me.

Vogt was wrong; I'd never got used to the sound of the interrogations.

Today, as I was driven down the Avenue Foch, the army were out on drill. Ranks of gleaming helmets all goose-stepping down the boulevard. I wondered if Obenauer or Schulz were amongst them, glad I was no longer part of that huge machine. It had once made me proud, but now it made me shiver, as if an arctic wind blew down my neck.

As I got out of the car, a tall man in shabby civilian clothes, a raincoat and hat, was getting out of a black car further down the road. He walked briskly ahead of me towards number eighty-four, and the guards exchanged a greeting with him before he went inside. There was something about the way he walked that was familiar. By the time I got inside though, there was no sign of him.

I'd forgotten about him by the time it came to lunchtime. Bauer and Schuster were in the habit of playing cards, and I sometimes joined them if the cells were quiet. Today we were playing for cigarettes as usual. The ornately plastered ceiling, from when this had been a palatial apartment, was already stained yellow with nicotine. I looked up over my hopeless hand at Schuster's wide beaming face as he laid down his run of four kings. His hands were scrubbed clean, and it was hard to believe he was the cause of the suffering I knew must go on behind those cell doors.

'Luck of the devil.' Bauer sulkily scraped up the cards and dealt another round.

I'd just picked up my hand, when laughing voices and footsteps in the corridor made us swivel to look towards the open door. It was a black-uniformed SS officer, with the man in the raincoat I'd seen earlier. The officer turned to look into the room, and the guards immediately stood to attention and barked out 'Heil Hitler!' Instinctively, I followed suit.

The moment was like a snapshot. Behind the officer, Jérôme's eyes met mine and his smile died. His eyes flashed in astonishment. Immediately, his expression changed to one of indifference. He didn't acknowledge me, or give any indication he'd ever seen me before. He didn't speak a word, but turned his head away, pretending to study the view from the window behind.

'Is Herr Vogt in his office?' the officer asked.

'Yes, sir,' Bauer answered.

'Best enjoy your break then, those cells will soon be heaving.'

They moved on. What was Jérôme doing here? He'd been speaking German only a moment ago. I replayed the moment in my head. He wasn't expecting to see me, and I'd blown his cover. Like me, he was obviously under the pay of the Germans. When had he changed sides? Had he been a spy all along? But in this case, unlike with me, Félix, Antoine and Berenice couldn't know.

'Your turn,' Bauer's voice broke into my thoughts.

'What?' I glanced at my hand and threw down the first card.

'Fool,' he said. 'What are you doing? I win.'

I didn't care; I had too much to think about. Jérôme might denounce me to Vogt. One thing was clear; it wouldn't be long before Vogt found out I was also working for the French, if he didn't know already. The files I had copied, the transmissions I'd falsified; they all came back to me with sickening clarity.

I needed breathing space. 'Call of nature, lads,' I said, throwing down my cards.

In a daze, I went into the cubicle and locked the door. My hands shook. I pressed them against the icy tiles of the wall.

I'd have to run. Now was the time. I'd just walk out of there before anyone knew I'd gone. What then? I'd have the Nazi army and the French Resistance after me. No time to think. I had to act.

I took a deep breath and opened the cubicle door. I stepped out into the corridor and bumped straight into Freitag.

'Exciting times,' he said, grinning down at me. 'We had a tip-off. The cells are full, and Vogt can't do it all. Vogt says you're to go in and translate for the interrogations in five and seven.'

'What?' I felt blood drain from my face.

He waited for me to walk ahead of him in the narrow corridor. Shit, I couldn't turn and run now.

I headed into the office aiming for nonchalance, my heart thudding wildly.

Freitag pointed. 'There's paper and a clipboard on the shelf just there. Bauer and Schuster have just been briefed to expect you, and they're waiting. Files are in the pigeonholes over there. Numbers five and seven.'

I found the files and opened them. In number five was René Fireille, a man accused of secretly giving a Jew his ration book. M'sieur Fireille was also suspected of being a member of the Communist Party. His file was thin, but the second file was much thicker.

I glanced at the name, but had to read it again. 'Berenice Severin.'

It couldn't be her. I flicked it open. A passport photo. Berenice was staring ahead in that glassy way of all passport photographs. A typewritten memo was attached. 'Jewish family Bechstein discovered in the cellar of her business. Interrogate and execute.'

CHAPTER 27

Fireille was a pale young man in broken spectacles who already seemed to have been beaten around the head, as one of his eyes was half-closed and his ear was dripping blood. He shrank back in terrified silence before Schuster even opened his mouth. In the cell next door Bauer was in with Vogt and a member of the SS, and the noises from there were enough to make bile rise in my throat.

Schuster tied Fireille to a chair with little protest and began his questioning. My job was to translate the questions into French and then translate the French back into German and make notes. I sat as far away as I could and shrank in my shirt, as if by doing so I might isolate myself from what might happen next, as Schuster began his work. It was clear he enjoyed this intimidation; a strange fire lit his eyes; a pungent smell of his sweat inside the serge of his uniform filled the room.

I did my best to make Schuster's questions sound reasonable, but Fireille was incoherent, his eyes wide with terror.

'I don't know any Jews. I just keep myself to myself. I have a wife and children. I'd never do anything…'

'But your ration book was found in Auerbach's pocket. How do you explain that?' No matter how measured my questions, Fireille's eyes stayed fixed on Schuster pacing behind me, his body coiled like a compressed spring.

Schuster frowned at me. 'You're not like Vogt,' he said. 'You're taking too much nonsense. We need to do it quicker. I'll show you.'

I wondered if he'd a bet on it, or whether it was just his anxiety to cause pain.

It took less than fifteen minutes to establish that Fireille was a member of the Communist Party and force him to supply us with names and addresses. Of course, it helped that Schuster produced a tray of pliers, knives and a bloodstained hammer, and threatened to hit him in the jaw with it until his teeth fell out.

That, and the animal screams from next door, soon obtained the result, though it wasn't the result Schuster wanted.

'He was no fun,' he said to me as he locked the cell door again and we emerged back into the light of the corridor. 'He didn't put up a fight.' Schuster cracked his knuckles. It felt like a preparation, and my stomach swooped with fear for Berenice.

Time was running out. There was only one chance for Berenice, and I didn't know if I could do it or whether she'd be in any state to know what was happening. The only chance of her escape depended on my impeccable timing. The thought of it made me light-headed.

Concentrate, Fred. I wiped my hands down my trousers; they were damp and sticky with sweat. If it went wrong, we'd both end up dead.

'I need a smoke,' Schuster said, pocketing the key. He headed for the guardroom. I went back to my desk and took out Berenice's file. In it, I read that she had been a suspect for years. The file had a page about her son, Pierre, and a note to cross-reference it with his file. So they still didn't know Antoine was Pierre. I wondered if he was in one of the other cells. Shit, what a mess.

I followed Schuster's rolling walk back to the guardroom. On the way back, one of the cell doors opened and Vogt, followed by Bauer and another guard, crowded out of the door dragging a short, dark-haired man with them. Even though his face was a mess, and one arm seemed to be broken, I recognised Félix straight away.

He saw me staring, and in one contemptuous movement he hawked and spat. The blood and phlegm landed on my shoe. 'Rot in hell, you bastard.'

The men dragged him away. Vogt said, 'Do you know him?'

'Never seen him before,' I said. 'Who is he?'

'Félix Armand. Head of a Resistance group. He's not talking now, but he will. After they give him the water treatment.'

My face stiffened. Vogt's scrutiny of me was just a little too long, before he walked off towards his office. He knows.

My blood stopped in my veins. Should I run? And leave Berenice behind?

Félix thought it was me who'd betrayed them. He didn't know about Jérôme. So that meant Berenice probably didn't either.

Stay calm. Do nothing to arouse their suspicion. Behave normally.

Christ, how could I do that?

'Pass me the file,' Schuster said. 'Bauer says the woman in number seven is Pierre Severin's mother. The one in number five just let it slip.'

Oh Félix. I turned my head so he couldn't see my reaction. When I turned back, Schuster was pawing Berenice's file, and the sight of his predatory attention made me cringe. The waiting to go into that cell tightened the tendons in my neck until my shoulders were as hard as a rock. I picked at the stuffing in the threadbare arm of the chair, and in desperation I took a cigarette from Schuster's pack and inhaled the stink into my lungs. I held it, feeling the fizz of it hit my veins, then blew out. Better. I was calmer. Knew what I must do. I felt the weight of the gun dragging on my inside jacket pocket.

'We need to find out where her son's hiding, and get names out of her. Names of who supplies the false papers. This one's a fighter. Bauer says she scratched like hell. He found the death capsule in the fold of her ear. Still, if she wants to be dead, she'll be dead soon enough. But not before we've found out what we need. You can just leave it to me — you just translate what she says, all right? I can handle her.'

Crazy. He was congratulating himself on being able to intimidate her, a woman twice his age. He pulled himself up taller, unlocked the door.

Berenice looked smaller than I remembered, like an old woman. Dark shadows hung under her eyes and her hair was limp, bedraggled. She was wearing her familiar café outfit of grey blouse and black skirt, but the skirt was ripped and the blouse had a sleeve torn. Blue bruises made a map on her arms, which were tied behind her back with what looked to be her own shoelaces. Her flat black shoes gaped open.

Before Schuster could speak, I spoke rapidly in French: 'You don't know me. Do exactly what I say and I'll get us both out of here.'

'Like you got us in here, you mean?' Berenice said bitterly.

'What's she saying?' Schuster was displeased. He liked to do the talking.

'I said, "This is a German officer, you must do exactly what he says," and I won't translate her reply.'

Berenice turned her head away. I wasn't sure if she'd understood any of my German, but her mouth turned down in disgust.

Schuster paced. He was annoyed, but I could see he was unsure of my status. Was I representing Vogt, in which case I was his superior, or was I just his assistant? 'You'd best leave it to me,' he said. 'I'm used to this. You can sit over there and write down what she says, all right?'

I smiled reassuringly at him, went to the chair near the door and opened the file.

He unbuckled his belt and wrapped it round his hand.

My mouth went dry. I swallowed, then took out my pencil and pad, as if I was about to take notes.

'Where is your son, Pierre Severin?' Schuster asked.

I didn't need to translate. The question was clear enough.

'No idea,' Berenice said, eyes blazing. 'Last time I heard of him he was in Rouen.'

'Rouen? Is that what she says?'

'Yes,' I said.

'Liar.' He let out a few inches of belt and swung it. His arm was long and the buckle hissed before it sliced across her forehead.

Berenice's head snapped sideways before returning to upright. Her eyes spilled tears but she didn't cry out.

Dear God. I winced, but Schuster didn't see; he was rewinding it for another shot.

'Tell her Félix Armand has been executed,' Schuster said. 'Say he refused to give us names. Because of that, we'll kill another fifty French civilians. Fifty more if she doesn't speak.'

Was it an empty threat? Would they really kill civilians for this? I'd no way of knowing. I didn't want to tell her that. I tried to put all my intention into my hurried words, hoping if I spoke quickly enough Schuster wouldn't catch the words. 'Listen. Félix didn't give you up. Jérôme betrayed you. If you know where Antoine is, say nothing. Make something up, anything, and I'll try to get you out.'

Had she understood? Something in her eyes changed. I could see her thinking, weighing up whether to believe me. I hoped she was reading the minute signals I was trying to convey.

All this within the space of a few short seconds. This time the belt caught her a slice on the cheek. The noise she made was a gasp like a sigh. Blood dribbled from the split onto her blouse. She spoke with venom in French. 'I'll die rather than tell you anything, Édouard Vibert. I don't believe you. You betrayed us.'

'She says her son has gone over into the Vichy zone,' I said, frantically improvising. 'A small town called Ambert.'

'Stupid bitch,' Schuster said.

He withdrew his fist with the coiled belt wrapped round it and punched her hard in the mouth. 'That's for telling us lies.'

For the second time, my hand went to the cold weight of my gun. Not yet.

I released my hand from the grip. Unable to use her hands, Berenice doubled over and slumped forward until she slipped to the ground. I felt so sick I thought I might faint.

More senseless beating, kicks with his boots, until my neck was so knotted and tense my head throbbed. Berenice cried out something unintelligible. Then, 'He's in Ambert,' she said, '76 Rue Allemand.'

'We've got an address,' I said thickly. 'And the son'll give us everything else. File says we've to take her to the woods. And we can have a smoke on the way back.'

'Can't do it by firing squad,' he said. 'French law forbids us to execute women by the gun, unless they're Jews.'

'What, then?'

'We can shoot the bitch if she tries to escape. And she will, when she sees the trench.'

The law was supposed to prevent barbarity. I couldn't believe Schuster was talking of it as if it were some normal everyday duty. The hard coldness of my gun repulsed me, but I'd have only one chance, when it would be me or Schuster. Could I do it? I really didn't know.

Berenice could barely stand, and she was too woozy to struggle, but she let us drag her, stumbling, her hands still tied behind her back. Her feet tripped on the stairs, her eyes dazed and unfocussed. I concentrated on holding her up, my breath coming fast with the extra weight. We walked on through the gate to the Bois de Boulogne, past the bored-looking guards with machine guns. They watched us pass with indifference as if we were just ordinary passers-by. On, through the shade of the trees, past big old oaks with skeletal branches bearing a few brown leaves. The lack of birdsong made the shadows too silent, and our feet scuffed the dry ground.

Finally we came to a deep trench. The trees around it were scarred with bullet holes. I didn't look in. The stench of putrefying flesh told me everything I needed to know. Berenice suddenly seemed to realise what was happening and started to struggle.

Oh God, I couldn't let her run, Schuster would shoot her. I clung onto her arm, desperately pressed my fingers there so it would hurt. I hissed in French, 'Stay still. We only get one chance, d'you hear?'

'Run, bitch,' Schuster said, pulling his gun from its holster.

My fingers clutched her sleeve. I heard the fabric rip.

'What are you doing?' Schuster said.

He turned to look at me, and in that moment Berenice broke away. My hand slipped in and out of my pocket like butter, and in one smooth movement I fired.

The shot echoed in the sultry air, the reverberation bouncing off the trees and sounding over and over. Schuster clutched his chest, his face a mild expression of wounded surprise. He took a single step towards me, with his mouth open, about to speak. I found myself about to answer him, but then he toppled sideways away from me.

The moment seemed to stretch as his feet left the ground, so that the pattern of the sole of his boots imprinted itself in my memory.

There was a dull thud as he fell. I looked over the edge. Schuster was spread-eagled over a tangle of other bodies. The buttons of his uniform glinted around the red hole in his chest. One leg was splayed up towards me. His eyes were open, staring up at the empty sky.

The adrenalin came after, like a shot of morphine, making everything grainy, unreal.

I began to shake, as if my knees were made of cotton wool.

Point-blank range. The words repeated in my head. I shot him at point-blank range.

The fact he was dead stunned me.

I turned, confused, to see Berenice running towards the dark of the woods.

CHAPTER 28

She wouldn't stand a chance if anyone saw her. Not with her hands tied and the terrible state of her face. I stumbled after her. She was about fifteen yards ahead of me, dodging in and out of the trees. Suddenly she stopped, crouched down.

Her warning made me drop flat on the ground behind a pocket of woody scrub. Along one of the paths came a platoon of soldiers who were obviously out on manoeuvres. They passed close by, heading towards the Avenue Foch. I had to hope they wouldn't see Schuster's boot sticking out of that trench. My plan, before the reality, had been to change clothes with Schuster, even though he was a bigger man. A German uniform would have given us breathing space to get away, a way of pretending Berenice was my prisoner.

But Berenice had her own idea. She was running again now, awkwardly, her hands still tied. I chased after her, not daring to call out. She was faster than I thought she would be, despite everything. But I was fitter, stronger and unencumbered. I launched myself towards her and we fell in a crashing rugby tackle.

I had hold of her round the waist. 'Let go of me,' she hissed, kicking at my groin.

'At least let me untie your hands. You won't get anywhere like that.'

She squinted up at me through a swollen eye. 'You had a gun. Why didn't you shoot him earlier?'

'And risk the whole of Avenue Foch descending on us? I'm sorry I couldn't stop him... Oh what's the use? There's no time to explain. When Schuster doesn't go back, and I'm gone, the German Army will be after us.'

She sat up, her breath still coming fast. Her eyes bored into mine. 'Untie me then.'

We crawled over to a patch of undergrowth where we'd be out of sight. Freeing her was harder than it looked; her struggle had tightened the knots, and my hands felt like they belonged to someone else. 'Shit. I can't do it.'

'Have you got matches?'

I took out the matches with the Nazi symbol on the cover that Vogt had given me. Her mouth curled in disgust, but I ignored her and crawled behind her back. I struck one match after another and held them to the leather laces. In my haste, I burned her arm, and she winced but made no sound.

When she was free, she rubbed her swollen wrists before putting a hand on my arm. 'Was it really Jérôme?'

I nodded. 'Sorry. I saw him at Avenue Foch with the Gestapo.'

'The piece of shit.' She put a hand to her face, drew in a sharp breath.

'You need something for that. Does it hurt?'

'What the hell do you think?' She was tying her shoes together as best she could with the remnants of the laces.

I looked over my shoulder. 'We need to move.'

'Wait until dark,' she said. 'I don't look dressed for Paris in the afternoon.'

'No. They'll have dogs. We've got to get under cover somewhere. Not my apartment or the café.'

A shout from the direction of the trench.

German voices. 'Over here.' 'Fetch help.'

Cold shivers ran up my back. 'They've found him.'

'The Seine. The Quai Carnot,' Berenice said. 'We'll try to get a boat.'

'You go, Berenice. You know Paris. I'm going to make it much harder for you to disappear.'

'I feel like company. Come on.' She grabbed my arm and we began to hurry northwards, skirting the trees, keeping out of sight.

'Which way?'

We turned down a wooded path only to see two German soldiers on patrol coming towards us. We backtracked, and one of them called out, 'Hey! You!'

As we turned back we saw more soldiers behind them, dozens of them in formation. The Bois de Boulogne was the Wehrmacht's training ground.

Berenice yanked my arm and we plunged into the undergrowth. To our right we heard the noise of men's boots on the footpaths, but we kept on dodging our way though. Behind us, to the right, there was movement between the bare trees and the glint of helmets and rifles.

Panting hard, we emerged on the other side of the thicket onto a broad path beside the river. Downstream, we saw German guards close to a bridge, to the left no one.

'Walk quietly,' I said, 'as if we're just out for a stroll.' We walked upriver, looking for a place to cross. 'The bridges will all be guarded. Can you swim?'

'Only ladies breaststroke.' She stared at the fast-flowing brown murk of the Seine. 'I don't know if I can swim that. And if we do, you'll lose your papers.'

'Useless anyway, given the whole of the German Army will be looking for me.'

The lower bridge was in sight. We walked briskly towards it, but even from here I could see the grey-green helmets of troops.

An order from behind me: 'Halt!'

A soldier was on the path about a hundred yards behind us. More soldiers burst from the thicket.

I grabbed Berenice's arm and we skidded down the bank. I kicked off my shoes, shrugged off my jacket. 'Your shoes!' I gasped.

She pulled them off and, half falling, we staggered into the freezing water. The shock made me gasp. The current was strong and dragged us downriver towards the soldiers. I splashed out in a front crawl, keeping Berenice ahead and to the left of me, but she was already tiring.

Braat-a-tat! A rain of machine-gun fire skimmed the water just behind me.

I didn't dare look back, just kept on swimming, the dark peat smell of the river in my lungs, the cold making my breath ragged. I floundered, trying to reach Berenice, who was drifting upriver away from me, going nowhere. 'Turn on your back,' I gasped. 'I'll help you.'

She rolled over and her head momentarily disappeared.

I scrabbled and splashed for her with one arm and towed her, not caring if her head was in or out of the water. She coughed and struggled. More machine-gun fire bouncing fountains off the water. Something hit me in the shoulder, sinking me, until I resurfaced to the fact that one arm was weak and wouldn't pull.

Berenice, seeing the bank ahead, found extra strength from somewhere and hauled herself towards a pontoon with small boats bobbing alongside. Spluttering, we dragged ourselves up, water cascading from our clothes. Behind us, bullets still rained into the water.

I glanced to the right: soldiers running towards us.

To the left: more men running.

We shot across the road towards a side street. On the corner opposite me was a café. A man with a white moustache was sitting at a table outside, smoking. '*Les bicyclettes! La bas!*' he said in an urgent whisper.

'Thank you,' I yelled.

'*Vive La France!*'

We followed his eyes. Just around the corner, several bicycles were propped against the wall. As soon as I stopped running, the air swam around me like I was still underwater. Berenice was already wheeling a cycle out as I grabbed the handlebars with a slippery hand. As I looked down to put my bare feet on the pedals, I saw a trickle of blood in the water still sluicing from my clothes.

We set off pedalling like crazy, in and out of alleyways. I clung on with one hand; the right one didn't seem to work so well. After fifteen minutes of frantic legwork, Berenice leapt off and threw her cycle into a side street.

She led me down into an alleyway, and as we came out, I saw we were opposite a churchyard. We wove our way uphill past ancient trees and decrepit mausoleums and bone-houses. My feet kept stubbing on the steps; my toes were numb with cold. By now I was panting hard, my arm hanging like a dead weight. Berenice climbed steadily upwards, her skirt stuck to her legs as she pulled herself up by the stone walls.

God, she was tough. Finally, she paused at the top of a flight of stairs. She ducked down between two crumbling tombs.

'Where the hell are we?' I asked.

'Mont-Valérien cemetery. Site of an old Catholic monastery. We can see people coming from up here, but we can't go any further. Too dangerous. There's the old Fort up there, and it's been taken over by the Boche.'

I looked down towards Paris. I could even see the Eiffel Tower in the haze of the city. It didn't look like a city at war. It looked peaceful in the late afternoon light, the Seine curving around it as if to protect it.

'You've been shot in the shoulder,' Berenice said. Her voice was slurred because her lip was swollen.

'I know. My right arm won't work properly. Is it bad?'

She came around to look and I felt her touch my shoulder. There was a sting of pain. I winced.

'The bullet's still in there,' she said. 'Good thing too, you would have bled more otherwise.'

'Have you a plan?'

'No. You?'

'Staying alive seems like a good idea.'

I peered down the hill. 'Can you see anyone?'

'I think we lost them. We should rest here,' she said. 'Once it's dark, we can move, try to find help.'

'Who will help us? Whoever tries will write their own death sentence.'

'There will be someone,' she said stubbornly. 'France looks after her own.'

I looked at her face, a mess of dried blood and bruising. 'I said before ... go alone. I'm the one they're looking for. Even before Jérôme, Vogt knew; he knew I was working for the French. It was only a matter of time.'

'I would be a corpse in that trench if it wasn't for you.'

'No. I saved myself. It was the end of the line, and I knew it was my only chance to run.'

'We go together.' She turned away from me, stared down the hill.

'I don't know. Who will want to take me in? They said they'd shoot more civilians for every German lost. That's the tactic; use terror to control the people, make them feel responsible.'

She didn't reply. And in my mind's eye I saw Schuster, cigarette burning in the ashtray before him, grinning at me over a hand of cards. I hadn't meant to kill him, yet my hand had leapt to the gun almost like a reflex. How had I known that was the moment? The speed of his death had rocked me to the core. And the fact that flesh was so soft and weak. I hadn't known men could kill each other so easily.

I took the pistol from my pocket and laid it on the tomb next to me. Then we waited until night fell and the curfew bell was long past. As we waited, I dozed, and Schuster's face turned into the face of my brother, Horst. I hoped to God some bastard Frenchman hadn't put a gun to his head.

CHAPTER 29

Berenice had a map of Paris ingrained in her head, and without it we would never have been able to negotiate the alleyways of Paris and find our way back to the city. Even with her injuries, she strode doggedly on. I had ceased to think. I had just followed her blindly where she led me, watching our backs and keeping out of the way of the night patrols. We were both bone-tired by the time we arrived at a black front door in a small street of tall tenement houses. Berenice tapped softly on the door.

It opened a crack and a familiar wrinkled face peered out. Sebastien.

His smile died on seeing Berenice's face. Wordlessly, he pulled her in, and once I was inside he shut the door and bolted it.

'Thank God. We heard you'd been taken,' he said. 'The café's swarming with Germans. They've taken all your belongings. The Bechsteins have been put on a train — east.'

'Sebastien?' A woman with her grey hair scraped back under a hairnet appeared. She was in a rose-flowered nightdress and dressing gown.

'This is my wife, Marthe,' Sebastien said. 'You know Berenice, and this is Édouard, who beats me at chess.'

'They can't stay here.' Marthe folded her arms across her chest. 'Look at them. And he's got a bullet in his back. You can't tell me they'll be no trouble.'

'It'll just be one night, won't it, Édouard?' Sebastien said.

'We'd be really grateful,' I said, aiming for reasonableness. 'We've had quite a day.' How ludicrous it sounded to be making polite conversation. Yet, instinct told me that begging would only make us seem more desperate.

Marthe ignored me. 'I don't like it, Sebastien. You told me the Gestapo closed down her café. Do you want the Gestapo here?'

'Look at them,' Sebastien said sharply. He indicated where Berenice had slumped into a chair. 'Do you think they'd come to us if they had anywhere else to go? Then they get a welcome like yours. Shame on you. They're staying, and if you don't like it you can find another husband.'

Marthe turned without a word. Her feet could be heard clomping up the stairs.

'She's just crotchety,' Sebastien said. 'You woke her from her beauty sleep. She'll be all right in the morning.'

In fact, we stayed six weeks, until January 1943. Sebastien rallied more friends from the Resistance and got a doctor to take out the bullet and stitch us up. We couldn't go out and we knew how much it cost them to feed us and supply us with new clothes and shoes. But Marthe was a proficient seamstress, and she was able to alter a skirt and jersey to fit Berenice and let down one of Sebastien's old coats to fit me. We were both thinner, both haggard with the lack of proper food and the worry. The clothes Marthe supplied were dowdy and unremarkable.

'Better this way,' she said. 'Safer not to be pretty or fashionable.'

Berenice sighed, and said, 'So now I am no longer a Parisienne.'

How had I never realised that Sebastien and Henri were part of the network? I suppose, because they were old, I'd overlooked them. But old men were less likely to be conscripted to work camps, and Sebastien had contacts who supplied us with new papers to travel out of the occupied zone into Vichy France. Sebastien told Berenice that Pierre, who I knew as Antoine, was in Marseille already and had a safe house where we could go.

'It would be better to get out of France,' I said. 'We could try for Geneva, neutral territory. There's a chance they'll give us refugee status.'

Berenice looked at me as if I'd lost my mind. 'I'm going to Marseille. If you want to go to Switzerland, then that's your choice. But I'm not going to run away and sit on some border doing nothing. Not when my son's still in France.'

'But why jump from a frying pan into a fire? Pétain's in the pocket of the Nazis. It will be just the same there as here in Paris. Wouldn't you rather wake up with food on the table and the feeling nobody will shoot you in the back?'

'I'd rather be in France. The Swiss are two steps away from Nazism anyway.'

'Now you're being ridiculous.'

'I've said I'm not going to Switzerland. If you don't want to come to Marseille, I can go alone.'

Sebastien, who had been listening to this conversation, stood up from his chair, his arms outstretched. 'Now, now. Stop this foolish argument. The country's divided enough without you two adding to it. Sleep on it, both of you.'

I couldn't sleep that night. If I went to Switzerland, I might be able to get word to Céline, and I'd be out of this damned mess altogether. The thought of it beckoned me, like a sort of paradise. Yet Berenice had trusted me; she'd been my only friend since I arrived in France. It was her Resistance contacts that had sewed up my shoulder and risked discovery and death for me. Surely I owed them something? And I hated the idea of Berenice travelling alone with nobody to watch her back. Just the thought of abandoning her filled me with guilt.

Finally, I came up with a compromise. I'd go with her to Marseille, just until she made contact with Antoine, then I'd leave as soon as I could and try to make it across country to Switzerland. She didn't thank me when I told her. Even this she saw as a desertion of duty.

'You have no snow skills,' she said. 'Going that way will kill you.'

'I have to be somewhere where I can breathe,' I said stubbornly. Perhaps in time, when this whole miserable war was over, Céline could join me in Switzerland. As a deserter and a traitor, I could never go back to Germany, and it festered like a raw wound that I might never be able to look at my parents' faces again.

I missed them with a visceral ache. I had thought I was German, that Germany represented a certain sort of righteous, upstanding goodness; an identity I took pride in. Now I realised that a patriotic identity was a kind of trap that shut you off from other people.

The Gestapo, my own countrymen, were searching for us; that much we heard. We had to move twice whilst they conducted house-to-house searches. They had issued photographs, and because of this we had both grown our hair longer and I had grown a moustache. Berenice's face was almost back to normal, and Marthe had supplied her with powder and lipstick and a low-brimmed hat to help disguise the scars and the bruising.

Berenice was anxious to go to Antoine, but we knew we could only cross the Demarcation line if we had an identity card, an Ausweis. These could only be obtained from the German occupation authorities after stringent identity checks, so we knew we'd have to cross the border off the road. We'd travel to Dijon by train, and after that we'd be escorted by various Resistance contacts until we reached Marseille, the only functioning port in the unoccupied zone and crowded with refugees like us. Hard to believe, but the port was still trading and was the only gateway out of France.

The day we left the sky was heavy with unshed rain. Marthe hugged us both a little too tightly, something that made me think it was a final goodbye. Sebastien shook my hand up and down, and said, 'I'll miss our chess.' It was the closest he could come to an admission of affection.

We walked along the street to the station as if treading on eggshells. Every noise made me wince. Berenice was supposed to be my mother, in her frumpy skirt and battered hat. I was the son, on my way back to a farm where we were working the land for the German Army. We'd memorised our new identities, reciting them over and over. Marie and Paul Corbet: mother and son. My third identity in as many years. It surprised me that this bag of bones could be known as so many things.

To be out on the street for as little time as possible, we'd left it until the last minute, given there could be a queue for the train. At the Gare de Lyon, SS men were checking everyone's papers. I glanced at Berenice, who was white under her powder. Her fingers pulled obsessively at the rough brown scarf around her neck. The last time she'd seen men like this, they'd almost killed her. I prayed she would hold up.

We queued with the rest. All of us thin, hungry and scared. I clung to the suitcase that contained only an old blanket. Fear hung in the air like a miasma. At the turnstile, I pushed

Berenice ahead. If there was trouble, I wanted her to have a chance to run.

I saw her brace herself and pull back her shoulders as she opened the flap of the identity card. The SS man, a portly man with skin scarred by acne, only glanced before he waved her through. She turned to catch my eye in triumph.

Don't, I thought. *Just keep walking.*

The acne-cheeked man held out his hand, and I dropped my papers into his fleshy palm. He looked up at my face to check the picture, and I tried to remain impassive, though I could feel cold sweat breaking out round my collar.

'Farm labourer?' he asked me.

I smiled, pretending not to understand.

'Farm? You work on farm?'

'*Oui.*'

He nodded, folded my identity paper back together and passed it back. As he did so, he grabbed my hand. I saw him glance at it and immediately realised my mistake. My hand was not the calloused hand of a farm labourer.

'I've been ill,' I said in French, floundering, 'many months.' I coughed, releasing a cloud of white steam. 'Bad lungs. *Krank.*'

He stepped away, as if I might be infectious, before waving me through. My blood racing in my veins, I walked as briskly as I could towards Berenice, who had paused near one of the iron columns. I sneaked a look back to the turnstile. Acne-face was pointing me out to two other men on his side of the gate. The men were in civilian clothes, suits and heavy overcoats, but they had the upright bearing of policemen. Gestapo.

'Walk quickly,' I said. 'They've seen something suspicious about us.'

We hurried down the platform and the guard waved his flag and blew the whistle. The men were following us rapidly towards the train.

'Get on,' I said.

She leapt in through the doors. And I followed, just in time to slam the door as the train shunted off. I stuck my head out of the window. I could only see one Gestapo man. Where was the other?

'Stay here a moment. One of them might be on the train,' I said.

We waited, but nobody appeared.

'I think we're all right; let's find a carriage,' I said. The train was less busy than I expected. Paris had emptied over the past year, and the carriages were sparsely populated. I chose one where there was a down-at-heel old woman cradling a shopping basket on her knee. Next to her feet, two cloth bags bulged with what looked like old clothes and shoes.

The train was speeding now with bursts of steam and a clickety-clack. I gave Berenice a reassuring look and saw her shoulders drop. Had we lost them? Once out of the station, rain streaked the windows and the train wound through bare countryside, past empty fields and skeletal trees. The compartment was icy cold; we hugged our hands under our arms.

At Sens station, a station with no shelter, the train shuddered to a halt and a few more damp and bedraggled passengers got on. A man in an overcoat climbed into our compartment and sat down. He had nothing with him, no newspaper, no briefcase, no luggage of any description. The woman with the basket ignored him and continued to gaze out of the window.

I caught Berenice's eye.

She raised an eyebrow but I daren't tell her what was on my mind. The man couldn't have got on at Sens because his overcoat was still dry. He must have got on at Paris and only now moved into our compartment. But why?

I continued to stare out of the window, aware that something was very wrong, and probably that something was us. Was this one of the Gestapo men from the Gare de Lyon, or was I mistaken? Perhaps he was just an ordinary French businessman visiting the city.

As the train cut through the landscape, my eyes kept flicking to him. He barely moved. He didn't light a cigarette or try to sleep. He kept his eyes open, occasionally checking his wristwatch or glancing out of the open compartment door.

How far to Auxerre? We'd have to run for it. If they had suspicions about us, there'd probably be Gestapo at the other end. He was nearest the door. If he was armed, we'd be in trouble.

Just before Auxerre, I turned to him and spoke in French. 'What a terrible day. Should have brought my umbrella. Is it this bad in Dijon?'

The man didn't answer, but Berenice replied, 'Let's hope not.'

The train was slowing. The woman with the basket stood up. 'Your stop?' I asked.

'Yes,' she said, grasping one of the cloth bundles.

'Maman will help you,' I said.

Berenice shot me a look but stood up and helped the old woman towards the door. In one swift movement I grabbed the other bag and leapt out of the compartment, slamming the door shut. Seizing Berenice by the arm I turned and ran down the train, throwing the bag into the narrow corridor behind me.

Shutting the door gave us precious seconds.

A shot. The man in the overcoat was forcing his way past the old woman's bags.

Opposite the next compartment, I hauled open the door window, leaned out and twisted the handle.

The door swung open. Though we'd slowed, to me the ground was still flying past at a terrifying speed.

'I can't,' Berenice said as I pushed her to the edge.

'You must.'

The man had scrambled over the bags and was trying to keep his footing as the train lurched around a corner. A connecting door to the compartment opened and a uniformed ticket inspector appeared. 'What's going on? What was that noise?'

Our pursuer paused, gun held before him.

The guard didn't seem to see the gun. 'Shut that door!' he shouted at us. 'It's forbidden to open the doors until we reach a station.'

Then he turned to look again. '*Quest-ce que —*'

'Get out of my way,' the man said, the gun pointing at his chest.

The guard slipped back behind the compartment door.

Berenice needed no more encouragement — she leapt. It took me so much by surprise that it was a good two seconds before I followed her. My bad shoulder hit the ground with a crack, but I rolled free just in time to see our man hovering by the flapping door. He hung half out of the door, pointed his gun and fired, but the shot went wide.

Just at that moment, the train lurched around a corner and the man lost his footing. He tried to cling to the door, but that last desperate grab made him fall awkwardly onto the track.

His screams were drowned by the noise of the train. I closed my eyes as he disappeared underneath it.

I sat up, panting.

Berenice limped towards me. 'Did he jump?' she asked, looking wildly around.

'He fell under the train.'

'My God. Is he alive?'

'I don't know. I'll have to go and look. Wait there.'

'Twisted my damn knee,' she said.

I walked warily towards the tracks. There was no movement from the man on the rails. I could see blood and bone.

A few moments later, I was back with Berenice. 'He's dead,' I said. 'But I got this.' I passed her the Gestapo tag I'd taken from around his neck.

She examined the brass eagle and swastika on one side and the lettering with '*Geheime Staatspolizei*' on the reverse. 'No papers?'

'No. I searched him thoroughly.' I swallowed. It had been a horrible job. 'I guess he just wasn't expecting to travel.'

She passed the Gestapo tag back. 'I never figured you'd be one for souvenirs.'

I let her comment pass. 'Let's go. You can lean on me.' I put my arm under her shoulder.

'Did you find his gun?'

'No, it could be anywhere. Didn't want to waste time looking.'

'I used to like hiking,' she said, 'when I was younger. How far to our contact near the Demarcation line?'

'Don't know. Thirty kilometres?'

'*Merde*. It's going to be a long night.'

Crossing France with no map, in the pitch-black, and keeping a wary eye for Allied bombers or German troops wasn't easy, especially as Berenice was obviously in pain. She limped on beside me, never complaining. Several times we stopped, unable to fathom where we were, but by dawn we were soaked to the skin and shivering. I needed her just as much as she needed me. Without her, my faith in getting out of France alive would have probably deserted me.

Our contact was an aristocratic Englishman called Reginald Huntingdon, complete with a prim moustache and a burgundy silk smoking jacket, like an escapee from an Oscar Wilde play. Berenice's expression at the sight of him made me want to laugh. The house, with a fairy-tale tower and big arched door was a stately pile that you might call a small chateau.

Reginald seemed unsurprised at our bedraggled appearance and showed us to an enormous bathroom with gurgling pipework and an antiquated-looking bathtub. 'Now, old chaps, get yourself hot baths, and then I'll feed you. You must be off the premises by nine thirty at the latest though, as M'sieur Petit, the head of the Dijon Feldgendarmerie, and his SS pals are coming for a breakfast meeting.'

I swallowed my resentment that if you had enough money you seemed to belong to some sort of club that transcended the war. We bathed and stripped to our underwear, and then, draped in huge towels, we set our clothes to dry in front of his enormous kitchen range. We were waited on by an old-fashioned English butler, Harris, who was delighted that I could speak English.

Over eggs and bread, I asked him if he knew anything about the occupation of Jersey.

'Sorry, sir, I'm afraid not. Only the same as here; Jews have been removed and anyone English deported to Germany.'

'What about everyone else?'

'Like here, I suppose. Mr Huntingdon does what he can. He'll help Allied airmen, give them a safe place and so on. But we have to pay lip service to the Boche or they'll requisition the house. Fortunately, Mr Huntingdon speaks good German, and he has a full wine cellar, so it smooths the way. They use him in their meetings to translate for M'sieur Petit.'

Another whose knowledge of the language had placed him on a knife-edge. We were interrupted by the sound of cars arriving outside.

The butler went to peer from the window. 'They're early.'

'Is there a back way out?'

'Not without risk. They always station a man outside the back to deter people from coming in. But you'll be quite safe in the bedrooms upstairs. Follow me, please.'

We swiped our clothes from the clothes horse before the range and followed his upright figure up the narrow servant stairs. Quite unhurried, he led us across a carpeted landing and into a large bedroom. 'I'd lock the door if I were you, sir.' He put a hand to his lips and whispered, 'Quiet as mice.'

Berenice was dressing, but I padded over to the window and, keeping well behind the curtain, peered out.

There were three cars. The one with a miniature Nazi flag fluttering from the front had obviously housed the black-clad SS officers. The second was a French Citroën covered in dust and scrapes. From the third, a large man in a Wehrmacht uniform was just climbing out, his shiny boots and flapping cavalry trousers emerging first. Something about the way he stood and stretched his back arrested me. I watched as he crossed the yard and gave the obligatory 'Heil Hitler'. He rubbed his nose with a knuckle and it reminded me of Schulz. I stared a bit longer.

'Come away,' hissed Berenice. 'They'll see you.'

'A moment more.' By now I was certain it was Schulz, though heavier and with a bristling air of authority. Well, who would have thought it? He'd risen in the ranks, stripes on his shoulder and a peaked cap. These men were easy with each other, jovial. They greeted Reginald with claps on the back and smiles.

Schulz would know me if he saw me. I gnawed on a fingernail, wondering whether to tell Berenice. I saw her suddenly in a way I hadn't before, the toll that all this was taking on her. The creases around her eyes, her hollow cheeks. She looked sixty, not forty-five.

'D'you think it's all right?' she asked. She meant, could we trust Reginald?

'I hope so. We just have to keep quiet and sit it out.' I heard the men come in below and begin a conversation over the clatter of cups and cutlery. The smell of frying mushrooms wafted up through the cracks in the floorboards.

I pointed at the floor and lay down to hear what they said. Berenice followed suit, but the floorboard creaked under her. We froze, held our breath.

The conversation continued beneath us, perfectly audible. They hadn't heard us.

'We need two thousand gendarmes from you for this operation,' one of the men said.

Reginald translated this into French, and immediately the higher voice of M'sieur Petit replied in French. 'Impossible. Pétain has already deployed seven-hundred of my men to police the border into Switzerland. Crime's running out of control here in Dijon. We can't cope. Ask him where I'm expected to find these men.'

'He says he hasn't that many men,' Reginald said in heavily accented German.

'He can recruit more.' The man speaking had his mouth full. A pause. 'Tell him it's a short-term operation, just a few days at most. We are redesigning the whole harbour area and evacuating the population. To do that, we must seal the entire port from behind, drive the undesirables towards the sea and cut off all their escape routes.'

'He says perhaps you might recruit more officers,' Reginald said coaxingly. 'He'll only need them for a few days, he says.'

Petit's voice. 'Will they need to be armed? I can't arm raw recruits! Anyway, what sort of duties is he talking about?'

A pause a moment, then Reginald spoke again in German. 'He wants to know what tasks they'll be assigned.'

'Schulz, can you pass the butter? What was I saying? Oh yes, the police chief René Bousquet, his superior, has guaranteed us a strong police presence to escort undesirables to the trains and load them up. There'll be many thousand if our intelligence is correct. Tell him we intend to purge the harbour area of Jews and resisters once and for all.'

'I see. And who will M'sieur Petit answer to?' Reginald asked.

'Schulz here will be in charge of operations on the ground. Tell M'sieur Petit his men will be detailed to check identity papers in the second arrondissement. His will be one of fifteen constabularies brought in for the purpose. And of course, afterwards, his men will supervise transport to the trains. Tell him the operation must remain secret if we are to smoke them all out.'

Berenice was raising her eyebrows at me questioningly, wanting to know what was going on. I shook my head, anxious to hear every word.

M'sieur Petit's voice had risen in pitch again. 'Did I hear him say trains? We're not having anything to do with that. The transport network is a shambles! Timetables ignored, bombs on the line. It's quite impossible.'

'Be calm, M'sieur. He is only asking you to supervise evacuation transport. From what I can gather, it's all been agreed from above by René Bousquet. They anticipate many thousands will need to be transported out of Marseille, and it has to be done in an orderly way.'

'I know what they're doing,' Petit said. 'I can't get my men to be party to this. They won't want to be responsible for deporting French citizens to their stinking camps. My officers don't like doing it, and I can't get volunteers. Not now the word's out where they go.'

'Be careful,' Reginald said. 'They understand more than you think. And if I know Hauptmann Graf, I'm afraid he will not take no for an answer. Best agree, my friend, and then we'll make some alternate plan.'

'Let me in on your discussion, won't you, Reginald?' the gruff voice insisted.

'Your reputation has preceded you, gentlemen. He's worried because his men know that nobody who goes on the trains ever comes back. He worries you'll be taking good Frenchmen without cause.'

'Tell him there is always room on the transport for police chiefs who stand in the way of peace and order.'

There was silence. Even the chink of cutlery on plates stopped.

'What did he say?' Petit asked.

'You'd best do as he says,' Reginald said. In a low voice, 'As your friend, I'm advising you here and now to keep your mouth shut and agree to his plans.'

A scrape of a chair. 'Sorry, Reginald.' A moment later, the door banged. Outside, there was the grind of a Citroen engine, then the crunch of gravel as it drove away.

'God in heaven,' Hauptmann Graf said. 'He's an odious little man. Will he come round?'

'I'll have a word with him,' Reginald said, 'explain what it means if he won't comply. Don't worry, I'll talk him into it.'

'If not, I meant what I said. This operation is vital.'

For the first time I heard Schulz's voice. 'He'll be grateful to us when it's done. Once the place is evacuated and the criminal element removed, then we will demolish the whole area and rebuild so the infestation can never return. I've seen the architect's plans; they're glorious. Cafés and open parks, wide boulevards and plane trees for shade. It will regenerate the port, bring more tourists to Marseille.'

From the noises below, it was clear that the men continued to eat and make small talk about cafés and wine and the opera. We stayed stiff and still until we heard the cars drive away.

'What was all that about?' Berenice asked.

I was throwing on my clothes. 'We need to get to Marseille as soon as we can.' I didn't mention Schulz.

'Why? What's going on?'

'The Nazis are planning some sort of round-up. We need to warn Antoine; get him out of there.'

In the kitchen we found Reginald, now immaculately attired in a suit and tie and reeking of cologne, still drinking his last cup of coffee. I spoke to him in French, so Berenice would understand. 'We heard,' I said. 'We have friends in Marseille.'

'Oh dear. I did wonder if that's where you were heading.'

'Do you know what the schedule is?' Berenice asked.

'January twenty-third, Graf told me. Four days away.'

'That soon?'

'Things move quickly when Germans want them done.'

'Can you help us?' Berenice asked. 'Drive us to Marseille?'

'I'm afraid not, dear lady. I deal in information only. I provide a safe house and a judiciously loose tongue as far as German plans are concerned. To do more would risk all the other networks I have a finger in. If this safe house was lost, if I ceased to be a friend to the Germans, many more lives would be at risk. You do see, don't you?'

'But my son is in Marseille. Won't you reconsider?'

Reginald bit his lip, removed the napkin from his lap and folded it. 'Sorry, can't be done. But the safe house will still be here if it works out for you. Harris can drive you to a place where there's a footpath to Marseille, and I'll supply you with a map. It's a day's walk, that's all.'

CHAPTER 30

By the time we arrived at Marseille, it was more than forty-eight hours later. Heavy rain made the footpaths muddy, and Berenice's knee had been so sore that we'd had to find shelter. I guessed she'd torn a ligament, but there was no time to rest. We'd slept fitfully in a country bus shelter just outside the city. Entering Marseille was a case of dodging patrols and the checkpoints that might ask us for our papers. Now that the Germans had ceased to pretend France had a free zone, it was impossible to move anywhere without being subject to Nazi inspection, and we knew that any encounter was too risky for us to contemplate.

The roads to the city were already cordoned off, and soldiers and police were erecting more barriers. We saw families leaving with handcarts piled high with their belongings. So much displacement everywhere we went. We took the winding route through narrow alleys and it was midday when we crept into the city, a humid muggy day with damp from the sea hanging above the streets like a veil. The closer we got to the salty smell of the sea, the more the streets were filled with activity: ragged refugees lugging bundles, heading for the port. We kept our heads down and tried to look purposeful.

The empty shop windows were plastered with printed notices saying 'Preparation for Evacuation of the Port of Marseille'. We paused to read one. All French people from the second arrondissement were to be rehomed for the redevelopment of the harbour area. Citizens should prepare to be evacuated.

All we had was an address, so we had to ask for directions, picking who to ask with care. We avoided the prostitutes loitering in broad daylight on the corners of the tabacs, waiting for German trade. I approached a man leaning out of a window. He shut it fast, but not before I'd seen his black beard and Jewish ringlets.

'Which way to the Rue Coutellerie?' Berenice asked a stooped old woman with a barrow full of what looked like old iron and scrap metal.

'This way; I show you.' We followed her as she clanked down the cobbled street.

We waved her adieu, stopped outside a four-storey house and, checking we hadn't been followed, stepped into the entrance lobby. There was a smell of cheap perfume and damp coats.

'Which floor?' I asked.

Berenice shrugged, and limped to the nearest door. When we knocked nobody answered, though we could hear whispered voices behind. It was the same with all the doors.

'Guess they're scared,' I said. 'Would you open your door to strangers?'

On the first floor we struck lucky. The door opened a crack, and a woman's eyes, rather too black with mascara, peered out. 'We're looking for Pierre Severin,' Berenice said. 'Tall, thin, brown hair, about your age.'

'Don't know.' Her accent sounded Polish. She pushed the strap of her flesh-coloured slip back on her shoulder, a cigarette dangling from her red-lipsticked mouth. She took a long drag before deigning to speak. 'Could be upstairs. Many young men there. Number nineteen.'

We continued to climb the stairs. The iron numbers on the door hung askew.

Berenice knocked.

'Who is it?' said a terse male voice from inside.

'I'm looking for Pierre Severin. Or Antoine. He sometimes calls himself Antoine.'

Muffled voices. 'What do you want?'

'I'm his mother.'

More angry voices from behind the door, until it suddenly swung open and an arm shot out to drag Berenice inside. When I followed her in, a knife appeared over my shoulder and was pressed to my throat. Two men held Berenice. My first impression was that the room was full of young men, though in reality it was only three. All bearded, all smelling of sweat. All on high alert. Dirty mattresses littered the floor and a machine gun faced the window. Other weapons leant against the corners, boxes of ammo, and what looked like coils of wire.

'What the hell?' Antoine shook Berenice, eyes blazing. 'I got a letter from the gendarmerie. It said you'd been shot whilst running away.'

Berenice wrestled herself free. 'That's what they intended to do, darling, but it didn't work out that way. We've been on the run since then. Sebastien helped us. We couldn't tell a soul; there's notices out for us all over Paris.'

'It's all right, Guillaume, I know them.'

The knife loosened and the two men slunk away, eyes curious, as they returned to lounging on the mattresses.

Antoine ran his hand through his long dark hair. 'For God's sake! You could've let me know. I thought you were dead.'

'We daren't,' Berenice said. 'It would have put Sebastien and Marthe at risk. We had to lie low. And until Sebastien told me, I'd no idea where you were.'

'You weren't supposed to know. No one was supposed to know.'

'What the hell's he doing here?'

'He helped me. It was Jérôme, not Édouard, who betrayed us.'

'You say they're looking for you. Who? The Sûreté?'

'Gestapo, but —'

'You risked bringing them here?' One of the men stood, the shorter thick-set one with the knife.

'Cool down,' Antoine said, restraining him with a hand on his arm. 'This is Lucien —' he pointed to his other friend — 'and you can call him Guillaume.'

'We came to warn you,' I said. 'There's going to be a Nazi round-up. Berenice thought —'

'Did anyone follow you?' Lucien asked.

'No. We were pretty careful. Look, you need to listen to what we're telling you. They're drafting thousands of police in here to clear the whole area. Every building will be searched. Every Jew will be sent to Drancy and then to Auschwitz. Every anti-fascist, every communist, homosexual, resister, prostitute, anyone they don't like the look of will be on those cattle trucks with them.' I explained what we'd heard and how.

Guillaume lit a cigarette. He was a short, wiry youth with a Roman nose and a restless air. His fingers and upper lip were stained yellow with nicotine. 'Yeah. We know. Notices went up yesterday saying the houses were going to be evacuated. We're meeting tonight with the rest of the cell to make a plan.'

'They said the day after tomorrow,' I said. 'But I'm worried. They're beginning to seal the city already. Uniformed police are already massing near the main boulevard. No one will be able to leave by the northern routes except under escort. They're calling it an evacuation, but we all know what it really is.

Systematic persecution. Everyone will have to show their papers.'

'No chance. They'll know me from my papers. There's a warrant out for Antoine Fournier. And I'm not the only one. We're all wanted men.'

'We can't warn everyone,' Lucien said. 'Think what will happen if we do. Mass panic. We need to wait for the rest of the cell before we make a plan.'

'No. There's no time,' I said. 'You need to get out now. The net's closing already.'

'It's perfect,' Guillaume said, pacing back and forth. 'Now's our chance to fight. They think we don't know they're coming, and now's our chance to show the bastard Boche we're a proper fighting force. We'll get word to everyone we know. But it could be bloody, Antoine. Your mother should go.'

'Are you crazy? It's not just a few men! It's every Nazi and every police force for miles around.' Berenice took hold of Antoine's arm. 'Please. It's time to save yourself whilst there's still time.'

'Save myself? What about the rest? The ones who are left? The Jews hiding in the next-door apartment? The refugees from fascist Italy? Don't they deserve some sort of protection?'

'You can't save them all,' I said. 'There are too many police, and the Nazi soldiers are drilled like a bloody machine. It would be suicide.'

Antoine stepped back, positioned himself next to Guillaume. 'I'm not leaving. We knew this was coming; the moment where we'd have to fight for France or die.'

Berenice snorted. 'Don't be ridiculous —'

'Don't you understand?' Antoine's cheeks were flushed with anger. 'This is Marseille! The hub of the Revolution, where

French peasants stood up against oppression. *Liberté, égalité, fraternité.* Shall we abandon it now?'

'Berenice…' I tried to intervene by pressing my hand to her shoulder. 'We need to go. If they find us, there'll be no mercy.'

'You go,' she said, shaking me off. 'Go to your fine Swiss mountain. I'll stay here with my son.'

Antoine turned on her. 'Don't be a fool, Mother. I never asked you to come. I don't want you here with your bourgeois ideas of what is good for me.'

'Being alive! That's what's good for you!' she blazed.

'I disagree,' Guillaume said. 'Principles are more important than life.' He rested his long thin arm around Antoine's shoulder.

'I'm not going,' Berenice said. 'You'll have to tear me from your side.'

Antoine made a face of disgust. 'I'm not five years old anymore. I don't need this.'

Lucien sighed. 'Listen. The best thing we can do is find out where the checkpoints are, which streets are closing, get some idea of the geography, of how the Nazis are working. Then, when we meet the others tonight we'll be better informed. I suggest we take a few streets each, see what we can find out. Note any escape routes that are still open. Talk to our contacts if we can. Get them to meet here tonight.'

Guillaume reached into a holdall and drew out a well-thumbed map of the town and unfolded it. I hunkered down over it whilst we divvied up the area around the harbour. I didn't like it. Every instinct told me to get out of there as fast as I could. But I knew Berenice by now; she was single-minded and stubborn.

Twenty minutes later, we split up on the streets of Marseille.

Marseille was heaving. From the different accents I could hear as I headed to the seafront, refugees had converged here from all over the world: Belgians, Czechs, Poles and Spaniards. By the port on the wide tree-lined pavement, I stood for a moment staring at a row of empty green buses, and, opposite, a row of canvas-topped trucks. On the cobbles under the trees, black-cloaked gendarmes were setting up trestle tables and chairs.

'Not there, further over,' a voice behind me ordered in German. Automatically I turned. And I was face to face with Schulz.

His eyes lit up in astonishment. 'God in Heaven! Is it...? Fred? Fred Huber! What are you doing here?'

'Same as you, I expect,' I said. 'Getting everyone out of here.'

He looked me up and down. I knew I looked a wreck. Close up, he was bigger and more solid than I remembered. 'I didn't know you were in Marseille,' he said. 'Still in the same line of work?'

'Translations, yes. And undercover work, as you can see.' I gestured down at my filthy trousers. 'I've just been drafted in. You know, we probably shouldn't speak. It might blow my cover.' I knew I was blabbering as I grasped for some sort of normality.

'I never expected to see you again,' he said. 'I was sure you'd be dead by now. Men in your position don't usually last that long.'

'Oh, after Obenauer, everything else seemed a piece of cake.'

He laughed. Then he took out a revolver and pointed it at me. 'Better make this look good, eh? Head down there to that bench and we can sit.'

I walked, aware of his heavy tread behind me, and sat on the bench.

He sat beside me, the gun in his hand. I tried to ignore it, but its presence brought up the hairs on the back of my neck. 'Look at you!' I pointed to his stripes. 'You've done well for yourself,' I said, the words dry in my mouth. 'How's Ingrid?'

He turned to face me, so close I could see the pores on his nose. 'Don't ask. She didn't wait for me.' His mouth twitched. 'Still, good riddance. Plenty of pretty girls in France. I've never gone short.'

He didn't ask about Céline, though I could almost see the thought pass his eyes. He seemed to be struggling for words. The world seemed like a sad pretence, as if we were all playing roles in some game we didn't understand.

'It's good to see you, Fred,' he said, rubbing the side of his nose in his familiar habit. 'Seems a long time since the Hotel in Cherbourg. Remember when Obenauer pinched your breakfast?'

I found myself smiling, as if he really was my friend after all this. 'God, yes.'

There was a kind of sadness in his eyes. Nostalgia perhaps. I saw him control it and replace it with cheery good humour. 'He was a bastard, wasn't he? Wonder where he is now.'

'Some high-up Nazi command, I expect. The bastards always rise high in the ranks.' The pause made me realise I'd inadvertently insulted him. His hand moved to cradle the revolver. I tried not to fixate on it.

I stood up, anxious to get away. 'Well, it's been nice to —'

'Where are you staying?' he asked, standing to bar my way. 'Maybe we could meet for a beer. Catch up.'

'Good idea,' I said, falsely enthusiastic. 'Where?'

'The German mess at the Hotel de Ville. I'm telling you, it's the best imported schnapps outside Germany. It'll have to be the day after tomorrow, though. Give me twenty-four hours; I've a busy two nights ahead.'

'Tell me about it.'

'What about Tuesday, shall we say eight o'clock?'

'I'll be there. Better get on now though, I've more houses to search.'

'You working alone? Who're you under?'

I made up a name. 'Hansen. Good chap. I'd better get back to him.'

Schulz was watching me rather too closely. I had the impression I'd made some sort of mistake. I stood up and began to walk away. 'See you later,' I said, having no intention of ever going near him again.

'Till Tuesday,' he said. He fingered his revolver a moment before holstering it. 'Heil Hitler!' he said quietly. He didn't salute.

I let my breath out and strode purposefully away down a side street until I was out of sight of the main road. Then I stopped, pressed my hands to my knees, taking lungfuls of sea air. The whole episode had been profoundly disturbing.

I didn't mention Schulz when we reconvened at the apartment. All that night Antoine and Lucien argued, and various young men came and went, knocking with their peculiar password of five knocks on the apartment door. Maps of Marseille were laid out on the floor, positions of Resistance members logged and marked.

I was the only one who wanted to leave Marseille. The group had a peculiar loyalty to the town that baffled me. And after the curfew, every hour that went by, the noose was getting tighter and the window of escape shrinking. Several times I tried to get Berenice to see reason, but she would not leave Antoine.

I glanced at where Berenice was sleeping, on the edge of a filthy mattress, close to Antoine but not touching. Guillaume lay on his other side, long limbs thrown over the edge of the mattress as they slept, fully dressed, guns within reach. Lucien, the third man, remained on guard all night. He gestured at me to lie down and sleep, but although I lay down, I was too restless to drop off.

Despite a dark sense of foreboding, leaving Berenice here would feel like a betrayal. If I left alone, I would always wonder what I could have done if I'd stayed. Whether I could have made a difference. Somewhere, Céline was waiting for me, at home, but the thought of her seemed so far away. I hadn't escaped all this way only to give myself right into the hands of the Nazis at the last moment. But the encounter with Schulz had put the fear of God into me. I'd sensed the Helmuth Schulz I'd known in Cherbourg was no more. Just like the baker Fred Huber had somehow become the Resistance man Édouard Vibert.

I pressed my hands into my eyes. I was so tired, yet I daren't sleep. The air was oppressive, like clouds massing before a storm. The hours ticked by. Common sense told me that if I stayed, I would die.

Yet still I didn't leave.

As dawn broke, I went to the window. 'Forgive me, Céline,' I whispered.

My eye was caught by a movement at the other end of the street. German Wehrmacht. I glanced the other way. A cordon of policemen at the other end of the street. Shit. They were here already.

CHAPTER 31

'Germans!' The room erupted into action.

Berenice was still groggy but leapt to her feet and wrapped her coat tighter as Antoine took a look out of the window. Already the soldiers had moved another block down the street, bullying an old couple and some dark-clad refugees ahead of them.

'We need to get out of here,' Guillaume said. 'If they find our weapons, we'll be dead men. Just take the revolvers and the pistols. Anything small you can carry.'

I grabbed a revolver, and fumbling in haste, I loaded it.

'Make a run for it,' Lucien said. 'Head for the épicerie on the corner of Magdalene.'

We knocked on every door as we leapt down the stairs, shouting in French, 'Hurry, get out, Nazi search party!'

Doors opened and closed. But others were already alerted and there was a mad scramble to get out and down the stairs. Ahead of us, a dark-haired woman, who I guessed was Jewish, threw her suitcase to the bottom of the stairs before hurtling after it.

A glance right and left showed the street littered with people dragging out their belongings. Bedding tied into bundles. Perambulators with wailing babies.

The first wave of evicted people passed, heading down towards the harbour, with two German soldiers, rifles at the ready, right behind them. We dodged back into the lobby.

As soon as they passed, Antoine dived out of the doorway. I took Berenice's arm and we pelted after them. There was a shout in German as we went, but we ducked away. Antoine skidded to a stop and turned into a narrow funnel of a street.

We went round the back, to a yard and into an empty grocery shop, the épicerie with a boarded-up shopfront.

Lucien and Guillaume crowded in after us. The cold-store window, which stank of damp and plaster, looked out onto the main boulevard of the Rue de la Magdalene. Guillaume stationed himself there and pointed a gun out of this narrow aperture.

Moments later he turned back, eyes wide. 'We can't fight them. It's a whole platoon.'

I put my eye to the crack between the wood and the door. The crump, crump of marching feet. In the distance, there was the slamming of doors, shouts, and cries. A thump and a thud on the boarded-up window right next to my shoulder. I imagined soldiers battering it with their rifles. We kept silent.

The noise of machine-gun fire. My stomach clenched. Through the sliver of light I saw a German had fallen, and his friend had dodged behind a tabac booth and was searching for the source of the gunfire.

It wasn't from our men, but clearly someone else had taken a shot at them.

More gunfire, and this time I heard German voices outside the back of the shop.

I saw Berenice whip round, then the back door crashed open fast as a boot kicked it open.

Guillaume, angry as a hornet, turned from his post and fired. The Nazi fell.

We were too stunned to react. Thoughts blundered round my head. If he didn't come out, they'd come in.

'Run,' I shouted to Guillaume.

A shadow by the cold-store window. Something black flew in through the opening. I saw it was a grenade the instant before the world lit up in neon. An almighty explosion rocked the ground and shattered the glass window. Guillaume was thrown like a rag doll into a heap on the ground.

'Guillaume?' My ears rang from the explosion. I put my gun down on the floor and joined Antoine, who was crouched over him.

Blood was everywhere. Guillaume's arm was a bloody stump, his chest a mass of blood and bone. His unmoving eyes stared out at us in surprise.

'We can't do anything,' I said. 'Let's go!'

Through the smoke, the empty window was dark with Germans climbing in.

'Maman!' Antoine grasped Berenice by the arm and dragged her out through the back door.

Lucien and I dived after them; shots ricocheted on the wall behind me.

Out. Panting for breath. A frantic look up and down.

The street was crammed with police and soldiers and frightened refugees.

'Édouard, here!' Berenice cried.

Antoine and Berenice had been caught by the second wave of Wehrmacht and were being herded down towards the quay.

There, rows of gendarmes in black capes and hats were waiting to check their papers.

'Get out of here,' I said to Lucien. Within seconds he had melted into the crowd.

The explosion had made my mind sharp. The desk ahead with its row of gendarmes seemed cut out, as if it were a scene in an old-fashioned stereoscope. I walked briskly after Antoine and Berenice. Berenice had the false papers Sebastien had given her, but it would be the end for Antoine. He'd get arrested for certain when he couldn't produce his papers.

And then it would be the end for Berenice. They couldn't arrest him, not without her reaction giving her away. She'd never leave him. A row of buses stood nearby, engines idling. I glanced to the other side of the street, towards the canvas-topped trucks and the Germans in heavy greatcoats surrounding a queue of the poorest, the thinnest, the most ragged. The police were shoving them aboard the trucks. I guessed these were the transport for the camps.

A call from behind me: 'Schnell!'

It made me startle and turn.

I'd been so fixed on what was ahead I hadn't heard them. Two more soldiers came up behind me, neither of them more than seventeen years old, bright-eyed with battle fever, faces pink with excitement. One of them jabbed a rifle into my back. I fell in beside Berenice.

She gripped my arm momentarily, her fingers digging into my wrist. Then she let go. We didn't look at each other, but that grip pained me; it was her goodbye.

A homburg-hatted old man, just ahead of Berenice, shifted restlessly from foot to foot as the gendarme scrutinised his papers. From the angry gesticulation at the table, it was clear they did not meet their requirements.

The gendarme summoned a soldier who was watching the proceedings. There were a few more moments of protest from the man in the hat before the soldier swung the butt of his rifle into the old man's groin. The man folded in half, his legs buckled and he fell, his hat rolling away. One of the young men behind me ran over and kicked him in the face with obvious relish before two soldiers dragged him across the street like a refuse sack and hoisted him into the truck.

Nobody reacted. Everyone looked away. But I could feel the fear seep like water in the silence.

Antoine had stepped behind Berenice to make her go first. I saw her turn, dread etched in her eyes, and a wordless exchange passed between them. The hem of her coat trembled, though her face betrayed nothing.

That's it, I thought. Don't arouse their suspicion.

She clung to Antoine's arm, but he pushed her forward. I guessed he wanted to give her a chance before his inevitable arrest.

'Papers, and be quick,' the gendarme said.

Berenice placed her false papers on the table. The gendarme, a man whose manner reeked of impatience, said, 'Marie Corbet?'

'Oui.'

In the harbour ahead, a ship hooted its horn. The noise made everyone startle. We'd all forgotten that normal life was carrying on.

Now. Whilst they were distracted. 'Excuse me,' I tapped Antoine on the back. 'You dropped these.' I thrust my papers towards him.

His eyes widened. I shoved my pass into his hand.

The gendarme stamped her pass and gestured Berenice off towards the buses. 'Next.'

Antoine leaned over to put my papers on the table. His empty fists opened and closed like two beating hearts.

'Henri Corbet, farmer.' He glanced to where Berenice was hovering, waiting. 'This is who? Your mother?'

'Yes,' Berenice interrupted. 'My son. His beard has grown, hein?'

The gendarme squinted at my picture and frowned.

A bead of sweat formed on my lip. I licked it away. The gendarme looked from Antoine to Berenice. The family resemblance was clear.

The stamp came down on his pass. 'Get on that bus over there. Next.'

I'd unobtrusively moved myself further back in the queue. Antoine and Berenice had climbed aboard the bus, and Berenice's anguished white face watched me through the blur of the window. Moments later, the bus shunted into gear and drove off, leaving a pall of exhaust fumes behind it. I was now behind a French family, complete with ageing widowed grandmother.

There was no escape. I'd no papers, and no gun, but I had the Gestapo tag. I had to try something.

I stepped out from the queue, pulled myself upright. '*Achtung! Weiterfahren!*' I gestured at the people in the queue towards the desk.

Immediately I was surrounded by German officers. A perspiring soldier with a jutting chin loomed over me. 'What is this?'

I aimed for an air of relaxation, gave a lazy salute. 'Heil Hitler! Siegfried Huber. Gestapo.' I flashed the tag from my pocket. 'General Schulz wants these people moving more quickly, or we won't get this arrondissement cleared by the end of the day.' I prayed my rapid German would buy me some time. 'I suggest we move this bigger queue into two smaller ones, and set up another table over there.' I began to gesture to the crowd, '*Schnell! Links fahren!*' I turned to the sweating soldier with the big chin. 'Do you speak French? It's a shambles. Get them to move to the left.' I pointed at one of the other men. 'You. Go and fetch another table.'

My natural German and feigned air of authority must have worked, because the men took my orders and began to organise the queue into two separate groups. I continued to direct the men, acting like a supervisor, then followed them over as they set up the table and persuaded one of the gendarmes to stand behind it.

A hand on my back.

'Siegfried Huber.'

I startled and turned at the familiar voice.

Schulz kept his hand on my shoulder, pinning it in place. 'Except you're not just Huber, are you? You are Édouard Vibert. Member of the French Resistance and a traitor who killed one of our best men.' Schulz's voice was soft. 'And now you are supposedly Gestapo.'

I saw the sweating soldier watching us. He must have fetched Schulz.

'I knew who you were all along,' Schulz said sadly. 'The real Gestapo have been searching for you for weeks. I followed the story with particular interest, was always a little proud that I knew you, this wolf in sheep's clothing, but I never actually thought we'd meet again. You wouldn't have had a drink with me, would you? I would have waited in vain.'

'In another time and place, I would have gladly bought you a drink, Helmuth. I only did what you would have done in my place.'

'No. I would not betray my countrymen so easily.' He gave a rueful smile. 'You always thought me a bit stupid. No, don't deny it. But now you are the stupid one. You will be charged with desertion and killing a fellow officer.'

The trial was what I expected. Short, brutal and uncompromising. I was to be made an example to any other Nazi who thought of disobeying orders. With several others I was loaded into a truck and driven under armed guard for several hours. To my surprise, we arrived on the outskirts of Paris. In the distance, the familiar skyline beckoned me. We were told our execution was to take place at 6am the next day, and the SS officers shepherded us towards a small disused chapel — a single room about twelve feet long, empty of pews or furniture. Just inside the door was a heap of open coffins, constructed out of cheap boxwood and stained brown with blood.

'Where are we?' I asked one of the other men.

'Saint-Valérien park just outside Paris.'

I smiled then. It was the very place Berenice had taken us to after we ran from the Bois de Boulogne.

It seemed odd to have come full circle. I hoped Berenice and Antoine had got out of Marseille. Seven of us were put in there to await our deaths. I didn't know what they'd done. Maybe some were members of the French Resistance. Maybe some were German deserters like me. None of us spoke. We each had our own thoughts and respected the other men. One wept quietly in the corner; one prayed, his hands clasped together in that futile begging gesture you see in medieval paintings. One man spent his time scratching his name into the walls for posterity with a button, wearing out the cuff of his shirt.

I sat and thought back, realising that my time on Jersey with Céline had been my heaven, and that if there was nothing after this life, then I had had plenty of joy. My death would be quick, unlike those sent to work to death in Nazi work camps, or Jews slaughtered like cattle. My thoughts went to my parents and to Horst. All of them thinking they were good German citizens, and yet something about their ideas had gone awry, and I couldn't explain it in any way that made sense.

I watched the man praying with envy. I had no easy God to believe in. There was only life. I remembered the Arbeiterjugend oaths that we had to take when we were children at school, the ones that said we should die for our country. We didn't know what it meant then. And I still had no idea. What was my country?

Just a bunch of memories; an idea of what it was to be German.

Bratwurst and Sauerkraut.

Houseplants and Lederhosen.

Wagner and Goethe.

Way before six o'clock, I was waiting, all my senses alert. Outside, I heard a trill of birdsong, and a slant of sunshine crept in through the slit of window in the apse. When the SS Blackshirts came, they led us at gunpoint to the execution place, a circular brake of trees before which seven posts were lined up.

Before us, twenty men knelt at their machine guns. It looked curiously beautiful, the symmetry of the trees and the guns. A clean arena of death. An SS officer tied my hands behind me to the rough post. Many previous shots had splintered it. Strangely, not to be the first to be waiting here gave me courage.

They tied a blindfold around my eyes, a heavy black cloth, and I looked out into the dark and silence, life pulsing through my veins.

One of the prisoners yelled out, '*Bonne chance!*'

It made me laugh. I held my breath. They always give the order with a raised arm, so you never know when it will come.

CHAPTER 32

April 1943

Céline

Horst wasn't the kind of man who had any domestic skills, and even if he had, he would still have expected to be waited on. He could be charming, but only to get his own way, and in some respects he was like a child, bullying one minute and cajoling the next. His presence filled the house. He took the spot nearest the fire, the biggest portion of food, and spent long hours in the washroom shaving and leaving his mess of soap and bristles. Of course, I was to wash without such niceties as soap.

Now we were no longer baking, he left his wet greatcoat hanging on the hook where Fred's aprons used to hang. That was enough to hurt, but once I couldn't help noticing dark splodges near the hem, stains that could be blood. I dared not say a thing to him; he was an unpredictable predator. And without my glasses, I supposed I must have looked like a peering, mouse-like creature, trying not to jump at her own shadow.

Rachel, of course, was in the hiding place whenever Horst was in, and her presence made me constantly on edge. Every time he went upstairs alone, I held my breath. But so far, months had gone by and he had paid the room where I slept little attention, except for a rap on the door when he expected me to go to him.

One wet April day, Horst was out, and Rachel was stretching her limbs next to the window.

'Don't stand so close,' I said. 'Someone might see you.'

'I have to have a little light,' she said. 'Have you any idea how much I long to see the sea? To stretch or run, or see the seasons change. I envy you the rain, and the wind. It's all right for you, you can cycle into town, go for a blow on the top of the hill.'

'Huh. I spend most of the time queueing. And when I get to the front of the queue, there's just a miserable piece of pork belly — more fat and gristle than meat.'

'Still, you're a part of life. I'm just waiting. Waiting to die, or waiting to live.'

I saw her wistful look, and it churned me up inside. When I had to go out for provisions I cycled up the bluff of the hill, out into the lanes. My body was unused to pedalling so hard, and I soon grew out of breath and had to jump off and push. The hedgerows still bore patches of late bluebells, rosy-red campion, and, in the scrub, pink thrift. The rain had stopped, and the sun peeked from the scudding clouds. I gathered up a big bunch of dripping flowers and put them in my bicycle basket. If Rachel couldn't go out to nature, I would have to bring it to her.

I freewheeled down the hill, into the wind, and for once the tension loosened and I felt a kind of freedom, until I saw the humps of the gun turrets where previously there had been only trees.

When I finally got back after the shopping, I filled a striped blue jug with flowers and put them on the table, then took a smaller matching jug upstairs.

Rachel looked up from the bed, where she was reading.

'For you,' I said, holding them out with a mock bow.

'Oh, aren't they gorgeous!' She took hold of the jug and held it on her lap. After quite a few minutes she said, 'You know, I never really appreciated bluebells before. Can I take them into my lair?'

'Go ahead. Though you won't see them in the dark.'

'I have my torch for when you're both downstairs. And it will make it more like home.'

I nodded, turning away, bitter that a two-foot-six cupboard should have to be someone's home.

Having Rachel upstairs meant I could never relax. I was afraid of the slightest sound when Horst was in the house. Only when he was out could I let out my breath and release the knot in my shoulders. It was bizarre how after a few months, the situation assumed a strange kind of normality. It was helped by the fact that Horst was in the house less and less time, as his duties became harder.

The fortification of the island demanded enormous numbers of enslaved workers, and many German officers were working longer hours to keep them building. Summer had arrived, and despite the scorching summer heat they were pushing on with the building works.

A soft knock at the door. Wolfgang. I had grown to know his knock.

Wolfgang was a godsend; his medical duties enabled him to drive around the island, and he helped us by stealing extra rations from the German stores whenever he could.

I rushed to usher Wolfgang in as quickly as I could, fearful that the neighbours would tell Horst about this other mysterious German that spent so much time here.

'Sorry, I couldn't get away last week,' he said.

'No matter, you're here now. Good to see you, Wolfgang. Rachel's missed you.'

His eyes lit up. 'Such a beautiful day,' he said. 'The sea so blue. I wish I could take her driving, but it is too much risk.' He held out a parcel. 'It is dried sausage. *Wurst*. Not good sausage, tough. All I could get today.'

I took the parcel. 'I'm so grateful. Every little helps. Where did you park?'

'Round the back by the store. Don't worry, Mrs Galen can't see it. Can I go up?'

I nodded and watched him lope up the stairs. Above me I heard scuffling as Rachel emerged, and then voices.

It always made me uneasy. In one way, it was none of my business what they did upstairs, and I felt glad Rachel should have a little company other than my own, but in another, I felt responsible for Rachel in a way that tied my stomach in knots.

As I hid the parcel in one of my gumboots by the back door, I heard the creak of bedsprings and laughter from upstairs, and the sound made my chest hurt; it had been so long since I'd laughed. I went to the kitchen and put the kettle on, standing by it as it began to boil.

The soft purr of an engine. I yanked the whistling kettle off the hob and listened. A car. Only Germans had cars now. I shot to the window. Horst's car had just pulled up, and a driver was climbing out to open the door for him.

I dumped the steaming kettle on the window ledge and yelled up the stairs, 'Horst's back!'

Wolfgang's panicked face appeared over the bannister.

'He's back,' I said.

'Why?' He seemed unable to take it in.

297

'I don't know! Just get out of here. Out the back way.'

He almost flew down the stairs. Thank God I'd left the keys in the door.

The front door opened, and Horst pushed past me without speaking. His face was white.

Upstairs, a scraping sound on the linoleum as Rachel went back into hiding.

'You've left the back door open,' Horst said. He stared at me, his mouth working as if he wanted to say something, but nothing came out.

'Yes. Sorry. It's the heat,' I improvised. 'It's so hot.' I banged the door shut, glad to see Wolfgang had driven away.

'You're home early,' I said, to distract him.

I wondered if he were drunk again, or worse, ill. He looked different. Drained. Some sort of sixth sense at this change made my spine tingle.

I carried on making the tea as he headed for the stairs, fear coiling in my guts and all my senses tuned to the rooms above me. I heard the drag of the legs of his chair, and then a strange sound I'd never heard before. A groan and a sob. Horst was crying.

I listened harder. It was definitely him. Muffled sobs and the noise of someone blowing his nose.

By the time he came down, I could smell whiskey fumes and he was even more unsteady on his feet. His eyes were red-rimmed and half-closed.

'What is it?' I asked. 'What's happened?'

'It's all your fault. You gave him this foolish idea, turned him from being good German to stupid Englishman.'

I backed away from his belligerent glare.

'And now look, what shall I tell my parents? It will kill them.' His shoulders heaved in another sob. 'It's Siegfried. He's dead.'

The world seemed to stop. I saw very clearly the shabbiness of the room, and this man in a grey-green uniform with the haunted eyes, the way his neck bulged over his collar where it was too tight.

As the words sunk in, my chest constricted, like a ball of paper you crumple in your hand. 'What are you saying? What about Fred?' I rushed over, grasped him by the sleeve.

He flung his arm out to dislodge me, catching me a slap on the face.

'He deserted and they shot him.' He punched a hand into the wall, over and over. Then turned, his face raw with pain. 'My own brother. A coward. What was he thinking?'

It couldn't be true. I refused to believe it. This wasn't happening.

'How do you know? Where is he? What happened?' So many questions, and Horst was just blubbing again in front of me, great wet tears that he scrubbed away with his sleeve. 'They tell me today. The shame of it. Like I am traitor. Like I am responsible for it.' His shoulders heaved again. 'They sent a letter to my mother. They will send you one too.'

'Who shot him? Who? His own side?' I couldn't take it in.

Horst took our wedding photograph from the mantel and stared into it. 'He should never have married you. He was all right until he met you.'

'Don't!' I said, reaching out, seeing what was coming.

Too late. He threw the photograph down. It hit the hearth and I saw shards of glass skitter from the broken frame.

I ran to pick up the pieces.

My head whirled. I found myself staring into our young faces. Fred with his proud smile, all neat, with a buttonhole in his lapel; me — windblown, my veil blowing sideways above my smiling face. How had it come to this?

I looked up at Horst who had slumped into a chair, his head pressed into his hands. He raised his eyes to mine. His lip trembled before he spoke. 'The bloody fool. We used to play at soldiers when we were small. He always used to follow me. I was the leader. Now I have no-one to lead.' He shook his head, suddenly maudlin.

He was sorry for himself, I realised. Not for Fred, not for me, not for anyone else.

The thought made me calm. As if from a great distance, I watched him pick up the telephone and call for his driver to return.

'I will rise above this *Fleck*,' he said to me, drawing himself up tall. He said the word *Fleck* — stain, with disgust. 'I will prove it to them I am great soldier. They will all see how hard I work for the Reich.'

Fifteen minutes later, the car was back, and he staggered out and into it. I guessed he was going to work. He never once offered me any kind of condolence.

When he had gone I was able to sweep up the broken glass, and by the time Rachel crept downstairs, I was sitting in the armchair, clutching the precious photograph to my chest.

'I heard him bawling,' she said. 'It scared me. What's going on?'

'He says Fred is dead.' The words seemed unreal, as if someone else was speaking. 'Executed for desertion.'

Rachel came over and put her arms around me. 'Oh, no. Oh, Céline.'

I leaned into her scrawny arms and willed the tears to come, but I was still too shaken to weep for him.

'I can't cry,' I said. 'I should cry, but I can't damn well feel anything.'

'Are you sure it's true?'

I nodded numbly. 'Horst was certain. But it's so unfair. That he should be gone, and Horst still here. Like some sort of twisted joke.'

'Come on,' she said. 'I'll make tea. You've had a shock.'

She made the tea and sat with me, forcing me to gulp the scalding liquid down. My hands were trembling, and suddenly I wondered how I'd go on, and why my life was worth living. Rachel caught my mood.

'He'd want you to survive it,' was all she said.

Later that night I lay alone in bed, still clutching the photograph. *What were you doing?* I said to him. *What made you get yourself shot? Why didn't you come home safe?*

I looked into his smiling eyes and couldn't find an answer. Sleep wouldn't come. Tears wouldn't come. I heard Horst come in in the small hours and clatter upstairs, heard his grunt as he collapsed into bed. Suddenly the whole point of struggling on, of living with this man, was too exhausting. I could have curled up and slept for a thousand years. It was so tempting to just give Rachel up, surrender her to the Nazis, take whatever punishment was coming.

But I knew I couldn't do that to Rachel.

Grieving is a strange process. One day you can carry on as if everything is the same, the next something will catch you short. I hid the photograph away, for I never wanted Horst to touch it again, and at night I lay hugging Fred's old striped pyjamas, and just the thought of him wearing them made me cry so hard that Horst banged on the wall to make me stop.

Mostly I bottled it all up. To have Rachel on the other side of the partition, and Horst in the next bedroom meant I could have no privacy. My feelings were like a weight, a lump of black lead that made every simple action an effort. I was suffocated, as if I couldn't breathe. Horst himself never referred to Fred again. It was as if he had never had a brother at all.

Horst didn't like me to cry in front of him, so all my weeping was done in snatched moments. I began to feel I might go mad if the war didn't stop soon.

It was a few more months before he insisted I share his bed. At first it was a kiss and a grope, but over time it soon progressed to him wanting more.

When I refused, he said, 'Come on, life will be much pleasanter for us both.'

The way he said it left me in no doubt that it was a threat. After the first night, he took it as his right. He'd thrash on top of me in a desperate sort of way, as if he was trying to blot everything out of existence, even me. My body protested. It closed up, tightened, shrank away from him. He knew, and he didn't like it.

'Talk to me,' he said, his hands pinning down my shoulders.

'I don't know what to talk about,' I faltered.

'Tell me you love it.'

'I can't, I —'

His fist came out and my cheek exploded in pain. The first time he hit me like that, I was so shocked I cried out.

Later, when he'd gone to work, Rachel saw the bruise on my cheek. 'Bastard. I heard him.'

'It's nothing.'

'You mustn't let him. You'll have to try to keep out of his way.'

'Easier said than done.'

She paused, sat down at the table opposite me, and pushed her hair back out of her eyes. 'You look exhausted, Céline.' A silence. 'You're so thin, giving me half your rations. And if I wasn't here, you could just move away. But you have to be here to feed me, to empty my chamber pot into the privy, to keep him distracted enough not to know there's a Jew right under his roof.'

'I wouldn't have it any other way,' I said. 'But sometimes I think I can't bear it anymore, and I wonder ... well, I wonder if we'll ever be able to stop.'

'Me too. And I fantasize about the British winning the war and putting a bullet through his head.'

CHAPTER 33

Horst's footsteps approached the shop door and my guts shrivelled inside me. It was November now, and after all this time, I knew how those Russian men felt to be slaves. The food was ready on the table as he'd demanded, and I knew I should be grateful for the fact he had supplied a rind of bacon, potatoes and turnip, with which I had made a stew. I imagined his face would frown at it, the way he usually did.

On his way past, he put the newspaper down deliberately in front of me, and of course I read the headlines, as he intended me to do. Two old ladies from St Brelade — Suzanne Malherbe and Lucille Schwab — had been sentenced to death for distributing anti-German propaganda. Their leaflets had apparently been written as if written by a German officer and signed '*The soldier without a name*'. Good for them.

Horst threw his cap down on the settee and went to wash. He didn't even acknowledge me. It struck me that this was like the worst kind of a marriage, except that I hadn't even volunteered for it. Fred now seemed like a distant dream from a golden past. I couldn't bear to think of him anymore. The thought that he'd been another German in jack boots stuck in my throat and filled me with hate, but at the same time the thought that I'd never see him again made me crumble. There seemed to be two Freds in my mind, and it didn't seem safe to love either of them.

By the time Horst had washed, I was at the kitchen table. The fact that we hardly spoke now made every sound in the house even more obvious. I jumped at every fall of soot in the chimney, at every gurgle from the pipes, at every noise of children passing in the street outside. Although I knew Rachel was well aware of how she mustn't even breathe loudly, the simple fact of her being hidden there behind the partition still made every creak heart-stopping. And after so long, I was resigned to it with a kind of numb endurance.

'I hate this wet weather,' Horst said. 'Jersey roads are very bad. A lot of work when cars and trucks are stuck in mud.'

'I know,' I said. 'We aren't used to so much traffic.'

I cringed. Every statement I made felt like an accusation.

Horst regarded me coldly. 'If I had want opinion from you, I would have ask you.' He glared at me and continued to eat. When the plate was empty, he pushed it away. 'This food is terrible. Don't Jersey women know how to cook?'

'I did my best with what we had.'

'Miserable little island. The farmers cheat us. We know you do it. Only today we had a letter. Someone tell us that Flanders Farm is cheating us with the milk.'

I was silent; it was always best to let him talk if I didn't want a fist across my face.

He stood up. 'They have one more cow there than we have known. Not anymore. Cow has gone to slaughter. The woman she is deported. She will be on her way to *Konzentrationslager.*' He gave a burp of a laugh. 'Maybe slaughter for her too.'

'Surely not. Mrs Flanders is an old woman. Maybe she didn't know how many cows she had.'

He gave me a look that would shrivel anything within five yards. 'We are not stupid. She knew of course. Now she pays the price.'

Much as I disliked Mrs Flanders, for I was convinced it was she who had colluded with the Galens about daubing my windows, she was one of us, and I had a sneaking admiration for her too. She had defied the Germans in a way I hadn't. But then, maybe she hadn't been forced to have one living under her roof. Resistance was easy if you were at a distance. Close up, it was hard, and even harder if you had a big secret to keep.

I set to cleaning away the plates, and I heard him go up to the bedroom. My tension increased as it always did when I thought of Rachel only a few feet away from him. And if I was terrified, how must she feel? However bad things got, I couldn't imagine actually informing on her.

Above me, the thud of Horst's pacing footsteps was followed by the smell of cigar smoke drifting down. Obviously he could still get cigars, and the bedside table always had a bottle of whiskey or brandy on it. This was his usual pattern. He would be up there with his papers and his lists of men.

One day when he was out, Rachel and I took a look at his ledger. We hardly dared to open it, thinking that somehow he would know, but finally we plucked up the courage. In it were long lists of men, each one named and numbered. Over the months, we'd taken to looking at these lists every day. They were obviously the lists of men labouring at the quarry, and they held a strange fascination for us. Every day, more would be crossed out.

Yevgenievich, Drugov
Kautsky, Zubarev
Leonidovich, Konstantin
Frolov, Mikhalitsyn
Stepanovich, Gleb

'Dead men,' Rachel said, resting her finger on one of the names.

'So many,' I said.

Just seeing that scratched line through their names filled

me with anger. They would have family somewhere wondering where they were, and now they were reduced to this one line that erased them from existence. It always made me think of Fred, and I'd have to swallow hard to push him from my mind.

Upstairs I heard the chink of a glass. Horst would be drinking again. The evenings were one long silent scream of waiting. I didn't dare go anywhere, because wherever I went I was spat at and called 'Jerrybag'. And I was ashamed of the bruises on my face.

The bakery had closed altogether. There was too little flour for bread to bake now, and even the Germans were looking thinner. Since the Allied invasion of Normandy, Jersey had been cut off by both Britain and Germany. The effect on Horst of being abandoned by his Führer made him angry and resentful, and I was an easy target for his disappointment.

At the same hour every night, Horst called me from the top of the stairs. At first this had been a request. Then it had become his right. Now it was an exercise in punishment.

When I heard him call, I put down my book. So soon? Things must be bad at the camp. Wearily, I braced myself for what was to come. I'd try to please him, and that way the pain and humiliation would be less.

When I got upstairs he was waiting by the window, stubbing out his cigar on the sill. I wanted to tell him to use an ashtray like a civilised human being. He saw my expression, and smiling slightly, he continued to grind the butt into the paint as he watched my face.

'I don't like that dress,' he said. 'Where is the one I buy for you?'

I began to walk from the room.

'No. Undress here first.'

Fear and the cold had already made gooseflesh of my arms. Please God, let him not be rough today.

Awkwardly, I took off my cardigan and unbuttoned the dress. Horst himself never undressed. There was power in that uniform, in his black shiny boots, and he knew it. I tried to seem calm, because my fear made him worse.

Once I was shivering in my corselette and pants, I made to leave the room.

'Wait.'

I backed away, knowing what was coming.

'You're a whore, Céline. A dirty little whore.' He came towards me and hooked a finger under my chin. 'What would my brother think if he could see you now, in your underwear, begging for it?'

'Please, Horst…' I tried to find the man behind the twisted leering expression. The man I'd known in Vienna, the smiling youth who formally shook my hand. But he was gone, and this man was something I had no answer for. His boredom, his rage, his pleasure in hurting, as if it somehow healed the hurt in him, were all impenetrable.

'You know what happens to whores, don't you?' He grabbed my arm and swung back his fist. When it connected with my face I felt nothing, just the force of falling backwards, the crack of my skull against the wall. I tasted the iron of blood in my mouth before a boot landed in my stomach, and a flower of pain spread outwards until I heard my own cry. I slipped to the ground, felt him drag me into the middle of the floor, and then he was upon me.

CHAPTER 34

For months it went on. I had to use a rubber cap in case I should fall with child, and I put it in every single day. It cost me Fred's Sunday suit on the black market and the anguish that went with it. I'd never be able to look at a man again without revulsion. The war would soon be over, they promised us. Both Rachel and I were getting desperate, not sure how much longer we could go on, living on borrowed time.

It wasn't until May 1945 that the Germans surrendered in Europe. The news came to me whispered from another woman as I queued to get one of the precious Red Cross parcels that England had finally sent.

I hurried home, a new spring in my step, anxious to share some of the parcel and the good news with Rachel. When I got there, we were able to open a tin of Rowntree's cocoa and have a cup of it. We toasted the British troops in cocoa, and hugged.

The noise of an engine outside stopped our celebration.

'It's Horst's car,' I said, peering out of the window. 'Wolfgang's just helping him out. Quick!'

Rachel slithered back under the bed, and I piled the boxes and shoes around the door to her hiding place. I bolted back downstairs and managed to swill out the cups just in time.

'What's that smell?' Horst said as he came in.

The cocoa packet was still on the table.

'Red Cross parcel,' I said. 'It's cocoa. I couldn't resist. Shall I make you some?'

He took a look at the contents laid out on the table: the canned meat, powdered milk, the tin of Klim.

'English shit,' he said. He swept his arm across the table and everything went to the ground.

Of course. I should have realised. The news of the defeat of the Germans would have reached Horst too. He went up to his room and I heard the door slam.

When he came back to eat, he stank of whiskey, and even the meat roll and tinned vegetables couldn't pacify him.

'You think you're so clever, you English, *ja*? What you look at?'

'Nothing, Horst.'

He stood suddenly and pulled me back by the hair.

'Upstairs,' he said.

I did as he asked. It will soon be over, I thought. This war will soon end.

'Lie down.'

I squeezed my eyes shut, let the fight seep out of me. Let him. Then it would be over. He would fall into his usual stupor and sleep. This grunting, groaning animal that stank of cigars was nothing to do with me.

It was taking too long. He was usually spent by now. A blow to my chest, a fist like a hammer.

'Move, can't you?' he shouted, shaking me until my head rattled. 'Do you think I want to do this with a dead thing? Move.'

I tried to move, but his weight pressed me down, like a butterfly on a pin. I made one intense effort. Life, that was what mattered. To stay alive. For Rachel. With horror, I felt him grow soft inside me.

He slid out of me. Incensed now, he rolled me off the bed. I landed in a sprawl, my face crushed towards the linoleum floor.

I tried to turn my head and caught a glimpse of the barrel of a gun.

Christ. He meant to kill me.

A hand grasped my hair, yanking, until my neck might snap. 'They say the Führer is lost, and we are still stuck in this place. I'm tired of you,' he said. 'I don't see why I have to see your face another day.'

'No! Think of Fred. What would he say?' My voice was thick, desperate.

'Fred is dead. He was a traitor. He gave up on Germany because of you. Because of women like you and men like him, we are lost. He paid the price, and so will you.' He cocked the trigger and the sound of it was loud in my ears. The gun pressed against my temple.

A flash of something steel across Horst's neck. Several things happened at once. He tried to twist, but he buckled towards me, knocking me off balance so I fell with a crash, the breath forced from my lungs. Horst's head hit the ground next to mine. His mouth made a sound like a groan, but his eyes were blankly open, and a gush of red was everywhere. Blood. The stink of it like iron and heat, and the gun skittering from his open hand.

At the same time, I pushed his weight off me and turned. Rachel swayed there, white-faced, a sharp kitchen knife in her hand.

I sat up woozily.

More blood pooled around Horst's neck. He writhed a moment more, then was still.

'You killed him.' The words stuck to my lips in a whisper.

Rachel quietly put down the knife on the floor. 'Every night I've covered my ears, trying to block out the sound of him. His shouts, his taunts. I swore I'd go mad if he hit you again, and I'd just had enough. I couldn't take any more. He would've shot you.'

'It's the finish for us,' I said.

'I know. I'm sorry. I didn't mean it to end this way.' She knelt beside me and we gripped each other tight. Her ribs trembled under her nightdress.

'We were so close to making it,' I said.

CHAPTER 35

In a frenzy, we scrubbed every trace of blood from the floor and wrapped Horst's neck to stem the flow. In death, he looked calm, just another blond man in uniform.

'What makes one man so different from another?' Rachel said. 'They have the same bones, the same flesh. And yet one can be kind and another cruel. Where does it come from, kindness?'

'I don't know. Fred used to worship his older brother,' I said.

She gave a dismissive snort. I stared at the soles of Horst's boots, marvelling that I felt nothing for him. This was Fred's brother lying here, and I could remember how full of life he'd been as a young man. How full of life we'd all been, when we were young. A great sadness washed over me.

'They'll be here soon, though, to collect him in the car,' Rachel said.

'I know.' It hadn't escaped me that we had a dead German actually in the house.

'What shall we do? It would be no use pretending it was an accident,' Rachel said. 'Nobody cuts their own throat, do they?'

'We could hide him.' I made an effort to be practical, and cast my eyes around the room.

'The partition,' Rachel said. 'It's the obvious answer. It's my fault after all. It'll give us a few more hours to think of something.'

I shook my head. 'You can't have him in there with you. That's macabre. And anyway, as soon as they realise he's missing, there'll be a search, you know that?'

'So you'd better tell the driver he decided to walk to town and left for St Helier already.'

'No. If I do that, it puts him here. I've a better idea. I'll act worried and tell them Horst didn't come home.'

'But they know he did,' Rachel said. 'Wolfgang drove him — you saw him help Horst out of the car.'

'But it's Wolfgang. Will he tell?'

'I don't know. I just can't think anymore.'

She looked so tired and forlorn that I went to give her a hug. 'Brace up. One thing at a time. Let's get him out of the way.'

He was a heavy man to lift, and we had to drag him. More blood; more mopping up.

Once he was behind the partition, I checked his room, moved a rug over the damp patch on the floorboards and washed up the plates in the kitchen. On tenterhooks, we scoured the house, looking for tell-tale signs he'd been home last night. Of course, we found his coat on the hook and his hat on the settee. I hid them under my mattress. *Please, let them not search us,* I thought.

When the knock came at the door the next day, I was ready. It was a young man, the one who usually came for him in the mornings.

I acted flustered. 'I'm sorry, but he isn't here. I'm so worried. He didn't come home last night.'

'Not come home?' The soldier looked like he didn't understand.

'I was expecting him as usual, but he didn't come. Maybe he spent the night at a hotel? When you see him, will you ask him to telephone me?'

'Yes. This I will do.' Then he frowned. 'Your face, what has happened to it?'

I thought quickly. 'I was set upon by some people. They punched me and called me "Jerrybag" because Hauptmann Huber lives here.'

'Hauptmann Huber will be angry. What people? I will find them, they will be punished.'

'I don't know their names. I didn't see their faces, it was dark...' I was rambling but couldn't stop. Panic was hot in my throat.

'Don't be frightened. We will take care of you, Frau Huber. I will see to it.'

'Thank you.'

I shut the door and sagged against it with relief.

'What is going on? Where is Hauptmann Huber?' Wolfgang asked. It was midday by the time he came, and his face was creased with worry. 'Is he ill?'

I shook my head.

'The men are restless; he has not arrived for work. I made an excuse and come to ask you.'

'Come in,' I said, ushering him past the shop counter and into the sitting room.

'Is Rachel all right?'

'Yes —' Rachel appeared from upstairs — 'I'm fine. But we have a problem.'

'Where's Huber? They told me he had not been home last night, but I know I brought him here and watched him come through this door.'

'He's dead,' Rachel said flatly.

Wolfgang's face dropped. 'No.' He glanced at me as if I might deny it. 'What happened to your face?'

Rachel and I looked at each other. 'We need to bury him somewhere,' Rachel said. 'Can you help us?'

Wolfgang sat back on the chair, his face grey. 'Show me,' he said. 'I must know it all.'

Rachel took him upstairs, and I heard the bed castors creak across the floor, and her voice explaining.

When he came down, he was even more grave. 'If they find out he's dead, we will all be executed. Every person on Jersey will be at risk. They will kill you one by one until you confess.'

'Then they mustn't know he's dead,' I said. 'He must just disappear somehow.'

'How many days I wish for that to happen,' Wolfgang said. 'But not like this. This is too … too difficult.'

'Then we are finished.' Rachel went to Wolfgang and laid a hand on his arm. 'You are a good man, Wolfgang. We are grateful for your help. And we cannot expect more than you have already given.'

He took her hand and kissed it. They looked at each other a long while, and he ran a finger down the side of her cheek until she took hold of his hand and pressed it to her chest.

'If I do this, I do it for you,' Wolfgang said. After a few moments' thought, he went on, 'If I could get him to the sea, we could bury him there and hope that nobody finds him.'

'No,' I said. 'He might wash up somewhere.'

'If he didn't have his uniform, they wouldn't know it was him,' Wolfgang said. 'Many Todt workers, they are thrown into the sea.'

I was momentarily shocked. But then I realised it was the answer.

'Don't go to the door if anyone comes,' he said. 'I must go now. I will say I took him to a hotel and have not seen him since.'

The next day, I searched Tilly's room for a box of old gardening clothes that used to belong to Fred. I had to harden myself to use them. When I held them to my chest they smelt of icing sugar and pastry, of earth and manure, and even now the fact that Fred was dead and that I'd never see him again took my breath. I didn't dare think what he would make of me using his clothes for this purpose.

Rachel took Horst's uniform and burned it in the range. We dressed Horst in the ragged clothes and bound his feet with strips of cloth. The sight of him was both repulsive and sad. He was stiff, so it wasn't an easy task. But finally it was done.

That night, Wolfgang drove up to the back door in the car. 'They are searching for Huber everywhere. Yesterday was talk of him deserting his post. Today they suspect something. Tomorrow they will search house to house. You'd better be ready.'

Under the cover of dark, Wolfgang dragged Horst into the car. No one would be surprised to see an OT officer manhandling a prisoner's corpse.

After Wolfgang had gone, we cleared out the range and scraped the buttons and brass from the bottom of the firebox into a paper bag.

Rachel didn't say much. She was worried about Wolfgang, and all night we expected a knock at the door, but none came. When I looked out of the window, I saw the moon rising slim over the rooftops and heard the boom of guns from somewhere far off at sea.

At dawn, I took a trowel and went down the lane to bury the paper bag. I stopped at a damp ditch and dug a hole good and deep. Once I'd covered it over, I stamped down the earth and dragged rough grass over it. As I was hurrying home, a lone soldier passed me. He gestured to me to look in my basket.

'Nothing,' I said.

He saw the empty basket and trowel straight away. 'You dig potatoes?' he asked hopefully. His thin and bony wrists protruded from his uniform. He looked about seventeen years old, but his face was gaunt and his eyes shadowed.

'Yes. But none left.' I shrugged.

'Same. Same for us,' he said. 'No food anywhere.' And he walked on by. After he'd gone, I found tears were rolling down my face. I wasn't sure why I was crying, but perhaps it was for some lost innocence, for the way war had turned us all into less than we were before, and for that boy's army adventure being so much less than he'd hoped for.

When I got back, two armed soldiers were already on guard outside my house. They stopped me at the door until I shouted, 'Ich bin Frau Huber!' at them, and they reluctantly let me pass. Immediately I could hear boots on the upstairs floorboards and my wardrobe door's familiar creak before it banged shut. I hurried through the shop and searched in vain for Wolfgang's friendly face, but there was no sign of him. Another armed soldier stood by the fireplace, and Oberstleutnant Fischer, thinner and more tired-looking, sat on the arm of the chair in my sitting room. My senses were so on fire with listening I barely heard his first words.

'I am sorry about the door,' he said in German. 'My men are a little enthusiastic. They hear how the war goes and they are angry.'

'I was out searching for food,' I replied, also in German. I kept up the pretence, aware of the bangs and scuffles from the rest of the house, my stomach clenched tight, expecting any moment to hear Rachel's cry.

I sat down and crossed my legs in a semblance of calm. 'Any news of Horst?' I tried to keep my eyes ahead and not on the stairs.

'No.' Fischer looked at me closely. 'I thought we might establish the last time you saw him. He wasn't a man to shirk his duty. So, to speak plain, we think something might have befallen him.'

I kept my gaze wide and innocent.

'You don't think…?'

'It is war, Frau Huber.' He sounded weary. 'A good man disappears, and we must ask questions.'

'I suppose so,' I said. Upstairs, the slow scrape of furniture being dragged across the floor. I could barely breathe.

He sighed. 'The news from Germany is bad. So many cities ruined, destroyed by this war. Dresden, it is rubble. Berlin too, a Pompeii. And what was it for, this great crusade? Thousands dead, thousands lost. A Europe in ruins.'

I was silent. He seemed to have shrunk into himself.

'Your husband, is he still in France?'

'No … he … he didn't make it.'

He closed his eyes. I had to wait a good while before he spoke. 'My condolences, Frau Huber. Such a bloody waste.'

'*Oberstleutnant! Etwas hier.*' The soldier on the stairs summoned him with a sharp movement of the head.

Fischer didn't seem to hear him.

'What is it?' I stood up too fast. My voice came out dry as feathers.

'*Kommen Sie,*' the soldier replied.

Oberstleutnant Fischer snapped back into himself and took to the stairs, with me following behind. I could barely see through the door for helmeted men. One of them pushed me aside into my bedroom as they hammered on the false wall.

What must Rachel be feeling, locked behind there? I knew they would find the hinged door as soon as the bed was moved, and they were dragging everything aside. My hand came to my mouth as a sob escaped.

A sudden shout of triumph made my heart plummet to my shoes.

Crashes and the splinter of wood. They kicked down the partition and dragged Rachel out. Surprisingly, she was calm, even dignified.

'Who is this?' Fischer said.

'A cousin,' I said.

Rachel shook her head at me. 'I'm sorry, Céline.' She turned to Fischer, raised her chin. 'I am Rachel Cohen.'

'Identity card?' he asked.

She shook her head. The soldier who was holding her slapped her hard across the face. She reeled, but recovered herself enough to speak. 'You have it already.'

'Don't hurt her,' I said, but two men held me back.

Fischer stared at her a moment. 'I remember. You are the Jew from the bank.'

'She has a name! Rachel Cohen,' I said.

'Well, Fräulein Cohen, you are under arrest and it is time to go. Take her to the car, men.'

They bustled her down the stairs, hands behind her back. She called out, 'I made her do it. She didn't want to hide me, but I forced her.'

I tried to follow, but Fischer caught me by the arm. 'Best not, Frau Huber.'

'Wait! Where are you taking her?' I wrenched my arm away.

He sighed. 'Where all the Jews must go.'

'Please, Herr Fischer.' I spoke in rapid German. 'Germany has lost. You know this now, and we are just waiting for the

320

announcement. You are the last outpost of the Führer's men. Already we almost have victory in Europe. Why ruin another life?'

'Because I must do my duty to the end. You have been helping an undesirable. So, there will be a trial for you as soon as the paperwork is completed, and we will follow the correct procedure.'

'But it's madness. Today you have the power, but in a few hours it will all change! The British are coming, and you will have to surrender. Forget you found her. Just a few hours, that's all I ask.'

'No, Frau Huber. I need my certainties. If I fail in my duty now, I will always wonder why I did not fail in it earlier. Could I have saved more souls? Once orders are no longer orders, then the whole bloody muddle of war becomes a pointless thing. Your husband died for the Reich; he and many more like him. I owe it to them, don't you agree?'

'He would have wanted you to save her,' I said hotly.

'Perhaps at the beginning of the war. We are all different men at the beginning of the war. We all have compassion then.'

An engine revved up outside, followed by the noise of trucks starting up. He walked downstairs with a heavy tread. I followed and watched in stunned silence as he put on his cap. When he got to the door, he turned back. 'My men will fix this door. When they send for you, you will report as requested. Goodbye, Frau Huber.'

With the slam of the door, my chest caved in towards my ribs. I ran to the shop window and watched the car drive away. Rachel's small dark head was dwarfed by the men in the car. The two open-topped trucks full of helmeted men flanked it, either side. So many men for one small person.

I went upstairs and looked through the door to Rachel's room. The partition was splintered, and torn bits of paper littered the floor, but scrawled in wax crayon on the back of the wall hundreds, no thousands, of times, over and over, was a red letter 'V'.

Behind the ruined wall, the long makeshift bed still bore the imprint of Rachel's warm body. The Tilley lamp was still on, and the book she had been reading lay open, face down. *The Midnight Folk* by John Masefield, the green embossed hardback I'd had when I was seven years old, and kept, even though it was tatty, because I was fond of it. I picked it up and read the familiar lines:

Waking up, he rubbed his eyes: it was broad daylight; but no one was there. Someone was scraping and calling inside the wainscot, just below where the pistols hung. There was something odd about the daylight; it was brighter than usual; all things looked more real than usual.

'Can't you open the door, Kay?' the voice asked.

There never had been a door there; but now that Kay looked, there was a little door, all studded with knobs of iron. Just as he got down to it, it opened towards him; there before him was Nibbins, the black cat.

'Come along Kay,' Nibbins said, 'we can just do it while they're at the banquet; but don't make more noise than you must.'

Kay peeped through the door. It opened from a little narrow passage in the thickness of the wall.

'Where does it lead to?' he asked.

'Come and see,' Nibbins said.

CHAPTER 36

I hardly slept, thinking of Rachel huddled in a cell somewhere, and the more good news we had, the more restless I became, doubting if the official announcement of victory in Europe would ever come. If it didn't, then my trial would no doubt sentence me to a long journey to Germany, but this time, as a proven enemy of the state, it certainly wouldn't be a pleasure cruise.

When I heard the metallic bang of the letterbox, I ran to fetch the newspaper, hoping for news about where Rachel was being held. It was just one sheet — a full-page spread from the Bailiff, Coutanche, urging everyone to listen to the broadcast from the BBC. It would be relayed in St Helier from loudspeakers, but we shouldn't hoist Union flags until after the end of hostilities announcement came.

Was this it? Was this really it? Had we killed a man for nothing? I had to hear it with my own ears. I walked shakily towards the town, but nothing seemed to have changed; in the distance, the stark silhouettes of German soldiers with rifles were manning the gun towers.

But the square before the Pomme d'Or hotel was different. Before I even got there, I was jostled forward into a road packed to bursting. Then I realised, there were no German soldiers stopping us from gathering. The noise of voices was like the whooshing rush of sea over pebbles, everyone speaking at once.

Goodness, the whole of Jersey must be here! When the crackling voice of Churchill finally came through the loudspeakers, the crowd around me erupted into cheers, but were quickly hushed to a pregnant silence by Churchill's voice.

'Hostilities will end officially at one minute after midnight tonight — Tuesday, 8th May — but in the interests of saving lives, the "cease fire" began yesterday, to be sounded all along the front, and our dear Channel Islands are also to be freed today.'

At the words 'Our dear Channel Islands' the crowd went wild.

The elderly man next to me lifted me up and swung me round and planted a smacking kiss on my lips.

A skinny woman in a battered felt hat tutted. '"Dear Channel Islands" indeed. If we were that dear, why didn't they help us? We've been bullied and half-starved for the last five years.'

'But it's over,' I yelled. 'No more "verboten"!'

And, finally, even she had to smile.

It was impossible to hear the rest of the speech; it was just a background fuzz against the whoops and shouts all around me. Silence fell again for the Bailiff, who mounted the podium amid a great cheer and clapping of hands to tell us that the navy were already on their way from England to arrange the surrender of the German forces on the islands.

I wondered where Rachel was. It seemed a bitter blow that she couldn't be here with me, and that she'd been taken so near the end. I cursed Fischer and his pig-headed devotion to duty. But the mood of jubilation was infectious, and I was soon joining in the singing of English songs, with tears running down my face. The curfew was forgotten. Nobody slept. We couldn't. We were high on adrenalin and hope.

After the jubilation, the bakery seemed a sad, empty shell. I ran my hand along the bare counter and thought back to before the war, to the smell of apple pie and Fred's cheerful face. I didn't go upstairs. I couldn't face the splintered wall, the painful memories, or the room where Horst had died. Nothing would be the same again; I could never get that back. This place would always be a place of both light and shadow. I kept wondering where Fred died, whether Horst had been right, and that he'd really been shot, or whether Horst had just said that to hurt me. Somehow, I'd have to find out.

The next day, more huge crowds filled the roadway below the Pomme d'Or, which had been selected as the new Jersey Allied headquarters. With the rest, I longed for the actual landing of the British troops.

When they finally arrived, the sight of brown uniforms disembarking made me crumple with relief. Right in front of me, a young London Tommy was mobbed, as people surrounded him, anxious for news about relatives or friends or conditions in England. Curfew and all other restrictions were completely forgotten. Grey-green uniforms were replaced by brown and khaki as the Germans hid in their billets or aboard their ships. White crosses sprang up on the German ships and guns.

Queues of dejected Germans crowded the beaches as prisoners of war. Their defeat played out in the dejected set of their shoulders and their trailing feet. How quickly power could turn one nation into a bully, and how soon that power evaporated, running through their fingers like a fistful of sand. I strained to see the Germans' faces, wondering if Wolfgang was amongst them, and hoped he would be treated well, glad I never had to witness those last desperate moments as he hurled Horst's body into the sea.

Behind me, a familiar voice rang out. 'There she is, the Jerrybag!'

I turned. It was as if everything happened in slow motion. Mrs Hedges pointed an accusing finger at me, and from the crowd, a group of men and women burst out and grabbed me by the shoulders.

All I could see were the wide-open angry mouths shouting at me as my arm was almost wrested from its socket. One of my shoes fell off as I scraped along the pavement, resisting as I was pushed and pulled forward.

'Stop!' I shouted.

But nobody listened. The crowd were chanting, 'Whore, whore.'

Outside the barber's shop, someone kicked me forward. I was surrounded by a sea of faces. In the crowd I saw Mrs Soulier, her arms folded across her chest, shouting with the rest. Four men were holding another poor woman down. She had a placard around her neck with the word 'Jerrybag' scrawled on it. Blood dripped from cuts on her scalp as the barber hacked off her hair.

She looked up at me.

'I did what I had to do,' she said. Her eyes met mine, and we exchanged a glance of understanding.

They dragged her off the chair, and they would have thrown her in the water, but for the fact she twisted and leapt away. I watched her run through the crowd as they kicked and spat at her and threw stones, but I didn't see much more because someone grabbed my shoulders and pressed me down hard onto the chair.

Rough hands pinioned my arms to my side, and the sharp edge of a cardboard placard scratched across my face. I felt my hair tugged away from my scalp. There was a clash of scissor blades, and a whisper of hair fell past my face.

'Stop!' A familiar voice from the crowd. 'Leave her alone!' Rachel. I turned my head to try to see her, but it was jerked back by a slap on the face. Thank God. She was still here on Jersey and not on a ship to Germany.

'Stop!' she cried again; this time she'd made it through the crowd, and stood before us, hands on hips, her face contorted and red with anger.

The grip on my arms didn't loosen, though I struggled.

'Mr Scott, she saved my life. She hid me all that time. You've got to listen! The Germans were just a cover. I'd be dead by now if it wasn't for her kindness.'

A man's voice from behind me: 'She's a sympathiser! Mrs Hedges says she's married to a German.'

'She's a widow,' yelled Rachel. 'Her husband died fighting, you imbeciles! Let go of her!'

The grip on one of my arms loosened, and Mr Scott from the bank stepped forward. 'Miss Cohen. The Germans told me you were dead.'

'I was in hiding,' Rachel said. 'Please, Mr Scott. Let Céline go. She's suffered at their hands more than most. I know because I saw it.'

'She could have said no.'

'So what would you do with a gun at your head?'

'Jerrybag!' came a lone female voice from the crowd.

Rachel turned, eyes blazing. 'If she's a Jerrybag, then so is every last woman on the island. We've all had to collude with them one way or another to stay alive, haven't we?' She glanced round the surly faces. 'Well, haven't we?'

Something about her conviction, her steely glare, made the crowd fall silent.

'We've all suffered at their hands,' Mr Scott said. 'They imprisoned me for six months for employing you.'

'So let's not make ourselves as bad as them,' Rachel retorted.

Rachel plucked the placard from around my neck and cast it on the ground. 'And before you call anyone else names, look to your own consciences.' She pulled me up from the chair.

'Jerrybag!' the same woman called again.

Rachel rounded on her. 'You stupid woman. The war's over. Do you really want it to go on? They give us peace, and you want to fight your own people? Good people who've never done anything to harm you?'

Silence.

'Come on, Céline, we're going home.'

When I stood up, nobody stopped me. Rachel's hand on my arm was steady and strong. With as much dignity as I could muster with only one shoe, we walked through the crowd.

'If you want it, Miss Cohen, your position's still open at the bank,' called Mr Scott.

'Thank you,' Rachel called back over her shoulder. 'I'll be in on Monday.'

Our safety seemed too fragile to risk stopping, and I was too scared to speak. We didn't even turn to look at each other until we reached the top of the hill. Then, wordlessly, we hugged.

'I thought they'd scalp you,' Rachel said. 'I was more terrified of them than the Germans!'

'Liar,' I said. 'Anyway, I needed a haircut.'

Our fear was too tender yet for laughter. She squeezed my arm and interlaced her fingers in mine. I stared out to sea, then my gaze shifted to the fragile border between land and ocean, between Jersey and the rest of the world.

Rachel's eyes were trained on the grey landing craft filling the bay, at the queues of soldiers leaving. 'I can't believe they came at all,' she said. 'And now I can't believe they've gone.'

'It seems unreal, the difference a single day can make,' I said. 'And that some piece of paper signed in another part of the world can turn things on their head.'

She let go. 'I'll miss Wolfgang. He was ... he was not like the others.'

'That man — he'd do anything for you, the great soft thing. He knows he can find you here on Jersey, and maybe he'll come back one day,' I said. 'It seems odd that soon those beaches will be emptied of mines, and the children will be back to dig sandcastles and play hopscotch and eat ice creams. And no one will remember.'

'I'll remember,' Rachel said. 'I'll remember that even in the worst of times, there are still good people.'

'I'm not sure. When people ask us what part Jersey played in the war, we'll just seem like cowards.'

'There's more than one way to fight though, isn't there? Like not buckling under and giving up.'

I smiled. 'It's not very heroic.'

'Heroic isn't what matters; it's survival that matters; to witness it and then move on. To be here to build a new and different future.' She reached out to wrap her arm round my waist.

'You sound like Churchill,' I said. 'You've missed your calling.'

'Let's go home,' Rachel said. 'When the British let me out of the jail, they gave me a little present.' She put her hand in her pocket and drew out a twist of white paper containing a black powdery substance.

'What is it? Gosh, I'll have to buy new glasses.'

'You don't need them for this. It's the most English thing you can imagine.'

I sniffed it. 'Tea!'

We limped back towards the bakery arm in arm, through the bright summer sun that smelt of hot tarmac, as the shouts and cheers from the town grew fainter.

EPILOGUE

Céline

The scars of the occupation ran deep. Rachel heard nothing more of her parents. Nobody spoke of it, but we presumed they were dead. Her horror when we learned of the extermination of so many Jews, in places like Auschwitz, made it feel impossible to talk to her of Fred. My attempts to find out what had happened to him were in vain, as all my letters went unanswered. Germany was in chaos, and the subject of the Germans was closed. Nobody wanted to talk of them; the people of Jersey wanted to pretend it had never happened. Like everyone else, I had to become thick-skinned about my own pain.

I ran the bakery single-handed, worked long days, and slept exhausted at night, trying not to think of the past. Rachel lodged with me and went off to the bank every day. She was quieter now, and serious, and grateful for the security it offered her. We rubbed along well; with her I didn't need to explain my occasional black moods or my nightmares.

One late Friday afternoon, I was just tallying the till when the door opened and an unfamiliar customer came in. She hesitated, as if she was weighing up her surroundings, before coming to the counter.

'Sorry, we've not much left I'm afraid,' I said.

'It doesn't matter,' she said, in French.

I paused in my counting, curious. She was an older woman, with a lined forehead, and creases around the edges of her eyes that spoke of both laughter and tears. Salt and pepper hair stood straight up from her forehead under a brown felt hat.

'Are you Céline?' she asked in French.

'That's me,' I said, shutting the till drawer.

'Thank God. It's taken me a long time to pluck up the courage to come and see you. I'm Berenice Severin.'

The name meant nothing to me.

'Is there somewhere private we can talk?'

'What's it about?' I was suspicious.

'It's about your husband, Siegfried Huber.'

The name sent a jolt to my heart. I turned the shop sign to *Closed* without a word and led her to the sitting room.

'Is he alive?' were my first words.

She gave a small shake of the head. 'It's taken a while to search the records to find out what happened to him.'

I exhaled and sat down heavily in the chair. I was wary of this unknown woman. 'Somebody else told me he was dead … but what do you know about it … I mean, how can you be sure?'

'May I?' She indicated the chair and sat opposite me, leaning forward, her hands clasped on her knees. 'What a lovely room,' she said.

'Tell me what you know.'

'We knew your husband as Édouard,' she said. 'He sacrificed his own life for my son. And as a result, he was executed by the SS on January twenty-seventh 1943. His execution is on record with those of the Mouvement de Libération Nationale. The French Resistance.'

'You must have the wrong person. Fred was conscripted …
into the German Army,' I said.

She leaned forward, a gentleness in her expression. 'No. He
talked of you often, of this bakery here in Jersey. There is no
mistaking you. He was a hero. A hero of the French
Resistance.'

'But how can that be? You said you knew him as Édouard.
Are you sure it was him?'

'Do you have any of that English tea? It's a long story.'

I made tea and several hours later she had finished. I was
reeling, my head filled with French names and places. From
knowing nothing, suddenly there was too much for me to take
in.

She put her teacup down and reached into her handbag. 'I
thought you would like to see these,' she said. 'Really, I would
like to have shown Édouard. But you are the next best thing.
You know, he always wanted to get home to you. He wanted
to go to Switzerland into neutral territory, but I dissuaded him.
I've always regretted it. If I hadn't —'

'We all have regrets,' I said.

She pressed her lips together and passed me the first of
several photographs. 'This is Pierre, my son. Édouard, your
Fred, knew him as Antoine. Here he is, with his wife Eloise.
They met on the evacuation bus when we fled Marseille. And
these are my grandchildren.'

I stared at the young man in the photos, at his brilliant smile.
The children were on a beach next to a giant sandcastle. A little
girl of about four, in a checked frock clutching a bucket. A
toddler in rompers squinting at the camera whilst digging a
hole.

'Édouard saved my life three times. Once when I was arrested and questioned by the Gestapo. Once when a man tried to shoot us on a train. And once when he gave Pierre his papers. Without him, Pierre and I would have both been on the train to the death camps. I know it is little consolation to you, but he gave us our lives. You should be very proud.'

Berenice was staying in St Helier in a small boarding house on the seafront. When she'd gone, with promises to tell me more tomorrow, I left the shop and walked up the hill, anxious for some time alone before Rachel returned from work. My heart was full of Fred. It was as if something inside me had melted. All these years I'd been terrified he'd become like his brother, Horst. That I was wrong to care where he was, or what had happened to him. Now my shame had gone, and I was able to love him again. It would never bring him back, but the thought that, all along, he'd been the Fred I knew, made my heart ache.

My Fred. Like me, he'd made hard decisions. He would never come home, but in some sense his story had reclaimed his right to be here. He'd fought for freedom in a way I could never have imagined.

I stopped on the brow of the hill in the late evening light and gazed back over the island he'd loved. The gun turrets were still there, used by children as dens instead of by men with machine guns. In the distance, caramel-coloured cattle grazed, and farms were growing flowers, as they used to do, not just beet and potatoes. Flanders Farm had planted lavender, and the purple haze of flowers scented the air with its sharp tang. Perhaps I'd bake the French specialities that Fred used to love so much. Croissants and pain au chocolat. Even Viennese pastries … one day.

I imagined him back in the bakery, blowing his burnt fingers after taking a tray from the oven. I imagined him taking off his shoes and socks after a hard day, with an 'aah' of pleasure. I smiled and cried a little, then shook my head.

'Chin up, Céline,' I said to myself, hearing Fred's voice plain as plain.

Outside the front door, I paused. I can do it, I thought. His death need not be for nothing. I can brave the past and find my future.

A NOTE FROM THE AUTHOR

Thank you for reading and I hope you enjoyed *THE OCCUPATION*. During World War Two, the Channel Islands were the only part of the British Isles to be occupied by the Germans. This story is based on several true accounts, although I have welded them together and compressed them into a fictional narrative. For more on Jersey's Occupation, I thoroughly recommend Madeleine Bunting's excellent book, *The Model Occupation*. For an overview, the BBC history site has several pages on this topic. Though fictional, Céline and Rachel's story was inspired by the true story of Dorothea Weber, who helped her Jewish friend Hedwig Bercu by hiding her from the Germans. More on this surprising real life story can be found here. Fred's story in France is entirely fictional. Amongst others, the following books were very helpful in giving me the research background for his story:

The Gestapo — Frank McDonough

Suite Française — Irène Némirovsky

Les Parisiennes — Anne Sebba

Avenue of Spies — Alex Kershaw

The Resistance — Matthew Cobb

Fighters in the Shadows — Robert Gildea

If you've enjoyed *The Occupation*, I would really appreciate an online review on **Goodreads** or **Amazon**, which will help other readers to discover it. I love to chat to other readers about what I'm reading too, so do look me up on my Facebook page: **AuthorDeborahSwift** or on Twitter: **@swiftstory**.

Deborah Swift

www.deborahswift.com

ACKNOWLEDGEMENTS

My thanks go to the whole Sapere Books team for bringing this novel to publication. Huge thanks to Amy Durant of Sapere Books and to independent editor Richard Sheehan for their insightful editing. I would also like to thank the other writers of The Darkest Hour Anthology where the story first appeared, and who were the first readers to offer me feedback and suggest that the shorter story could be expanded into a novel. Particular thanks to Marion Kummerow, who organized the anthology and helped with German translation.

Sapere Books is an exciting new publisher of brilliant fiction and popular history.

To find out more about our latest releases and our monthly bargain books visit our website: **saperebooks.com**